A FAMILIAR MAGIC

E.M.

CHAPTER ONE

This party was such a bad idea. I kept a wary eye on the rowdy teenagers dancing perilously close to the bonfire and wrapped my arms tighter around my middle. I tried to ignore my growing anxiety, but no amount of stale beer or loud music could hide the subtle change in the air. The glow of the once vibrant, summer evening rapidly faded as if the very life was strangled out of it. I hadn't noticed at first, but now it was impossible to ignore. The ocean breeze pushed against my skin in urgency, howling a warning that I couldn't decipher. My toes dug deeper in the sand, trying to claim the last bit of fading warmth from the sun and I shivered again. Being alone out in the open no longer seemed like such a great idea, but sitting by the fire wasn't an option, though it would be safer. Joining the crowd would be seen as an open invitation for someone to come talk to me, and I'd rather face whatever lurked past the fire's edge than subject myself to even more torment. I thought that in coming tonight I could prove I belonged, that I wasn't so different. I was a normal teenager. Thirty minutes into tonight's festivities and I knew I could never be like them.

Braxton would call it being difficult—*had* called me that at least three times already tonight, but what did he know? He was nothing but a privileged boy from South Miami with unlimited access to daddy's money. He had no clue of the nightmares that stalked the shadows of this city; none of them did. Not for the first time, I rolled my eyes at how gullible humans were. They find a dead body with a torn-out throat and label it a robbery gone bad. An abandoned house filled with bloodless corpses? That had to be a cult. They got demon possessions right but were blind to a majority of them and had no idea how to properly exorcise the spirit. How their species managed to survive this long was beyond me.

A strong breeze taunted the burning driftwood until it collapsed in on itself, sending ashes and embers dancing across the sand. I tilted my head and sniffed, recognizing the scent of something *other* on the wind. My heart skipped and then took off as I tried to pin down the source of the smell. My nose burned from the stench of something charred and rotted and I pushed away the small voice in my head that begged me to run. My pupils dilated as I allowed enough of the change through my iron control to see in the dark. The murky corners and recesses of the beach came into focus with that small shift, but no monsters jumped out at me, only severely drunk teenagers. Another ocean breeze fanned the bonfire, and someone called out for more driftwood.

You're being paranoid, Kaya.

I berated myself and ducked further into my hoodie, hiding all but my face and a few wisps of my white hair. The moon reflected off those free strands and I watched them glow like a beacon. Frowning, I tucked them away and turned to face the approaching footsteps. Only a few inches taller than me, Braxton made up for his lack of height with cute looks and an ample amount of muscle. His blonde hair reflected off the firelight with an orange hue, and a dimple appeared on his right cheek when he caught me staring.

"Did you see how long I held that keg stand? No one's gonna come close to beating my record."

I threw on my fakest smile and gave him an over-exaggerated thumbs up. "Your parents must be so proud." Seriously, what had I seen in him?

He grinned and stepped closer, missing my sarcasm entirely. "I care more about what you think," he whispered, snaking an arm around my waist.

I pushed my hands against his chest when he got too close and tried not to cringe at the acrid stench of beer on his breath. Now was one of those times I wished I didn't have enhanced senses. What possessed me into thinking this boy was cute?

"Braxton, I want to go home." His nuzzling my ear was more annoying than sexy, and I pushed harder against his him until there was enough space between us for him to see I was serious. "Braxton. Home. Now."

His face crumpled in what I'm sure he thought was an adorable pout. "Aw come on, babe. You haven't even finished your beer."

Said beer still filled half a cup and was nestled in the sand by my foot. I wrinkled my nose at his use of a pet name and kicked the cup over.

"There, no more beer. Let's go."

I brushed past his stunned expression and headed toward the parking lot. I kept my chin down against the stinging sand, but my eyes still scanned the shadows. Braxton's annoying advances were distracting enough, but they couldn't hold up against instinct, and mine told me that something *other* mingled in the crowd tonight. I had no plans to stick around and see what it was. I held my flip flops in one hand and tried to brush the sand off my feet with the other. Braxton's shiny GTO sat right where we parked it, but its headlights were dull and its engine silent.

I held in a few choice words as I swung to face the brown-eyed boy that was one second away from seeing me seriously pissed off. Braxton leaned against the lamppost with a half grin and I tried not to shudder as his eyes raked over my bare legs. Growling, I pulled my hoodie as low as I could, but it made no difference.

"Braxton," his eyes lifted to mine and I didn't like what I saw there. I'd been told alcohol made humans susceptible to their own inner-beasts, but this was the first time the focus was on me. My lip curled at the challenge. "Braxton, give me your keys. I'll drive us home."

My eyes darted to the key ring hanging from his pocket and I took a step closer, my hand slowly reaching, fingertips shaking —not from fear, but as a reaction. The animal inside me sensed the *other* being and the growing danger made it harder to keep her in check. Any closer and whatever was out there would be able to sense me too.

I wasn't prepared for how fast he moved, and that was stupid on my part. Sensei always warned me to be on my guard and I'd failed my first test. Braxton's hand engulfed my wrist entirely, his fingers overlapping and leaving no soft point to break out of. That didn't stop me from trying, though.

"Let go!" I demanded, putting as much authority into my tone as I could. It worked on my students at the dojo but didn't seem to have an effect on him.

"They said you'd play hard to get, but I didn't listen to them," Braxton laughed and yanked me against his chest in one swift pull. His muscles strained against the sleeves of his shirt and rather than be attracted, I saw them for the danger they represented. I brought my free hand up to slap him, but he caught it before it could make contact. "I told them you were just shy, that once I had you alone, you'd want what all the other girls did."

I didn't have to ask him who he meant by *them*—Avry and Zeke. The three of them had younger siblings that I taught at the dojo, that's how I'd met them. With no other friends my age and no company besides Sensei, I jumped at their invitation to go to the party tonight.

Stupid. Stupid stupid stupid.

Was I so needy and starved for attention that I threw all my common sense out the window? The answer was apparently yes, because I ignored all my instincts and all Sensei's teachings and jumped in the car without a look back. Now I was paying the price.

"So what do you say, Kaya? Let's have a little fun like I know you've been dying to do, and then I'll take you home. Scout's honor."

Braxton had never been a scout a day in his life, but he was about to earn his first badge in getting his ass kicked. I closed the last few inches between us and pressed my hips tightly against his. I bit back my smirk at his sharp intake of breath and gave him a coy smile instead.

"I never thought I'd be doing this," I purred, and his heartrate kicked into overdrive.

"Oh yeah?" he relaxed his grip on my wrists and I wrapped my arms around his neck.

I wound my fingers deep into his hair and gave a gentle tug until he groaned and let my breath ghost over his ear as I spoke again.

"I can't believe it." I leaned away and he let me, watching me with half-lidded eyes to see what I'd do next.

"Can't believe what, babe?" he asked.

My fists tightened in his hair seconds before my knee met

his crotch. The air left his lungs with an audible *whoosh* as he curled down to cup himself.

"I can't believe you were stupid enough to think you could get away with assaulting me. I *teach* your little brother karate, you dumbass!"

Braxton was curled into a ball on the blacktop and I worried that I might have hit him too hard; humans could be fragile. Then I remembered he deserved it. A chilling howl pierced through both the street traffic and music from the beach party. The shrill note caused the hair on my neck to stand on end and I knew without a shadow of a doubt that I'd run out of time. Braxton's delay had cost me and the animal inside me knew it too.

She quietly paced and waited for the demon to show itself, her growl a challenge I fought to keep behind my lips. My pupils widened, and my nostrils flared, but I didn't allow any other aspects of the change. My fingernails ached with the pressure of my claws behind them and my skin broke out in goosebumps as I fought to keep myself in check. Another howl, closer this time, and my body shook with the sheer will of holding back. Dammit, how did it find me?

Think, Kaya. Think!

I spun and reached for Braxton, who was still crying on the ground. I dug through his pockets, ignoring his curses and cries of pain, as I looked for his car keys. My hands shook, and my fingers fumbled, but I felt the cool kiss of metal against my skin and almost wept with relief. The keys jingled like a mini dinner bell as I ran to the car. One after another they each failed until even the last key wouldn't open the door. With a frustrated cry, I hurled *someone's* keys out into the sand and knelt back down beside Braxton.

"Where are your keys, Braxton?" I held him by the front of his shirt and shook him so hard his head looked like it would snap off. Dropping him before I accidentally broke his neck, I stood and walked a few paces away to see if he'd dropped them when I broke his nuts. "Shit," I whispered, the whine getting stuck in my throat.

This was bad, very bad. I wasn't ready to take on a demon by myself! With every passing second, I could feel the demon grow closer and my animal half was about to lose her shit. The giant bonfire looked inviting and safe, especially with all the humans still gathered around it, but that was the very reason why I couldn't go over there. Whether or not I was ready, and whether or not I was fully trained—spoiler alert, I wasn't— it was my responsibility to protect humanity from the demons. It was literally my birthright, the sole purpose for my being on earth. The problem was, I didn't know what kind of demon was out there, and the stupid boy next to me didn't deserve my protection.

"Get yourself together, Kaya. You can do this."

My little pep talk did nothing to calm me down, but I forced my feet to move anyway until I was on the opposite side of the parking lot and far away from the juicy, but still shitty human. The honking horns of Miami's night traffic blurred the lights to my right, and the ocean lapped in a picturesque calm to my left. Before me was a small copse of trees that I knew backed onto a private neighborhood, and that's where the demon came for me. At first the shadows hid all the attributes I needed to see, but the stench couldn't be dulled by darkness and I knew the demon arrived heartbeats before I saw it.

I'd only ever seen a demon once before in my life, and that was a night I preferred not to think about. Still, my body couldn't help but react in much the same way it had when I was thirteen, pure terror. My knees trembled, and my palms grew damp as the fear wound its way through my body. I gasped when my lungs demanded oxygen, only to hold my breath again as the stench of the demon wafted closer. A wolf was the first thing I saw, its teeth brighter than my own hair and larger than my hand. Smoke curled around its snout as fire dripped from its mouth.

I wanted to close my eyes and pretend that monsters didn't exist. I didn't want to see the rest of the demon, didn't want to confirm what years of stories and teachings told me I was looking at, but it kept coming. Stepping from the shadows, the massive canine body morphed into a serpent's tail that arched over its back, the rattles filling my ears with their deadly drone. It was a motherfucking Amon demon.

I was so dead. It took two fully trained warriors to bring one of these guys down and I was nothing but a teenaged runaway. I wasn't trained. Without a witch's magic, I couldn't even stun the demon long enough to cut off its tail, which surprisingly was the only way to kill it. The Amon demon sniffed the warm air like the scent of my fear was a delicious appetizer, before licking its chops and hissing at me.

"What are you doing, little familiar, so far from home?" Its raspy voice scraped the inside of my head like nails on a chalk-board and I clenched my jaw against the pain. The demon took another step closer and inhaled, *"How loud will you scream for me, as I tear the flesh off your bones?"*

Any closer and the demon's fire breath would burn me to a crisp. I wasn't sure if the demon liked his dinner raw or well done, but I wasn't going to stick around and find out. I tapped into the speed and strength of my animal half and bolted from the parking lot. With every step, my animal demanded I let her lose, but a large cat would quickly stand out in the city and I didn't need to be hunted by more than what was already on my heels. My bare feet slammed against the concrete sidewalk, but I barely felt the pain. The demon wasn't far behind and had the added luxury of being invisible to humans; I didn't see this cat and mouse game lasting very long.

Knowing that a full shift was my only hope at surviving, I made a last-minute turn into the Oleta River State Park and lost myself amongst the trees. The undergrowth and ferns grew thick the further in I ran, and I used every bit of the shadows they offered to gain more distance between myself and the Amon demon. I could hear its heavy steps behind me, and the rattling of its tail told me I wasn't as far ahead as I hoped. The change wasn't something that came easy to me, no matter how hard my animal was fighting to get out. I'd spent the last six months fighting with every fiber of my humanity to keep my *other* self tucked away, to not lose control around the humans, and all those walls I'd built weren't easy to break through now. Even though I desperately needed to. I called claws to my hands first and used them to slash at the branches and small trees blocking my path.

I tried to call forth the rest of my animal, but my fear and pounding heart made it too hard. My thoughts swirled with panic, mental cries to run faster, to shift, to hide—they all blocked the path I needed to find the doorway in my mind that led to my change. A serpent's tail slammed into the tree above my head and I cried out. The broken branches crashed from above with jagged teeth and I threw myself to the side to keep from being crushed. I scrambled to my feet, slipping on rocks and mud and watched the demon stalk closer. With a canal at my back, I had nowhere else to go and I couldn't even get a patch of fur to sprout on my skin.

This was it, without shifting I stood no chance and my seventeen short years flashed before my eyes in a wave of color. My clawed hands felt heavy, like any second they would sink to the ground in defeat. But the thought of giving up stoked an inner fire that lay dormant since the last time I faced a demon.

"Poor baby familiar," the demon crooned. *"Will you cry for me? They taste so much better when they cry."*

My eyes stung with moisture that I refused to let fall. I didn't want to die, but I'd be damned if I'd go out a coward; the demon didn't deserve the satisfaction. I locked my knees and fisted my hands at my side, waiting for the inevitable death I knew I couldn't outrun. Maybe if I timed it right, I could duck beneath its swinging tail. Or would it attack me with its teeth first? I met its stare with a wild grin and brought my claws up, ready to at least try.

"Well? Come on then!" I taunted. "What are you waiting for, an invitation?"

With a heated snarl, the demon pounced... and then recoiled, shaking its head. Red sparks flickered in the corner of my vision but when I looked, I only saw the fire dripping from the demon's maw.

"You will pay for that," the demon growled and sprung again.

I had just enough time to throw my hands up before the demon was struck with a flying boulder. The tree to my left split in half as the demon's body broke right through it. I froze, blinked, and blinked again. What the hell just happened? The Amon howled his fury and stalked toward me, his eyes sharp and intently scanning for whoever intervened with his dinner. Two muscular men and two full grown lions exploded from the trees in a flash of golden fur and swaths of black. I instinctively took a step back as I recognized the uniforms, witches and their partners. They surrounded the Amon, the lions roaring with malice as their witch counterparts rose their arms in a chant. Even with an advantage of numbers, the newcomers had a tough time of it and couldn't get close enough to land a killing blow. The demon's tail whipped fiercely over its body and to the side, spearing toward one of the lions, while white hot flames spewed from its mouth towards the witches.

Their vials of defensive potions fell from their hands and were destroyed on the ground below, useless without a spell and a target. The lions had no safe opening to strike without the witch's magic and the Amon couldn't get close enough to kill one of the witches because of their familiars. The standoff wasn't going to last much longer, and I didn't want to be here to see who won; neither option was good for me.

As I toed my foot to the side, careful not to draw attention my way, the change slowly left my body, leaving my fingernails dull and my eyesight horrible. Exhaustion ran heavy through my limbs, even though I hadn't completed a full shift, the small change still took a lot out of me. My legs shook hard enough to knock me on my ass, and I wondered if I'd expended more energy than I'd originally thought, but when the ground beneath me continued to roll, I knew it wasn't coming from me. Across the clearing, a tree unrooted and floated in the air above another witch. His black hair was darker than I remembered, but I knew those eyes, that face. Prince Auden, second son of the Wardwell line, flung the tree with nothing but a flick of his hand and smirked when it impaled the Amon demon.

Pinned to the ground, the lions wasted no time and got to work ripping the demon apart. The sounds of torn flesh and painful cries would echo in my head tonight, I knew, but that wasn't what worried me at the moment. Prince Auden was staring at me, staring like he remembered exactly who I was and why I was a wanted fugitive of my people. Before he could ensnare me with his power, I bolted through the trees and ran for my life. Literally. Something told me it wasn't a coincidence that the prince happened to be here just in time to save me, which meant, they'd finally found me. The bustling city of Miami kept me hidden these past four years and I hated to leave it, but if I wanted to stay alive long enough to see my eighteenth birthday, I needed to make myself disappear. Again.

CHAPTER TWO

My mouth flooded with saliva as another round of vomit burned past my throat. I'd made it as far as this dumpster in the back alley behind the dojo, before my stomach rebelled and I winced as another dry heave forced me to double over. Wiping my mouth with the back of my hand, I shuffled the final steps to the back door and dug out my key. Trembling hands and a burnt-out streetlight made it hard to line everything up, but I finally got the door open and sighed in relief when I locked it behind me.

I leaned against the door and held my breath, listening for any signs that I was followed. I was pretty sure I lost the witches somewhere in the Art Deco District, but that was only fifteen minutes away from here and no matter which way I looked at it, I knew I had no other choice. I was going to have to leave Miami. The empty dojo I called my home was a silent room of shadows as I cut across the mats to the thin door in the back. Once a storage room, it was converted after Sensei found me scrounging for scraps in his dumpster when I was thirteen. He took me in and trained me, taught me everything I needed to know to survive on my own. Within these walls was the safest

I'd ever felt since that night, until now. Between the demon and the arrival of the witches, my sense of security was irrevocably shaken.

My stomach churned again as I thought about what I'd seen tonight. No amount of childhood stories or the meager education I'd received back home could've prepared me for that. Demons were so much more than the dark scribbles they'd been reduced to in my textbooks, but I'd already learned that firsthand. What really shook me tonight was seeing Prince Auden. I sincerely hoped he hadn't recognized me, but a quick look in the mirror deflated those hopes real quick. My pale hair hung free from the confines of my hoodie, the edges dancing around my waist. I wasn't sure when the strands had fallen free tonight, but if the prince saw it...well, there weren't many people my age with white hair. Fear still coursed through me and made my eyes appear bigger than they actually were, the light blue crystal clear even in the dim lighting. My eyelashes were dark and my lips a light pink — the only splashes of color I naturally possessed. I stood out even amongst my own kind and the more unique details I noticed, the more I knew my chances of going undetected dwindled.

I turned on one of the showers in the locker room, letting the steam billow through the stalls and then scrubbed at my skin until it bloomed pink as I tried to wash away the stench of demon and despair. I needed to come up with a plan; a way out of the city by sunrise, where to go, and what to do once I got there. A teardrop escaped at the thought of starting over again and once the tears started, I couldn't stop them. Tucked into a corner of the stall, I cried. I cried for the little girl forced from her home with nowhere else to go. I cried for that same girl, all grown up with no choice but to run again. The fear and anxiety poured from my very skin to meld with the water swirling around the drain until my tears ran on empty and I was able to think clearly.

I was tired of hiding and suppressing half of who I really was, but until I was eighteen and able to blend better into human society, or until I could master a full shift to defend myself, staying on the run would better protect me. I knew how to avoid demons and was successful until tonight, but the witches were another problem entirely. They weren't going to just let me go and Prince Auden could be very determined when he wanted to be. Despite the fact that my brain was running on fumes and there were a million other things I needed to be thinking about, I could only focus on one thing; the prince. Long buried memories from my childhood reminded me that we'd been friends once. There was plenty of laughter and mischief when I thought of Auden, but the happy feeling never lasted long when I dwelled on memories of the past and all too soon my broken heart throbbed hard enough to remind me of why things changed. I'd killed my best friend and run from the consequences; I didn't deserve happiness in my life anymore.

It took less than an hour to pack the rest of my meager belongings into my now empty sparring bag. I glanced wistfully at my gear in the corner, but it served no use where I was going. Before walking out the door, I penned a letter to Sensei, thanking him for his generosity and apologizing for disappearing like I was— I may have also swiped a few weapons from the walls and promised to find a way to return them some day. There was no sign of daybreak, so the streets were quiet, which served me well. Demons and other nasties preferred to hide from Florida's blazing sun, but I knew there was still a chance I'd run into one. I kept that in the back of my mind as I began my journey west. The options were endless, since my people didn't stray far from the bayous of Louisiana, but my luck would be better in quirky cities with a wide mix of characters; it was easier to blend in. I bought the next bus ticket to Los Angeles and tried to compose myself as I settled into one of the creaky chairs at the bus terminal. Two hours. I had to sit here for two hours before my bus was scheduled to arrive. My knee bounced repeatedly, shaking the entire row of chairs next to me until the old lady at the end shot me a dirty look. I winced and tried to calm down, but it was easier said than done. With every minute that passed, more of the city awoke and the harder it would be to spot the prince. He could be hiding in the crowd at the bagel shop across the street, or lurking by the buses, waiting for the chance to snatch me out of the line.

My paranoia grew with each imagined scenario until I thought the old lady was going to stab me with her knitting needles. But I couldn't help it. Lack of sleep and a healthy dose of anxiety meant I couldn't shut my brain off. An hour later, I lunged from my chair when I started to get twitchy and paced up and down the aisle instead. When my stomach reminded me I hadn't eaten since before the party last night, I made my way to the vending machines. The old lady's relief at my disappearance was palpable and I stuck my tongue out at her, even though she couldn't see me from around the corner. Some sticky buns and a pack of gum were all I could stomach, but they did the trick. The rush of sugar was a welcome high that felt normal enough to calm me down. A usual day for me was filled with copious amounts of sugar that struggled to keep pace with my overactive metabolism.

The bus station bathrooms weren't too bad, and the sinks had warm water that I used to clean the icing from my fingers. The bathroom door slammed open hard enough to spook the woman beside me and her jerky movements splashed soap into my eyes. I cursed through the burn.

"Get out."

My fists ceased rubbing against my eyes and the burning

began anew, but I was too frozen to do anything about it. I recognized that voice. Through stinging tears, I watched as Prince Auden let the woman squeeze past him before he shut the door and bolted the lock. The only way out of this bathroom was through that door or the small window behind me, both options had a dismal chance of success.

"Kaya." My name on his lips was like a punch to the gut; he *did* remember me.

I felt his gaze like a finger lightly trailing on my skin and I squirmed, trying to escape what it made me feel. The still dripping faucet was the only sound besides my heavy breathing as I waited to see how this would unfold. My dagger was a solid presence at the small of my back and there were a few throwing knives in my boots, but they weren't much comfort. I didn't want to hurt the prince, despite the way he was looking at me right now. His glare and curled lip dripped with disgust as he surveyed me in my cut off shorts and another hoodie. But there was something swimming behind that revulsion, a heat that caused me to squirm all over again.

My eyes had a mind of their own and initiated a thorough examination without my permission. But once I started looking, I couldn't make myself stop. Prince Auden was attractive—like frame his face and hang it over my bed attractive. He had full brows that arched over warm eyes, lined with gold. His onyx curls swept over his forehead and down his jaw, framing high cheekbones and full lips. The gray shirt he wore left little to the imagination and I greedily outlined each defined muscle until they disappeared behind the weapons hanging from his belt.

"My eyes are up here." His voice was soft but laced with a growl and my gaze jumped to his in shock.

"I-It's been a long time," I blurted out in a sad excuse. "You grew up."

My cheeks burned with mortification. You grew up? Who the hell said that besides psychos and stalkers? Ugh, if I could drown myself in one of those toilets right now... The last time I saw Auden, he was sixteen and he sure as hell didn't look like *that.* I felt like a peasant standing in front of him.

His lips thinned, and those beautiful eyes darkened. "Is that why you look almost ready to pounce on me?"

Now my cheeks burned for a different reason as my mouth dropped open. "I do not!" Surely, I wasn't that obvious.

He laughed, low and deep. "Like a cat in heat."

Any remaining attraction I felt toward him dissolved with my next breath and just like that, I remembered the very real danger I was in. I shouldn't have been ogling him anyway; he was the enemy now. Or, I was depending on how you looked at it. I glanced around the room and took a step back, trying to distance myself and make him think I was looking for a way out of here. In reality, my hand was slowly reaching for the knife I had tucked away. He didn't fall for my ruse and his eyes narrowed in on my arm just as my fingers wrapped around the handle.

"What are you—" His nostrils flared as he darted forward. "Oh no you don't."

I brought the knife up between us with only a foot to spare, but I wasn't fully committed to using it. The prince saw my hesitation and took advantage. He grabbed my wrist and stepped into me, pinning me against the tile. When I didn't immediately release the knife, he slammed my hand against the wall hard enough to make me drop it and it clattered harmlessly to the floor. I cursed, that was my favorite knife. Struggling against his grip, I twisted and tried to kick, but I had no leverage. His hips pressed against mine as he pinned my second arm with the first above my head. I froze. Stunned, I sucked in a lung-full of air and held it, eyes wide. His soft chuckle caused a chain reaction of goosebumps. Dark lashes fanned his cheeks as he watched me with hooded eyes. This close, I was sure he could feel my heart racing, a healthy dose of fear and undeniable attraction spurring it into a gallop.

"It was a nice try, sweetheart, but you and I both know that wouldn't have worked against me." His warm breath tickled my ear as he spoke, confusing my body even more. "I wouldn't try shifting either," he warned. "I'll put you down before you even sprout a claw."

That wasn't a problem, seeing as I couldn't shift, but he didn't know that. He also seriously underestimated me if he thought a knife was my only means of protecting myself. Sensei taught me better than that. Prince Auden planted his free hand on the wall beside my head, closing the distance between us even more until our breaths mingled. I glanced at his lips and then back to his eyes. Repeat. Why was he so close? His breath hitched as he leaned down, and I watched transfixed as his tongue darted out to wet his bottom lip. The grip on my wrists lessened but they were still pinned to the wall as he stretched them even higher, forcing my chest to thrust out more between us. Before he could do anything else, I turned and bit into the fleshy part of his forearm.

His skin was ripped from my mouth on a shout and I ignored the copper tang of blood on my teeth. I had to keep moving or I would lose the element of surprise. I yanked my wrists out of his hold and grabbed two fistfuls of his t-shirt. Planting my foot behind his ankle, I pulled with every ounce of supernatural strength I had in me and swung him over my hip into the porcelain sinks. I wanted to look over my shoulder and see the damage I'd caused; was he badly hurt? Were those golden eyes now burning dark with fury? There was no time to see as I unlocked the door and bolted into the crowded bus terminal. I came tearing around the corner like the hounds of hell were on my heels, but I had no care for the strange looks my actions garnered, my only thoughts were to get to my bag and get as far away as possible. Steps away from the isle where I left my things, I caught a glimpse of Auden's back up. They sat near the lady with the knitting needles as she bored them to tears with her animated tales of sock making. Dressed in all black, they sat too straight in their chairs, their muscles too tense, as their eyes scanned the terminal. Their fake smiles kept the old woman rambling on, but I knew they weren't listening to a single word she said. The two dots tattooed beneath their left ears only confirmed my suspicions. I used to look forward to the day I received my tattoos, but now the marks instilled fear rather than pride. The first dot was a little bit bigger and awarded at graduation, the second, more coveted dot, was bestowed when you paired with a partner. That meant there were two lion familiars somewhere in this crowd as well.

Abandoning my belongings, I ran outside and pushed my way through to the line for my bus. Thankfully, I kept the ticket in my pocket instead of my backpack. I was the last one to step on, so the only available seats left were in the front. I snagged the one with a window and hunched down under my hoodie. The hair on my arms rose when I saw Auden step outside. Even from here, I could see a thin trail of blood trickle down the side of his face from a cut on his temple. I ducked lower and made sure my hair wasn't visible as I watched the other two witches and their familiars join the hunt. They were easy to spot amongst the crowd, sleek and precise as they were. Moving like a well-trained unit, they forced their way onto bus after bus, searching for their runaway victim with a speed that made me nervous.

There were only two buses left before they got to my row and if they found me here, I lost. The brakes squeaked and hissed as the driver closed the doors and set the gear to drive.

Our wheels began rolling and I prayed for them to go faster because Auden was staring at us now. Staring at me. At my window, like he could see me hiding behind the tinted glass. His feet ate up the space between our row and the one he was on, moving far quicker than this damn Greyhound.

"Kaya!" He shouted, moving at a trot now, and then a run.

His hands rained down on the side of the bus, just under where I sat, and our eyes locked. The bus didn't stop though and eventually it reached a speed that he couldn't keep up with. My gaze never left his as we made our exit from the terminal, but there was a promise buried within his mask of fury and I felt it down to my bones. Escaping Auden wasn't going to be that easy.

CHAPTER THREE

The rough stone of the community's outer wall tore the skin on the palms of my hands, but I ignored the sting and kept climbing. The ledge on the top was covered with slick moss from all the thunderstorms this past month and I made sure to have a firm grip before I pulled myself the rest of the way over. The bayou stretched out for miles on the other side and I grinned, the untamed freedom was what we were after tonight.

"Get your ass up here, Asher!" I shouted at the dark-haired boy below and he flipped me off. It always took him a bit to compose himself before he started to climb and even though I knew he couldn't help it, I teased him each time. "The Crown Prince is afraid of heights?" I mocked. "What will *the people think?"*

Asher slammed a shaking hand down on the ledge and I grabbed his shirt to help haul him up.

"Not the Crown *Prince, Kaya. I'm third in line for the throne." His face was a bit pale as he took in the bayou from this high up, but his shaking stopped.*

"I know, dummy." I replied. "I'm only teasing you."

Asher took off his glasses and polished them with his shirt, a habit he couldn't escape thanks to the humidity that strangled us with zero relief each day. I tried to convince him to get contacts, but he swore up and down that he could read faster in his glasses. I rolled my eyes. He was such a nerd. As a witch of the Royal line, he was expected to be an example for others our age; to excel at fighting, spell casting, and demonology. Instead, he rarely left the library and I had to bribe him to use his powers. As different as we were, our friendship worked. I brought him out of his shell, and he kept me from falling behind when it came to all the bookish crap. He was my person; the only one on the planet who knew my secrets and my dreams. The only one who listened to me and never thought I was stupid for wanting more—irresponsible, maybe. But never stupid. He was quirky and a know-it-all, not the least bit athletic, and knew when I was lying before I even got the words out, but he was my best friend in the whole world and I'd kill for him any day.

"Have you ever wondered what's out there?" I asked, staring wistfully past our boundaries.

My whole life was spent behind these walls and it was never a problem until last year. When my mom passed, the relationship between me and my father grew strained and I found myself wishing for some distraction from his endless expectations. I brought Asher to the top of this wall more often now, but tonight was the first time I actually contemplated descending to the other side.

"Graduation will come soon enough," Asher stated, very matter-of-fact. "You'll spend plenty of time away then."

"I don't want to wait until I'm nineteen for adventure," I whined. "I want to experience it now!" Feeling inspired and just a tad reckless, I climbed down the wall and set my feet outside the community for the first time.

"Kaya, what are you doing? Get back up here!" Asher's eyes bugged out behind his frames, but for once his stern demands couldn't make me listen.

I took in a deep breath of moist, boggy air. I felt free, and it wasn't so much that things were immediately different on this side of the wall, but just the knowledge that I was physically outside the community—finally— made me want to go further.

"Don't be such a baby, Ash."

He was already scaling the wall and probably preparing a lecture as he did. Ever the one to follow the rules, he participated in my half-baked schemes reluctantly, but I knew he would never let me wander outside the community alone. If taking advantage of that made me a bad friend, I could live with the consequences. He scurried to my side and gave a pleading glance back to the wall before actually taking in the scenery around us.

"We're not supposed to be out here. What if there's a demon?" He whispered.

I tried not to let his whining get to me, I was asking a lot of him. "When's the last time you saw a demon?" I asked, already knowing the answer. Never. Neither of us had ever seen one.

Demons fed on the aura found in all living things and they usually lived and hunted close to their main food source: humans. The easy prey drew them in by the droves and our job was to go and wipe them out. Of course, humans were McDonalds compared to the aura found in a witch or familiar—or any other supernatural creature— but why work for your food when you don't have to? I pushed ahead, avoiding the pockets of mud, and forced him to keep my pace. I didn't plan on keeping us out here all night—I just needed a little bit longer before we turned back. Our squelching footsteps were overwhelmed by the chirping cicadas, I couldn't even hear myself think they were so loud. Perfect. I sighed and reached out to run my fingers over the hanging Spanish moss. Why did my father insist on keeping this from me? What was so terrible about the bayou that I had to stay confined behind the enchanted walls until I graduated?

"I'm starting to think our elders use the stories of demons to scare us into following their rules. They probably went extinct." I pushed further into the swamp, careful to make sure I stepped on solid ground.

"Kaya." Asher's voice was quiet, like how it got when he was about to lecture me.

My eyes rolled skyward. "I know, I know. Your precious textbooks say otherwise, but think for yourself, Ash. The warriors that graduated last year said they still *haven't seen one. What does that tell you?"*

"Kaya!"

I didn't expect the shout—Asher never raised his voice—and I turned, assuming he was stuck again. It took precious seconds for my mind to catch up to the reality before me, and when it did, I couldn't stop the scream that escaped my numb lips. The freakishly long appendages were the first thing I noticed—there were six— and one of them held the still form of my best friend. His face was frozen in a mask of horror and his head twisted at an unnatural angle. The demon's mouth was a spiral hole of serrated teeth, but I swear it grinned at me. Its fat tongue was discolored and dripping with saliva as it tasted Asher's skin in one long, slow lick. The monster clicked its pleasure and another round of clicks and whistles answered from the trees. The air warped around me, red and thick with humidity, but I gave no thought to the strangeness of it.

Demons were outside the community. Demons killed my best friend. Demons...there were demons...

I jerked awake when a heavy hand landed on my shoulder and stared right into the aging face of another passenger. Little creases of worry lined the corners of her eyes as she slowly withdrew her arm.

"Are you alright, child?" She asked, with a thin voice. "You were crying out in your sleep and thrashing all crazy like. I've heard your supposed to wake a person if you catch them like that." She brought a hand to her chin and scratched. "Or maybe you're supposed to leave them be."

My heart had yet to calm down and the nightmare still held me firmly in its grasp, but I managed to somehow thank the lady and she backed away to her seat with a smile. Under my hoodie, my skin was damp, and my hair stuck to my forehead like it had been plastered there. The cool glass of the window felt good against my clammy skin and I watched the miles fly by, unable to close my eyes again. Why now? I hadn't had that nightmare in years, so long I'd almost forgotten how exhausting it could be, and I knew from experience that it wouldn't let me go for a while yet. If it was a figment of my imagination, it probably would've been easier to get rid of, but it wasn't. That night would plague me until my dying days, trapping me in a perpetual hell until I finally joined the others of my kind that deserved such a fate. Asher shouldn't have died that night. He should still be curled up on a chair in the library, memorizing a book we weren't required to read and lecturing me for not taking an interest in our destiny. He should be a normal seventeen-year-old boy, crushing on girls and getting nervous for his last year of training before being chosen by a familiar. Not that he ever had to worry, he always knew I'd choose him.

But Asher had no choices now, I'd stripped them all away the night I forced him past the wall. I had no idea demons truly existed, even though I'd been taught the exact opposite my entire life. I was so cocky and full of myself that I thought I knew better than the entire history of our people. My selfishness got my best friend killed. And now his brother had come to collect on his justice.

I had no idea how long I could outrun him. Auden wasn't stupid, he'd figure out what bus I was on and where it was going in no time. I only had a head start. The question was, how much of a head start? I'd been too scared to get off at any of the stops, petrified that Auden would be there waiting. So far, there was no sign of the witches, but that could change. My legs were cramping, and my ass cheeks fell asleep hours ago, but both were ideal compared to what tortures awaited me at Auden's hand. A shiver snaked down my spine when I thought of him, and I drifted back to the confusion that surrounded my feelings of the prince. He had to hate me for what happened to his little brother, and I couldn't blame him, but his actions contradicted themselves. His attitude and how he spoke to me in the bathroom supported my theory of hate, but how he touched me, what I felt when he had me pressed against the wall, were exact opposites. And I couldn't deny how I reacted, even now thinking about it, another shiver caused me to shimmy in my seat. The wild cat inside me purred her approval, but I ignored her. There was nothing between Auden and me but animosity and a bit of attraction. The stones were cast long ago and there was no escaping the fallout.

The bus pulled into a small rest stop that had a cute little café attached. The red and white checkered curtains screamed Texas and promised a homecooked meal for the weary traveler. I felt, more than heard, my stomach growl with frustration. I had no money for even a cup of coffee, so it would be another hour spent chewing gum. My fellow passengers disembarked to stretch their legs, and I watched them through the window as they crossed the empty parking lot and disappeared. I sighed and stood from my seat to pace the isle. The lights from the café threw distorted shadows across the chairs as I leaned down to touch my toes and stretch my stiff back.

"You're all that's left, little lady."

I jerked back up with enough force to rival a spring-loaded pistol and grabbed at my chest in an attempt to calm my racing heart. The driver stood by the steering wheel with one hand on the pressure lock to the doors. He looked expectant and I tried to collect my thoughts enough to give him some kind of reply.

"All passengers must disembark here for the allotted hour,"

he continued. "It's my scheduled break and I have to clear the vehicle before locking the doors."

I glanced out the window at the now busy café and chewed on the corner of my lip. It was on the tip of my tongue to tell him no, but I didn't want to cause any problems. I slowly shuffled toward the front, continuously sneaking glances out the window as I did. The driver took note of how skittish I was being and tried to reassure me.

"You'll be plenty safe in there, honey. Don't you worry." He winked, but it did nothing to ease my fears. "Mama June don't tolerate any kind of shady business in her café."

I snorted as I tiptoed down the stairs and peeked out the door. This dude had no idea of the "shady business" that went down in places like these every day. The second my foot landed on the gravel lot, I bolted for the women's restroom. The facilities were located on the exterior of the building, but no one jumped out as I made the mad dash. The irony wasn't lost on me that I was seeking shelter in the last place Auden had me cornered, but luckily it was a single stall bathroom and the lock anchored from the inside. My gasps echoed in the small room and I gripped the corners of the ceramic sink as a wave of nausea sent my head spinning. That little burst of energy fed on the last of my reserves, and the little stick of cinnamon gum I popped in my mouth did nothing to replenish it. Delicious smells wafted in through the vent in the ceiling and I groaned with need. Fried chicken. Holy fuck what I wouldn't do for some of that right now. On cue, my stomach clenched, and nausea rolled again. I sank to the floor, not giving two shits about what kind of germs were fornicating on it and wrapped my arms around my knees. I burrowed my face into the sleeves of my hoodie and tried not to cry.

I'd been hungry before, living on the streets of Miami, and survived. I could do it again. Once I reached Los Angeles, I could beg for some cash while I searched for a job. Until then, I had to suck it up and focus on the more critical issues, *getting* there. A knock on the door broke me free from my planning and grounded me in the present.

"Just a minute!" I shouted and flushed the empty toilet before turning on the sink.

I took a good look at my reflection and used some of the tap water to scrub away the funk that stuck to me after my nightmare. With my hair fully tucked inside my hood again, I unlocked the door and peered through the crack. An impatient middle-aged woman taped her foot like it would get me to move faster.

"It's about time," she huffed, when I opened the door to let her pass.

She slammed it behind me, and I turned to face the no longer empty parking lot. Two other Greyhounds pulled up and began unloading their passengers. My mouth went dry as I moved amongst them, scanning each face I passed. No one had warrior tattoos as far as I could tell, but that didn't stop my heart from racing each time a stranger glanced my way. I moved between them like a waif, small and barely noticeable as I fought to maintain a steady pace. The closer I got to the buses, the fewer people I passed, until I was once again alone. By the time I reached my bus, the lights from the café were mostly obscured, but the dark made a perfect place to hide. Just ask the demons, they used it to their advantage all the time. Why couldn't I?

After fifteen minutes of leaning against the bus, I heard the scuff of an approaching footstep. Finally! I was wondering if I had to wait for the rest of the passengers to line up or something before the driver would let us back on. I stepped toward the doors as the old man rounded the neighboring Greyhound but froze when I saw black hair instead of grey and a wicked smirk in place of a kind smile.

"Auden," his name rushed out on a wheeze as I took a step back.

The cut on his temple from our last encounter no longer bled, but a dark bruise marred his otherwise flawless appearance. He didn't look the least bit tousled after hunting me through four different states—the asshole didn't even look tired! Meanwhile, my hair felt greasy enough to make French fries and I ran on fumes. How in the hell was that fair? The crunch of rocks beneath my shoe gave way each step I took as Auden slowly stalked me further between the buses. That smirk never left his face as his eyes scanned me from head to toe and my skin pebbled in goosebumps. My claws pierced the tender skin under my fingernails as I tried to keep my animal-half restrained, but there was no holding her back. My canines slowly elongated until twin pinpricks stung my lower lip. The scent of my own fear only fueled my cat's fight or flight instincts. I knew exactly which she'd choose but ripping out the prince's throat wouldn't solve my problems, only make them worse.

I held on to my waning control and spun. The gravel slipped under my heel, but I quickly corrected myself and bolted in the opposite direction of those calculating golden eyes. He caught me by the picnic tables with a strong tackle that knocked the breath from my lungs and rolled us at the last second so I wouldn't take the brunt of the damage. It still fucking hurt. I broke free on the landing and scrambled to my knees, my fingers clawing at the dirt for some leverage to stand. Auden's arm wrapped around my waist when I didn't move quick enough and I was wrenched back. Before I could blink, he had me on my back with my arms pinned on either side of my head, getting tangled in my hair as it spilled around my shoulders in one thick wave. The prince straddled my waist and the corner of his mouth pulled back in a sly grin.

He leaned down, so close his nose brushed the curve of my cheek. "You didn't think it was going to be that easy, did you?"

His tone was taunting, and I wanted nothing more than to wipe that smug grin off his face, but I relaxed in his hold, knowing if I gave away what I was about to do, he'd overpower me again.

"How'd you find me?" I asked, honestly curious.

"You're serious?" He frowned, and then chuckled like I was intentionally being adorable. "Sweetheart, we've been following your bus since it left the depo." I groaned and he laughed again, relaxing his grip on my wrists just a bit. "Don't be too hard on yourself, I'm a fully trained warrior and you're..."

"A disgraced runaway?" I offered and he shook his head, his smile falling.

"That wasn't what I was going to say."

"How about traitor? Prisoner?" I slowly slid my left foot to the outside of his ankle, careful to keep my movements smooth and precise.

His lips pursed, and he shook his head. "I don't know why you did what you did, but you had to know we'd come for you eventually."

I did know. I lived every day of my life these last four years, looking over my shoulder knowing my past would catch up to me sooner or later. That's why I hadn't just sat on my ass and waited for it like a pathetic victim. I'd trained, and trained, and then trained some more. I broke bones and iced bruises, tore muscles and then rebuilt them to respond to whatever crazy demand I asked of them. I made *myself* a warrior, a secret weapon that no one expected to come in such a disarming package. And I couldn't wait to unleash her. Without warning, I jerked my right hand up while simultaneously pulling my left hand down. Auden was caught off balance just enough for me to lift my hips and roll us over. Now on top, I gave him a fleeting smile before slamming my elbow into the side of his jaw.

I vaulted over him and aimed for the trees, hoping to lose him somewhere in the acres of wilderness that surrounded us. My senses picked up on an extra scent a second too late, and a tawny lion prowled toward me from under a low-hanging branch. There was a challenge in her gaze, one my cat was ready to answer, but we wouldn't win that fight. I skidded to a halt and held my open hands up by my head. I couldn't stop the hiss that escaped as she inched closer. A low growl responded from behind me and I looked back to see the male lion sitting on his haunches, jaws open in warning.

"You just don't learn," Auden, flanked by the two other witches from Miami, sauntered up behind the large feline. "I'm beginning to think you're not very bright."

I bared my teeth at his approach but knew better than to move my hands. "And I'm beginning to think you're just a tool. Don't you have anything better to do than harass me?"

My hostile attitude did nothing to deter him and I found my hands handcuffed behind my back faster than I could say son-of-a-bitch. Before helping me into the backseat of his car, Auden tilted his head, regarding me like one would a puzzle they had yet to master.

"I thought it was a fluke before but it's not, is it?" His fingers reached out to play with a wayward lock of my hair, following the silky strand as it curled past my shoulder. His eyes searched mine and I was surprised to see respect reflecting back at me. "You're trained."

He didn't have to look so surprised. "If you move that hand any lower, you'll find out just how much."

The prince grinned and guided my head through the open door. "Buckle up, Kaya. It's a long trip back home."

CHAPTER
FOUR

My eyes burned as I watched the trees pass outside my window in a mix of brown and green blurs. The SUV rocked down the interstate at not even a mile over the speed limit, but it still felt like time was moving too fast. The minute Auden cuffed me and buckled me in the back seat, I knew my fate; I just wasn't prepared to meet it yet. I counted each mile marker as we grew closer to the state line and racked my overworked brain for a way out of this. Short of throwing myself out of a moving vehicle, I was shit out of luck. One of the other witches released my hands a couple hours ago —thankfully— but it wasn't like taking on five-to-one odds was a good idea either. Nope. I was irrevocably screwed.

My sigh drew Auden's gaze from the passenger seat in front of me. His eyes burned with their ghostly touch, but he didn't say anything. It had been the same for hours—every twitch, scooch, cough, blink—I felt his stare. He'd yet to say a word. No one had. Apparently, everyone in the car played The Quiet Game on expert level. The silence didn't bother me too much, since my head felt like it could split open at any moment, but the lack of distractions left me alone with restless thoughts.

And a crap ton of guilt. Four years was a long time to stay away, and I already anticipated the negative response my return would garner. That wasn't the problem. More than pain or guilt, it was the *fear* that kept me away. Fear that every street held a memory strong enough to break me in two, or that the sound of midnight cicadas would torment rather than soothe. Asher and I left our mark on every corner of that community and the thought of seeing his ghost everywhere I turned caused the breath to catch in my throat and a painful knot to tighten around my heart.

Of course, they would probably take me straight to the prison cells when we arrived, so there was a chance I wouldn't see much of the community at all. And that made me panic for entirely different reasons. I clenched my eyes and tried to breathe, both wishing I could just get it over with and dreading the moment. My stomach growled and then rolled with a wave of nausea. The throbbing in my head increased until I thought I'd faint, and then ebbed away to a dull ache. I felt everyone's gaze on me this time, but it was the boy with the piercing eyes who spoke.

"When was the last time you ate?" Auden looked almost angry that he had to ask, and I tried—and failed— not to glare.

"My stomach wasn't *that* loud." I grumbled, and he raised a brow, still expecting an answer. I sighed and rolled my eyes toward the top of the car. "Fine. I had some Honey Buns at the bus depo in Miami."

I didn't think it was possible, but his glare grew darker. "That was over twenty-four hours ago."

I shrugged. What did he expect me to do about it? It was his fault I was on the run again to begin with.

"When was your last *actual* meal before that?" He asked, and I frowned as I tried to remember.

I'd had a sandwich for lunch before teaching afternoon

classes, but then skipped dinner to go to that party with Braxton and his friends. The Honey Buns were the last thing I ate before getting on the bus, and the ride to Texas took a whole day so—damn. I hadn't had a solid meal in almost two days. No wonder it felt like someone was carving out my stomach with a spoon. Said organ clenched at the reminder and I tried to keep the pain from my face. At my long silence and lack of an answer, Auden faced forward again with a curse. He directed us off the interstate not even two minutes later.

"Cuff her," he ordered, and the witch beside me managed to lock the cool metal around one of my wrists before I jerked away. Crouched up against my door, my eyes dared him to come closer.

"Why the hell are you cuffing me again?" I shouted. My rising anger increased the already unbearable pressure in my head.

Auden gave me a pointed look around the headrest, as if my current behavior was exactly why. I didn't care. Having my arms secured behind me sucked. Not only was it uncomfortable and I already felt like shit, but it made me feel vulnerable in a way I hadn't felt in a long time.

"What if I promise to play nice?" I asked through gritted teeth, while keeping an eye on the witch next to me.

The SUV pulled into the back lot of a generic steakhouse and Auden hopped out. I watched the witch carefully, but he didn't move to grab me. I should've been watching my back. My door flew open and I fell into a set of strong arms. My head spun at the rapid movement, but Auden tightened his hold around my waist until my shoulders met the solid wall of his chest. I took in a deep breath and was overwhelmed by his scent; earthy and sweet, like daytime rain in the heat of summer. With a gentle push, I was once again sitting upright; Auden still pressed against me. His hand slid across my stomach and I held back a shiver as his fingers danced down my arm to my wrist. My eyes closed and swayed a little until I felt Auden's breath stir the hair at my temple. The small touch of his cheek against mine grounded me through the maelstrom of sensations ravaging my body. I wasn't sure if the fluttering in my stomach was the good kind, or a sign that I was going to be sick, but the *click* of metal as it tightened around my wrist answered for me.

I was definitely going to be sick. Right after I kicked Auden's ass.

"Take. them. off." My growl was lethal. Feral. The animal inside me did not like being restrained.

"Not a chance," he whispered, and his lips just barely grazed the shell of my ear.

I jerked away with a snarl and pulled on the cuffs until my shoulders hurt. Auden's large hand covered both of my own until I stopped struggling. He helped me settle more comfortably in the seat before closing the door.

"Behave," he ordered through the open window, and I scoffed.

"Where the hell would I go with my hands cuffed behind me?"

The one side of his mouth curled into a smug grin. "Exactly."

He disappeared into the steakhouse without another word as I sat there fuming. I was surrounded by two witches and their partners, was restraining me really necessary? I wasn't stupid. I'd probably not even make it out of the parking lot. Auden knew me better than I thought, though, because I would've at least tried. Forty-five minutes later, we were back on the road in a car that smelled like heaven, with my hands still cuffed behind my back. And for good reason. Claws broke free from the tips of my fingers I was so pissed. Auden still held the juicy burger in front of my lips as I imagined those claws piercing his eyes.

"And how am I supposed to eat that?" I asked, my voice dangerously calm.

He smirked. "I'm holding it, aren't I?"

"No. *Hell* no." I bared my teeth. "I'm not going to sit here like an invalid while you feed me. Just uncuff me."

He blatantly ignored my request and moved the burger closer to my lips. "They say hand feeding is a critical way to form bonding between beast and master."

"I don't want to bond with you!"

He shrugged and took a bite out of my burger. "Suit yourself."

I watched as he polished off *my* burger, my stomach squeezing in a painful tantrum. It took a while for me to calm down and for my claws to retract. I knew the leather behind me would bear the scars of my fury. Asshole. Auden was such a complete and utter asshole. My body shook with residual anger and my vision swam when I looked out the window. Woah. I frowned. My head felt woozy, like it was full of liquid that sloshed around when I turned. But that couldn't be right because I was so parched that my mouth and throat were scratchy. Auden's acute gaze met my dazed one and I watched his lips move as he asked me a question. It looked like he was saying my name, but I couldn't be sure. He reached back across the center console to tap my cheek as he spoke louder.

"How long has it been since you've had something to drink?" When I didn't answer, he frowned. "Surely not as long as you've been without food?"

I think I shrugged, because he cursed—again— and we pulled over. The witch next to me opened the door and got out, allowing Auden to slide into his vacant seat.

"Being able to shift means your body burns through more

calories and nutrients than even *I* do. Keeping hydrated is especially important after shifting. Even partial shifts," he lectured, eyeing the claw marks in my seat. "Don't you remember that from school?"

I didn't have the energy to remind him that I never made it to those classes, or that I really haven't been able to shift yet—a secret I hoped to keep. He opened a water bottle and brought it to my lips, but I couldn't get my mouth to open. My hands were still trapped behind my back and that stubborn part of me hated having to depend on him.

He tilted the bottle higher until I could feel the cool water. "I swear, Kaya. Don't fight me just this once and drink dammit."

My face scrunched. He sounded genuinely worried, but I chalked it up to him being vexed about not completing his mission. If something happened to me now, he wouldn't be able to see justice served. My desperation won out either way and I allowed the water to glide past my lips. Once I started, I couldn't stop and was soon chugging the whole bottle. Some of the fear left Auden's gaze as I drank, but I was too focused on quenching my thirst to dwell on it. He stopped me after one bottle and held his hand out to the side until a burger was placed in his palm. I glared at him as he unwrapped it. I *knew* he hadn't eaten all of them. My stomach gurgled again at the sight of the sandwich, but when Auden ripped a piece off and brought it to my lips, I only stared at him. He raised a brow when I refused to open my mouth, but patiently waited for my stomach to override my brain. Which it did. Quickly. I opened and he pulled back an inch.

"Don't bite," he warned, and then placed the morsel on my tongue.

My lips closed around his fingers as he pulled back, but I was past the point of caring. The flavor exploded and I groaned. Once I swallowed, Auden had another piece waiting for me. He set it in my mouth. My lips grazed his finger. Repeat. We were both blushing as I finished the burger, but neither one of us looked away. Not when he balled up the empty wrapper. Not even when the SUV started to sway down the interstate again. With a huff, Auden was the first to break free, and once his eyes left mine, the spell was broken. He made no move to reclaim his seat up front, but instead settled deeper into the leather and fixed his gaze out the window. He didn't speak to me again, even though the tick in his jaw gave away his awareness of me watching.

I thought I'd find it hard to relax with him sitting so close. My senses were heightened, and his scent zinged through me like a livewire, forcing my shoulders to strain against the cuffs as my inner beast took notice.

Down girl.

I slowly released the breath I'd been holding. My muscles were still tense, so I turned my attention to relaxing them until the confusing boy next to me was the last thing on my mind.

I DRIFTED— hovered somewhere in the middle of conscious and not, in the in-between where dreams and reality swirled into wants and desires. I adjusted my head until it rested at a slight angle, the surface beneath me firm but not uncomfortable. The soothing, consistent croon of the tires and gentle sway of the SUV lulled me even further, until even the biting metal still restricting my arms became a distant irritation. I was comfortable and surrounded in warmth, like I was cocooned in sunshine and a pleasant, earthy scent teased my senses. The sensations lured my mind to wandering. Like a lock had been turned, memories from days long past roamed free with no sense of time or direction.

Maybe it was the feeling of sunshine on my skin, or the light fragrance of a rainstorm that I couldn't shake, but I found myself bound to a memory so unlike the others that haunted me. I remembered it was hot out, the humidity a constant companion in the bayou, but it was cool under the tree we were climbing. We were young back then; a year or so shy of being considered teenagers. It was a rough time for both of us. My mom passed away that year and Asher had finally started to feel the pressure of being a prince. Maybe that's why I teased him so hard for stopping on the lowest branch—I was channeling my pre-teen angst over my mother into trying to help Asher overcome his fear of heights. Or I was just being a bitch. Either way, I left him clinging to the relative safety down below while I shot for the top. I aimed for those tiny branches in the canopy, the ones that bent under your weight with the potential to snap at any moment. The adrenaline was exciting and addictive, plenty strong enough to smother the hurt I was working so hard to escape from feeling.

Following through had never been a problem for me, not even back then. It was what came after that I never thought about. The consequences. Sitting at the top was everything I thought it would be; breathtaking, exhilarating, and completely free. Coming back down was an entirely different experience. My muscles froze and locked around the tree trunk when the branches grew further apart. It was such a long way *down*, how had I even gotten this high? Even now I recalled the overwhelming terror, my racing heart, and how Asher's face swam as my vision spun. Before I could work through my fears as we'd been taught, Asher panicked and ran for help. I felt sick to my stomach thinking of my father finding me like this, but that wasn't who Asher brought. His older brother Auden stood at the base of the tree and looked up at me with such a beautiful smile that I almost swooned right off the branch. At fifteen, Auden was all lean muscle and shaggy hair.

He'd already moved into the intermediate training classes, so I hardly saw him at school anymore, but he always seemed to be there when we needed him. I watched him from my place hidden in the leaves, my hands going numb from my death grip on the bark, but he never once made fun of me for getting scared. He stood there with his arms held out and a promise to catch me dancing behind his smile. The feeling of being in his arms was all I dreamed about for a year after that. Even my shirt smelt like him, freakin summer raindrops for weeks and I refused to wash it even after the scent faded. Heights never bothered me again. He never realized it, but Auden gave me confidence that day. And knowing he would always be there to catch me only made me more reckless.

Gentle fingers brushed the hair from my cheek to tuck it behind my ear and I shivered. Goosebumps pebbled down my arms as I held my breath. There was a pause and then the fingers were back, trailing through my hair in an almost absent-minded caress. My eyes were still closed but I was fully awake now. The remaining wisps of my memories faded with every brush of those fingers, leaving behind only a faint, rich aroma that reminded me of the damp earth that lingered after a shower. The scent disappeared with my next breath, just as fleeting.

"I know you're awake."

My eyes flew open. That hand made another pass through my hair and I could no longer deny it. That scent...the touch... Auden was *petting* me. Holy. Fucking. Shit. A horde of ants marching down my shirt wouldn't have made me move faster. I jerked away, my body recoiling like it was on fire. And it kind of was. I was sure my cheeks were red enough to rival a burning ember and the rest of me wasn't fairing much better, what with Auden watching me with that arrogant grin. My thoughts were racing. I'd fallen asleep on him. His hand...his fingers... they'd been— I shook my head but couldn't untangle what I felt with what it could possibly mean. He was supposed to hate me.

"Did you have a good nap?" Auden teased, his eyes glowing with mirth.

My blush deepened. "I need to use the bathroom," I blurted, and immediately wished I could pull the words back.

Why did I blab the weirdest shit when I was around him? To his credit, he didn't make fun of my inopportune announcement, only shook his head and kept that damn grin on his face —the one that said he knew something I didn't. Whatever. As long as he stayed on that side of the car, I could deal with it. Silence followed as we exited the interstate and pulled into a rest stop. Only one other car was parked in the lot and I swallowed my disappointment. There went any chance I had of blending in with a crowd. It shouldn't have come as a surprise; it was dark out. Most people with common sense wouldn't willingly pull off here this late at night. The area wasn't well lit and aside from a couple picnic tables, the facilities were shadowed by thick trees that echoed with what had to be thousands of crickets.

It was actually kind of beautiful, for all that it was secluded. The air was warm and fragrant with the scent of pine, pushed by a gentle breeze rustling the stoic trees.

"Call in our location," Auden ordered, and the others exited the car to scout the area.

Auden opened my door and wrapped his hand around my elbow to steady me as I stepped down. The second my feet hit the pavement, I half turned so he could get to the lock.

"I promise to be a good girl this time," I winked over my shoulder.

"Cute," he scowled, and grabbed the chain between the cuffs.

He used it to direct me up the sidewalk and toward the sign for the woman's restroom. Just before the door, I dug in my heels and refused to move one step further, despite the fact that my bladder truly was desperate at this point.

"I know guys can get away with hands-free miracles," I sneered. "But us girls work with a different set of anatomy. You need to uncuff me." He opened his mouth to argue, I could tell, but I cut him off. "I'm not stupid enough to try and run, Auden. Seriously."

With a sigh and a warning glare, he turned me around to fiddle with the lock.

"Layla will be in there with you," he warned, stepping close enough that I could feel the heat from his body.

Arms now free, I spun around and moved toward the door. Auden slammed his hand on the wall in front of me, blocking my path. He brought his other up as well, effectively caging me in.

"Don't give me a reason to come in there." His voice was gruff and low, with the hint of a dare. Like he *wanted* me to mess up. "Remember what happened last time."

It was my turn to smirk. "You mean when I escaped and knocked you on your ass?"

His head tilted and a few locks of hair fell forward, adding to the intensity of his stare. "I won't underestimate you again," he promised, and moved closer. "But I'd love another chance to see what you can do."

There was a question in that statement, one I was nowhere near ready to answer. Despite the slight tremble in my legs, I ducked under his arm and escaped into the girl's room. My privacy didn't last long as a familiar—who I assumed was Layla — followed me in a short time later. She didn't say anything as she leaned against the sinks, arms crossed. So, it was going to be like that. As a fellow shifter, it hurt that I couldn't turn to her for support, but I understood. To her, I was a traitor. Not liking how that made me feel, I buried the pain and ducked into a stall.

Auden was waiting by the SUV when we came out, cuffs swinging around his finger. I grimaced as we got closer.

"Do you have to?" The question ended on a whine and I winced. I didn't want to come across as weak, but just the thought of putting my arms behind my back again made me want to cry. Auden must have seen something on my face, even though I tried my best to maintain a cool exterior.

"Tell you what," he held his hand out and I reluctantly lifted my arm. "I'll only lock the one side."

He clicked the metal around my wrist and then the other half around the door handle after helping me back in the car. I studied his face as he buckled the seatbelt across my lap.

"Just like that?" I asked, unable to keep my grateful mouth shut. "No warnings of what will happen if I try to fight it?"

He shook his head. "It's called a compromise. I'll make you more comfortable if you stop being a pain in my ass."

Before I could reply with a smartass comment, one of the other witches approached and whispered something in Auden's ear. His eyes widened at whatever it was, and he turned away from me.

"Here?" I heard him ask in disbelief. "Is she sure?"

There was a response, but I couldn't make out the rest of the conversation. Unease prickled the back of my neck and I fought the shiver that rolled down my spine. Auden sent him off to wherever the others disappeared and climbed into the front seat.

"What's going on?" I asked, as I watched the witch silently fade into the trees.

There was a slight breeze wafting in through the cracked windows, but I couldn't scent the others anymore. Auden didn't look at me when he answered, he was too busy staring at the same place I was.

"Layla said she scented a demon near the restrooms when she escorted you."

"What?" I shrieked. "And she's just now saying something?"

"Relax, Kaya. It was an old trace; at least a few hours." He was watching me in the rearview mirror now, so he had a full view of my crazy.

I threw my free hand in the air and rolled my eyes. "Three hours wasn't that long ago. What if it comes back?"

Auden shrugged like it wasn't a big deal. "Then we'll handle it."

My jaw dropped. It was inconceivable to me that he would be so nonchalant about a demon being so close to us. I knew that fully trained witches and their partners actively hunted them, but...still, it was a *demon*. Not dealing with the demon meant it would continue to torment and kill countless victims before we'd potentially have another shot, yet I still found myself wanting to run full speed in the opposite direction. Protecting humanity was drilled into us at birth; no one else in the community would've thought about running. Even more proof that I no longer belonged.

CHAPTER FIVE

We sat there for a while, listening to the cricket's chirp. The immediate threat wore off when we saw no sign of the demon, but anticipation still lingered as we waited for the others to return. With the windows cracked, I tuned in to the nighttime routine of the forest creatures and their colorful symphony clashed with the deafening silence in the car.

My thoughts veered back to worries over what would happen when we reached the community in a few hours. What would the others think when they saw me? I pictured an angry mob at the gates, fists raised and fingers pointed, demanding my head for the loss of their beloved prince. Over dramatic? Most likely, but not out of the realm of possibility. There weren't many of us left now so our people were close knit more out of necessity than intention. Even if they didn't know yet, my return wouldn't go unnoticed for long.

"What's going to happen to me when we get back?" My voice was small; quiet in the silent car.

I heard more than saw Auden shift in his seat and I knew he

was watching me even before I looked up. His eyes were shuttered—I found no comfort in them.

"You can't escape justice, Kaya." He wasn't being cruel, but his words stung nonetheless. "You know my father is a fair king, and the Council will punish what befits the crime."

That's what worried me. Murder wasn't rewarded with a slap on the wrist; I fully expected to be put on display and used as an example to any other abhorrent individuals dwelling in the underbelly of our population. Exile didn't exist in our world due to risk of exposure so, my options were either death or life in prison. Neither appealed to me. I looked out the window again, wishing for the freedom the moonlight and summer air offered. I sniffed and my nostrils flared at the acrid odor oozing toward us from the trees.

"It'll be okay," Auden tried to comfort me, but we both knew his words were empty. It was out of his hands now. "When we get back—"

I held up my hand, cutting off whatever he was about to promise. I couldn't listen to him and hear what was happening outside at the same time. I felt his fingers wrap around mine.

"Kaya, I'm just—"

"They've stopped," I whispered, and his hand grasped mine tighter until I looked at him, pupils split from the small shift I couldn't stop.

"What do you sense?" he asked, instantly alert.

Doubt crept in when I realized I couldn't say. The crickets were quiet, that's what caught my attention, but that wasn't proof of anything. I didn't know how to explain the hair on my neck standing on end or how I could feel my animal half pacing inside me, eager to get at whatever lurked behind the tree line. Auden unlocked the doors and I reached forward, clutching at his shirt.

"It's probably nothing," I babbled, feeling more stupid than

I ever had before. And that was saying something. "I don't know what I'm talking about. They're just bugs. I shouldn't have said anything."

Auden let me ramble. He didn't taunt or tease me for asking him to stay, but instead told me he was going to do a perimeter search just in case.

"Trust your instincts, Kaya," he spoke through the window.

I hadn't noticed the lingering trace of demon earlier, how could he trust my instincts now? I watched him as he circled the car and moved toward the restrooms. Every muscle in my body went rigid when I lost sight of him behind the building and I had to force myself to calm down. Dry leaves scratched the sidewalk as another breeze blew them by, but now I couldn't hear Auden's footsteps. I pulled myself up on my knees and brought my ear closer to the crack in the window. Still nothing. It could mean he walked out of range, but I couldn't fight the feeling that something wasn't right. It was more than the awareness of being watched; it was in my gut; it was down to my very *bones*. The next breeze that blew through the car only confirmed my suspicions.

Demon.

The air was choked with the rotten stench of it. It was so potent I knew it couldn't be far. Why hadn't I heard any fighting? I strained closer to the top of the window, but the cuff bit into the skin of my wrist and I hissed. Dammit, I should've asked Auden to unlock it before he left. Deep down I knew he would've said no. I didn't want to acknowledge it, but he wouldn't risk his prize getting away, even with the potential danger. The car jolted and rocked, the roof caving in under the weight of something very large on top of it.

"Auden?" I called out, hoping it was him, or one of the others, but no one responded.

Slowly, I pressed my face to the glass, trying in vain to see what was above me. A string of clicks and whistles punctured the stillness and I jerked away from the window. The SUV suddenly felt too small and my instinct to run only made my confinement worse. Sweat dotted my brow as I tried not to panic. I failed when a thick goop of saliva seeped down my window and I lost the hold on my emotions. I yanked against my seatbelt, ignoring the ache it caused in my arm as I blindly searched for the release button. The demon's drool ate at the glass and I watched in horror when began to disintegrate.

"Shit. Shit. Shit."

The seatbelt came off with a soft *click*, but the cuff was another story. I pulled as hard as I could and tried to strategically squeeze my hand out somehow, but the damn thing wouldn't break. Claws sprouted and retracted with every other breath. My fangs elongated until I couldn't hide them behind my lips and I growled when a drop of the saliva made it through the window to land on my arm. At the smell of my blood, the demon screeched, and I cried out. The sound pierced my ears like a high-pitched frequency. A claw, topped with sharp barbs, wiggled its way through the slowly melting window. Looking more like a pincer, the four fingers were fused into two sets on either side, and they clacked together as the demon reached for its prey.

Half leaning over the car, the demon's six eyes watched me with a sickening glee. Its arms were longer from the elbow joint down and it used that extra reach to strike at me. I screamed as its pincer ripped at my skin and latched on. My hold on my animal disappeared with the utter agony that spread down my arm. It burned and I tossed my head as I tried to escape the never-ending pain. By some miracle, I broke free and scrambled to the floor between the seats, my injured arm still offered up like a sacrifice thanks to the cuff. From my new vantage point, I could see all of the demon's contorted legs through the windows as it sprawled over the top of the car like a gigantic spider. Its arm reached closer and more of its acidic saliva dripped inside. When the glass finally cracked under the pressure, the demon arm retreated…only to ram through the center of the window, causing the last of it to shatter on impact. I threw my arms up to protect my face and a shockwave went through the already broken car. The door on the other side blew off its hinges and there was Auden, eyes blazing with fury.

His rescue was just a second too late, and the demon got ahold of me again. Its pincer tore a chunk out of my shoulder and vomit flooded the back of my throat.

"Auden!" I screamed, the pain making my voice shrill.

The demon chittered and moved in for the kill, but I kept my gaze locked on Auden as I waited for it to strike. The cuff around my wrist unlocked and my arm fell to the seat. With another wave of Auden's hand, I found myself sliding across the leather, out the side door, and into his arms. The demon shrieked its fury at losing its dinner, and I knew it wasn't done with us yet.

"I've got you," Auden murmured, setting me down on my feet.

My lower lip trembled, but I kept my jaw locked so I wouldn't cry. My arm, shoulder, and head were now throbbing in tandem.

"How do we kill it?" I panted, even as I wondered if it was possible.

It was only the two of us now, seeing as the others hadn't appeared at the commotion. I tried not to dwell on what that meant when we were facing a similar fate. Auden pulled a wicked knife from his belt. The metal gleamed in the moonlight as he turned to face the pissed off demon.

"*You* do nothing," he ordered, keeping me out of sight behind him. "*I'm* going to stab it through the head with this."

I didn't get to argue before he ran headfirst at the monstrosity now only feet away. The demon had climbed off the ruined SUV, so Auden wove through its many legs. His skill left me awestruck, briefly distracting me from the danger at hand. I'd never seen anyone move with such swiftness. He stalked and struck with the cunning grace of a feline—with the skill that I *should* have in order to help him. I could only watch, heart in my throat, as he fought to get close enough to use that knife. With so many legs, it wasn't an easy feat and he was obviously tiring. Between one leap and the next, the demon jabbed with its pincer and struck Auden in the chest. I was running before he even hit the ground.

"No!" he roared, his hand held up to keep me at bay, but it was too late.

I knelt beside him as another pincer descended upon us. Auden raised his arm again and with a grunt of pain, his power sent me sliding across the asphalt and out of the way. I think some part of me fractured when I saw the demon hoist Auden in the air by his neck like a rag doll. It was Asher all over again. But unlike that night, I was no longer helpless. My claws were back, curling my fingers with how forcefully they sprang from my fingertips. From deep within, my animal snarled, and it tore from my chest like a battle cry. I was moving then, leaping and climbing up those grotesque legs, sinking my claws into its squishy abdomen as I tore my way to its head. It didn't have a chance to so much as twitch before I was there—claws shredding and cracking— *puncturing* down into its skull. The demon gave one last keening cry before it collapsed, its legs curling underneath it like a dead bug.

I stayed on top of it. My claws retreated, leaving my bare hand half inside the demon's scrambled brains, but I was past the point of caring. Our blood mixed as the burning on my right side reached intolerable levels.

"Kaya." Auden's voice called to me from the other end of a long tunnel. Too far for me to answer back, but I somehow found the strength to pry open my eyes. His face was bruised and speckled with blood, but no less beautiful. "It's okay now, Kaya. You're going to be okay."

Who was he trying to convince? As I staved off the awaiting darkness, I wondered if he was going to be upset that I couldn't stand trial for killing his brother, or if this would be penance enough.

My shoulder was on fire. Deep rooted flames licked down my arm, searing skin and muscle until even my fingertips throbbed. The pain was mind-numbing. I thrashed against my captors, but my kicks couldn't break me free and I was left screaming as another wave of heat charred what was left of my control. The animal inside me roared and my captors cursed when my hooked claws shredded skin.

"Shit! What the fuck?"

More hands fumbled over my arms and legs until my struggles caused my own skin to tear and I roared again.

"She broke the restraints!"

"Someone tranq her!"

I snarled at the thought and my teeth hit air when I tried to bite the asshole who suggested putting me out. Another round of flames. I bucked against their hold, wanting the stranger's hands off me nearly as bad as I wanted the pain to stop. Their grips only tightened. A whine escaped past my lips when a hand squeezed my wrist a little too hard.

"Ease up, asshole, you're hurting her."

I recognized that voice. My lids cracked open and my eyes rolled wildly as I looked for him. Several faces blurred in elongated sneers and worried frowns. Where is—*there.* Auden's dark locks fell partially over one eye and his lips were pressed into a hard line as he held me down with both hands on my shoulders.

"It hurts," I mewled, as tears mixed with the snot and blood already staining my shirt.

"I know, sweetheart," his voice was gentle, but he didn't let up on his grip. "It's the poison."

Poison? Images flooded my mind through the pain. A rest stop. Glass breaking. Screams. *The demon.* My shoulder being punctured by its sharp pincers. I remembered Auden suffered from a similar strike, but he pressed into me like the same poison wasn't coursing through his veins. For the first time, I took note of where I was. Or, tried to. Auden and four other faces held me down, my back pressed against something firm but soft, and a bright light shone right in my face with the glare of a thousand suns. Where was I? I craned my neck trying to see, but the movement pulled at my shoulder and I growled.

"Let me up," I demanded, as the weight of their stares and hands began to truly register. Auden's frown deepened, but he didn't budge.

He gave a slight shake of his head. "I can't do that."

I tried to fight off the panic, at least long enough for him to explain himself. Maybe he had reasons. Maybe we were somewhere up high, and he was preventing me from falling to my death. Highly unlikely, but I needed something to hold onto for why this was happening. Auden's fingers tensed and seemed to clamp down harder just as another face appeared beside his. The man was older, a characteristic easily distinguished by his graying hair, but it was the way Auden obeyed his direction that told me he was the one in charge.

"Use more strength, son. You can't hurt her more than she already is."

Auden's hands pressed deeper at his command and my lip curled at the pain. Well, that was obviously a lie. The added pressure on my shoulder slowly grew until the flames were back, starting from my fingers this time and working their way up. My claws ripped into whatever material I lay on top of, an involuntary reaction to the sting. The hands on my arms and legs renewed their holds with gusto and the simmering panic within me ruptured.

"Auden." I didn't recognize my voice. It was reedy and thin, like I couldn't get enough air.

My back bowed and the hands pulled me down again. My animal was close to the surface now, fueled by my hysteria. Tuffs of fur broke out across my limbs and face. The pinch in my gums told me my fangs were still loose and my normally muted senses were on overdrive. Which only made my shoulder hurt worse.

"Hold her still!"

More pressure. More pain. I screamed when a needle came into view and my thrashing increased.

"Auden!" I pleaded.

I broke an arm free and swiped my claws at the man with the needle. I didn't care if he was in charge, he was *not* sticking me with that thing. My first strike missed, and I wasted no time trying again, but Auden caught my wrist before it made contact. Pinning my hand on my stomach, he gritted his teeth against my show of strength and kept me still.

"Auden, please." My voice broke as my eyes widened.

"Shh," he whispered in my ear, and I fought to contain my sobs. He pulled back to look at me, his face so close I could see the few freckles dusting his skin. "I've got you," he promised.

His words had the desired effect, sweeping the fight right out of my limbs until I lay deflated on the table. Almost like a trained reaction, my body responded before I had the chance to think about it. Some part of me, a huge part, still trusted him. The certainty in his eyes is what I held on to; the promise of safety and the knowledge that he wouldn't let me down.

Until he gave a stiff nod and the man beside him moved closer.

He tricked me; the realization hit me like a bucket of ice water, stealing the breath from my lungs with the sting of it. He calmed me down just enough for the others to get a better hold on me and now I was well and truly trapped. I fought with every ounce of strength I had left, but it was no use. The pinch in my arm was nothing compared to the pain I already suffered, but the weightlessness that followed was new. My breathing slowed and my mind detached from the rest of my body. Inside, my animal slept and with every peaceful breath we took, the claws retracted, and my muscles relaxed. The forceful hands slowly lifted off me, no longer anchoring me. A pair of golden eyes burned into mine until I couldn't even follow my own thoughts, but one word stuck with me as I floated away; betrayal.

CHAPTER SIX

Sleep eluded me. I watched the shadows move across the walls with every passing hour, feeling time slip away and knowing I could do nothing to stop it. I was exhausted and my eyes burned with every blink, but I couldn't close them. The ghosts of this room sat too close for me to rest. The beige walls were as barren as before—even with the obvious fresh coat of paint, the heavy fumes couldn't mask the smell that clung to this place; sterile and not at all comforting. I was in the infirmary. I was *back*. The monitor beeped from the spike in my pulse and I closed my eyes to try and hide from the truth a little longer.

I knew I'd end up here eventually—it was inevitable from the second Auden handcuffed me—but I thought I'd have the chance to slowly come to terms with it. Not be outside the walls one minute and find myself trapped inside them the next. I inhaled and slowly released my breath a few times, then opened my eyes again. It was easier to take it in the second time and I instead focused on *why* I was here. My entire right arm was wrapped in gauze, but I felt no pain. I vividly remembered the demon attack and the agony its many pincers could cause. I killed it after it hurt Auden; I knew that for sure. That kind of rage wasn't easy to forget. Neither was the feel of its brains getting trapped beneath my claws. I lifted a hand to see if any of the disgusting goop remained but couldn't bring my arm higher than my hip.

Dread settled somewhere deep in my gut as I pulled on my arm again. And again. The siderails of my bed shook with the force of my distressed pulls and my heart climbed higher up my throat with each failed attempt to be free. Another set of cuffs adorned my wrists, the squishy kind usually reserved for the more... mental patients. A quick kick told me my ankles weren't given the same treatment and I nearly cried with relief. I didn't do well with confinement or being helpless in general. Having my strength ripped from me was my literal definition of hell. And my biggest fear. Horrible things happen when you give up control, or when its forced from you. My mom and Asher were only a couple examples and my current situation was yet another to add to the list. Having my legs free meant there was a still a chance at escape, and I held that thought in my mind as I talked myself down from a panic attack.

Breathe. They haven't fully *confined you.*

Not like they did to get me here. With every useless tug on my wrists, I felt a pair of invisible hands holding me down; I saw a pair of golden eyes that promised freedom and then severed that hope with one unyielding push. Anger rose through the storm inside me and I latched onto it, basking in the memory of his betrayal rather than let myself spiral. Hours must have passed, but the annoying clock on the wall said it had only been thirty minutes. I counted the ticks. I should've closed my eyes and forced myself to sleep—I needed the rest—but when I finally stopped thinking about what was coming, or stopped jumping at every sound outside my door, my brain thought it would be fun to think about Asher.

Growing up, my antics brought us to the infirmary more often than not. It was never for anything worse than some broken bones, thankfully, and we were discharged with plenty of time left in the day to get into more trouble. But on the rare occasions that I had to withstand an overnight stay, Asher would sneak in and sit by my bed through the night. He once told me he did it because he liked knowing he could protect me too. There was nothing remotely dangerous about the infirmary, but I let him think it was brave.

What I wouldn't give to have him beside me right now, to hear the rustling of paper as he read some ridiculously boring book. I didn't realize how much I relied on him or how deeply my childhood was anchored to how I viewed the world with him my by side. Not until I lost him. I deserved everything that's happened to me and all the things still yet to come. I truly did. Footsteps outside sent my heart into a gallop. Multiple shadows passed under my door, but only one stopped in front of it. I braced myself for the King's Guard to bust in and carry me away for sentencing, but the man standing in front of me was no guard. His white coat screamed doctor and his fake smile set off alarm bells.

A vision of him ordering Auden to hold me still while he readied a needle had me scowling before he could open his mouth to greet me.

That's right. I remember you, asshole.

He wasn't as old as I'd originally thought, maybe early fifties, with a strong jaw. The laugh lines around his eyes and mouth told me he was quick to smile, but I couldn't shake the vision of him standing over me, back-lit by the light, as his hand lowered that needle closer to my skin. If my hostility bothered him, he didn't show it. He pulled a chair alongside my bed like nothing was wrong and maintained that damn smile as he sat down.

"Miss Thornton—may I call you Kaya?" The scowl was a permanent fixture on my face, and I had no plans to change it. In fact, I worked on glaring even harder. After an uncomfortable cough, he moved on. "Miss Thornton, then. I'm Dr. Ellis and I've overseen your care since you and the prince were brought in last night. Do you remember what happened?"

Was he serious? Like I could forget being mauled by a demon and *then* being tranqed like a wild animal. My cheeks burned at the memory. But I gave no response. I didn't even blink.

"You, young lady, are very lucky to be alive," he told me with a smile, like it was such an accomplishment. Like I wasn't thrust in the path of the demon to begin with, and then forced here when its poison left me incapacitated. "One more hour without antivenom, Miss Thornton, and you would've died."

I hadn't realized I was that bad off. I'll never forget the burning fire that engulfed my arm after being clawed, but I wondered how Auden faired. Did they have to hold him down too as it burned him from the inside out? Dr. Ellis sighed with impatience and I stopped thinking about Auden.

"Perhaps you can tell me your pain level, on a scale of one to ten?" It was a freakin fifteen, but I wasn't going to tell him that. The incessant ticking of the clock filled the silence until I turned my ire to it as well, wishing the power of my glare alone could knock it off the wall. Dr. Ellis didn't seem bothered one bit and I tried to show I was just as indifferent, even if I was going crazy on the inside. My nerves were frayed and playing mind games with the doc only shredded them further.

"I'm only trying to help you, Kaya. I'm here to aid you through this as you transition back to being the happy girl you were before."

I snorted and rolled my eyes, unable to hold back how ridiculous I thought his charade was. He knew nothing about me or who I was before. That thin folder in his lap told him outdated data about a thirteen-year-old that no longer existed and I was confident there was nothing in there but the basic profile collected on every student. He knew nothing of my home life before I left, the gaping hole that's festered in me since losing Asher, and aside from noticing how pissed off I was, he had no idea what thoughts tortured me now. And I sure as hell wasn't planning on telling him. When his attempt at being friendly failed, he tried another approach.

"Let's try a different topic then, shall we? Something other than last night." He kept that manila folder open in his lap. "We know you've started your cycle because we saw your claws as we—" he glanced at my restraints but made no move to take them off. "What we don't know yet is what breed you've presented as. Auden said he never saw you fully shift."

My brows rose. Like a change of topic was going to make me spill my guts to him. Why bother trying? He looked like he was honestly trying to get me to open up, but I was bound to get a guilty verdict. Execution was not off the table. Maybe they planned life imprisonment instead, so they needed me healthy? Either way, I didn't feel inclined to answer. The doctor sighed and closed my file. Despite my less than forthcoming attitude, the room lacked tension. Dr. Ellis reclined in his chair like he had all day, and who knows, maybe he did.

"I appreciate you allowing me to speak with you today," his smile was looking more genuine by the minute, but anger was still firmly rooted within me. "We *do* need to update your history since your records end abruptly at age thirteen. Everything seemed to be in order up until then. Have you had any past traumas we should know about? Excluding what brought you here, of course." I kept my jaw clenched. He laughed, "Ah yes, the silent treatment continues. Regardless, the blood tests will answer most of our questions. Will you allow us to collect a sample?"

The door gently opened behind him and a nurse squeezed past with a small tray. It appeared too well planned, like the nurse had been waiting outside this whole time, listening in for his cue. Dr. Ellis watched me as she moved closer and began to set up her equipment. The needle flashed in the fluorescent lights and I glared at him again.

He responded with a charming smile. "You'll understand if I'm not the one holding the needle this time, hm?"

"This will only pinch a moment," the nurse told me, leaning closer.

My tongue finally came unglued and I moved my arm away as much as the restraints would allow. "I'd really rather you didn't."

It was like I'd hit the pause button and they both froze. Dr. Ellis opened his mouth, then closed it, obviously surprised at my decision to speak, let alone deny him, but he quickly recovered.

"I'm afraid you have no choice in the matter," he replied, his voice firm, but not unkind. "All students must have an updated chart each year, as I'm sure you remember." At my skepticism, he added, "It's only routine lab work."

"Can you take these off at least?" I asked, shaking the restraints.

He shook his head, "Unfortunately no, my dear. It's protocol to have a patient on a twenty-four hour hold after a psychosis episode."

"After a what?"

He gave me a tight smile. "You attacked a nurse as she changed your dressings and scratched yourself pretty bad in the process."

I glanced down at all the gauze. "But I don't remember doing that."

The doctor nodded as if he expected my answer. "We weren't sure if it was a reaction from the poison or not. Hence the hold."

With my anger somewhat faded, I could tell he was being genuine in not wanting to upset me. I scented no dishonesty from him, and that was the only reason I allowed the nurse to draw blood without incident. When they left, I pulled on my restraints again. I knew the padded cuffs were temporary, and better than the metal ones Auden forced on me, but I still wanted them off. The need to pace, to *move*, was overwhelming and even though my legs were free, I felt trapped. Anxiety rose in me again. What if I had to pee? What if they came to carry me away and I had no way to defend myself? Knowing a mental breakdown was a very real possibility, I took a deep breath and relaxed against the pillow. That maddening ticking of the clock was ever-present in the background but after a time it started to blur into one long drone. With luck it would drown out the dark thoughts creeping on the edge of my sanity.

I LOOKED EVERYWHERE and finally found him sitting under the gazebo with his nose buried in a book. As usual. I huffed and walked faster. We were late again, and it annoyed me that I was going to be in trouble with my father all because Asher hated training. We were both thirteen this year and the intermediate training was significantly harder than what we were doing before. My muscles were in a permanent state of sore and new blisters cracked every time I moved my hands, but I loved it. I lived *for it. I felt myself growing stronger each day and if I kept at it, I knew I'd be approved to pair with Asher upon graduation. Then again, if we*

continued to be late to practice, we might not make it that far. I focused on reigning in my tempter as I approached. It was hard for me to not grab Asher by the shoulders and shake him for being so careless about our future, but I had to be careful with him. He didn't react well to confrontation. As the youngest prince, and with no real affinity for fighting, he would most likely be assigned to the government after graduation. And as his familiar, I would follow him. I'd be lucky to ever see a demon with that kind of assignment, but I couldn't picture myself anywhere but at his side. If that was somewhere behind a desk, then so be it.

I closed the last few feet to the gazebo and froze at the scene before me. Asher sat on the bench; his nose buried in a thick textbook as per usual. But what wasn't typical was Asiel standing in front of him. The oldest son of the Wardwell line was already nineteen and about to graduate with his partner. He stood taller than even Auden and shared the same black hair that decorated the heads of his brothers, but he lacked their compassion. Something inside him was rotten. I'd always thought so. He was quick to sneer and slow to forgive, not good qualities for our next ruler, in my opinion. I approached from behind and had a clear view to whatever tortures he planned to inflict on his brother today.

"You're supposed to bow to the Crown Prince when he addresses you." Asiel's voice was deep and filled with disdain as he looked down on his little brother.

Asher, to his credit, didn't even look up when he replied, "I'm a prince too, brother. And royal protocol dictates that I don't have to bow for anyone other than father. And traditionally only at a few functions each year."

It was a common response for Asher; educated, simple, and delivered with no emotional emphasis. A fact that I knew only pissed Asiel off more. For reasons still unknown, he couldn't stand his youngest brother and Asher's composed responses were a constant trigger for him. I didn't have time to say anything before Asiel brought his foot down on the textbook, sending the delicate papers flying. Asher's mouth dropped open on a cry as he lunged for the tome that was probably older than all our ages put together.

"Do you have any *idea what you just did!" So lost in his anger, Asher didn't notice the sick grin growing on his brother's face. But I did.*

I dove between them before Asiel's foot could strike something far more precious. I landed on my already sore knee as I brought both arms up, crossed in a block. The strength behind the kick caught me by surprise and I flew back, ass over head to land in a heap beside Asher. I was back on my feet within seconds and put myself squarely between the princes. That was no teasing hit. If it had made contact.... Asiel smirked as my eyes grew wider.

"Kaya, right on time," Asiel sneered. "You do always seem to show up at the worst possible moments."

I sensed Asher getting to his feet behind me, and I adjusted my stance to keep him covered.

"What are you playing at? That kick could have seriously hurt him!" I shouted, and Asiel frowned like he couldn't believe a thirteen-year-old was yelling at him. "Don't you get tired of always being an asshole?"

That was the wrong thing to say, and I knew it the second his frown went from being annoyed to royally pissed. Pun intended. He drew himself up to his full height, adding an extra couple inches of imposing intimidation before opening his mouth to deliver whatever he had up his sleeve to shut me up.

"This really isn't your place," he growled and took a step closer. "Remove yourself from my presence so that I can have a private *conversation with my brother."*

Asher's entire body trembled behind me and I knew my decision was made. I was disobeying a direct order by staying, but I couldn't leave now. What kind of familiar was I if I left my charge in what was obviously very real danger? Asiel's kick wasn't one for bruising; it was meant to break *something, and I refused to walk away and let him get another shot.*

"Fine," he growled. "I'll remove you myself."

He reached out one long arm and grabbed ahold of my hair. The thin strands quickly tangled around his fingers and I yelped. Instinctively, I clawed at his hand with both of mine, but he wouldn't let go. He pulled me closer, instead, until his lips were inches from my face. I'd never noticed how dark his eyes were—the center was solid black with hardly any of the telltale Wardwell gold shining through.

"I never promised to be gentle about it," Asiel laughed, before lifting me until my toes barely brushed the floor.

I was definitely screaming now, as chunks of my hair ripped the skin off my scalp. Asiel held me higher, like I weighed next to nothing, and continued to laugh while tears streamed down my face. I could hardly hear Asher's pleads over the sounds of my own cries, but somewhere in the back of my mind—behind the pain— a voice told me Asher was next, as soon as his brother finished with me. I couldn't let that happen. My foot struck out on reflex and laded a solid kick to Asiel's precious family jewels. He dropped me to cup his crotch, but it wasn't enough to take him down.

"You little bitch!"

Rage was all I saw. Not his hand flying for my face, or the murder burning in his glare. Only rage. Until Auden appeared between us, veins protruding from his arm as he caught his brother's strike midair. Asher and I cowered behind him as Asiel lost his shit.

"She'll hang for this, little brother! I swear on my crown."

I heard the threats but couldn't take my eyes off Auden. My hand gripped the back of his shirt as if he could block my fear by just being there. He glanced down over his shoulder and I quickly released him. Stepping back into Asher, I trembled at the look I saw on his face.

"I'll handle this," he promised, with a severity far too deliberate for a sixteen-year-old.

"Did you hear what I said?" Asiel was still screeching. "She struck *the Crown Prince! There's no saving her now."*

What he said was true; I'd committed a crime usually punishable by death. But my father was the head of the Shifter's Council, so I was sure it wouldn't come to that. Pretty sure, at least. Auden struggled to keep his older brother in check, and I could only watch, my feet rooted to the floor. When he glanced over his shoulder again and saw us standing there, Auden ordered Asher to move.

"Get her out of here," he commanded.

Asher grabbed my arm and pulled me with him down the steps. I knew I was making it difficult for him, but I couldn't pull my eyes away. Not until Auden's gaze met mine and I swear the gold in them shined.

"You'll be safe, Kaya. I promise." He dipped his chin and laced his tone with another command. "Go."

I vaulted from my troubled dreams at the sound of a creaking door and scanned the room for the new threat. The dim, evening sun tinted the walls with an amber glow and cast half my field of view in shadows. Hidden in those shadows, in the partially open doorway, stood Auden. Dressed in a clean pair of jeans and a shirt, he showed no signs of having almost died the night before. Envy burned through me when I glanced down at my thin hospital gown and medley of wrappings down my arms. I scowled and opened my mouth to point out the complete unfairness of it but held my breath when I saw his expression. He looked angry, with his furrowed brows and clenched jaw, as his eyes lowered and traced the shape of my legs under the sheet, then moved up to where my hands were secured to the bed rails and higher still. They lingered on my chest...a little too long and I was suddenly very aware of how cold it was in the room. I forced a dry swallow and felt him follow the subtle movements of my throat. When his gaze finally met mine, he stopped, and I felt that stare down to the ends of my hair. I couldn't even call him out for it; he wasn't the only one with wandering eyes.

Water drops still reflected in his hair from a recent shower and his shirt looked like adhesive as it clung to his damp skin. A small bulge on his shoulder could've been a bandage, but I wasn't sure, and he moved like it wasn't bothering him anyway. He even held a lunch tray in that hand. I tracked him as he set it down on the end table and took a seat in the chair Dr. Ellis left by my bed. He clicked the bedside lamp on as the room grew darker and I leaned away from the artificial light. This close, I couldn't bring myself to look at him. After my dream, it hurt too much. Those beautiful features that used to inspire so many daydreams now only reminded me of what I'd lost; his friendship, his respect, the safety that I felt even when he wasn't near.

After all this time, the sight of him still stirred feelings inside me that I wasn't sure I could trust anymore. I watched him watch me; his gaze was wary but gave nothing else away and the longer he sat there in silence, the more pissed off I became. A plethora of colorful words nearly shot from my mouth and I fought to hold them back. Any other time I'd scream them without a second thought, but the thick lump in my throat warned me it wouldn't be a good idea. His betrayal shouldn't hurt this much, we weren't friends. I guess I thought we'd reached some kind of truce. I thought that maybe some of the old Auden was back. I was wrong.

"Hey." He was the first to break the silence, but I only stared, unsure of the emotion building behind my lips. He frowned and leaned closer, looking at me with growing worry. "The doc said you were okay for visitors, that the sedation had worn off."

"It did," I snapped. "My mouth works fine; I just have nothing to say to you."

He looked almost hurt at my comment and his eyes churned

with confusion. "I thought we—last night—" he sighed. "Why are you so pissed at me?"

I laughed, but it lacked humor. "You fucking held me down and let them tranq me! You promised me. You said you—" That lump of tears grew and I looked away.

He rubbed the back of his head with a grimace. "I honestly didn't think you'd remember."

"That doesn't make it okay, Auden! They tied me up!" I pulled at the restraints until the bed shook.

"What do you expect me to say?" He was shouting now too. "You were a danger to yourself, clawing and biting everyone. The poison was *killing* you." He growled. "They needed to treat you and you wouldn't let anyone close enough to do it."

It was probably true. There was no way I'd react well to having so many people hold me down, and I remembered my claws catching on the skin of those who got too careless to avoid them.

"I would've let you close," I all but whispered and he froze. "You could've *asked*."

He fell back into the seat, the fight leaving him between one breath and the next, and I watched his hand inch closer until it rested over mine. "You weren't in your right mind. We did what was needed." He squeezed my fingers until I looked up. "I'd do it again if I had to."

Well. I guess that was that. My heart stuttered when he squeezed my hand again, but just as quick, he let go. The end table squeaked as he slid it closer and gestured at the lunch tray. I jingled the cuffs and he smirked.

"We made a good team last time." My glare only made him laugh harder. "I'm kidding. What if I loosen your restraints?" He asked, and the pressure on my wrist eased until I could lift my arm high enough to feed myself.

"You could always take them off completely." I suggested,

silently hoping our truce extended this far. "The poison's out of my system. I'm not going to hurt anyone."

He turned away to open my juice, but I saw him cringe. When he faced me again, the guilt was still on his face.

"The restraints are also there so you won't run."

Any thoughts I had of us becoming friends jumped ship at his statement. I almost forgot why I was here in the first place. Auden wasn't checking on me because he cared, he was ensuring his brother's murderer could stand trial. I was such an idiot.

"Kaya—" Auden began, but I cut off whatever promises he was getting ready to pitch.

"What's going to happen to me?"

"I don't know," he admitted.

"Don't lie." I bared my teeth, anger once again flowing freely.

His eyes widened. "I honestly don't know."

I pushed the tray away and juice sloshed over the rim of my cup. "Bullshit! You're the freaking prince! How do you *not* know?" Whatever. If he wanted to keep it a secret, then so be it. I wasn't going to beg.

I went to cross my arms, but the restraints weren't loose enough to allow that kind of movement so I clenched my fists at my side instead. Anger and hurt roared through me as I came to the realization that I truly didn't know the boy sitting beside me. He was a stranger now. A very pissed off stranger. His cheeks flamed red as he tried to get a hold of his temper; I guess one trait hadn't changed since childhood. When he finally gained enough control to speak, his voice was low and goosebumps broke out across my skin at the fury reaching toward me through his words.

"The Council hasn't stopped searching for you since the night you disappeared, and when they *finally* picked up on a lead, I was out of those gates before anyone could stop me. I don't know what's going to happen because I haven't *been* here to know." I pointedly looked away in an attempt to ignore him once more, but he furiously shook the side rail and the unexpected jolt brought our faces closer than before. The gold flecks swirled in his gaze as he growled at me. "I've spent months tracking you; countless nights spent tired, hungry, and away from home as I searched for one wayward shifter who didn't want to be found. *All* my time and attention was spent right here, in getting to this very moment. So, forgive me if I might not be privy to the consequences your selfish actions will reap."

His words slammed home, reminding me that the resentful boy sitting next to me was no longer my childhood friend and protector. He was the prince, a brother seeking vengeance, and I was the one who ruined everything. My eyes welled and I blinked to keep the tears from falling, but it was no use. He saw them anyway. His frown softened as one escaped and rolled down my cheek and I turned away before I could see his anger melt into pity. My actions were what brought us to this point, there was no one else to blame, and I didn't want his sympathy now just because he caught me crying.

A light touch on my cheek had my head turning, and his hand stayed there, forcing me to look at him as he spoke.

"You'll meet with my father, my brother, and the Council. It's up to them what happens from there. But I swear, Kaya, I'd tell you if I knew."

I nodded and he pulled away. The anger slowly receded but the fear that replaced it wasn't any easier to deal with. If Auden truly didn't know, then what the hell was going to happen to me?

CHAPTER SEVEN

My eyelids felt crusty and cumbersome, like they could no longer easily slide open and closed without a colossal effort, and it took all I had to not succumb to sleep. I'd hardly been able to rest these last few nights, too busy fretting and thinking up the worst possible outcomes that my trial would bring. There was something about being tied to a bed during your final hours before a probable execution that made it so *not* easy to sleep. I did as much tossing and turning as my restraints would allow but found no relief. Honestly, I couldn't turn my mind off and sleep wasn't going to happen even if I was one hundred percent comfortable anyway—just for the record, I wasn't. Only after exhausting myself did I ultimately fall into a fitful slumber. And now, when my eyes finally reacted to my desperate commands, I found myself wishing they hadn't. I didn't have to look at the clock ticking on the wall to know what was coming. The curtains on the window didn't need to be pulled back for me to see that a new day had risen. It was here, the moment I'd spent four years trying to avoid. I was as prepared as I'd ever be to face the king and his Council, but it didn't stop the fear and when Auden came to collect me in the pre-dawn hours, I was a complete wreck. His face was set in a grim mask that only deepened when two Royal Guards stepped up behind him.

"It's time," he declared, and the guards moved around him to approach my bed.

Their faces remained smooth and unchanging as they uncuffed me and I rubbed at the now bare skin. They were undamaged and sound, but the ghostly feel of the restraints remained, especially when I received no sympathy from Auden's gaze. He set a pair of clothes in my lap, the school's training uniform, and motioned toward the bathroom door behind me.

"Get cleaned up," he ordered, but I didn't move.

I held my gown closed as I stood and the new clothes clutched to my front like a shield. My feet didn't want to cooperate, however. They were turned toward the bathroom, but my eyes kept darting to the open door behind Auden. Bathroom or freedom? Guaranteed death or a chance to escape? My knee lifted and Auden's hand on my arm stopped me before I could take a step. He moved closer, until I could feel his breath tickle my cheek as he spoke.

"Please don't give them a reason to come in after you." His voice was quiet now, pleading, as his eyes briefly flicked toward the guards.

It was a brief moment of humanity in the otherwise stoic mask he was wearing, and it told me that some of the old Auden might still be in there somewhere. I didn't trust what would come out if I spoke, so I nodded that I understood and went to change. We didn't linger after that and I soon found myself following the guards to the front doors, flanked by a silent and moody Auden. I stopped just before going outside, my shoes shaking against the marble. Seeing the sunshine, feeling the heat, the smell of the earth—every molecule in my body screamed *home.* My body wanted to be out there. My animal half nearly pulled from my hold with the need to run free through the swamp, but I held her back. Fear kept me immobile. Not the fear of dying, but of seeing his face. I was terrified that I'd feel Asher's loss even harder outside the safety of these walls. Out there, the memories were bound to overwhelm me, and I wasn't ready for that. But I didn't have a choice.

Auden's large hand warmed the small of my back as he steered me outside and toward the unknown with a small push. I tried to keep my eyes averted and strictly on the ground—it didn't last long. I couldn't help myself and I was both surprised and not to see the community hadn't changed. Everything looked the same. Even the sounds were identical; shouts of greetings, children playing, the far-off clash of training by the school grounds. At first our walk went unnoticed, but I watched people do double takes when the sun reflected off my pale hair. I was a rarity amongst my kind, so it didn't take much for my name to be recalled from behind their mental cobwebs.

The path led through a small garden that marked the center of campus. Up ahead I heard the trickle of a fountain and the cacophony of conversations hidden just past the trees. My breaths came in short bursts as I thought about facing them. What curses would be thrown at me as I marched past them? Or would it be a suffocating silence under the weight of their glares? I was going to throw up. Auden pulled us to a stop at the curve of the path and the guards turned to him with matching frowns.

"We should take another route that doesn't go through the center of campus," he ordered, and steered me away from the garden path without even looking at me. The guard's swift grip on my elbow kept us from going far.

"The king commanded we stick to the main route," came the unapologetic reply.

Auden huffed and turned around. "Surely you recognize the logic of not taking her that way. We can secure her far easier with less people around."

"My orders are from the king."

There would be no detour. With a final sigh, Auden waved him on and once again stepped behind me. Somehow, I got my feet to move but my knees felt like Jell-O.

"Don't let them see you panic." Auden's whisper was just low enough for me to make out. "You're not cuffed and you're in a training uniform. For all they know, we're escorting you across campus to the dorms."

I appreciated his attempt to calm me, but it didn't stop the fear. There was a chance the Council kept the details of Asher's death a secret, but it was a slim one. I avoided gazes as we passed and focused on the ground. I worried that people would maul me on sight or at the very least throw insults, but other than be surprised, most just watched us pass. We slowly moved through the common areas and toward the amphitheater. The trees and vegetation grew thicker the further out we went and I sighed in relief when we left the gawking bystanders behind. Not much effort was put into landscaping outside the city center and the result left the few buildings over here all but smothered by nature. We were practically on top of the amphitheater before I saw it, hidden behind the moss and vines as it was. I stumbled when Auden once again pressed against my back, guiding me away from the imposing structure.

"Where are we going?" I asked, looking over my shoulder. "I thought I was on trial?"

Auden frowned but recovered and kept pushing me forward. "My father requested a more...private meeting, if that's what you're asking about."

Now it was my turn to frown, but there was no time for questions. The swamp water rose before us, lapping at the base of the cypress trees in gentle waves. Through the mud, a wooden bridge beckoned and offered safe passage over the mysteries that lurked below. I knew this bridge; knew where it ended and where the broken planks were. I knew just where to jump to make it sway and how to balance on the side rails all the way to the other bank. Asher and I raced across every day on our way to school and again each evening after training. This bridge was the sole entrance and exit to the Ruling Island—so called because it was the lush chunk of land that housed the private homes of the Royal Family as well as the Council members and their families. It used to be my home.

"Auden, what's going on?" I didn't bother masking the way my voice shook.

"Exactly what I told you," he replied, and forced me to take that first step onto the bridge. "The king, my brother, and the Council are awaiting your presence in the meeting chamber."

Not the amphitheater? The fact that my trial wouldn't be a public display wasn't exactly a comfort. It sucked either way, but a public trial could be swayed by the public's response. Maybe the king anticipated a negative reaction to my execution.

"You didn't say all *that*," I hissed, but dutifully followed the guards across the bridge.

There were less than ten homes on the island, each grand and opulent; somehow able to evade the algae day in and day out. There were manicured lawns and bright balconies, delicate hanging moss and arched windows. No home was more lavish than that of the king, but the palace also housed the government offices, so much of its grandeur was lost on me. I spent my childhood running amok through those offices while my father ran the Council. The polished hardwood showed my same reflection, but with haunted eyes and I had to look away. No matter where I turned, my past was there, taunting me. We entered the center of the Council's chamber before I could compare more memories of before with the panicked realizations I was having now. I stood alone in front of the high bench surrounded by the scent of aged wood and dust, and stared at seven faces fixed on my every move. The king sat directly in the center and had the final say over my judgement today, but he wasn't who I looked at now.

Directly to his left sat a middle-aged familiar, the king's very own in fact. He was a tawny lion when he shifted and some of those attributes carried over into his human form. His deep blonde hair was threaded with strands of gold and bronze that flowed unchecked down his back. The laugh lines around his mouth and eyes were stale and silent, as they'd been since the night my mother died. He didn't stand as proud as he used to, or maybe he did but his age was showing. Either way, my father stared down at me like he was observing a stranger on trial, not his only daughter. There were no smiles or tears of joy. Damn, I'd even take a head nod—*something* to show he cared. Silence was all that greeted me, until the king cleared his throat. I hadn't noticed how long I stared at my father, but it was too long. I hastily bowed to the king and prince at his side, staying down longer than was required as an apology for my rude behavior. A relaxed chuckle was swiftly followed by the king's unmistakable timbre.

"Rise, Kaya, and let us look upon you."

I stood, a blush staining my cheeks as all the eyes in the room did just as the king commanded. I cautiously watched their reactions and waited for the anvil to drop. A majority of their faces held mild curiosity, including the king. At his right hand sat his eldest son, Asiel, a scowl marring his handsome face. All the men of the Wardwell line shared one obvious trait, their hair. Black as the darkest night, it ran true no matter how watered down the genes were. The king looked how I thought Auden would as he aged, thick dark hair with only a speckling of gray, kind eyes, and a firm jaw. He must hate me, but you'd never be able to tell by looking at him. His poker face was on solid display and it was deceiving in its softness. Asiel, on the other hand, had a thing or two to learn about hiding his thoughts. I felt his glare even before I saw it and it took everything in me to not return the favor. Insubordination wouldn't serve me well right now. Just shy of twenty-five, Asiel still carried the hate torch for me. I'd recognize that scowl anywhere and adding facial scruff to it did nothing to mask its potency. His jaw was firmer, his shoulders broader, but that insecure little prince still lurked inside.

"I send you out on a scouting mission and you come back with a missing childhood friend." The king declared with some amusement. "I'm eager to hear this story, my son."

Auden moved forward until he stood beside me, but his eyes didn't bother glancing my way. "I told you before I left, father, that I'd found her."

My heart jolted and I fought to keep my face relaxed. I thought the Council was the one looking for me.

"Indeed. And here she is." The king addressed me now. "Tell me, my dear, did you enjoy those years outside the safety of these walls?"

I was stunned, unsure how to answer. It felt like such a loaded question. Did I enjoy being out from under my father's endless expectations? Being away from the haunting memories of my mother and the happiness we could never seem to replicate in her absence? Without a shadow of a doubt. But never at the expense of Asher. This had to be a trick question, yet they all waited patiently for me to answer.

"N-no?" I didn't know how to get anything else out. Fortunately, the king looked past my tongue-tied response and moved on.

"Of course you didn't. My reports state the condition of

your return was marked critical due to a demon attack mere miles from our borders. Who in their right mind would choose that risk over the safety offered here?" I opened my mouth, but nothing came out. "Certainly not a fledgling familiar with incomplete training. No, I'm sure that experience was lesson enough on that matter, hm?" After a beat, I nodded, not sure what kind of answer he was expecting of me. "Now, on to the matter of your future." My heart stopped. "Your...absence has stunted your training and put you far behind the others your age. To add you to their ranks now would be irresponsible of me."

It was hard to understand him over the roaring in my ears, but I thought I heard him say the complete opposite of 'off with her head'.

"Sire, if I may?" An older familiar on the end leaned in to be heard, his greying hair tied back at his nape. "Our numbers have dramatically dropped these past years. Using every able-bodied fighter is a necessity."

"So, we would throw my daughter on the mercy of the demons and hope luck is on her side? I think not." My father all but snarled at the Councilor and the vehemence with which he defended my safety floored me.

In fact, this entire trial confused the hell out of me. They were supposed to argue over how to punish me, not how to squeeze me back into society. I expected an immediate death sentence, had resigned myself to it. The idea that my future wasn't going to be cut short today was both exhilarating and terrifying. Was it possible that they didn't know what I'd done? Did they think it a mere coincidence that a demon killed Asher and that I disappeared? My thoughts raced with the possibility.

"Councilor Thornton, we must think of our future. There are too few of us already," the familiar's voice pulled me back to the discussion at hand.

"I'm well aware of our numbers, Councilor Minos," my father rebuked. "I still vote no."

"There's other roles she can fill within the community," Asiel didn't raise his voice, but his words silenced the others, nonetheless. His eyes watched me closely and I tried not to fidget. "She's healthy and of reputable stock. In a couple years she'll be old enough to find a mate and help replenish our dwindling population."

Vomit hit the back of my throat. He didn't—he couldn't —*what*? He basically suggested I become a broodmare. Give me death. Seriously. I'd rather be six feet under, my soul answering for my crimes for eternity than be subjected to *that*. He couldn't do that, could he? Surely the Council would be opposed. And my father, he'd vote against it. But no one said anything. Fuck, were they actually considering it? Darkness closed on the edges of my vision. My throat tightened until I couldn't breathe, and a small whimper squeezed through my clenched teeth. Auden was in front of me in a blink, his large frame blocking me from the sickening gazes that were now appraising me for my breeding capabilities.

"She's trained," his words echoed across the chamber; echoed in my head and my next breath came easier. He was right. I was trained. I took down a demon; there was hope for me.

"Son, just being able to shift doesn't mean she's trained." The king fixed him with a glare. "You of all people should know that."

"She took down a Buer demon on her own, *without* fully shifting." Auden held his father's gaze. "And she saved my life doing it."

The bench was silent as he let that grenade drop. I gained enough control of myself to step out from behind Auden's shadow. After a moment of shocked silence, the king motioned for Auden to continue.

"It had me around the throat, seconds away from ripping out my heart," he explained. "Then, from out of nowhere Kaya literally climbed its body with nothing but claws and fangs and ripped into its skull with her bare hands. I'm sure the rescue squad gave full detail of the killing blow and what damage took down the demon. *She* did that." He stepped to the side and pointed at me. "Without a full shift, with an injured shoulder, *and* poison coursing through her veins. She. can. fight."

A lump fully blocked my throat as I fought to keep the emotion off my face while watching Auden. He'd gone to bat for me, against his father and the entire Council. Gone were the anger and distrust I'd grown used to seeing, in their place was this righteous pillar of support. I felt the shift in the room as the Council looked upon me once again. I wanted to fall right there from the weight of their stares, but I locked my knees and lifted my chin. Let them see my strength. Let them see past my mistakes. Please, let them see everything Auden claimed I was. The king appraised me with new eyes, interest lighting the golden flecks.

"Very well, I'll entertain the idea." The king all but growled, still not convinced. "But tell me, how do you expect this to work? She's far too behind to graduate into pairs with the others her age at the end of this next year. Capable fighter or no, she's not prepared to join the ranks or even train with them."

"So, we double her training until she's caught up," Auden shrugged like it was no big deal. "She can do it."

Asiel chuckled and the still undecided Councilors turned their attention to him. There was a sick twist to his smile that caused my palms to sweat. Since we were children, he'd wanted nothing but to get rid of me and here was his chance served on a silver platter. My squirming reaction to his breeding comment didn't go unnoticed and I knew he'd do everything he could to secure that as my future.

"As cute as the idea may sound, brother, we're limited on those skilled enough to train her on that level in such a short amount of time. And those that *are* capable, we need out in the field." The Council murmured at the logical flaw Asiel presented, even the king nodded in agreement. "Unfortunately, we just don't have the men to spare."

I shot a panicked glance at my father, hoping the tale of my abilities might spur him into supporting me, but he was nodding along with the rest of them. The betrayal wasn't unexpected, but it still hurt like hell.

"I'll train her."

"What?" The word was out of my mouth before I could stop it and Auden smirked at me with amusement.

"I can train you this next year and have you prepared to graduate with the others," he turned back to his father. "I have complete confidence in my abilities. And hers."

"I find it hard to believe that one of our best warriors has nothing better to do than tutor a fledgling shifter." Asiel wasn't the least bit okay with his brother's suggestion, if his sneer and sarcastic attitude was anything to go by.

But Auden wasn't the least bit phased. "There's nothing more important than the future of our people. If our numbers are already as low as you say then we can't afford to lose even one promising shifter."

A vein bulged in Asiel's forehead but it looked like the tides had changed as Councilor Minos's previous argument came back into play. After a close vote, it was decided that I would rejoin my class and the standard curriculum, plus extra trainings held daily with Auden. With his help, the goal was for me to graduate in a year with the others my age, much to my relief.

Dismissed, we were almost out the doors when Asiel's voice once again called out.

"One more thing, Prince Auden." It was Asiel. His scowl was still firmly in place at being outvoted on the subject of my future. "She has the opportunity to graduate, but we can't guarantee a witch will choose her. Her future will revert back to repopulation should she fail, along with any other unpartnered."

I didn't like the smile he turned on me but didn't dare disrespect him and risk changing their minds about giving me a second chance. I also didn't question what he meant by a witch choosing me. There was too much to process in my brain already.

"I wish you good luck, Kaya."

I called bullshit on that.

CHAPTER EIGHT

The well-manicured lawns of the island rolled out before me, but neither their beauty nor the incessant humidity could pull my mind away from the terrifying thoughts that besieged it now. Auden's firm hand on my elbow was the only thing keeping me from unceremoniously falling into the swamp. I thought I'd be leaving that room in chains, my trial all but a formality. Instead, I got what I wanted, my freedom. So then why did it scare the shit out of me? The bridge creaked and moaned beneath our steps and each groan of the wood pushed my thoughts back to that room—how too the Council's chairs creaked as they leaned forward to get a good look at me. Even now, I could feel their eyes. An involuntary shiver had Auden looking at me strangely, but I pushed forward until my feet were once again on the boggy ground.

"You could've warned me." I wanted to take the words back as soon as they left my mouth. Auden was just as surprised as I was at his brother's threats—I saw his face. But I couldn't help but lash out. If it weren't for him, I would be back in Miami where I was only stared at for being weird, not for having a solid bloodline for breeding.

Auden swung me around so fast whiplash was a very real possibility and his hand tightened on my arm enough to leave a bruise as he pulled me close.

"I'm not my brother's keeper." His tone had a bite to it, but his eyes swam with turmoil.

This close, our noses nearly touched. There was no hiding, no pretending to feel anything but the truth. I kept the frustration off my face, but it was there in my voice.

"I know, Auden. I—" I sighed and forced my eyes to meet his. "I'm sorry. I know you had nothing to do with your brother's decree. I don't even know why I accused you."

"You're afraid."

My hackles rose at the suggestion, but there was no use lying to him, or myself. His grip on my arm loosened and I stepped away. He cocked his head, watching me as I tried to come up with a response.

"Why do I get the feeling you're more afraid of your newfound freedom than you were about the uncertainty of going into that meeting?"

I scoffed at his choice of words and kept walking. The sandy path led back to town and I knew all the trails out here like the back of my hand. He could follow or not, but I wouldn't get lost.

"Freedom," I sneered. I wanted to vomit at the thought. "This isn't freedom, Auden. You heard them. I have till the end of the year to prove myself, or..." I couldn't even bring myself to say it. The decree was utterly barbaric and disgusting.

"You've got time to prepare before the Choosing, Kaya." I felt Auden looming behind me, his steps in sync with mine. He twirled me around to face him again and I had to grab his shoulders to keep from falling over. "You're not destined for the population pool. That I can promise you."

His empty promises did nothing but piss me off, which I was sure he could tell when I pushed him away with a snarl.

"What is this bullshit about a population pool anyway? And the Choosing?" I looked around at the community that felt so familiar but was so obviously different. "What the fuck is going on?"

My raised voice caught the attention of those passing by, but I didn't care. Let them answer if he wasn't going to. Auden roughly pushed me through the outer hall of the school. I recognized the courtyard we stumbled into, but now was not the time to reminisce about recess and the more carefree times. There was something off about this situation and I didn't like how vulnerable it made me feel to not understand the whole picture.

"You've been gone a long time, Kaya. Things have been rough, and we've had to adapt."

I threw my hands in the air. "By enforcing population growth! Do you even hear yourself?"

Too quick, he was in my face again. "You don't understand."

"Then explain it to me," I dared, gripping his arms and invading his personal space for a change.

Someone cleared their throat beside us, and we hastily broke apart. A teacher stood in the doorway, his face a mask of irritation.

"Shouting outside the classrooms while lessons are underway is most unseemly for you, my prince." The slight was delivered with a bow, but there was no mistaking the disapproval radiating off the older gentleman. His grey eyes turned to me, taking in my appearance and seeming to size me up all in one glance. "We expected you an hour ago, Miss Thornton. Come along now."

He held out an arm, gesturing me through the still open doorway. My head swiveled between the two of them while my intelligence tried to catch up.

"What?" Was the only word my mouth could form with so little working brain power. The teacher sighed.

"To class, Miss Thornton. Surely the fact that you are behind on your education has been made clear to you?"

Oh, it had alright. But that didn't explain what was happening right now.

"I thought I was going to my dorm."

"To do what? Waste another day you could otherwise be taking advantage of? I think not."

I glanced at Auden again, but he was backing away. The bastard was leaving me here. I imagined stabbing him with a thousand daggers.

"I don't even know which room is mine yet," came my feeble excuse.

The teacher rolled his eyes and gripped my good shoulder. There was no breaking his hold as he pushed me through the door.

"The dorms are where they've always been, and the House Matron will show you to your room after classes." His shoes clacked down the empty hallway, echoed by the squeaks from my sneakers. "You're already dressed out, and you'll find a locker full of supplies waiting for you after my class. Welcome back, Miss Thornton. Please find a seat."

Tripping into the room wasn't my best entrance, but at least no one laughed. No. They were all too busy staring. I sighed and took the first open seat I could find; it was thankfully in the back. It didn't protect me from the stares. I plastered on a fake smirk and tried to pretend that I didn't care.

"As you all can see, Miss Thornton has returned to us. She is far behind on the curriculum, so if you would all be so kind as to assist her when you can, I'm sure her acclimation back into our routine won't be as painful. Now, please open your textbooks to chapter five and we will continue our discussion on Vera demons."

Mr. Laveau was stubborn. He droned on through the lecture, though it was obvious no one paid attention. They were too busy sneaking looks at me. I recognized their faces but didn't bother acknowledging them. I wasn't close with anyone other than Asher before I left, so there were no friendships lost here. When the bell rang, I stayed in my seat, not wanting to be trampled or draw attention to myself in the hallway. The whispers had already started. A small paper slid across my desk and into my field of view.

"Your schedule," said Mr. Laveau. "You have training next and I suggest you hurry. Mr. Fox has not softened in the years you've been absent."

I sighed for what felt like the millionth time that day and left the safety of the classroom. I'd rather bear the weight of stares and rumors than risk the ire of Mr. Fox. He could be downright brutal when he wanted to be. I remembered my way around campus and found myself at the gym with minutes to spare. Like before, I was greeted with open curiosity. Not one for the spotlight, I retreated to the back of the room.

"Group up, you pack of lazy kits. This isn't your first day!" Mr. Fox's growl pushed the others into motion, and they paired up until there were only a few of us left on our own. "Ah, yes, Miss Thornton. I was told of your arrival." The chit chat in the room stopped as he approached me, his gaze measuring me in much the same way Mr. Laveau did. "You've kept in shape, so at least you're not behind on that front." His eyes landed on my bandaged arm and he frowned. "Let a beastie get a taste of you, I see. No shifting until you're cleared by the physician. Pair up with Cace for today and we'll see where you're at."

He snapped his fingers and a boy with shaggy, chestnut hair bounded up beside us. His smile was nice enough, so I returned it with a nod. Mr. Fox clapped his hands and addressed the rest of the class.

"Today seems as good a day as any to practice the basics, so no shifting. Each pair line up before a dummy and grab some jars. Let's see if your spell casting and teamwork have improved."

I watched the room explode in motion, but when Cace returned with our jars, I had no idea what to do. Cace picked up a small vial of green goo and looked back at me, expectantly.

"Um, do I grab one too or something?" He started laughing, but quickly cut it off with a cough when he saw I wasn't joking.

"Sorry, I forgot you hadn't built up to this." He showed me the vile of goo and pointed at the dummy. "Those things are spelled to attack us. I have to respond with a successful application of this fake potion to make it stop."

I nodded along as he explained. It sounded easy enough. "What do I do?"

"Well, you're my familiar for this drill. You watch my back, throw me potions if I miss, protect my blind spots, you know, the usual."

Right. Because this was all so very usual for a high school gym class.

"These are just the basics so we can learn to move around each other. Things will get smoothed out next year after the Choosing."

Again with that damn word. I wanted to ask him what it meant, but he already moved into position.

"You ready?" Cace asked, vial in hand.

I shrugged and moved into place beside him, watching for the dummy's first move. Cace's hand on my shoulder pushed me back a couple steps until I was behind him and off to the right.

"Remember, you help from back here."

My lip curled and I was about to ask if he had a superiority complex, but the dummy jolted to life. Its long, deflated arms swelled until they swung around its torso like furious snakes. Four of them. Cace bobbed and weaved as he looked for an opening, and I could already tell that that strategy would fail. He needed to throw the potion from afar and *then* move in. Maybe even use me as a distraction. I opened my mouth to warn him about the swinging arm on the right, but it got him before I could utter a sound. The vial broke and stained his pants, but he was otherwise unharmed.

"You're supposed to watch my back!" He shouted.

"I was going to warn you, but I was too far back to say anything in time."

"Then *move*," he glared, and my eyes narrowed.

"*Fine*."

Cace picked up another vial and stood in front of the dummy. I was to the side again, but when he moved, I moved with him. I let him bob and weave, even though it was still a stupid plan, and I focused on keeping the arms away from him. A wild limb swung toward us and I took its hit on my side with a grunt. Wrapping my arm around it, I pulled, tugging the dummy in a new direction. Unfortunately, Cace wasn't expecting that and the other set of arms knocked him on his ass. Another vial broke on his shirt.

"Kaya!" He roared, looking extra pissy this time.

Dropping the now limp arm, I fixed him with a glare of my own. "What?"

He closed his eyes and exhaled through his nose; it did nothing to calm him. "You don't fight the dummy. That's *my* job."

Was he serious?

"I stopped it from clobbering you!"

He huffed and pointed at his shirt. "You call this stopping it?

You should've moved after that block and continued to watch my back, not engage."

That didn't sound like teamwork at all. How could we take it down if I only blocked? When I asked, he only laughed at me.

"It's my job to destroy the demon, familiar. It's your job to protect me while I do it."

My face would've been comical if I wasn't so pissed off and about ten seconds away from punching him in the nuts. I wasn't his *sidekick*; I was his partner. There was no way in hell I was going to sit by and watch a demon destroy anyone. Not again. Practice or not. The dummy came back to life and before Cace could take a step, I charged at it. I didn't bother with a vial because potions were useless to my kind. I had all I needed inside me. With a kick of speed and strength from my animal, I launched over the dummy and landed in a crouch behind it. Its swinging arms were still focused on Cace, so I made quick work of seizing them and tying them together. The room was silent as I stepped out from behind the wiggling bows. Cace wore a scowl and I practically saw the steam escaping from his ears.

"Don't tell me to stand behind you again," I warned him with a smile.

He muttered under his breath and I swore it sounded like he said, "that's where you belong." But Mr. Fox was already addressing us, so I couldn't press the issue.

"A good use of your strength's, Kaya. Perhaps next time you can work as a team and kill the demon rather than turn it into a Christmas present, hm?"

Cace went back to glaring after our instructor left. I had nothing else to say to him though and he turned away before I could come up with something witty. Mr. Fox called an end to class and the dummy deflated for good this time.

"He's always been a bit of a sore loser." I turned to the voice and was greeted by a pair of sparkling green eyes and a face covered in goo. He smiled when I wrinkled my nose but didn't take offense. "My partner sucks too. I'm Bast," he said, offering a surprisingly clean hand.

"Kaya," I replied, and he smirked.

"Oh, I know. The gossip mill hasn't stopped about you, honey."

Great. "What are they saying about me?"

He shrugged and wiped his face off with a towel to reveal more of his mocha skin, then brought it higher over his head to get the goo trapped in his bronzed hair. "The usual; runaway, romance, secret baby."

"Secret baby!" I cried. "I was *thirteen*."

My outrage only fueled his mirth. "I never believed the rumors, of course."

"Of course."

"But I'd love to hear the real story sometime." He threw the towel at me and I barely caught it before it hit my face. He was gone before I could yell at him for it.

The room was nearly empty as the others left to get cleaned off before lunch. With a groan, I headed toward the girl's dorms and hoped there were a pair of clean clothes waiting for me.

CHAPTER
NINE

The whispers were everywhere. Whispers and the never-ending stares that followed. I got it; I was the new girl who wasn't so new. The long lost familiar; the wayward child returned home. I understood where their fascination and curiosity stemmed from, but it was still a little much. A group of girls my age chittered as I passed, and I fought the urge to run a hand over my hair to smooth it out. Thanks to Cace's inability to work well with others, half my body was covered with that fake potion goop—no part of my hair or face had been spared. A quick duck down the nearest path had me hidden from sight. It would take longer to get to the dorms this way, but I didn't mind the extra walk. I let my mind wander as I continued deeper into the trees. I'd taken this path many times growing up and was in no danger of getting lost. The crunch of gravel beneath my shoes confirmed my isolation and I breathed a sigh of relief. Alone at last. A light breeze blew in from the west and I inhaled all the summer scents that it carried with it.

You could tell what time of year it was without looking at a calendar. It was the thick humidity that clung to the air and the sweat running down your back. The buzzing of insects that lulled you into contentment while lounging at the pool. Water dripping down a cool glass of lemonade. Asher doing a cannon ball into the deep end and soaking you with a well-timed wave. I stumbled and caught myself as that memory wreaked havoc on my heart. Cursing, I stomped further down the path, furious at myself for letting that memory sneak through. I had to be more careful. Remembering Asher like that, after burying those thoughts for so long, was enough to shatter my heart all over again. I wouldn't survive the broken pieces it left behind. Not here. Not being back in this place.

The path I was on split into three as it wrapped around an overgrown garden. The walkways cut off and intersected in no distinct pattern, separating the old flowerbeds in a lingering attempt to protect them from wandering feet. The weeds had taken over. Vines and flowers were overgrown with no one to rein them in. Preferring the silence of strangled flowers to the gossip being forged back on campus, I took a seat on a sturdy bench and surveyed the forgotten landscape. It was wild and unkempt, yet the unruly vegetation didn't stray from the boundaries long ago set to entrap it, choosing rather to rebel in smaller ways—a root bursting through the brick here, an orchid hanging over the fencing there. I smiled, feeling a sense of kinship with the earth that was fighting so hard to reclaim itself. I never fit in, never felt the need to, and I had little doubt that that would ever change no matter my circumstances. So much was different and yet too much remained the same. The gossip mill always flowed around here, and it wouldn't be the first time I was the focus of it, but the brief comments made to me in class and after told me the dynamic of our little island was off balance. Cace was real clear about where he thought I belonged and showing him up was the highlight of my day. My smile slipped as I remembered my victory wouldn't last. The second my arm was cleared by the doctors; I'd have to shift, and they'd all see that I couldn't. Just like the rebellious plants in this garden, they were going to force me to mold into what they wanted, and it was going to be a long, arduous battle ahead when they realized I wouldn't go quietly.

The ground trembled and grew still, the small vibrations lingering in the soles of my shoes as I glanced around. Another tremor sent loose pebbles skipping across the walkway. The trees quaked and their leaves rustled, but nothing else stood out of place. Until the earth buckled. My very bones felt loose inside my body as I was tossed from the bench. I threw my hands out and sliced them open as I tried to grab anything I could. The sting of the small wounds faded to the back of my mind as I watched the worn path crack and roll in a large wave that knocked me back on my ass despite my hold on the trellis. Screams echoed through the now destroyed garden and rose higher than the moans of the disgruntled earth. I scrambled to my feet amid the shaking dirt and tripped my way toward the safety of campus. There'd never been an earthquake here, but my brain had no other excuse for what this could be. It looked like what happened in the movies, so who knew? Did Louisiana even get earthquakes?

I heard my name, softer than a feather on the wind, and not even a second later, Auden tore around the corner. The relief on his face when he saw me both warmed my heart and made me a tad cranky. Did he think I couldn't handle a little earthquake on my own? I wasn't a child. He stood in front of me before my next heartbeat, his eyes scanning every inch of me.

"Are you okay?" He took in my grimy hair and clothes, but thankfully didn't linger on the potion goop stuck to my cheek.

The earth rolled again before I could answer, and we fell into one another. Auden's arms wrapped around my waist, keeping us upright. Our chests were touching, close enough that I could feel each rapid breath as he pushed against me. He took a step back and wrapped a warm hand around one of my own.

"Come on, we've got to get you inside."

I let him drag me along but couldn't stop the random earthquake facts from bombarding my brain. "Isn't that the last place I should be during an earthquake? Trapped inside a building?"

Auden glanced back at me, confused, but slid to a stop when a hoard of scared students trailed by guards blocked our path.

"Shit. We can't go this way."

He just barely pulled us to the side in time for them to pass. The fear on their faces left no room for them to know who they nearly ran over, but one of the guards clearly recognized Auden and stopped before us while the others continued on. He gave a brief bow but was knocked out of it when the earth bucked again.

"How bad is it?" Auden asked, his voice level despite the chaos around us.

The guard briefly glanced at me, and then down to where Auden still held my hand, but answered. "Three have broken through the south wall, Your Highness. Two more on the east, but I'm not sure about anywhere else."

"Five?" Auden snarled. "How is that possible?"

"I-I'm not sure, Your Highness. I only know what I heard from the others."

A tendon popped along the corner of Auden's jaw as he scanned the swamp. The tremors were becoming fewer and far between, but there was still a very real air of danger hovering over us.

"This isn't an earthquake, is it?" I whispered, realizing we were facing something far more devastating.

The guard shot me a grave look, but before he could answer, Auden dismissed him and pushed us deeper into the tangled trees, perpendicular to where the students went running. The ground continued its tantrum, but either it wasn't as strong, or we were used to running on it because our travel was less hindered than before. We approached a small cement square sitting solidly on the forest floor and ducked against its single door.

"Auden, what's going on?" I asked, breathless as I huddled against the relative safety the squat building offered.

"I'll explain when we get inside," he growled, grabbing hold of the heavy lock and chain around the door handle.

With a swift blast of his power, the metal bent and slid apart and he promptly ushered me inside. Pitch black greeted me, coupled with a mildew scent that made my nose crinkle. The strike of flint was immediately followed by a dull glow and, after grabbing my hand again, Auden led us down the moldy steps and deeper into the darkness. The staircase itself was a marvel since Louisiana didn't have room to spare when it came to digging underground. The spells on this place had to be expansive to keep all the water out. We eventually opened up to a small chamber and once the other lanterns were lit the view before me blew my mind. Weapons of all sizes and types hung from the walls and on tables in the far corner. I opened one of the many trunks strewn about the room and found more weapons, armor, potion vials, and even some extra clothes.

"What is this place?" I asked, still exploring.

What I thought was just a single chamber was only the entrance to even more rooms. One was very obviously a small kitchen, a bathroom, and the largest chamber held beds. Rows and rows of bunkbeds.

"It's a weapons and supply cache, a safe room—you name it," Auden replied, as he tucked another knife into his belt and moved to the stairs.

"Wait!" I called after him. "You're leaving me here?"

He swept out an arm and gestured at the many trunks I'd already rummaged through. "There's plenty of supplies. You'll be safe here until I return."

"I don't even know where here is!" I shouted, my anger making itself fully known. Did he really plan to deposit me in this underground bunker and walk away without any explanation as to what was going on?

"I just told you—"

"You haven't told me shit," I growled, and stomped forward until I was right in his face. "And if you really think I'm going to stay put in this dank hole in the ground while something is obviously happening up there, then you don't know me at all."

Auden sighed and stepped away from the stairs. I fought to keep from smirking at that small victory and instead kept my scowl firmly glued in place.

"The shaking means that demons have made it through the barrier," he whispered, voice hard.

Shock now fully replaced anything I'd been feeling. Demons *inside* the barrier? "T-that's not possible." My voice wobbled and Auden gave a humorless laugh.

"It's very possible and it's not the first time it's happened. Over the past few years it's become more common." He leaned back against the damp wall; arms crossed in front of him as he watched my every reaction. "They used to only attack when the magic was at its weakest; when someone was coming in with a demon for interrogation or when the barrier itself was being renewed. They still try at those times but are somehow able to get in at other times too."

"Like now," I whispered.

Auden nodded. "Like now."

My body shook for an entirely different reason as I thought of demons being this close, of them being right above us, following our scent trail to that little metal door. I hated the knowing look Auden pinned me with, like he knew what thoughts were running through my head and he pitied me for them.

"My brother commissioned a number of these safe houses in the woods around campus for this very reason," he stepped closer, gentle and slow, like any sudden movement would spook me. "My father doesn't know about them yet since we haven't been able to properly test them."

"What?" And he was going to leave me in here as some sort of experiment?

"The concrete is ten feet thick on all sides and we're too far down for the demons to sense you, even with your injury." His hands came to rest lightly on my shoulders and my shaking stopped as his calming warmth seeped into my skin. The lantern's light brought out the gold in his eyes, making them dance like two burning embers as his gaze caught mine. "You're safe here."

His words were successful in calming me and as the panic left, my instinct to fight overwhelmed the orders from my brain to cower in a corner. I was terrified of what kind of demons could be out there, but I couldn't let Auden go against them alone. He may be a total asshat a majority of the time, but he was all I had left of Asher. And my best friend would never forgive me if I failed his brother the same way I failed him.

I grabbed Auden's arm as he turned to leave, "I'm coming with you."

His eyes widened at my statement, but thankfully, he didn't laugh. "You're injured," he calmly replied, glancing at the soiled gauze bound around my arm and across my chest. "You still bear the marks of your last tangle with a demon, it's best you remain here."

"I don't care if I have to fight with one arm tied behind my back," I argued. And technically, it wasn't far from the truth. "I won't let you go out there and face those things alone."

"It's cute that you're worried," he smirked and looked down at me. Actually smirked, like I was an adorable child playing at being a big kid. "But I'll be fine."

"Tell that to the demon I slayed that had your throat in its pincers."

His smirk fell and was replaced with a glare. "You don't know what kind of demons are out there, or how many. You might not get lucky again like you did a few nights ago."

"Lucky!" I sneered, but he was already backing away.

"Stay put, Kaya." He warned, his glare promising retribution if I disobeyed.

I watched him climb the stairs, laden down with weapons that I knew would only benefit him if he had the time to draw them. He needed a partner to watch his back, to distract the demons and give him enough time to use his steel.

"At least tell me your familiar is meeting you out there," I pleaded. "You need back up."

He stopped just before the turn in the stairway and looked over his shoulder with a wild grin. "I don't have a familiar. I work better alone."

And he left. He fucking left. The metal door sealed shut again with a solid *clang* and I was left alone in the silence. The earth didn't shake in here, whether because the rooms were spelled or the tremors themselves had stopped, I wasn't sure. I couldn't hear a single sound from above, no screams, no calls of an all clear, nothing. I remembered the fear on the students faces as they fled down the garden path. Hell, even the guards looked terrified. I knew, somewhere up there, Auden was running in the opposite direction, *toward* the danger that sent everyone else fleeing. Would there be other witches and their partners already fighting when he arrived? What if a demon found him before he could get to them? What if there were far more than the five we were told about and our forces were overrun?

Without their partner, a witch was severely handicapped in battle. They worked best as a team, regardless of what Auden thought about working better alone. I recalled all too clearly what he looked like trapped in a demon's death grip and I couldn't stand the thought of it happening again. So the question was, did I stay down here safe, and wait for his less than likely return? Or did I put my big girl pants on and help him kick some demon ass? It wouldn't just be a tongue thrashing I'd receive when Auden saw I disobeyed his order, and I was both afraid and slightly intrigued to find out what he'd do. The wounds on my shoulder throbbed, as if they knew there would be more of them on my body before the day was through.

"Fuck it," I whispered to the empty room, and made a beeline for the weapons.

CHAPTER
TEN

My body felt heavy, but in a good way. The extra weapons I grabbed weighed me down around my ankles and hips, but they wouldn't hinder my movements and I needed everything I could carry for what may lay ahead. I cracked open the metal door and took a few tentative steps out, freezing after only a few. It was too quiet, eerily so; an unnatural stillness that had my hair standing on end. Adrenaline coursed through me, causing my heart to race and my inner cat to take notice. I did a calculating scan of the area and my eyes kept darting back to the large cypress tree on the left. The little voice in my head screamed I was wasting time, that I needed to catch up to Auden, but my instincts were louder. Something was out there.

A flash of movement made me hold my breath, and I was thankful that my hand hadn't yet left the door; it still remained cracked so I could get back in quickly if I had to. My eyesight already shifted to feline, allowing for me to see in far greater detail. Without it, I wouldn't have noticed the small hand with curved fingers gripping the bark of that tree, or the rest of the distorted form that followed. It resembled a small child, but when you looked close enough, the proportions were off. The neck was a little too long, upper arms extended slightly further than the lower— the eyes were too sunken in, like he was starving. But I knew better. Raka demons always looked hungry and their appetite was insatiable. Their childlike appearance lured in prey with unsettling ease. However, they were anything but the innocent victims they portrayed themselves to be.

Their fingernails were venomous and potent enough to paralyze a grown man in less than thirty minutes. Plenty of time for them to track their prey and then devour the flesh from their bones. More leaves and branches rustled as the Raka moved closer. This particular breed of demon traveled in packs, and I'd counted fifteen so far. My heart raced and my limbs shook as I fought off the most minor changes, too scared to make even the slightest sound. They'd yet to notice me, hadn't so much as sniffed in my direction. When I glanced down, I saw why. Protection sigils were drawn in the dirt at my feet. The looped shapes were meant to ward off demons and create a barrier of some sort that kept them from sensing me. They were carved and reapplied weekly all around the island. I didn't know if they also applied to sound, so I hardly breathed until the last Raka demon disappeared into the trees.

When I could no longer hear them, I let out the breath I'd been holding and gently shut the door behind me, careful to keep the metal silent. I darted off in the opposite direction of the demons, who looked to be moving toward the dorms. Not really knowing where else to start, I retraced the path Auden and I took until I found myself once again in the destroyed garden that was only hours before vibrant with life. Now it was as stale and silent as the rest of the forest. Birds and insects made no sound and I'd yet to come across any wildlife. I fought back the growing fear and kept on, following one of the paths rather than keep to the tangled trees. I moved more swiftly on even ground. Minutes later, the old amphitheater stabbed out toward the clouds, looming over the trees like a gothic sanctuary.

The aged brick blended perfectly with the terrain, making it hard to see until you were right upon it, despite its massive size. Auden's scent was all over this place, and I followed it as it wrapped around the back, then through an open archway and into the darkened service tunnels. All the entrances and halls eventually led to the arena, so I was sure I'd stumble upon him eventually. The problem was predicting his attitude when I did. The sound of scuffling stones stopped me in the middle of the hall, halfway from where I'd just come and to the dull light up ahead that was the arena. My claws itched to be free as I slowly turned and came face to face with a small girl, looking no older than six. Her hair was matted, and her dress was faded and torn, but it was the blood she licked off her fingers that stopped my heart.

"Can you help me miss? I think I'm lost." The Raka asked, voice soft and whimsical. Even her smile was disarming and cute. The brief flashes of fangs behind those lips were a whole other story. "Where are you going?"

Her innocent words followed me as I gradually backed away. I kept my eyes on her the entire time, though she hadn't moved. She watched me with her head cocked to the side, like she couldn't grasp why her prey was attempting to escape.

"Why won't you help us?"

The voice behind me caused me to jump and I spun on the ball of my foot until my back was against the brick. I watched the Raka from of the corners of my eyes. Shit.

"She's not very nice," the other Raka hissed.

My elongated pupils made seeing in the dark easy and I was able to make out the details of the newest arrival. This one was a boy, wearing an extra-long shirt and torn pants. He appeared malnourished with sharp elbows and sunken cheeks, but his hands too were covered in blood so he must have recently fed. Either that or he had another victim lined up for later. The sounds of fighting echoed down the hall, ending in multiple shouts that sounded like Auden. I was out of time. Inching along the wall, I kept a wary eye on both demons as they moved closer. I fingered a knife at my belt, but the boy shook his head and lunged with a snarl before I could bring it up. His nails scraped across my wrist, causing me to yelp and drop the weapon. I watched my blood surge to the two small scratches and cursed. The Raka giggled. The invisible countdown to paralysis had begun. I was running out of time to help Auden and now that I was infected, the two little demons no longer held that much of a threat.

A savage grin split my face. "I have nails too, you little shit."

I struck, and swiped my claws right across his face, causing him to hiss and fall back. I didn't waste a single second and bolted to the side. Their growls faded as I ran toward the arena, but more were waiting when I arrived. Raka were everywhere. Smack in the middle of the pit, five Raka had Auden surrounded, with a few of their dead siblings scattered on the ground around them. The sound of slapping feet behind me told me the other two were closing fast and I'd soon be just as trapped. I ran to the center of the arena, just in time for Auden to throw a Raka right over me with a burst of power.

"Dammit, Kaya! I told you to stay put!" Fury didn't even begin to describe the look in his eyes when he saw me.

So focused on me, he didn't notice the Raka sneaking up behind him. Before I thought about what I was doing, a knife left my hand and embedded itself squarely in the demon's eye. It dropped dead and another moved to take its place. It was a true talent to somehow look pissed as hell while still dispatching demons, and Auden pulled it off flawlessly, but his death glares couldn't hide his injury. His left leg moved slower than it should. It had no range of motion to the point of him having to drag it whenever he moved.

"Can we discuss this later when I'm done saving your ass? *Again.*" My claws cut through the throat of a girl no older looking than seven. That was going to leave nightmares. "And *stop* glaring at me."

We made our way closer to one another despite the Raka trying to herd us in different directions. There were four left to go. Back to back now, we were both out of breath and I could scent Auden's blood.

"How long ago were you scratched?" I asked over my shoulder, still keeping an eye on the closest Raka.

Auden only grunted and threw his final potion, using his power to make sure it landed. A whispered spell was all it took for the Raka to go up in a screeching ball of flames.

"It's not too late for you to get out—" he started.

"Auden! How long?" I shouted, momentarily distracted, and the Raka before me took advantage.

I dodged the nails and grabbed its skinny arm. The Raka's eyes widened when I pulled him close and snapped his neck. I let the tiny body slump to the ground. It would still need to be burned, but that was one more down. Two to go.

"I've got maybe ten minutes left before complete paralysis," Auden finally answered. He didn't sound too happy about that admission, but I wasn't sure if it was because of our situation or that he had to admit it to *me*.

The last two Raka moved at once but were easily dispatched. They were lower level demons and their threat came from their venom and that they attacked in numbers. With no more scaling the walls, Auden collapsed with a groan; his leg finally giving out.

I crouched beside him, grabbing his arm and looping it around my neck. "Come on, there's still time to get you inside."

Auden shrugged me off and gave me a small push. "You go. You shouldn't be out here anyway."

I bit my tongue against all the things I was ready to call him and focused on trying to save his pompous ass instead.

"You're a sitting duck out here and we don't know how many more Raka are on campus or what other demons are lurking about." I showed him the scratches on my wrist. "One got me not long after you so I can't stand watch for long."

I expected mild panic, an 'I told you so', or at the very least his anger, but Auden only laughed. The chuckles ended in a coughing fit as the venom moved through his body.

"You really don't know anything, do you?" He was wheezing now, his breaths harder to take.

My mouth opened and closed, and my cheeks burned as if on fire. "How about being a little less of a dick to the girl who saved your life?"

Auden chuckled again, "Familiars are immune to Raka venom."

I let his words sink in as I glanced down at my arm. Immune? Well that was extremely lucky. Come to think of it, I hadn't felt any side effects of the scratches. My arm didn't feel numb or even in pain and I definitely still had full range of motion.

"You still don't have to be such an ass about it," I grumbled.

Auden's next coughing fit sent him flat on the ground, but it didn't stop his attitude. "If you refuse to listen, at least go find some help."

I got to my feet, brushed the dirt off my legs and glared at his prone form. The second I moved out of his line of sight I heard him sigh. He thought I'd actually do it. Leave him here vulnerable and alone. As if I'd listen to his chauvinistic orders. He wouldn't last three seconds if another demon came upon him in this state. I moved around the arena, picking up the fallen knives and other discarded weapons. When I could physically carry no more, I arranged them around us, within easy reach should I need them, and sat back down to wait. Red danced on the edges of my vision and I swung my gaze around the amphitheater looking for the threat. But we were alone as far as I could tell. I scooted closer to Auden just in case. Nothing was going to get through to the injured prince, not while I was still breathing. If Auden wanted to yell at me and berate me for disobeying his orders, then so be it. At least he'd still be in one piece to do it.

Moonlight shown through the holes in the roof of the amphitheater, casting the overlarge space in an unnerving light. Auden hadn't so much as twitched from his prone position on the ground and the muscles in my back were now paying for my loyalty. I rocked my hips back and forth to ease my poor ass that hadn't left the packed dirt. Stretching my arms above my head eased the tension in my back, but it returned minutes later.

"You know, if you accepted my help earlier, we might not be in this mess right now." My glare was firmly rooted on the paralyzed boy beside me. "At least the venom is keeping you from feeling the effects of this fucking floor."

I talked Auden's ears to bleeding in the hours we'd been stuck here, and had zero guilt about it. If I was here because of him then the least he could do was listen to my grievances. And there were many.

"Son of a bitch, all these scrapes itch like crazy!" I moaned, picking at the dried blood on my skin. "Be grateful you don't have to feel that either."

The venom paralyzed Auden's limbs and most other bodily functions but stopped short of killing him. Raka demons preferred eating live prey; there was no enjoyment if their victims weren't fully aware of what body parts were being devoured. Morbid. As. Shit. So, while he may look dead, he could very much hear everything I had to say. Unless he was asleep...which I had no way of knowing if he was.

I shoved his shoulder. "You better not be asleep, asshole. I want you to be able to recount every minute I spent saving your life."

The crickets and frogs were out in full force tonight, no longer hiding with the rest of the swamp's critters. That meant no more demons lurking about. None appeared around the amphitheater since I'd taken up watch at Auden's side, but still, I couldn't just leave him here. I sighed and began another round of stretches. Footsteps echoed off the walls of the tunnel in front of me and I scrambled to my feet as fast as my dead legs would carry me. Dagger in hand, I tried to ignore the sharp tingling down my calves as blood rushed to my toes.

Nothing will get to him. Nothing.

I made the silent vow over and over while I waited for the next monster to reveal itself. It took a moment to process what I was seeing but when it did, my shoulders slumped with relief.

"Fuck yes." A small group of guards stormed out of the small tunnel. They must've thought it was Christmas morning with the way I smiled at them. "I'm sure as hell glad to see you guys," I called out as they got closer.

A few of them smiled back but no one said anything as they split down the middle to reveal a lone figure dressed in the standard combat black.

"How did I know I'd find you by his side?"

Asiel. It took all my muscle control to keep the sneer off my face as he smirked at me. A single jerk of his chin sent a few guards forward to pick up their frozen prince. Asiel's lips twisted in a cruel smile and I felt his eyes on me as I moved to assist them.

The guard closest to me smiled, his eyes shining with respect as be brushed away my attempts. "We've got it from here, *moitié.*"

Moitié, or half; the old term for a witch's familiar. Bonded pairs were considered two halves of a whole; they moved, breathed, and fought as one. It was an honor to be recognized as such, even though I wasn't Auden's partner. Moisture stung my eyes at the compliment, but I had no chance to thank him. Ever the impatient douche, Asiel hurried us along and barked orders to get his brother to the infirmary. He didn't have to tell me twice; I didn't want to spend another second in this arena of death. For a fleeting moment, I wondered who would have the responsibility of cleaning up the remaining demon bodies. Asiel's dark shadow scattered those thoughts in the space of a single breath.

They carried Auden back through the tunnels, but his older brother didn't look in a hurry to follow him. His onyx hair was slicked back out of his face, showcasing his sharp cheekbones and narrow eyes.

"You should be inside with the other students, but you've never been one to follow the rules, have you?"

I didn't reply. Was he honestly upset that he found me standing guard over his brother? Who was I kidding—of course he was. I could lose an eyelash and it would be an afront to him if I hadn't bowed and asked his permission first.

"You better be careful, Kaya. That rebellious streak of yours won't be tolerated like it was when we were younger." He stepped closer, until his cloying aftershave clogged all my senses. My nose wrinkled in disgust. "One wrong move and I can convince my father to revoke your probation like...*that*." He punctuated the word with a lunge, and I tripped over my own feet trying to scuttle back.

His laugh rang across the now deserted arena as he leered over me. I kept my knees bent, ready to strike if needed, but remained on the ground. My hands stung from the new scrapes.

"No one said anything about probation," I growled through clenched teeth. My jaw ached with how hard I had it locked.

"It was implied," Asiel laughed again, and waved at a guard I hadn't noticed standing against the far wall. "Make sure she gets back to the dorms. We wouldn't want something to happen to my little brother's...friend on her way back."

He stepped away, just barely, to allow me room to stand. He was still far too close for comfort though and I didn't drag my feet moving to the exit. I felt those dark eyes on me until we turned the corner but couldn't relax even when we were out of sight. The guard was silent as we moved across the barren campus, like two wraths gliding over a graveyard of battle. And that's exactly what the campus had become. There was so much damage. Broken statues and benches, crumbling walls and shattered windows. Small fountains lay overturned and in pieces. Even the trees hadn't escaped unscathed.

Branches littered the walkways and bathed in drying pools of blood. An ungodly amount of them. This was carnage. This was destruction. But there wasn't a body to be found. Even as my sneakers left bloody tracks on the sidewalk, I couldn't find the source they led back to. I didn't even see a demon and there was enough black ichor and rancid sludge mixed with the ruby red to tell me plenty more than the Raka had made it through the barrier. Where were all the bodies? Why were they cleaned up and carted away but the aftereffects of their decay left for all to see? Not that there was anyone out here *to* see it.

My silent companion and I were the only souls moving about. As the guard led me past the gym and courtyard, through the training grounds and toward the empty girl's dorm, I followed blindly; too tired, too mentally drained to put up any fight over the insanity of it all. Demons absolutely *demolished* the community. I shuddered to think about what the residential side looked like. Gutted homes and broken families wasn't a picture I wanted to fall asleep with tonight. The imposing structure of the girl's dorm rose sharply before us. I'd never once thought of it as a tomb, but that's what it resembled tonight. The windows were shuttered and barred with no light squeezing under the cracks to welcome me inside. It was cold and deathly quiet.

The somber atmosphere fractured as the door slammed open under the guard's assault and I was pushed inside. The House Matron wasn't at her desk and no students lingered on the couches or near the game tables. Where the hell was everyone? A pit grew at the bottom of my stomach like a black hole. Worry and anxiety warred with one another for control. None of this seemed right. And yet, the guard pushed on, half dragging me now up the chipped wooden stairs and still not saying a word.

"What's going on?" I finally asked, my whisper as loud as a shout in the deserted hall. "Where is everyone?"

We came to a stop in front of a solid brass door with a twenty-two hung in front and I recognized the number from my class schedule. The guard did exactly as Asiel asked and delivered me to my room. I turned around to thank him and hopefully get an answer to my questions, but he was already gone. I watched his back disappear down the stairs with nary a sound. Asshole. Inside, I was greeted by an ordinary room, the layout and furnishings no different than the room I'd grown up in. The bed was tucked away in the corner, across from a sturdy dresser that bordered the door to the bathroom. A tiny nightstand sat beside the bed and a desk completed the furniture. A small window nestled between the bed and dresser, and...that was it. A basic dorm. There were no personal touches and the only clothing I knew I'd find in the drawers would be more training uniforms. I'd have to make a trip to my father's house to grab some things from my old room. I wouldn't fit in any of the clothes in that closet, but a colorful comforter and some pillows could help liven up the place.

The thought of having to see my father, to speak with him for the first time in four years almost drained what little energy I had left. Maybe I could time it while he was away in a meeting. A girl could hope, and the universe owed me a big ass favor by now. I didn't bother turning on a light as I moved into the adjacent bathroom. The small plug-in near the sink cast enough of a glow for me to get a decent look at my reflection and I cringed. By all that is holy, I looked like shit. I was beyond dirty. I was downright disgusting. Leftover practice potion, grime, blood, and who knew what other bodily fluids caked every visible inch of my skin and each fiber that made up my clothes.

There might have been one teensy little spot that wasn't *as* gross by my left boob and wasn't that just random as hell. The bandage around my arm was useless and more saturated in demon blood than my own. I stripped down and threw everything in the trash. Not even bothering to wait for the water to warm, I jumped under the spray and vigorously scrubbed until I could see my own clean skin underneath. Some of my stitches were torn and fresh blood oozed with every lift of my arm, but I didn't leave that shower until every speck of dirt was gone. The bottom of the tub would stain from this much filth, but I was past the point of caring. When I finally stepped out and donned a fresh towel, I forced myself to take stock of my injuries. There were definitely some new bruises and gashes; nothing a little hydrogen peroxide couldn't take care of.

By the way the stitches in my shoulder were torn, I knew it was going to scar. Surprisingly, the knowledge didn't bother me. A quick peek under the sink revealed the standard first-aid kit that came with each room. A little antibiotic ointment and some fresh gauze and I was as good as new. Not a minute too soon either, because my eyes closed the second my head hit the pillow. Asiel's sick smile and rivers of demon blood followed me into oblivion.

CHAPTER
ELEVEN

I awoke to thunder. The rumbling assault battered my senses even through the pillow I squeezed around my head and my cheek felt glued to the sheet via a puddle of drool. I felt like ass. Ass that got hit by a Tonka Truck, dragged for miles through fields of sharp objects, and left to rot. I rolled over, throwing the pillow off my head and pissing off my torn stitches in the process. The thunder outside was joined by a shrill screech that punctured my eardrums too consistently to be natural. I bolted upright and ignored the protests from the rest of my body. That was the bell. Had they forgotten to turn it off? Because there was no way we were expected to go to classes today. Right?

The barrage of footsteps and mindless conversation outside my door told me otherwise. I groaned and took my time standing. No dizziness blackened my vision and I saw that as a good sign. Flashes from the night before seemed less traumatic in the light of day, but I still thought it strange to let the vulnerable population resume daily activities less than twenty-four hours after a massive demon attack. Asiel's threat of probation was the only thing that had me reaching for a clean uniform, despite how much it hurt to put it on. As I moved to the bathroom to brush the nasty off my teeth, I made a mental list of what needed to be accomplished today: find out what happened to Auden, reach out to my father to plan a visit to my childhood home, and find out what the hell has been going on in this place since I've been gone. I knew exactly where to learn the info on the latter.

The cafeteria was as full and raucous as I remembered. Like most teenagers of any species, my classmates didn't find it too difficult to brush off the horrors of the previous day and instead focused on what truly mattered; copulating. My nose scrunched in disgust as I moved past a couple practically fornicating in the hall. The volume as I stepped through the doors was enough to bring back the headache I was just starting to lose. With teeth clenched, I got in line for breakfast and allowed my gaze to roam. More eyes were on me than not, but I ignored them. I grabbed my tray, laden down with I didn't even know what, and searched the crowded tables for somewhere to sit. When I spotted a moppy nest of brown curls, I smiled. The room seemed to suffocate itself as I sat my tray before the boy with shocked green eyes. Surely, he remembered me from yesterday.

Quiet conversations steadily resumed around us, but Bast watched me with a wary eye. A small purple bag landed on the table between us, smaller than my carton of OJ, but I knew what it was without having to touch it. A hex bag. Usually stuffed with chicken bones, an unbroken spider egg, and some kind of plant or herb, they were used to ward off evil and there were many *many* variations. Some deadly. Bast sighed and swatted it to the floor before returning to his hunched position over what looked like homework. A less than subtle glance over my shoulder told me where the bag came from as a table of mainly shifters and a few witches dissolved into fits of laughter. Nice to see they encouraged comradery in this place.

"Aren't you going to ask?" I looked at Bast and got a face full of frustration and defiance. Rather than feed his growing anger, I shrugged and kept eating. "It's their less than intelligent way of accusing me of being a demon."

I snorted and took a sip of my orange juice. "Cause that little bag will work."

Bast stared at me with an adorable head tilt, like there was something about me he couldn't figure out. "I could be, a demon that is, for all you know. Wouldn't you rather sit with your friends and not risk it?"

It sounded like a challenge the way he asked. Like he expected me to be like everyone else— to be like those idiots at the other table. Too bad that wasn't me. Once upon a time, maybe. Back when there was nothing else to do around here but train and give in to the drama. I've seen what life has to offer outside these walls and it was a sobering experience. One the other students should be painfully aware of given the events of yesterday. Life was way too short to worry about petty squabbles and maintaining your spot within the popular hierarchy. Bast seemed like he understood that, so I'd take my chances with him. After telling him a much shorter and less revealing version of that, he still appeared skeptical.

"But I could be. I could be a Shapeshifter playing spy right under your nose."

Jesus, was this kid *trying* to convince me? If he was a demon, I would eat my own socks. There was just no way.

My eyes narrowed as I set my face in a stern frown. "Demons don't usually try to convince people that they're demons. I'm not worried." Bast stared at me again, mouth slightly open. "Besides," I continued. "Even if you were, I'd probably still sit next to you. I've never been one to give a flying fuck about people's expectations of me."

Bast laughed this time, his eyes softening to the kind gaze I recognized. Movement behind me brought a flicker of worry back to them, and the smirk slipped from his face. "Now's your chance to prove it."

The large presence behind me wasn't threatening—it was more annoying than anything. I turned in my chair and greeted the newcomer with a half-smile, one that was polite but hopefully didn't offer an invitation. The boy was a shifter too, a lion if his coloring was anything to go by. His golden hair was streaked with different shades of yellows and browns and very flattering against the backdrop of his tanned skin and caramel eyes. He smiled wide, showing pristine canines that were only slightly sharper than a human's.

"Hey there," he greeted, completely ignoring Bast.

I glanced over to see his reaction at being intentionally disregarded, but he didn't seem to mind. He watched us with rapt attention. When I caught his eye, he rose a single brow and dropped a shoulder in a shrug. I turned back to the meathead beside me, only to catch him checking me out. Gross. Why were my boobs the first thing guys wanted to introduce themselves too? Properly annoyed now, I crossed my arms and waited for his eyes to move back to my face.

"Listen—"

"Lincoln," he supplied with another smile.

"Lincoln... Pressley?" I asked, surprised and honestly a little impressed. "The scrawny kid who almost couldn't finish the obstacles in age twelve?"

His cheeks bloomed at my obvious shock—Bast's snort didn't help—but he recovered quickly. Moving closer, he set a hand next to my tray and leaned a little too far into my personal space.

"A lot's changed since we were kids, Kaya. I'm at the top of our class now, guaranteed to be one of the first Chosen."

His words about being chosen nagged at the edge of my

thoughts but I pushed them aside, and then him. His scent still smothered our end of the table and my nostrils flared.

"I can see that," I replied. "Obviously."

"Why don't you join us over at my table and we can catch up?" He gestured behind him at the table of idiots I'd pegged as the ones who threw the hex bag.

"Is Bast invited?" I asked, my voice sickly sweet. "I wouldn't want to ditch my new friend on my first day back."

A cloud seemed to move across his face, tightening his features until his eyes lost their glow and his grin slipped. He slowly shook his head.

"Life will be easier for you this year if you befriend your own kind." His response landed with a bite that wasn't felt by me. Bast visibly flinched and if possible, hunched lower in his seat.

Lincoln spoke loud enough to be heard over the usual clamor of the cafeteria and now all eyes were on our little exchange. He didn't notice the attention, too focused on making Bast cower before him. I could feel the smaller boy's shaking from this side of the table, and well, bullying never sat well with me. The growl started deep in my chest and grew until it punctured whatever dominance game Lincoln was playing. His wide eyes mirrored my own. It was the first time my inner cat acted without a conscious intent on my part, and I wasn't sure how I felt about it. All familiars shifted into some breed of feline, be it a lion, cougar, lynx, or any other breed. Some got along easier in groups, while others were more solitary. Both had issues with dominance. It was how we worked out our hierarchy and place amongst our people. Apparently, my inner feline saw Lincoln as nothing more than a Tom Cat needing to be put in his place. Only he wasn't backing down.

Still functioning off pure instinct, I lunged, throwing myself between him and Bast with a snarl. The move had me half sitting on the table with my ass almost in my breakfast, but I blocked Bast from view. Lincoln, now forever dubbed douche bag, looked at me in shock, even as his own cat responded to my challenge with a growl of his own. Nobody moved. Every muscle in my body pulled taught, my claws stung beneath my nailbeds, begging for release.

I could tell Lincoln was in a similar state as he stared at me, his eyes hardening with every second I didn't back down. A fight between us could go either way right now, with how beat up I already was, but I'd give as good as I got. Unless he shifted. Then I was fucked.

"You're making a mistake. There's a lot that's changed since you've been gone." His breath tickled the hair by my forehead he was so close. "I'll give you one more chance."

My smile was savage, practically daring him to do something. "I'm perfectly fine here, Lincoln. So why don't you run along now before you do something that will force me to show you exactly what hasn't changed since I've been gone." I stepped into him, forcing his chin back if he didn't want to bash it against my head. "You're still that scrawny kid from age twelve. Don't make me kick your ass and prove it."

I detected the change in his scent before he made a move. Pure anger rolled off him in waves and I prepared myself for the attack I knew was coming. But it never did. One of Lincoln's friends wrapped an arm around his shoulders while whispering in his ear. Whatever he said worked and they backed away.

"I'll see you in training, little traitor. We'll see who's smiling then."

~

LITTLE TRAITOR. Lincoln's words bounced around my head like a wrecking ball, destroying everything in its path. Did he know?

About Asher? Or was I being overly sensitive to the word? Was is pure coincidence that he nailed exactly how I felt?

"I've never seen anyone put Lincoln in his place like that—well, except maybe the teachers." Bast bounced along beside me, hopping more on his tip toes than actually walking. "It was awesome!"

"So you've said about a thousand times already," I grumbled, my headache pulsing behind my right eye at full force.

I hadn't meant to start anything; coasting under the radar was my goal for this year. But I couldn't stand by while Bast was put down, no matter how annoying he was. That wasn't how I rolled. There was probably a better way to handle Lincoln, one that didn't involve threats and violence. Sensei would have told me to look for common ground, a mutual solution. Violence was always, *always* a last resort. I snorted. There'd been so much violence in my life this past week, the old man would've had me scrubbing the mats with a toothpick. It couldn't be avoided though. Our race was volatile in nature, always battling for dominance and carving out a pecking order amongst ourselves. Only the strong survived. Barbaric really. But when Lincoln flexed his power and brushed off my warning, it poked at something within me. I wanted to slice through his face with my claws and lick his blood off my fangs. What the hell did that say about me?

"Hellooo? I'm paying you *mounds* of compliments here. Are you even listening?" Bast's hand waving in my face had three seconds to move before I broke it. "You must be a large breed too, huh? That's why you were able to stand up to Lincoln." His smile was too bright for the mood I was in. "That's good. Too many have shifted into smaller breeds the past couple years. I heard my mom say it was a problem."

The look on my face was enough of a warning for him to back off and I took a deep breath, pushing my annoyance to the side. It wasn't his fault. He didn't know shifting was a sore spot for me. And bragging about your breed was one of the highlights for young familiars when they turned sixteen. The social ladder, our training assignments, even our mating interests all revolved around what breed we manifest as. And so far, no one knew what I was, which made me an even bigger topic of conversation. All they knew was I was strong enough to challenge Lincoln. What would they think when they learned the truth?

Bast waved another hand in front of me.

"Sorry," I told him, with a genuine half-smile. "I don't mean to keep spacing out. It's been a little rough being back."

His smile was sympathetic. "And to have a demon attack on your first day couldn't have been easy." He didn't know the half of it. His eyes lingered on the many scrapes and bruises the gauze and my uniform couldn't hide. "I heard you got stuck in it, rather than be in your dorm like the rest of us."

I was curious as to how he knew that, but it wasn't really a secret.

"Yeah." The small shrug pulled at my stitches. "Auden and I were ambushed at the amphitheater, but we took care of things."

I saw the sparkle in his eye a second before he started gushing. "Prince Auden is literally the *best* warrior in the community. Most kills, badass fighter, incredible power, and...it doesn't hurt that he's hotter than Satan's bathwater."

I sputtered a laugh as his eyebrows wiggled in reference to Auden's looks. I wasn't blind. The boy was drool worthy, but Bast obviously had a hero complex going on when it came to the prince.

"He's always been leaps ahead of the rest of us. I tried my best to keep up with him when we were younger and never even came close." I smiled at the memories; I had a little bit of a hero complex for him too back then.

"I forgot you grew up with the princes before you disappeared."

I tripped over my feet but quickly corrected myself. This conversation was getting dangerously close to a topic I was nowhere near ready to touch. The sun was shining, adding to the stifling heat that hadn't even reached its peak for the day, but inside I felt cold; frozen. I'd allowed myself to be comfortably lured into a normal conversation and look what happened. It always led back to the past. It was a small offhand comment, I shouldn't be shattering inside. But I was. Speaking about the past meant thinking about Asher, about what I missed about him and what he was missing now that he was dead. I broke eye contact with Bast, less he saw the inner turmoil I struggled with and looked around the room instead. We'd entered the side door of the gym, not bothering with the stairs since our class this morning was on the first floor. In one of the biggest rooms, actually. It was ordinary for today's purpose, but partitioning walls allowed for it to be even larger. This was where the age twelve obstacles were held, some non-official ceremonies, and a majority of the end of year tests. The fact that I'd taunted Lincoln about what happened in this very room years ago was one shitty coincidence. At twelve, we were tested on our speed and agility, familiar and witches alike, to see if we were up to par with what would begin our next level of training.

Since our abilities didn't kick in until sixteen, we were pretty even with the strength and stamina of the witches and to this day I wasn't sure how the instructors judged us. I do remember that Asher and I soared through those trials, mostly thanks to the grueling extra workouts I'd put us through in the weeks leading up to them. Asher was as far opposite as his brothers as you could get. He had to work extra hard to pass the physical demands of our education. But he had me. I just wish I could've come through for him when it counted.

A gentle shove on my shoulder knocked me from the memory and revealed our instructor gliding across the wooden floors, meticulously preparing the room for whatever she planned for today.

"Where do you keep going?" Bast asked, honest confusion splayed across his face.

"I was just thinking." I replied, still half caught up in my memories. "Why do we have classes today if there was just a demon attack?" I hadn't meant to ask that, my brain and mouth weren't exactly working in sync right now, but once I did, I realized I really wanted the answer.

Bast rolled his eyes. "Right? You'd think they'd give us a break. But nope. The Council voted to continue regular schedules as long as there was no major loss of life."

My eyes bugged out of my head. "No major loss of— there was monumental destruction and *pools* of blood last night." There was definitely loss of life yesterday. What was the Council waiting for?

"It's always like that," Bast said. "I guess it's the new normal."

I didn't know what to say to that. Unfortunately, the teacher started class before I could get more information. I hadn't noticed the other students traipse through the other set of doors, but they stood silent and attentive, shoulder to shoulder, as they waited for the woman before us to speak. The sun shone through the windows up high on the walls, out of reach from most damage we could cause, and the beams caught on glittering trails of dust that no amount of cleaning could erase. On the other side of the shafts of light stood our instructor. Her black hair was streaked with grey and pulled back in a bun tight enough to tug at the skin around her face. Her lips were pursed in a no-nonsense frown and I found myself hoping her cold eyes didn't land on me. No such luck. She worked her gaze down the line, snagging on me when she reached the end.

"For those of you who may not know." She was definitely talking to me. "My name is Instructor Lyra. Not Teacher, Teach, Instructor L, Ms. L, or any other variation you may try to come up with." Finally, that hard gaze left my face and scanned the rest of the class. "My job is to train you in the finer arts of being a familiar. To hone the deadly gifts your shifting allows you to wield. You will spend the better part of our time together in your animal forms so any questions will be held until the end of class."

My palms began to sweat as she continued. This was a shifting class. A *mandatory* shifting class where we learned all we could about our feline halves. The half I couldn't even reach. Something told me Instructor Lyra wouldn't be understanding if I told her I couldn't shift. I peered at my classmates, freezing just a little longer on Lincoln standing tall, front and center. They wouldn't be understanding either. If word got back to the Council, or worse, Asiel, that I was defective...I got nauseous just thinking about the consequences. The class dispersed at the instructor's order and Bast dragged me off to a far corner. By his pale complexion and nervous scent, he hated this as much as I did. I felt a little lighter knowing I wasn't alone in my feelings. A little. But not much. Instructor Lyra prowled toward us, her gate as smooth as any cat. The rest of the class already removed their clothes in preparation to shift. I felt their eyes on me. Waiting. Anticipating. Judging.

"Looks like you finally have someone to train with, Mr. Avet," she said, not at all dropping that severe mask she wore when addressing us.

Bast visibly shrunk under her scrutiny and I wondered if the students took their cues on how to treat him from this woman.

She looked like a person who stomped out weakness rather than help it grow stronger and the trembling boy at my side had seen his share of stomping. When she turned to me, the grey of her eyes pierced with their intensity. I refused to buckle. I wasn't sure how long we stood there, neither one willing to drop their stare but eventually the corner of her mouth twitched.

"I've heard of you, Miss Thornton." She said my name like she expected me to be...*more*. "There will be no special treatment for you in this class, no matter who your father is." As if I'd ever relied on special treatment, or the favoritism of my father. Hard to use something that didn't exist. I frowned but didn't bother correcting her. "Shift so I may see what we have to work with."

She flung her hand at me, like that little wave would magically change my form. Fairy Godmother she was not. I looked over at Bast, but he was still human. That order was just for me then.

"Are you hard of hearing or intentionally obtuse? Shift. Now."

The panic set in again as her demands drew more attention to our corner. She stood there, expectant and growing testier the longer I went without sprouting fur.

"My arm is too—" she smacked away the very arm I held out, her fingernails catching on the gauze. I hissed and my eyes flickered from the pain, changing from feline to human and back again like a seizure, before settling back to normal.

"Do I look blind to you, Miss Thornton? I can see that you are injured. That should not and will not stop you from shifting. Ever." She turned away and addressed the class, arms spread wide to gather them in for whatever show she was about to spin. And they eagerly waited. The tension grew as dozens of feline eyes settled on me like I was a fresh pound of meat.

Lincoln's tail twitched with pleasure as he observed me cradling my arm and I swallowed against the urge to hiss at him.

"Let this be a lesson to you all. There will inevitably come a time where you, and possibly your partner, will be injured; even gravely. That will *not* stop you from doing your duty. Being in your animal form will help you block out the pain and focus on the task at hand. Master this now and it will save you then." She was facing me again, her face and stance leaving no room for argument or failure. "I won't ask again. Shift."

There was nothing I could do but stand there. I didn't know *how* to do what she wanted.

"Shit, Kaya. Just do what she wants," Bast whispered, his nerves overpowered by his worry for me.

Instructor Lyra silenced him with a single lift of her finger. She didn't look at him. No. Her fury was pinpointed at me. "You would defy me." I didn't answer, couldn't. I was trying too damn hard to do what she asked, but no amount of fear or adrenaline was going to make my inner cat come forward. "You insolent, little—" her hand was raised, claws extended...until another hand wrapped around her wrist.

She spun with a snarl, but swiftly composed herself when she saw Auden standing there, backlighted by a ray of golden sun. He eyes gleamed beneath his lashes, a predator in his own right.

Instructor Lyra managed a slight tilt of her head. "My prince, to what do I owe the pleasure?"

If Auden noticed her barely withheld attitude, he didn't comment on it. He released her arm, "I'm terribly sorry to interrupt, Instructor, but I'm here for Miss Thornton. We had an appointment this morning and are now exceedingly late for it."

He didn't ask her permission, or even wait for her to acknowledge his excuse before he grabbed my good arm and led me from the room. I felt her seething behind us, but when I tried to turn back and look, Auden jerked me forward. We were out the doors and into the sunshine in the next heartbeat. I was used to his moody habits by now, so it didn't shock me that he had yet to even greet me. It was still annoying though. I tore my arm from his grasp, but he didn't make to grab me again. I tried as best I could to check him out while we walked. There was obvious bruising, but he moved like he hadn't been paralyzed for most of the night. He was sure footed and strong as hell—not even a limp as he led us through the woods. His lips formed a firm line, making his chin appear sharper as his face stayed frozen in a permanent glower. Great. We didn't have an appointment this morning, so, what was he so pissy about? Had he seen me in class? Maybe he sided with the instructor.

"Where are we going?" I asked, already out of breath from the less than forgiving pace he set.

"How long has your arm been bleeding like that?" He growled.

I scoffed. Typical of him to ignore my question. He was more agitated today, more brisk when he spoke. His hair curled past his ears as wild as ever, but the scowl on the face it framed was a new one. Not...quite angry.

"How long?" He asked again.

"It hasn't stopped since last night. I'm pretty sure I tore some stitches."

He swore and increased our pace, reaching for my arm again when the infirmary doors came into view. "You should've came here last night after dispatching the Raka instead of annoying me with your endless prattle."

I dodged his grasp and stomped in front of him, halting his steps. "Are you really mad at me for watching your back?" I shouted, incredulous. "What's your problem?"

"You shouldn't have had to!" He shouted back, and then

clenched his jaw until it ticked. When he spoke again, his voice was firm but shook with the anger he held back. "You should've been safe in your dorm like the other students. Or secure in that bunker. Where. I left. You."

I wanted to laugh at such a stupid argument, but I was too annoyed . "So let me get this straight. You're pissed that you needed help? Or that you needed help and *I* was the one who came through? Is that it?" I lowered my voice and tried to speak to his calmer nature. "Auden, *everyone* needs help sometimes and I refuse to walk away when I see that. Asher wouldn't have wanted—"

We both froze, our bodies somehow more tense now than when we were screaming at each other. I could hardly breath over the razor blades in my throat. It was the first time Asher had been mentioned and to hear his name echo in the space between us was like a blow to the gut. I couldn't look at Auden, but I felt his eyes on me. How they must look right now. More black than gold with the strength of his grief and anger. Hate. It was probably hate he was spearing me with. I turned away and started up the infirmary steps. Auden's hate I could handle, but it was seeing it through the eyes he shared with my best friend that I couldn't bear. Auden caught up with me as I signed my name on the clipboard at the empty desk.

"Kaya." There was so much pain in one word, enough to slice me open again. His touch was a gentle caress as he placed his fingers under my chin.

"Oh." The surprised orderly took one look at my battered body and soaked gauze, brushed off the awkward she stepped into, and got to work. "The doctor isn't going to like this. Please follow me."

She said nothing about the tension she obviously stepped right in the middle of. I guess I looked like shit enough for her to not care. Auden moved to follow us, a hulking shadow at my back. I shook my head.

"Just go," I whispered, barely able to even muster up those words.

"I'm coming with you," he swore.

When he again took a step, the orderly pointed to a chair in the small waiting room. "It's a private exam if you don't mind, Your Highness."

Auden looked ready to argue but she pushed on before he could say anything. Her calming hand was soft on my back and when I looked over at her, she winked. Maybe she noticed the mood after all. I nodded at the understanding I saw in her smile and tried to put the dark-haired prince out of my mind as we went into the exam room.

CHAPTER TWELVE

Auden still waited when we came out an hour later, doctor in tow. My arm throbbed in a weird wave of numb and then not under the new layer of gauze as the pain meds they used slowly wore off. Some of my stitches had indeed been torn, and the doctor glared at me the entire time he put the new ones in. Like it was my fault I was attacked by demons yesterday. The doc still appeared grumpy as we rounded the corner. Auden was on his feet in seconds, meeting us halfway.

"Is she okay?" he asked, with what I could have sworn sounded like real worry, but he wouldn't look at me.

I waved my good arm, with no effect. "*She's* right here. And I'm fine." They both tuned me out completely.

"She's training with you now I hear?" The doctor asked, and Auden nodded. "I've already warned her of her limits, but as her trainer, you should know too. Absolutely no shifting until those stitches are removed. She's already torn them once and I'm not in the habit of repeating my work."

I rolled my eyes. He wasn't the one that had to deal with the pain of torn stitches. So, he had to put a couple back in; cry me a river. That's literally his job.

"She can still exercise but be thoughtful of the limitations of that arm for at least a week. I'll mark her chart and inform her instructors if she'll be absent from their class," the Doc finished, and they shook hands, officially passing the baton of my care.

"Don't worry. I'll be keeping a very close eye on her from here on out," Auden replied, with a side glare at me.

There was a promise in that gaze, and I got both goosebumps and pissed off in the same breath. The doctor disappeared back around the corner before I could begrudgingly thank him for my new stitches and Auden had his hand on my back, steering us out the doors before I even knew what was going on. I tried to shrug him off, but his hand returned every time, warming my skin even through my shirt. He used gentle pushes to guide me and didn't rush us this time to get wherever we were going. We passed the gym and kept moving until the roof of the dorms rose above the trees.

"Are you taking me back to my room? What is this, time out?" I grumbled, not really fighting him. The throbbing in my arm wasn't going away and a nap *did* sound pretty nice.

Rather than answer, Auden kept steering me along one well-worn path after another, finally coming to a stop in a small clearing just to the right of the girl's dorm. The trees were thick here, making this place almost invisible they were so tightly woven together. The open ground in the center was bouncy, but solid and it expanded to a sky overhead that was blue and free of clouds. Private and yet open. The sun wouldn't shine directly over us until lunch so there was shade enough to keep the heat from being unbearable. I half expected a picnic blanket to be laid out it was so beautiful.

"What are we doing here, Auden?" I asked, a slight hitch in

my voice. There were too many reasons why he could want privacy, and I wasn't keen on facing any of them.

He dug a bag out of the ferns and the contents clacked together, like glass jars. Shit. Was this a picnic? My growing anxiety slowly ebbed as I watched him pull out vial after vial of different potions and set them equal distance apart.

"I figured we could take advantage of this time each morning to train, since you can't attend your usual scheduled class." He calmly watched me check out the vials and when I didn't argue he continued, "You're far behind your fellow classmates on many things, but the most important is recognizing the different potions we use. When you work closely with a witch, it's imperative that you're able to recognize the spell they're about to cast, and what the effects are of the potion they will throw."

"Makes sense," I admitted, moving closer. I was intrigued.

Seeing I wasn't going to fight him on this, Auden nodded. And so began his instructions. Each small bottle had a faint glow emanating from the inside as he moved them a safe distance apart from one another. The magic wasn't active until ignited with a word of power, but I couldn't tear my eyes away from them. They were beautiful. Thick, shimmery liquid in an array of different colors swirled behind the glass. Cobalt blue next to a teal so sharp it stung to look at it. The red and orange were vibrant and *alive,* while the purple and earthen green appeared silent, but with an edge. It was almost a shame to break them open, but I knew their affects could be just as stunning. The purple one called to me the most, its violet and lavender undertones almost peaceful in their dance.

"What's that one do?" I asked, pointing at it.

Auden followed my finger to the prettiest one. "The midnight potion. That's the last one we'll go over."

"Why?" I hated that he'd gone back to being difficult. It was beautiful out here, calming, and we worked with shiny vials. Why'd he have to go and ruin it? "It's a real dickish move to make it the last one just because I chose it."

He muttered something that sounded like very creative profanity and finished placing the last vial upon a medium sized rock before turning to face me. His shoulders were tense, arms crossed in front as he sized me up. A lone finger tapped across his bicep, but he didn't move from where he leaned against the tree.

"The *purple* one, as you elegantly call it, is a dreamless potion. It puts the target into a deep sleep and can accidentally infect those that get too close and breathe it in." He explained slowly, each word a small bite. "Which is why I'd planned to save it for last."

"Oh." My teeth unconsciously dug into my bottom lip as I tried to process his explanation through my annoyance. "You could've just said that."

He raised a single brow. "I'm pretty sure I just did."

Looks like his personality was permanently stuck on asshole. Fine.

I huffed and flicked a finger at the one next to it. "The teal one then. What's it do?"

The richness of the color was almost too much to bear when magnified under the glaring morning sun. Auden placed it near his foot at the base of the tree, so I assumed that was the one he wanted to start with. He bent down and swooped it up and the small bottle disappeared behind his long fingers.

"*This* is a freezing potion. Combined with the proper word of power, *kenbe*, it will freeze your target on the spot and allow for a less dangerous take down. The lasting effects can vary on the strength of the potion or that of the witch who threw it, as well as the type and strength of the demon, but they usually last for at least a solid thirty minutes."

Faster than I was ready for, Auden threw the potion at my feet. I hardly had time to scream before it imploded, and the icy liquid splashed against my bare legs. My head snapped back as the force of my anger grew into something truly impressive, but Auden's lips were moving, and the whispered word of power took affect with brutal efficiency. My limbs locked up like they were bound with iron. My jaw slammed shut, muffling my curses as if I'd been gagged. Which, technically, I guess I had been. Nothing hurt as I took stock of the rest of my body. The potion acted like an invisible net that kept me bound with a wave of concealed strength. My glare could burn holes in the sun, but Auden leisurely walked toward me like I wasn't a threat. Once he was in front of me, his lips split in a slow grin.

"Maybe we should start all our trainings like this." My muffled expletives fell way short of expressing how I felt. "Hmm? What was that?" Auden leaned in, bringing his ear closer until his scent nearly overwhelmed me. He turned his chin, bringing our lips near centimeters apart and then he hit me with another of his rare smiles. "It's too bad I have the antidote. I quite like not hearing you constantly argue."

I didn't try to say anything this time. His intentional needling wasn't enough to distract me from how close our lips were. A slight twitch, one small misstep on his part and they would touch. He seemed to realize it at the same time I did because his gaze caught on my mouth and his breathing grew ragged. I felt his fingertips lightly graze my jaw, his forefinger resting under my ear while his thumb rubbed across my chin. Our eyes met as he applied pressure and my lips parted, just enough for him to place a concealed vial to my lips. I caught a glimpse of milky white before it disappeared, over my tongue and down my throat. It had no taste and left no residue in my mouth, a ghost potion, but its results were instantaneous. As if someone cut the ropes that bound me, my body released and I toppled forward into Auden's awaiting arms.

Where I didn't stay.

Jerking back like I'd been stung; I wiped my mouth with the back of my hand and glowered. "What the hell was that?"

Auden strolled back to his post against the tree, acting not at all bothered by what just *almost* happened between us. But when he turned around, he couldn't hide the affects that moment had on him. His chest rose and fell in uneven breaths and his shoulders returned to their tense position.

"You need to know how the potion feels and how quickly it can take control. If you don't fully understand all the weapons in your arsenal, then you're fated to suffer at their misuse. I also wanted to demonstrate that some potions can be counteracted and how quickly that too can offer relief."

He spoke calmly, in an even tone that gave no room for me to unleash my anger. And he was right dammit. First-hand experience was always the best, even Sensei taught like that. But I never felt so unsettled after an example from Sensei. I never left training with my heart racing and my emotions so all over the place.

"You could have warned me first," my whisper was quiet, but strong, with just enough anger to back it.

Auden cocked his head to the side; a picture of unaffected. "Now, where would be the fun in that?"

We didn't stop at one potion. Auden made me choose another one, the orange, and thankfully didn't throw it at my feet this time. It probably had to do more with the fact that this was an *exploding* potion than the fact that he didn't want to piss me off further.

"The word of power for this one is *kraze,* and it packs a punch stronger than a small bomb if made and used correctly." He stood partially in front of me and threw the vial at a distant stone. The word of power blew it to tiny shards in seconds.

The red potion was next, its word of power *chalé.* The fire potion ignited a small bushel of swamp weeds that Auden easily put out with a wave of his hand, drawing water up from the earth with the pull of his power. On and on the demonstrations went— most of them too dangerous to risk throwing at me, thankfully. The small black vial, that bubbled and fizzed like soda when shook was filled with an acid mixture, one that didn't require a word of power, but the rusted yellow one did. I nicknamed that one Sticky Floor because once Auden said, *simante,* it was like the earth turned into a giant stick pad and I was the poor rat caught in the trap. Some heavy pulling and a lot of water was the only way to get me out and it proved Auden's newest point that even after a situation de-escalated with a potion, one couldn't wait to deal with the target. They could still escape.

The final vial sat patiently on the rock, its earthen tones deep and alluring. Auden rolled it between his hands, causing the potion to swirl and shift and catch the light in the most interesting way.

"This is a binding potion," he said, holding the vial still long enough for me to take a closer look at it. There were small specks floating inside, sparkling like the inside of a cracked gemstone.

"I thought you already showed me the binding potion?" I asked, wary as I remembered the feeling of being completely frozen.

"It's completely different than the first one," Auden explained. "For one thing, this particular potion can only be used outside. It has to make contact with the earth in order to work."

"That seems a little limiting. Why have a potion that only works in one type of place?"

I didn't like the grin he turned on me. I immediately stepped away, my eyes darting to the side to see what I could use as a shield, but we were in the center of the clearing. Auden causally dropped the potion between us, not even a drop landing on my skin and I breathed a sigh of relief.

"When a potion is as effective as this one, even its minor limitations can't counteract its uses." The corner of his lips tilted higher, and then he murmured, "*Mare.*"

Roots exploded from the earth and slithered across the ground to wrap around my feet, my ankles. They moved up my legs, binding and constricting like hungry snakes until finally— mercifully— coming to a stop around my collarbones. I thrashed and struggled, but the roots held firm, like they'd done for the trees for thousands of years.

"Auden," I growled, tired of playing these games.

He had a knife in his hand, the metal glinting when he moved it in the sun. Using the *very* pointy end, he casually cleaned the dirt and leftover potion grime from beneath his fingernails. My struggles slowed as I grew tired, but he continued like he hadn't heard me.

"I get the point," my voice was gruff with barely restrained irritation. "The potion works extremely well, and it doesn't have to touch the target, just the earth. Bravo. So cool. Now cut me loose!"

There wouldn't be an antidote for this potion, no, good ol fashioned hacking with a blade should do the trick. But Auden made no move to free me. It grew quiet as I waited for him to say or do something, anything. Only the sounds of the birds and distant classes in the training yards interrupted the tension riddled calm that settled over the clearing. Those blazing golden eyes that I hated to love, watched me. They lingered, taking in every detail and my stomach twisted in a delicious and embarrassing way.

"Us working together would go a lot smoother if you didn't argue with me every step of the way," Auden drawled, and I scoffed.

"It would also go a lot smoother if you didn't bite my head off one minute and then act a little *less* like a jackass the next," I shot back.

He didn't like being called a jackass, I could tell, but he silently shook his head and exhaled. The knife disappeared back into his belt as he calmly walked around me in slow, tight, circles. I could only move my head, and lost sight of him every time he passed behind me, but I would know exactly where he was even if I couldn't see him. I could *feel* him. The power that radiated off him—the heat. It wasn't something that could be overlooked, not unless one tried very hard. And trust me, I was trying.

"Our lesson for today is almost over," the low timbre of his voice came from my right. I didn't bother turning my head, I could track him without needing to see him. His scent was all around me now. I caught motion out of the corner of my eye, and then he was there in front of me again. "When I release you, I want you to go to your dorm and get some rest. I'll let the rest of your instructors know that you'll be taking the afternoon off."

A hiss escaped from between my clenched teeth at the audacity. I didn't want to go back to my dorm, like some grounded child, for the rest of the day. There was nothing to do in there but stare at the walls and *think*. I was actually looking forward to class later, Mr. Laveau's in particular. Learning about different demons as well as their origins and weaknesses gave me something to strive for. A goal to set before myself. I was going to become the best familiar the academy had ever put out. I was going to be faster, stronger, and more cunning than anyone who came before me. Let a demon try to hurt someone I cared about then. They wouldn't stand a chance.

"You already know I hate when you boss me around, so why continue to do it?" I warned, the scorn barely concealing my true emotions. "Release me."

He ignored my demand, turning instead to sit on the boulder across from me, one knee bent like he had all the time in the world to just sit and stare at me. I squirmed beneath the roots.

"Auden," I growled. "Let. Me. Go."

"I don't think I will," he purred, and the sound shot straight to my stomach, filling it with butterflies. "At least, not until I get some answers."

"I thought we were training! Not playing twenty questions." I scoffed and rolled my eyes, but inside I felt the stirring of panic. What answers did he seek? And why did I have to be restrained for him to get them?

My struggles resumed, fruitless and futile, as my fight or flight response was triggered. Whatever he wanted to discuss was important enough for him to lure me out here under the guise of training, to bind me in some—-ridiculously strong plants, honestly—to find answers to whatever he couldn't ask me any of the fifty million other times we've been alone. My self-preservation told me this wasn't a conversation I was going to enjoy. Auden sat calmly on the large rock and watched me squirm from beneath hooded eyes. I saw the flecks of gold even from here and it caused my pulse to race faster.

"Why did you run that night?" His voice was soft, but it carried over to me as if he shouted. It rang in my head like a bell and I was so caught off guard that I ceased my battle against the roots.

We stared at one another, him with endless patience and me with growing anger. He did *not* just ask me that. I got one ankle free, scraping it raw in the process, only for another root to slither around it and grow up my calf.

"*Ugh,* Auden!" I all but screamed. "Tell this *stupid* plant that I don't like hugs from things covered in dirt."

He said nothing as I twisted and pulled. Still nothing as the roots continued to grow wherever I broke free.

"Why did you run that night?" he asked, again.

I was beyond pissed off at this point. Beyond frustrated and beyond filtering my mouth. The panic was a growing wave within me, and I didn't know how much longer I could keep it at bay. Why did he have to ask about that night? It was all I could do to not let the grisly images cloud my vision, but each time he brought it up, they crept closer. I stopped moving and gulped down the humid swamp air before once again attacking the overgrown houseplant.

"You fucking know why," I panted. He had to know. Him and every other soul on this island.

"I don't think I do," he replied, finally moving from that damned rock. Only, he was coming closer now and I didn't think it was to cut me loose. "Just when I think I've got you figured out; you surprise me. I'm done guessing. Now," he was less than a foot away. "You tell me. What happened?"

His eyes glowed brighter the longer I remained silent. I could see the fury and hurt, the distrust in his gaze. I could practically taste it, it was so potent. There would be no talking myself out of this, no distractions to grab his attention. Nowhere to run or hide from that penetrating scrutiny. My throat clogged with tears, causing my breaths to come in shorter and faster.

"Why are you doing this?" I whispered. "Can't you ask me something else? Anything else?"

"Fine. Why do your eyes remain dull even after you've rested?" He countered, and I tried not to let the change of topic throw me. "Why do they only burn when you're fighting, either with a demon or with me?" He stepped closer, his gaze ensnaring me even when I wanted to hide from their intensity.

My heart slowed and then took off. Sweat beaded at my temples and drifted down into my hair. I kept my breaths silent, and the roots covered the rapid rise and fall of my chest, but I was sure Auden could tell I was mere moments away from hyperventilating. I knew he watched me; I mean, his eyes were on me all the time. But I assumed it was because he was worried that I'd try to run again, and then later because of the demon attack, my injury...

He'd been watching me far closer than I ever could've anticipated. He *studied* me, until here we were, him blurting out tells that I didn't even know I had.

"This isn't answer a question with a question. I'm not playing games here," I was breathless, anxious. I didn't want to talk about this.

Auden only stared—silent, waiting. Something flickered in his gaze that told me he could see past all the barricades I tried putting up. His face was set in concentration as he made a soft sound and took a step closer.

"It's Asher, isn't it?"

I squeezed my eyes shut against the rising flood of tears and swallowed the raw scream that built. His name undid me every time. It was like getting stabbed each time I heard it, but when it came from Auden's lips...I couldn't stand it.

Killer. Murderer. Betrayer. Killer. Murderer. Betrayer. Killermurdererbetrayer. Killermurdererbetrayer.

The voices in my head drowned out the sound of everything

else. They spiraled around me, tugging me deeper into their torturous funnel until I wasn't sure I deserved to find my way out again. A soft growl, the only sound that punctured the void, made me open my eyes. Amber and gold weaved together beneath darkened brows creased with concern. A tender hand brushed the hair from my face, continuing the caress down my cheek, before it curled around and cupped the back of my neck.

"What are you battling so hard in there?" He murmured, resting his forehead on mine.

We shared breaths, each one bursting from me in a choppy attempt to calm myself, only to be drawn in and exhaled again in one soothing wave by Auden. I wasn't sure how long we stood like that, him free and centered and me, bound and erratic.

"Let me go." My voice was barely audible, but it grew each time I used it until I was shouting. "Let me go! Let me go!"

I thrashed against my bindings, not caring that I tore skin or caused more of those stupid roots to grow around me. Auden clenched his jaw, as if he was pained by my screams. I was sure it was disappointment at my refusing to answer. The shakes started not long after the tears broke free and Auden's steady hand behind my neck drifted back to my jaw. More firm pressure against my chin and a purple vial appeared against my lips, the beauty of the liquid inside so at odds with the inky dark spreading through my mind.

"I'm so sorry, Kaya," Auden breathed, tipping the vial until it emptied. A softly whispered, "*Dòmi,*" was all it took and I floated away on a soft cloud that rumbled with darkness.

CHAPTER
THIRTEEN

The soft, feathered pillow beneath my cheek was more of a shock than a comfort and my eyes jolted wide, instantly alert to my surroundings. Pale walls as unique as Styrofoam stared back at me with a bored plainness. The sturdy wooden furniture looked stale and motionless, if not a little messy. Just as I'd left it. I was in my room—the scents of my sheets were familiar, but confusing. How had I gotten here?

I'd woken far too many times over the last week unsure of where I was, with my thoughts too muddled about what took place before I lost consciousness. That habit needed to stop now. I squinted against the harsh strip of sunlight that struck my face through the crack in the blinds and forced my thoughts to organize into a reliable timeline of what I last remembered. I was outside amongst the trees...or, was I wrapped in them? Small movements of the sheets against my skin told me the soreness in my arms and legs wasn't residual from a dream. It felt like I'd been in a battle with sandpaper. The roots!

I was bound in roots from Auden's stupid spell as he forced some medieval form of potion education upon me. I'd been unable to move more than a wiggle as he circled me and rambled on about something. I couldn't recall exactly what he said, but my body remembered the heat of him being so close, followed by the burning anger of his eyes piercing past my defenses over...something... there was a flash of amethyst and then cool oblivion. Had he knocked me out? I sat up, the comforter and sheets pooling in my lap as I gingerly felt my head for any sore spots. My skull felt fine, so he hadn't struck me with anything. My fingers pressed around my ears and toward my temple, making sure.

"Kaya." The soft voice came from the far corner, causing me to scream and nearly stab myself in the eye with one of my fingers.

The corner was deep in shadows, but as my racing heart thumped out of control, I slowly made out familiar features. As the figure uncurled from the chair, his black hair was the last part of him revealed by the few rays of sun striking that far across the room. Auden's gilded eyes captured and reflected the light like a cat's as he moved around my bed.

"What in the hell, Auden?" My shriek was somehow half a whisper, as if I was too scared to break the silence my room was shrouded in.

"I didn't mean to startle you," he replied, his voice rough like he too just woke.

I took a closer look at his shaggy hair and unkempt t-shirt. His uniform was creased with hundreds of wrinkles, evidence that he'd been sitting there a while and the yawn he didn't bother hiding was further proof.

"Were you *sleeping* in that corner?" I squeaked halfway through the question, both shocked and embarrassed. Auden yawned again and shrugged. "B-but why?" I sputtered.

A blush worked its way across his cheeks to match my own. "I came by at breakfast and you didn't answer." He brought a hand up to rub the back of his neck but didn't look away. "Some people have an adverse reaction to the dreamless potion and when I saw you were still asleep; I got a little worried. I decided to watch and make sure you were okay." He briefly glanced at the empty chair. "I guess I fell asleep at some point."

I didn't say anything. Couldn't. Too many thoughts were fighting for dominance. He watched me sleep. Did I snore? I casually wiped the back of my hand over my mouth. At least I hadn't been drooling. I'm sure my hair looked like a family of opossums moved in and decorated, but he'd seen me look far worse. My cheeks still burned. Ugh, how embarrassing. He sat there and watched me? Who knows what I did? Oh god. What if I farted? I imagined him leaning over me, concerned about the effects of the potion, when suddenly I—wait a damn minute. The dreamless potion. That jackhat *did* knock me out! He'd trapped me with the binding potion and held his own interrogation about the night I ran away. Thankfully, this time my anger far outweighed the panic that usually grew when I thought about that night. He forced that potion past my lips, intentionally, without knowing how it would affect me. He manipulated me to get answers, traumatizing me in the process. My cheeks burned for an entirely different reason now.

My hands closed into fists, crumpling the sheets as I calculated how graceful I could be at untangling my legs *and* kicking his ass. Auden's eyes flicked between my clenched fists and my face and he cautiously raised his hands.

"Now just hear me out—"

"How did you get in?" My voice was steel, and I was ready to claw at his face, but I wanted the full story first.

"Kaya—"

"Boys aren't allowed in the dorms," I interrupted. "I'll ask again; how did you get in?"

He sighed and ran a nervous hand through his hair. "The Dorm Matron let me in. I told her I had to drop something off."

My brows rose at how easy it was for him to gain access. It was information that I stored away for later. Was it so easy because of who he was or was the Matron lax in her duties? I wondered if the same excuse could get someone else in. It would be nice to have someone over to hang out who was actually invited. Auden saw the gears turning and his eyes narrowed.

"Don't even think about it," he warned. "I'm the only male allowed in here."

I raised a brow at the possessive statement, but he didn't break eye contact. "Whatever." It wasn't worth arguing over. I didn't need his permission. And besides, how would he know?

I threw my legs over the side of the bed, forcing Auden to step away. The comforter was thrown aside next, revealing my dirty jean shorts. At least he hadn't tried to undress me after roofying me. Only half a creeper then.

"You could've just not given me the potion." There it was.

He'd already explained its affects; going into a dreamless sleep wasn't something that had to be experienced to be understood.

"You were learning," he argued anyway. "And... I knew you weren't sleeping well, which would've interfered with future trainings to get you up to speed." He crossed his arms and leaned a hip against the nightstand, making the lamp wobble. "There's obviously a lot of baggage you've yet to deal with." And I'd been screaming like a total nutcase, is what he meant to say but didn't.

I scoffed and stood. My head barely came up to his shoulder, but I put as much warning into my glare as I could. "I don't want to talk about it."

He dipped his chin in a look that told me he saw right through my false bravado. I ignored it and pushed past him to my dresser. My stomach chose that moment to growl louder than a mountain lion and some of the tension in the room leeched away.

Auden laughed, "Go get a shower and then I'll take you to lunch."

I pulled fresh clothes from the drawer and tried to keep my underwear wrapped up in the shirt I grabbed.

"I know where the cafeteria is, Auden. I can get there perfectly fine on my own." I slammed the drawer shut a little harder than necessary.

"It's okay to accept help every now and again," he sounded amused. "Maybe I just want to hang out."

I moved to the bathroom and set my clothes on the counter, keeping my back to him. "Pot. Kettle. Black." I turned the shower on full steam and pushed on the door. "Maybe I don't want to hang out with the guy who poisoned me."

Auden's hand slammed on the wood, keeping only about half a foot of space open. "I didn't poison you," he growled.

I shrugged. "You definitely enjoyed throwing various potions at me."

He scanned my face, looking past my scowl and trying to see what I was hiding beneath. "Just the other day I couldn't get you to go away when I told you to, and now you want nothing to do with me. Why are you intentionally being difficult?"

Oh, I don't know, maybe it had something to do with my embarrassing spiral of despair yesterday and the fact that he pushed me into it.

My response was to kick him in the shin, and he loosened his hold on the door long enough for me to shut and lock it. I heard him sigh on the other side and waited for him to leave before undressing and getting in the shower. As I scrubbed away a day's worth of sleep and old potion residue, I pushed away the nagging voice that told me Auden was being genuine. It sounded like he really wanted to have lunch, but I didn't want to start up a friendship. I knew without a doubt it would be too easy to pick up where we left off, and if I was being honest with myself, it had already started. When he wasn't pissing me off, intentional or otherwise, I trusted him and enjoyed being around him. What happened yesterday did nothing to change that. The looks I caught him giving me, the smiles, the way my heart raced. He looked out for me and was *still* trying to protect me. No. All the signs were there that more was building between us than just an instructor and trainee relationship. Maybe the foundation of our childhood hadn't fully disappeared after all.

THE SKY WAS dark and grey when I left the dorms and it mirrored my mood with an eerie perfection. A strong, cool wind lifted the hair off my neck. Damp leaves and rich earth—signs that we were in for a massive summer storm. The air felt charged with unshed fury and I jogged the rest of the way, dashing inside the school with seconds to spare. Thick, hefty raindrops battered the windows just as the thunder announced its presence. Mother Nature sounded pissed off. Well, she could join the freaking club. She could even get premium membership if she hit Auden with a lightning bolt.

I let out a sigh and paused at the doors to the cafeteria. It was a feat in and of itself just to get my anger down to the level it was at now. Thankfully, the shower had thick walls, or my entire floor would've heard the curses coming out of my mouth after I'd slammed the door in Auden's face. I didn't know where my attitude came from or why it simmered inside me now, anxiously awaiting its chance to pounce. Usually, my temper was cool and glacial. It slowly grew and melted away unless something pissed me off enough to fracture it. But with Auden,

I felt like an inferno, blazing and churning in a fiery twister that threatened to burn down everything around me. What was it about him?

I made it through the line and, lunch in hand, searched for a place to sit. There were still a few stares from my nosier classmates, but most had gotten over the news of my arrival fairly quickly. A few empty seats caught my attention, but I didn't want to intrude or be forced to make small talk with someone I didn't care to get to know.

The rough sound of metal scraping against the linoleum was —thankfully— barely loud enough for me and the other students nearby to hear. It was more the open chair that was kicked in front of me that caught my attention. Auden leaned away, one arm draped along the back of his chair, and gestured at the ugly green plastic. Most of the room was too caught up in their own conversations to notice me awkwardly standing there, but those closest to the action watched with open curiosity. My cheeks warmed at the unwanted attention and I glared at the dark-haired boy that caused it. His grin only pissed me off more. There was no way in hell I could sit through lunch with him and *not* attempt to bash his head in with my lunch tray. So, I scanned the room until I found the one person who hadn't made me want to jump off a bridge since I'd arrived.

Blatantly stepping around the chair, I strolled to the other side of the room, fighting the whole way to keep my steps steady and light. Bast's deep, green eyes widened slightly when I sat across from him and I fought the urge to roll mine. Honestly. After yesterday it shouldn't be a surprise that I enjoyed his company.

I raised a brow. "This seat taken or something?"

He snapped out of it with a small shake of his head and gave me a sly smirk. "No...but I think you were supposed to sit somewhere else."

My head swung to the right, following where Bast pointed. The corner of Auden's mouth pulled down, seemingly tied to a string attached to his brow. The glower he sent my way could've melted the ice caps if global warming hadn't beaten him to it. I responded with one of my own and showed him the finger before turning back around. I still felt his eyes and Bast's whistle only made it harder to shake off his stare.

"Someone's in trouble," Bast sang, not bothering to hide his grin, or lower his voice.

"What else is new?" I grumbled.

"Trouble in paradise?"

I threw a fry and Bast caught it in his mouth. His smug look made me want to throw something bigger, but I was hungry, and lunch was almost over. I had a mission today and now even less time to complete it. I refused to be sidetracked.

"I have questions," I told Bast, while also giving him the side-eye. He knew better than to throw that slimy tomato at me. At least, I think he did.

He wisely lowered his hand; tomato safely back on his tray. "Only if you answer mine first."

I nodded. That was fair. As long as it didn't get too personal. Bast took a second before asking, his face scrunched in an adorable frown. He looked like he was gathering courage, but when his frown turned into a smirk, I knew I was wrong. I thought he was a demure, kind, misunderstood kid. No. He was mischievous and sneaky.

"What's up with you and Mr. Tall, Dark and Second in line for the throne?"

My mouth dropped open as I hunched in my seat. "Absolutely nothing!" I glanced to the side, scared Auden might have heard. He had a creepy way of showing up when he wasn't wanted. I didn't need him thinking that I was over here gossiping about him. "He's just training me so I can catch up in time for the Choosing. Which *someone* still needs to tell me what the hell that even is, by the way."

He waved his hand between us, like he was shooing a fly. "We'll get to that. What I want to know, is why you're denying the obvious chemistry between you and that hunk of a man?" He squinted at me and whispered to himself, "Is it denial? Or is she oblivious to the currents of straight panty dropping tension that flow between them?"

"Why are you talking like that? I'm right here."

"Stop avoiding the question." Another shooing motion. "How can you sit here, across from me, when you have *that* demanding your attention?"

I pushed my half-eaten tray away with a huff. "There's a lot of history between me and Auden and right now he could... one day... be a friend . *Maybe*. But that's all I'll say on the subject."

He definitely only made my heart race when he was pissing me off. And that didn't count. Right?

"Fine. Moving on." He didn't sound at all like he was moving on. "You could be the most popular familiar on campus, you know?"

I shrugged. What did I care about popularity? "I'm assuming all the same people that were popular growing up are still at the top of the totem pole; with a few new additions," I added, thinking about Lincoln. "I never paid attention to the who's who on campus."

Bast was shaking his head before I finished. "Girl, you better start caring. Only class ranking is based off merit. The rest of the Choosing is a popularity contest."

"Again, I ask what the hell is the Choosing? And since when is there a ranking?"

"How do you still not know what the Choosing is? According to our teachers, its literally what we should be striving for our entire lives."

I was only gone for four years, but that was apparently enough time for some major things to change. I could understand that, after all, I changed a lot myself. I had a feeling, though, that this wasn't change for the better and Bast's explanation only confirmed it. It all tied in with our low numbers and steadily declining population. This was the solution to ensuring only our best went after the demons and the rest built back our numbers. It didn't make much sense. Wouldn't you rather pass on the genes of your best fighters instead of those deemed not good enough? But what did I know?

"You're fucking with me!"

"Shhh," Bast winced as the students at the table next to us glared at him.

I didn't mean to draw any more negative attention his way, but I was floored; shocked. Literally there were no words.

"Let me get this straight," I said, lowering my voice this time. "At the end of the year, all the familiars and witches are ranked separately based off the last four years of our schooling. And then at the Choosing, the highest ranked witches get, what, the first pick of the litter? And then we're chosen down the line like elementary kickball teams?"

Bast frowned at the comparison. "Well, there's a little more to it than that. The Council and Prince Asiel have to approve the pairing, but basically that's how it works."

I didn't think I could be more shocked, but I was wrong. "Asiel? Why does Asiel have any say in the pairings?"

He looked at me like I'd lost some screws. "Maybe because he's the Crown Prince?" He took a bite out of his chicken tender and waved it around, adding, "It was also his idea in the first place."

That shouldn't have surprised me. The unfairness, the division of our society into a caste system, and the pure stupidity of it all screamed Asiel. Was our society really so bad off that we had to resort to this? It was a desecration to our traditions. A familiar chose the witch, that's the way it's always been. And there was no shame in it taking years to find the right partner. It was a life-long commitment and a great honor.

"You haven't been through the community yet, have you?" Bast's green eyes lost its usual glow. "There are still some places that haven't been rebuilt since that night."

"I feel like I'm missing a huge part of the story here," I replied, but I had an inkling that I knew where this was headed.

"You are," Bast confirmed.

The bell rang and the room filled with the sounds of chairs scraping and sneakers squeaking against the linoleum; effectively drowning out whatever he was about to say next. With a tilt of his head, Bast gestured for me to follow him. Our next class, Demonology, wasn't a far walk from the cafeteria—only one flight of stairs to be exact— but it was my last class of the day since I couldn't take part in the more physical classes that filled our afternoons.

"Why don't we hang out tonight?" I blurted right outside the classroom door.

Students pushed past us with annoyed glares as we stood in their way, but Bast's surprised face and my burning cheeks went unnoticed by anyone else but us.

"Unless you don't want to, I mean," I shrugged like it wasn't a big deal, but inside my heart was racing. I'd never had to actively try and make a friend before, and the one time I tried to step out of my comfort zone and into a social circle, I ended up with a demon on my ass and Auden's cuffs around my wrists.

"No, no." Bast swallowed and then shot me a genuine smile. "I'd love to."

He mirrored my sigh of relief and we shared an awkward look of understanding before breaking into fits of laughter.

"This door will close promptly in one minute, no matter

who is standing in the doorway making that raucous." Mr. Laveau stood behind his desk with a stern brow raised.

The next hour flew by as we learned about Revenants. This was my favorite class by far, and not just because Mr. Laveau was a fair and knowledgeable instructor. The subject matter was one I was very interested in. In this class, filled with both races, we learned about the wide array of different demons, their class systems, powers, physical attributes, and most importantly, how to kill them. We then practiced the physical act later in the afternoon.

"An adult's wingspan can reach roughly two meters, far surpassing the average seize of our male familiars, and are tipped with sharp barbs designed to pierce and slice." Mr. Laveau pointed to the image of the Revenant taking up the front wall of the classroom. The tip of one wing projected all the way onto the ceiling and I shuddered at the thought of encountering one in person. "It's hide appears smooth but is actually composed of thousands of tiny scales that overlap and protect it like a suit of armor. No man-made weapon we have can penetrate it. But some of our potions are effective and a familiar's claws shred through its hide like scissors to paper."

The student beside me, a witch named Mason, raised his hand, his face frozen in a mask of disbelief.

"So, you're telling me that neither a sword nor a gun can kill it, but a familiar's claws can?" He scoffed. "That doesn't even make sense."

I, and every other feline shifter in that room, glared at him. I almost offered to demonstrate how sharp my claws could be, but Mr. Laveau beat me to it. As an older witch, he was around long before this new Choosing bullshit was established, but I still had no idea where he fell on his opinions of it. Was he for the near subjugation of half our society, or against it? The two tattoos behind his ear told me he was paired or had been at one point. He knew first-hand what that relationship was like.

"Was there something wrong with what I said, Mr. Marsh?" Our instructor stepped closer, until the projection of the Revenant covered half his face in an eerie grey light. "Is there a reason you think a familiar's claws shouldn't be able to save you from certain death?"

A couple sniggers punctuated the silence and Mason huffed, like what he had to say was obvious.

"They're a lesser species, sir. Bred and predestined to assist us as *we* protect humanity from demons. It makes no sense that against such a formidable foe they would be more powerful."

I think my jaw touched my desk. He didn't just say that. That little shit, who looked like a toothpick with mini muscles, did *not* just say I was a lesser species. Was this the crap the school spewed now? I glanced around the room and nearly growled at the mixed reactions I saw. A couple other familiars silently snarled at the thought of being lesser, but most didn't react at all. Like this was an actual fact they'd come to accept. Some witches were even nodding along at the nonsense. What the actual fuck happened to this place?

"The only lesser species, Mr. Marsh, are the demons we are charged with destroying. Familiars are our partners and deserve the respect that position merits." Mr. Laveau didn't raise his voice, but there was an unyielding glint to his gaze that barred no room for argument. "As to why their claws will work but not something as powerful as a knife or any other weapon you might wield; some of our scientists believe it comes down to nature. A familiar's origins are rooted in the creation of life, their animal half a direct unpolluted product of Mother Earth, and as such is seen as the very opposite of the Revenant itself."

"Unless you're Bastion."

The class broke out in another fit of snickers and Bast sunk lower in his seat, his curls falling over half his face in a poor attempt at a shield. I caught the eye of a few nearest me and my glare shut them right up, but I didn't see who made the comment to begin with.

"That's enough," Mr. Laveau's disapproval cut through the rest of the chatter, but the damage was already done.

The bell rang and Bast bolted from his seat before I could get to him. My glower did little to keep the attention away from me—in fact, it might have encouraged some of the gossip—and I increased my speed until I was all but jogging out of the school and into the heavy downpour outside. The rain was warm when it hit me, but it came down in sheets so strong that it stung. Fuck this school. Fuck my classmates. And fuck being back here. I missed Sensei and the peace of the dojo. I missed the respect from my students and their parents. Respect that was sorely lacking here. But mostly, I missed how uncomplicated my life was before that stupid party. I stomped through a large puddle, splattering my sneakers and pants with mud and sighed. I should've fought harder to get away.

CHAPTER
FOURTEEN

The storm still raged outside, pounding relentlessly against the window and casting shadows of raindrops across the wall. The heavy lightening randomly lit up the room, and from where I stood in the shower, it was just enough light to see where the shampoo sat on the shelf. I hadn't bothered to turn on the lights when I got to my dorm. I preferred the dark atmosphere the thunderstorm provided and allowed its haunting lullaby to converge with the warm water, heating my muscles until I left the shower feeling like a puddle of goo. The silence was a welcome reprieve to the crazy mess of the last twenty-four hours.

It was the first time since I'd returned that I was able to just...be. No worrying about how the Council would punish me. No handcuffs. I had a blissful chunk of time where no one stared at me and I wasn't watching over my shoulder for the next unexpected strike. I'd had about all I could take for the week, and I still needed to go home and see my father. That was going to be super fun, I could tell. Standing in the doorway to the bathroom, I took in a deep breath and slowly let it out. The wind whistled and howled through the trees, shaking them hard enough they scratched at the windows. I didn't have to look to know that the sky was black and the rain came down sideways like thousands of heat-seeking missiles. Aside from the flashing light and rolling thunder, it was a calm bubble in here. A boring, calm, basic bubble. My eyes roamed, taking in the dismal plainness of the dorm and I found another emotion taking over. My old room was covered, floor to ceiling, with pictures of me and Asher; our adventures captured on film since the days we toddled around in diapers. I looked at empty corners where I remembered hanging pictures of my mom, happy and smiling. The barren walls that stared back at me now hit harder than the silence. Harder than the loneliness that's followed me every day since I was thirteen.

Lightening flashed and my gaze caught on a small lump, virtually camouflaged by the standard issued black comforter. I lunged for it before my brain fully registered what it was. My bag. I thought I'd lost it forever after leaving it at the Miami bus depo, but here it was. All my things were inside; clothes, extra shoes, toiletries, even my meager cash. I frantically dug some more, the knot in my throat growing larger with every pocket found empty, but—there. In the very front zipper was my favorite knife. The one Sensei gave me. When Auden knocked it from my hands, I didn't have time to grab it before making my escape. Then later, on the bus, I mourned its loss and resigned myself to never seeing it again. My eyes burned from Auden's unexpected kindness as I pulled out a clean pair of leggings and an oversized shirt. I brought them to my face and inhaled. Tears sprung free as the comforting scent washed over me. I missed home.

I wasn't sure how long I sat in my towel, crying over my clothes, but when I finished the rain was down to a trickle. Mild thunder still preceded each lightning strike even though the storm was obviously on its way out. Goosebumps dotted my skin and I quickly shimmied into my now wrinkled clothes, causing the stitches in my shoulder to pull as I brought my shirt over my head. Halfway through re-bandaging my arm, there was a knock on my door. I ignored it, hoping whoever it was would go away, but Auden stuck his head in a couple minutes later and I scowled.

"That door was locked," I grumbled, trying to tear the gauze with my teeth as I spoke.

"I have a key," he replied, letting himself all the way in the room.

"Of course, you do." I didn't waste energy on being surprised.

It wasn't easy to tie a knot with one hand and your mouth, in the dark. Auden offered to help, and my stubborn pride shooed him away each time, before I finally gave in and allowed him to kneel beside me. His fingers were warm as they gently brushed against my skin. His scent mixed with the heady fullness of the storm outside until I almost couldn't tell them apart, even with him this close. I kept my gaze down and away as he finished up.

Please don't blush. Please don't blush. I repeated the mantra over in my head. My damn cheeks and I were going to have a serious talk if they couldn't control themselves around him. I didn't need him thinking I was nervous or something equally as stupid. It was utter nonsense anyway. I was only reacting to the awkwardness between us. Perfectly normal.

"Come on," Auden stood and held out his hand.

I almost refused but didn't want to start a fight. He let go as soon as I was on my feet and we were out of my dorm and in the hallway before I even thought to question where he was taking me. The hallway was empty, lacking even the echoes of voices from the common room. Our footsteps caused the aged wood to creak as Auden led me to the left and around the corner, down a dimly lit corridor I hadn't even known was here, until he stopped in front of a thin door with an aged handle.

"How do you know so much about the girl's dorms?" I asked, as he pulled an ancient looking key from his pocket. "Seriously. I've lived in this building since I was eight and never knew about this."

The door in question led to an even thinner and darker stairwell that had seen better days. Auden's answering grin was downright *sinful* and I questioned my morals as I followed him into the dust ridden dark.

"Is this where you kill me and store my body?"

Auden came to an abrupt stop and looked back over his shoulder. "Is this where I *what*?"

I shrugged and ducked under his arm, taking the lead up the staircase. "It's a perfectly reasonable question."

After a second, I heard his steps resume on the cracked wood. "There was absolutely no reason in that question. None whatsoever."

On and up the stairs continued, growing more narrow the higher we went. Soon, both my shoulders were nearly touching the walls, so I knew Auden had to be walking almost sideways. I fought the urge to turn back and look.

"You bring me to an ancient hole in the wall—"

"It's obviously a stairwell."

"That no one but you even knows about, during the middle of a thunderstorm, when no one can hear me scream—"

"Who said anything about screaming?"

"And you think *I'm* weird for asking where you're going to hide my body?"

"Technically, you didn't ask where. Just if."

"Semantics." I stopped at the top, unable to go any further until Auden pulled out that key of his.

There was hardly any room for me in front of the door and it took an uncomfortable amount of scooting and brushing against one another until we got into a position that allowed Auden to reach the door. Unfortunately, it also forced the entire front of my body to press against the ridiculously defined front of his. While his arm brushed my waist with each attempt to fit the key into the lock. I was more than thankful that the lightbulb above us was more or less on its last leg. The copper inside barely glowed and sputtered constantly. In these cramped conditions, there was no hiding how my cheeks burned or how fast my breaths were coming.

"Please, take your time. I enjoy being repeatedly stabbed in the ass with a key."

Auden snorted. "Well, if you hadn't pushed past me, I'd be in front of the keyhole and the door would be open by now." A couple more subtle movements with his hand and I heard a click. "Got it."

The attic smelt musty and was just as dark as the stairwell, until Auden flipped a switch that bathed us in warm light. At least this bulb was working. Old cobwebs draped their sticky strings near my head. The luminescent strands also shimmered near the window at the other end of the room, immersed in lightning. Junk, covered in years of dust, was piled in the corners and off to the side, leaving plenty of room for a large rectangle of mats, some punching bags, small mitts, and an array of weapons. Auden already removed his shoes and stood in the middle of those mats, looking at me expectantly.

"I don't get it." And I truly didn't. Had he done all this? For me?

"What is there to get?" Auden smirked. "Your ass, here." He pointed in front of him. "Then we train."

I cautiously slipped out of my shoes, eyeing him with a growing sense of unease. He went against his father, brother, and most of the Council to get me reinstated as a student. He wouldn't jeopardize that now, would he?

"Auden," I said his name slowly. "Familiars aren't trained to fight with anything but our claws and fangs, nothing more than the basics really. You know that."

"It's not forbidden," he said with a shrug and stepped closer to where I hovered at the edge of the mats.

"But it is extremely frowned upon," I reminded him. "The others see it as an afront to our animal natures. If they find out I'm more than competent at kicking your ass in human form...I honestly don't know what they'd say."

Besides my precarious standing with the Council, there was another voice in the back of my mind that made me question if this was a wise idea. Asiel all but promised that I was only hanging onto my probation by a thin thread. Would this be strong enough to make it snap? With enough disgruntled comments from the other shifters, my probation could swiftly come to an end. Auden circled me, slowly herding me to the center of the mats. It reminded me of how he stalked me outside when I was bound with roots, and I tried not to let those thoughts overwhelm me. This was different than last time. There were no potions here.

"None of that bothered you when you learned how to fight to begin with. Obviously." Auden argued, and then lunged toward me.

I didn't expect the attack and backpedaled so hard only the punching bag kept me from falling on my ass. I ducked and threw myself to the side just in time for Auden's well aimed punch to miss me. It rocked the bag instead, but he was already facing me again; ready for round two.

"I couldn't shift yet! I was just a kid with no other way to protect herself. What else should I have done?" I growled, still avoiding him.

I made the mistake of moving too close, and Auden swiftly reached out and grabbed a handful of my shirt. Tightening his grip, he pulled me closer until the tips of my toes dragged across the floor.

A slight glance at the gauze peeking out of my sleeve and another smirk. "You can't shift now either. So, what are you going to do about it?"

If he only knew. I reacted on instinct, spurred on by a bit of anger and a large sprinkling of pride. Gripping his shoulders, I pulled down and brought my knee up at the same time. Auden dodged the strike, like I knew he would, but it distracted him and loosened his hold enough for me to grab his neck and pull on it while throwing my weight to the side. We both went down; Auden a little harder than me and on his stomach. I recovered first and rolled, throwing my leg over his waist. I scrambled to grab his arm and pin it behind his back, pushing his wrist up between his shoulder blades. Auden stopped struggling and I leaned down, forcing all my weight on his arm.

"Now what are *you* going to do about it?" I whispered in his ear.

His shoulders shook and for a moment I worried that I somehow hurt him. Muffled chuckles grew into full bellied laughter and I pulled his wrist harder on principle.

"What's so funny?" I asked, exasperated.

His shoulders trembled as he tried to calm himself enough to speak. "You're like a kitten; savage and a little painful, but not dangerous."

"I am *not*," I growled.

The laughter stopped. In a flash I was on my back, Auden's considerably heavier frame nearly crushing me. One second he was making me into a pancake, and the next he was hovering over me, pinning my arms above my head.

"What's so funny is you thought you could hold me down."

Our faces were mere inches apart. Strands of his hair tickled my cheeks, their caress almost as distracting as the gold swirling in his eyes. I could smell the peppermint of this toothpaste as well as the woodsy scent of his shampoo. I was drowning in him. He wasn't fairing much better. I could hear as well as feel when his breathing picked up; every hitch, every slow breath he took to control himself, I could feel as well as my own. The corner of his mouth kicked up in half a smile as I felt him shift his weight. He held both my wrists in one of his hands and brought the other one down. He grazed the curve of my cheek, the side of my jaw, and up my chin before booping me on my nose with his finger.

My mouth dropped open, emitting strangled sounds as I choked on my anger. Eventually, I found my voice.

"No, you didn't!" I screamed, shaking my head back and forth and kicking my feet to try and break free. "I'm not a child anymore, Auden." I bucked my hips like a wild woman but couldn't throw him off. "And I always *hated* when you did that."

Auden laughed so hard I didn't know how he managed to keep me pinned. Whenever he finally stopped, one look at my face sent him off on another fit.

"I'm sorry, I'm sorry. I couldn't resist," he apologized between breaths. He released my wrists and raised both arms. "Truce, I promise."

Training took on a more serious note after that. Partly because I was still annoyed, but mostly because according to Auden, I "wasn't as badass as you think you are". I wanted to disagree—did, actually; vehemently—but as much as I hated to admit it, he wasn't wrong. After over an hour of sparring, I was out of surprises. Auden now knew all my moves. And as he loved to prove, he could anticipate and block every single one of them. I was good; Sensei wouldn't have let me teach if I wasn't. Auden was just...better. His reflexes were ridiculous, and his speed didn't take away from his strength and accuracy. I tried. Really tried to kick his ass, but Auden *dominated*. It was an embarrassing blow to my ego for sure.

"That's enough for today," Auden decreed, not even out of breath.

Meanwhile, I was panting like a birth coach in a Lamaze class. My earlier shower did nothing for my stank now. My hair would definitely need to be rewashed and that almost annoyed me as much as Auden kicking my ass. It wasn't easy to scrub your scalp when stitches were pulling at your shoulder. I quietly put on my shoes while he put the punching mitts away.

"I'm going to assume same time and place tomorrow?" I asked, with a mixed feeling of dread and, was that *excitement*? No. Definitely not.

Auden walked through a stray cobweb and frantically wiped it away before replying. "We'll pick back up on Monday. You can have the weekend off."

"That's kind of you," I called after his retreating form, but he was already out the door and heading down the stairs.

That was irrefutably disappointment I felt. But it wasn't over getting a break from the hot and cold prince beside me. I'd been begging for a day off from him since he found me. No. The disappointment was about not having any plans for the weekend. Wandering campus didn't sound inviting in the least, sitting alone in my dorm was sad and pathetic, and as much as Bast claimed to like me, I'm sure seeing my face for the whole weekend wasn't what he had in mind when I asked him to hang out. My frustration lasted until I got back to my room, where it multiplied tenfold. There on my floor, standing out in stark clarity against the dark carpet, was a plain white envelope.

My lip curled as I stared at it; slid under my door like a juvenile prank. But there was nothing juvenile about the name on the back of it, nor of the script it was written. I'd recognize my father's meticulous handwriting anywhere. Here for over a week and this is his first point of contact? A damn letter? I threw the envelope like a frisbee before I could crumple it further. My back was already turned, and my feet steered me to the shower before it landed. Hot water went a long way to soothe my new bruises but did nothing to cool my temper. And no amount of curses or picking at scabbing stitches could distract me from what was in that letter.

I gave up and stomped from the steamy bathroom, a damp towel wrapped around me. I created a puddle on the carpet but that was the least of my worries at this point. The fancy card stock soaked up the water from my fingers like a plant in the desert. The sharp corners wilted, and I smiled, taking great joy in ruining something so pressed and neat. A joy that always frustrated my father to no end. My smile grew.

It didn't last long. Only one word and three numbers were embossed in gold on the card. Dinner. No questions of how I was doing. No question mark to *ask* if I wanted to join. It was a demand. He didn't even sign it. My father everyone; the illustrious, self-entitled asshole with a penchant for lavish stationary. I already planned to stop by the house sometime soon, so it wasn't like this was a big inconvenience. But I hoped to avoid him and go on my own terms. Instead, I've been summoned. Nothing made me not want to do something more than being told I had to do it.

I crumpled the letter and tossed it in the trash. If he wanted me to come to dinner, he should've tried actually *inviting* me. It was time for him to stop treating me like a child. No more demands. No more belittling. Who cared that everything I owned, outside of what was in my pack, came from him? What did it matter that he was legally in control of me until I turned twenty and graduated? None of that meant I had to put up with his blatant disrespect. I crossed my arms and glared at the ball of card stock in the trash, trying in vain to set it on fire with my mind. Like it was somehow the fault of that little bit of paper that my father and I had a horrible relationship. Sighing, I gave up and reached for the letter. Who was I kidding? I was going to that dinner.

Bast found me an hour later, still in my towel and still trying to destroy that letter with some kind of telekinetic ability. To his credit, he only commented on my being practically naked.

"You know I don't swing that way, right?" His grin was playful.

I rolled my eyes and slammed the bathroom door. I rushed to slip on some clothes, not paying attention to what I was putting on. "I was distracted," I called through the door.

"By this letter?" Came the response.

When I opened the door, Bast sat on my bed, the wrinkled letter pinched between his fingers.

"If this is how Auden finally asked you out, then I seriously underestimated his game." He shook his head. "Such a shame."

I snatched the letter from his hand and threw it back in the trash. "It's from my father. Growing up, family dinners were at the same time every Sunday. A tradition my mom started." I slumped down on the bed beside him. I hadn't talked about my mom in years. "When she died, my father demanded we continue like nothing changed. But those dinners soon became painful and just another chance for him to tell me how unimpressed he was with me."

"Ouch," Bast whispered.

I shrugged. "I'm pretty sure he can't stand the sight of me. I remind him too much of her."

"Then why still have the dinners?"

I laughed, but it was breathless and strained. "Who knows.

But if I want more clothes and supplies for my dorm, I have to go play nice."

Bast took that opportunity to look around my pitiful room. He tried to keep the grimace off his face, but I was slowly learning his tells. And right now, he didn't approve. He took in a deep breath and let it out before turning to face me fully. I startled back at the seriousness of his expression, but he grabbed both of my hands to keep me still.

"My mom runs a thrift shop on the edge of the community. Nothing there is new, but there's a lot of cool, good quality clothes and trinkets. You should be able to revamp your wardrobe and not come out looking homeless."

I snorted. "I've been homeless. Looking like it doesn't bother me."

Bast didn't laugh. His frown went from somber to pained. "I like you. You're the first friend I've had in over a year and I don't want to let you go so easily."

Now I was confused. "Why would I go?"

I squeezed his hands when he didn't answer, but he just shook his head. Whatever secrets he kept he wasn't willing to tell me yet.

"I'm not the most popular guy around here, as I'm sure you've noticed," he forced a laugh. "My mom isn't well-liked either. She's...tolerated is more the word. Because she serves a need."

"With her shop?" I asked, gently. I was afraid any second he was going to bolt he was shaking so badly.

Bast nodded. "She's the go between for us and the outside. People in the community donate used things to her shop, but if they want something from outside the wards, they place an order with her. Every two weeks she leaves to collect the orders."

“That must be dangerous,” I said. “Her leaving the safety of the wards so often. I can see why you worry.”

He let out a genuine laugh this time and settled. “You’re really sweet, but my mom can take care of herself. I just wished all the people she risks her life for respected what she did for them.”

I wasn’t sure what secrets Bast kept that made him fear the loss of our new friendship, but if his mom was anything like him, I couldn’t wait to meet her.

“So, when do you want to go?” I asked, hoping my eagerness would soothe his fears.

It got a small smile out of him. “We can go tomorrow. Make a day of it.” His grin turned feral. “Besides, you need a dress for the Choosing this weekend.”

CHAPTER FIFTEEN

My first taste of freedom since my return and even the weather celebrated. The sun was out in full force. And in a bout of pure rarity, the humidity was only half what it usually was. Which meant my hair didn't look like I stuck my finger in an electrical socket for once. Score. I left it down and twirled a piece of it around my finger while I waited for Bast. I sat on a bench in the overgrown garden near the dorms. There were still too many weeds to make out what used to grow here, but I enjoyed the chaos.

What was left of the brick walkway was now crumbled into tiny pieces and swept off to the side along with the broken trellis. But the bench still stood, so that was something, I guess. I moved away from the dark thoughts of demon attacks that followed and instead made a mental list of what I needed from my shopping trip today. Clothes mainly. But I wouldn't mind something to put on my walls other than white paint. Toiletries were provided so I didn't have to splurge there. Maybe I could smuggle in an iPod. Electronics weren't allowed on campus—too distracting we were told—but a girl could try.

"Sorry I'm late!" Bast slid on mud as he tore full speed into the garden. He righted himself and grabbed onto the bench, trying to catch his breath. "Someone...nailed another...hex bag... to my door."

I eyed the little purple bag hanging from his belt. "So, you made it into a keychain?"

"Whoever sent this one must be young," he swiveled his hips with a grin, making it swing. "It's your basic repulsion spell. Not dangerous at all."

We made our way out of the garden and onto one of the lesser walked paths away from campus. Not many took this route, but it was maintained enough that my shoes weren't sinking in the mud.

"Even the underclassmen are pranking you now?" And this didn't bother him? "I thought it was just Lincoln and his Dick Brigade."

Bast forced a laugh. "They might be the ring leaders of the pranks on campus, but the whole community wants me gone. Our laws about leaving are the only thing keeping them from throwing me out the gates."

I stopped walking. "That's just..."

He shrugged and started up again. "It's whatever."

"It's not, Bast." I grabbed his shoulder, pulling him to a stop once more. "We have to do something about this."

Even with the sun darkening his bronzed complexion, I saw the blush staining his cheeks. The glassy look in his eye.

"There's nothing anyone can do," he sniffed. "Better to just let it go and not draw attention to it."

He pushed us along the path at a much faster pace. The sound of not-so-far-off voices making him nervous after our conversation. We were both quiet. Him from shame or embarrassment— he wouldn't even look at me—and myself from pure anger. I wanted to beat the shit out of everyone who ever said or did anything to make him feel like that. He still refused to tell me why the others harassed him, which was okay. He would tell me in his own time. Until then, there wasn't much I could do but be his shield when I could. His sword too if it came down to it. It came as a shock how protective I was over him. A boy I barely knew. Something drew me to him, a kindred soul that knew his own share of pain and carried it better than I could.

We continued on in silence, both lost in our thoughts, until I looked up from the tangled path and saw...nothing. Wariness creeped in, born from years on the run.

"Where are we going?" I asked, looking around.

I half expected something to jump out of the trees and I wished I had the foresight to bring my knife. But, silly me, I thought it might come across threatening. I wouldn't be making that mistake again.

"My mom's shop is just a little further," Bast replied, moving past me.

"The shopping district is in the heart of the community, Bast. We should've left the path fifteen minutes back that way." I growled, pointing in the direction we'd come.

"My mom's place isn't in the shopping district." He kept pushing forward, moving trees and brush as the path grew wilder and more unkempt.

And I mean really wild. The path was no more than a worn gaming trail by now. The mud was sparse, but that didn't make traversing the swamp any easier. I tripped more times than I cared to admit and almost caught my face on a thorny branch. When I walked through a low hanging spider web, I'd had enough.

"Bast!" I screeched, frantically brushing the sticky strands from my hair. If my fingers found a spider, he was so dead. "Please tell me we're there."

He didn't have to tell me. Nestled amongst the wild moss

and drooping trees was a lone, rundown building. The walls were made of different types of wood all patched together and the roof was completely covered in rich, green lichen. The building appeared shorter, but with it hidden like it was, it was hard to tell its true size.

"This is an outpost," I whispered, my eyes still gathering detail. I was almost one hundred percent positive though.

Outposts were scattered around the perimeter of our land. Rotating pairs of witches and their partners took turns manning them when not on duty outside the wards. They served a variety of purposes but were mainly used as halfway houses when moving in and out of the community on assignment. There were also rumors of dungeons beneath the floorboards where they held demons and wayward students for questioning. Of course, the latter was just a story whispered around common room fires to scare the youngsters. Hopefully.

"It used to be," Bast admitted. "Now it's home."

"You grew up in an outpost?"

There were like twelve pairs of guards at an outpost at any given time. There was hardly enough room for *them*, let alone a child. Was his mother working and had to keep him with her? I shook my head. That didn't make sense. Children were housed in the campus dorms if they had no family to watch them while their parents were on duty.

"I can see the wheels spinning," Bast chuckled.

I nodded, mouth still slightly agape. "All the questions."

His grin was cheeky. "I lived your typical, pristine childhood nestled in the loving bosom of the community. Days were spent training at the school and my evenings spent running amuck with the other kids my age. I moved into the dorms at age eight like everyone else."

"So then how is this home?" I was now thoroughly confused.

The corners of his mouth dipped down, his lips tightening. "*This* is how far our neighbors chased my mother after I turned sixteen."

My mouth was now fully open; dropped wide enough to catch a whole host of nasty bugs. Chased. He said they *chased* his mom all the way out here. I couldn't help but conjure images of raging villagers with pitchforks and torches. It sounded so...medieval.

"You better have a good reason for being out here, young man. And for why you brought *her* with you."

I spun around at the intrusion and locked eyes with one pissed off familiar. She was striking; middle aged with rich blonde hair a few shades lighter than the tangled streaks that painted Bast's curls. A quick glance showed she was strapped down with enough weapons to be an Amazon warrior. Small scars decorated her skin—visible even from here—and I knew instantly that those weapons weren't just for show. She stomped her way over to us, breaking the small foliage in her path. I felt Bast shrink a little next to me, but he wore a grin on his face when I looked over.

"Hey, mom."

I did a double take, eyes growing wider by the second. This was Bast's mom? When he spoke of her, I pictured a gentle female that now spent her days running a thrift store on the outskirts of town. Someone kind, quiet and sweet like Bast. The woman before me was none of those things. Her eyes pierced sharper than any weapon she had stashed on her and paired with the muscles flexing in her arms—no. This woman wasn't soft. By the way she was stalking toward us like that, I'd bet all the money in my pocket she was a cougar. I fixed my face, which I'm sure was still frozen in disbelief, and tried a polite greeting.

"Hello, Ma'am. Thank yo—"

"I'm not going to ask again. What is she doing here?"

A blink. That was all I managed as I watched Bast's mom barrel past me like I was nothing more than another weed for her to stomp on. Bast no longer grinned and all hope of me sleeping in something tonight besides another training uniform flew away with each harsh whisper.

"She just wants to buy some clothes," Bast whined. "I didn't think it would be this big a deal."

His mom replied with a soft string of curses. "No, you didn't think. Her father runs the Council. What do you think he'll do to us if something happened to her? It's not safe out here."

"But—"

"Take her back, Bastion. Now."

Bast's mom marched past me again, not even sparing a glance as she went. When I could no longer hear her footsteps, I turned back around.

"So, she was nice."

Red stained his cheeks. "I'm sorry. I didn't know she'd be like that."

I didn't blame him. If I hadn't witnessed their argument firsthand, I probably would have. But Bast looked absolutely mortified and I found myself growing more and more upset with his mom. He had a hard enough time making friends as it was. Did she treat everyone he brought home this way?

"Why was she so angry?" I asked, honestly confused.

"She doesn't like that I brought you this close to the border." He pointed behind me and sure enough, the stone wall rose above the trees. I couldn't tell if the sight of it made me feel safe or trapped. "We have a hard enough time getting by as it is. If something were to happen to you out here, your father and the Council would exile us for sure."

"But there's no such thing as exile," I countered.

His eyes flashed. "Exactly."

The earth shook as I realized what he meant. The Council —*my father*—would kill Bast and his mother. Fuck. No wonder his mom looked torn between strangling him and marching me out of here herself. It felt like the ground was about to give way beneath me. It would be hard to have a friendship with Bast if his mother didn't approve. Was I destined to be alone again? I deserved worse, I was sure, but...still. No one *wanted* to be alone.

"Kaya!" Bast snapped his fingers in my face.

I shook my head and realized I hadn't imagined the ground moving. It really was.

"Not again," I whined, and jumped over a deep crack splitting the bedrock.

The shaking wasn't quite as bad as last time and I wondered if it had to do with our proximity to the barrier. I looked over at the wall, half expecting to see it riddled with holes or turned into a pile of rubble. What I saw instead sucked way worse.

"Imps!" I shouted and grabbed Bast's arm to make sure he saw.

Imps were three foot tall, humanoid looking demons. They were lower ranking, usually moving in before a bigger, meaner boss. What they didn't have in power, they made up for in spite. Their clawed, bird-like feet were strong enough to gut you with a single swipe and made it easy for them to scale the solid stone barrier like it wasn't even there. It also made for a creepy sight. Those already over the wall angled their heads, listening. Sound was their strongest sense and your worst enemy. Even the smallest breath could be picked up by their long, pointed ears. And then you were truly fucked because the pair of horns on their head wasn't just for show. They liked to get stabby. The second group crested the wall, their beaks snapping in glee when they caught site of us.

One or two Imps wasn't a big deal, honestly. The problem

was they liked to gather in large numbers, preferring to overwhelm their victims and pull them apart.

"What the hell are you two doing just standing there?" Bast's mom bellowed from the door to the outpost. "Do you want to die today?"

We bolted. Every step brought us closer to the safety of the outpost, but also closer to the hoard of Imps now barreling down upon us. Thanks to a whole lot of luck, we reached the door first and Bast's mom ushered us inside before anchoring the lock. The room was dark, the only light coming from the small cracks around the shuttered windows, but I still made out the rows and rows of shelves filled to the brim with clothes and other items. It was like if a pawn shop and a hoarder's house had a baby. A more organized, useful baby.

"Take her downstairs, son. You know where the safe room is."

Bast already pulled me aside as his mother started to strip off her weapons and clothes. Wood quaked beneath the onslaught of Imps; the walls visibly shuddering under the ferocity of their attack. The heavy door shook once. Twice. Then in a never-ending convulsion as if it were about to break apart from its hinges. The solid, thick plank across the threshold rattled and splintered and the bars over the windows groaned as they failed to keep out the little arms with clawed hands that reached through to break the glass. There was no time to go downstairs. The demons had arrived.

Bast's mom thumped her fist three times on the floor. "We can't let them get inside!" she shouted. "We'll be overwhelmed!"

I hardly had time to wonder why she yelled at the floor when the door to downstairs burst open. Two burly men and one female rushed into the room, armed to the teeth and shouting orders.

"Check the windows!"

"Barricade them if you have to."

"Why the hell aren't you two downstairs yet?" *That* one was from Bast's mom. She shared a look with one of the men, glared at us, and then shifted. A cougar. I knew it.

One of the men—the one with deep, ginger locks—shifted into a tiger without even taking his clothes off. Shredded cotton littered the floor, mixed in with the broken glass and chips of wood from the door.

"Why send us downstairs? You obviously need help." I gestured at the ongoing destruction of the cabin.

I felt Bast wince beside me, but I wasn't worried about pissing anyone off. I was more worried about surviving the afternoon.

"Let's go." Thick fingers gripped the back of my neck and pushed. "This battle is no place for children."

I twisted to the side, glaring at the bossy voice who thought it was okay to get touchy. "Who the fuck are you?"

I didn't appreciate being manhandled. Overrun by demons or not, he would feel my fist in his junk if he touched me again. The man had a buzzed head on a thick neck. He took a step closer but didn't reach for me a second time. Probably reading the threat in my glare. With his jaw clenched, he motioned for the others to continue whatever they were doing. Maybe it was the stern disapproval radiating off his overly stiff shoulders, but I got the feeling this guy wasn't used to having his orders questioned.

"I am Captain Cesar, and you, girl, are just a student. Meaning I outrank you." I scoffed and he moved in. His speed caught me off guard and I backed into Bast. "You kids need to get your asses moving and do as I say. We can't do what we need to do and worry about protecting you at the same time. Now get—"

The cabin trembled and cut off what he was about to say next. The woman in their company tossed a potion out of the broken window and the cabin moved again. I couldn't hear what word of power she used, but I caught a glimpse of the second bottle she threw and knew the feel of the binding roots that would emerge. I remembered Auden telling me that potion only needed to touch the ground to work. By the sound of enraged snarls that echoed from outside, her potion was successful. The flutter of activity in the cabin ceased as they listened to the growing storm of pissed off demons. Bast's mom and the tiger paced anxiously by the door, eager to tear into the enemy.

Minutes passed and the attack on the cabin slowly stopped. But I knew they were still out there. Two witches and two familiars. Was that enough to handle what waited on the other side of that broken door?

Captain Cesar nodded once at the other witch and turned back to us. "Bolt that door and get downstairs. That's an order."

One final hard look at us and the adults moved. After a swift peek through a hole in the door, they rushed outside. Bast lunged and slammed the battered plank back into place and slowly stepped back. We warily watched the door, ears attuned to any sound that would tell us their fates. When the sounds of fighting grew fainter and further away, we assumed the adults were successful. There was nothing left to do but wait. Once again, I lamented my stupidity at leaving my knife.

"Does your mom have any weapons stashed here?" I asked Bast, after a quick glance around the room offered no obvious choices. The witches picked up the knives she dropped before they left.

He laughed and pointed to the basement door. Funny. "Looks like we'll be following Captain Cesar's orders after all," he snickered.

CHAPTER
SIXTEEN

"There's no way I'm going to cower downstairs while our people need help out there," I growled. Bast nodded, like he already knew I wasn't going to listen to the captain's order. "We go down there, load up on whatever weapons we can, then go kick some demon ass." I ticked off our objective as we moved around the cluttered storeroom floor.

It looked like there were plenty of clothes here I would have loved to buy, one hoodie in particular looked comfy as hell. But shopping was going to have to wait. Maybe after the adults saw how we could help, Bast's mom would let me shop as a thank you.

"Why do we need weapons when we can shift?" Bast asked, stopping halfway across the room. He spun to face me, adorably confused. "You're not planning on running out there like that, are you?"

A large blast from my right sent me airborne near to the ceiling, but gravity brought me back down just as quickly. Curled on my side, I gasped and tried to bring air into my bruised lungs. My ears rang and debris rained down, stinging as it hit my skin, but nothing felt broken. I searched for Bast in the now ruined cabin. Panic grew with every second I failed to spot him. I coughed, finally achieving a full breath only to choke on dust and crawled to where I spotted him. He was lucky enough to land against the wall with all the clothes.

I looked over at the door as I passed, terrified when I saw it no longer existed. The wood completely imploded and took a giant chunk of the wall with it. Outlined in the nonexistent doorway, was a man. Standing well over six feet, it was hard to tell where his skin ended and his armor began, both were jet black. Even his horned helmet. His chest armor, arm guards, and leg armor shined in the low light of the cabin, like a thick metal that even my claws wouldn't put a dent in. Where is leg armor ended, his talons began; curving with a wicked sharpness that spoke of shredding and stabbing. All that was bad enough, but it wasn't until he removed his helmet to reveal a reptilian like head bleached bone white that I knew we were well and truly screwed.

"Fuck," I whispered, and crawled as fast as I could toward Bast. Using the mess of the ramshackle room, I kept hidden until I reached a mountain of clothes in the corner large enough for the both of us to hide behind.

The demon stopped just inside the hole in the wall and scanned the room. As his head moved from side to side, his skin changed. The rich, inky black faded in and out as the light struck it at different angles, going from dark to a faded shadow in the span of a breath.

"Shit. Oh, shit," Bast breathed, his whole body shaking with fear.

I placed a hand on his shoulder, hoping to calm him. "Maybe we can sneak out behind him," I whispered.

"That's a *Shade*, Kaya," Bast hissed. "We're as good as dead."

He wasn't wrong and saying it out loud did nothing to curb

the overwhelming dread growing inside me. Shades were at the top of the demon food chain. The fact that one made it through our barrier was very, very bad. What else was lurking just outside our borders, waiting to come in? Worse, how many more of his kind were there?

The demon inhaled and the slits of his nose opened and closed as he scented the air.

"I can smell you, little familiarsss," his voice ended on a hiss. "Come out, come out, wherever you are."

Bast and I looked at each other with panic in our eyes. We had less than seconds before he found us. We were sitting ducks with no way to defend ourselves.

"We need weapons," I whispered in his ear, scared the demon would still hear me.

Bast looked at me like I was crazy. "We *are* the weapons, but even we can't defeat a Shade on our own."

The demon's boots made silent thuds against the wood floor, getting closer before stopping. Closer and then stop. I peeked over the clothes to find the Shade less than ten feet away, sniffing the air every couple steps. I grabbed Bast's shirt and tugged, dragging him with me as we quietly tried to stay behind whatever we could to keep hidden. As the demon moved, we mirrored him. Getting to the door was my goal, but I wasn't sure what would happen once we got outside. There was no chance of outrunning a Shade, especially out in the open. We were almost there. An arm's reach away really, before the inevitable happened. My shoe caught on something in one of the debris piles, causing me to trip Bast. He crashed into me and down we went. Sprawled on the floor right in front of the exit, we both looked back at the demon who eyed us with a feral grin.

"Fuck." I rolled and pulled Bast behind me. "Go!"

He fought my hold until he stood beside me. "Like I'm going to leave you to face him alone."

Tears gathered in my throat, both at his loyalty and the knowledge that we were both going to die here. Probably painfully. I picked up the nearest object, anything I could get my hands on, and started throwing. A shoe, broken wood, a thick iron nail; they all passed through him. The shade laughed, his skin smoky and transparent.

"That won't work," Bast growled, fur sprouting on his face. "Only a familiar can injure a Shade in their shadow form."

But a Shade couldn't retaliate in that form, the shadows causing his hands to go right through matter just like my weapons went right through him. He had to solidify if he wanted to attack. If I timed it right, I could hurt him. Thinking I ran out of weapons, the Shade's skin darkened to black. I fingered the broken glass in my hand, waiting for just the right moment. I threw it the second his skin stopped moving, aiming for his eye. It sliced his cheek instead and the sound that came out of him told me our time was up.

"Shift, Kaya!"

I heard the alarm in Bast's voice. He couldn't tell I was trying. That I'd thrown every ounce of my fear, and strength, and desperation at that little door inside my mind. The one that's been sealed shut since the first time I shifted last year. Nothing I did worked. My inner cat pushed from the other side and I could feel her fear, as potent as mine, but there was a mental block I just couldn't get over, even while I stared death in the face.

"I can't!" I sobbed and sank to my knees.

The sound of cloth tearing had me turning and I looked back at the largest, darkest wolf I've ever seen standing where Bast had been only moments before. His head stood taller than my shoulders and his paws were almost as big as my face, with claws to match. His teeth were bared, but not at me, at the demon still stalking us. Even knowing death stood just out of reach, I couldn't take my eyes off him. I mean, he was a *wolf.* Never in the history of our people has anyone, *ever*, shifted into a canine. Suddenly, many things about his life made sense.

I stood, ready to fight and die by his side. "If we survive this, you and I are going to have one hell of a talk."

We faced the Shade together. I crouched, nails lengthening and eyes splitting in the only form of the shift my messed-up mind would allow. The demon laughed.

"I'm not impressed." His voice sounded like smoke and suffering, like something that sneaks up from behind and strangles the life out of you. "I've heard of you, Little Familiar." I choked on a laugh, doubtful that this monster had ever heard of me. "The one who doesn't shift." This time I gulped. "And yet you've somehow managed to kill many of my brethren. Interesting."

I wouldn't call it interesting at all. I'd call it survival. But I didn't have time to stop and think about how or why this demon heard of me. Taking advantage of the Shade's distraction, Bast lunged and sank his teeth into the demon's arm between the pieces of armor. Blood flung about the room as the demon shook his arm, trying to dislodge the wolf's massive teeth. Before he could strike at Bast, I joined in, my own claws extended and aiming for the soft spot where the demon's neck met his shoulder.

My claws hooked in, slicing through flesh and muscle until they reached bone. The demon's blood poured down the front of both of us now, smoking and burning holes into my clothes. Where the foul liquid touched my skin, it stung. I wondered if that was normal, but I couldn't ponder the weirdness of it. The demon threw Bast like a hackysac.

"No!" I shouted, my hand reaching. The air shimmered

around Bast in dizzying sparks of red and gold and he landed with a high-pitched yelp on the other side of the room.

With his now free hand, the demon grabbed a fistful of my hair and pulled, exposing my throat. I screamed as needles lanced across my scalp and tried to dislodge my claws, but they were stuck deep. Each time I yanked my hand, the demon roared and pulled harder on my hair.

"Enough!"

The demon's face morphed. His canines elongated, glowing in contrast to his dark gums. His lips receded and disappeared, leaving only his bone white skull and gaping mouth, filled with serrated teeth ready to devour me. I screamed again when he pulled harder on my hair to keep my neck open. All my struggles got me nowhere. I felt his breath, hot on my skin. My eyes shifted back and forth from human to feline as I lost what little control I had on my animal. With that loss of control, my claws withdrew, and my hand slipped free. But too late. Fire. It swam through my veins like a sickness, touching and spreading to every part of my body. And the pain. Excruciating pain. No amount of screaming helped. The demon's teeth sank deeper into my shoulder. The sounds of him drinking would haunt my dreams forever and with each pull, the pain grew stronger, and I grew weaker. Suddenly, the demon broke away. He stared at me in a mixture of confusion and euphoria.

"What are you?" He whispered. Then with a growl, he lunged back toward my neck...and froze just millimeters away.

His fingers still tangled in my hair, but they didn't tighten or pull when I wiggled and broke away, falling to the floor. I landed on my ass and looked up, expecting to once again be within biting distance of those teeth. The demon didn't move. He was frozen, teeth bared, and fist holding onto nothing but torn strands of my hair.

"Kaya, move."

Behind me, Auden stood in what was left of the doorway. Pure fury etched on every inch of his face. Arm outstretched, he walked closer and I realized that he had the demon under his power. Veins bulged in the demon's neck as he tried to break free, but he was only capable of small movements; fingers twitching, arms jerking.

"I can't hold him much longer," Auden warned through gritted teeth. "Move your ass!"

"I can't leave Bast!" I shouted back, gesturing to where the now naked and human boy was passed out against the wall.

With a howl, the demon broke free and pitched toward me, his form shifting between solid and not. Auden swiftly regained control, but only just. I watched sweat bead at his temple and roll down the side of his face.

"Shit." His hand spasmed. "Get behind me."

I backpedaled on all fours and my hand moved over something cold and solid. Metal. I looked down and saw one of the pure iron bars that covered the windows and grabbed ahold of it.

Auden cursed. "If he goes to shadow, we're screwed."

"Then I hope this works," I scrambled to my feet and took aim.

"Hope what—Kaya!"

The demon broke free just as I hurled myself at him, the iron pole pointed out between us. My battle cry echoed louder than the demon's bellow as the pole pierced his stomach. It must have been luck or fate, because the iron landed in the small patch not protected by the demon's chest plate. And since he was mid-attack, he wasn't in his shadow form. We stared at one another, both shocked at what just occurred. Then I was moving again, pushing and running the demon through until the iron struck the wall behind him.

"Auden, hold him!"

The demon's arms and legs slammed against the battered wall and held, like his wrists and ankles were tied with invisible rope. I grinned. My claws were back and this time I knew just where to put them. I slashed at the demon's neck, hacking with all my remaining strength until its head toppled to the ground. I fell with it, and watched it roll into a pile of ruined clothes.

"I did it," I whispered, still not quite believing it. Shocked that I even survived.

My now blunt fingertips curled against the floor as I tried to stand, and my legs nearly gave out. Shock made them feel like jelly, but I needed to check on Bast. Auden slammed into me, almost taking me back down. His arms wrapped around me like a solid band and squeezed the breath from my lungs.

"Is anything broken?" He asked, frantically scanning my body for new injuries.

His hands brushed along my shoulders and lingered at the demon's bite, then down my arms, my ribs, my hips. His voice a constant breathless murmur of worry and his touch a steady gentle caress. I shook my head and his eyes met mine.

"What the hell were you thinking?" His voice was still quiet, but solid. Lethal. Each word whipped at me with a verbal sting. "You went after a Shade. A fucking *Shade*, Kaya!" He shook my shoulders, fear and frustration threading through the anger he unleased upon me. "I should kill you myself if you have a damn death wish." Another shake. "Do you realize you almost died?"

"Yes." At my quiet admission he stopped shaking me, but his hands remained a warm pressure on my shoulders. "But so did Bast. And so did you. I wasn't going to let that happen. I couldn't."

Auden dropped his hands and straightened, exhaling through his nose. His jaw clenched, making it appear more squared and a tic popped on one side. All the signs that he was pissed. But his eyes...the gold in them churned. My breaths came faster when he brought his hand up and gently tugged on a strand of hair. The movement pulled on my sore scalp, but I didn't react. I was too busy watching him, wondering how much closer we were going to get. Wondering what thoughts were drifting behind that gaze and hoping he couldn't hear how fast he made my heart race.

"Don't ever do something that stupid again, okay?"

My brows flew high before slamming back down over a frown. Did he just call me stupid? Did he think I wasn't capable of protecting my friends? I opened my mouth to tell him where he could shove his orders, but his hand covered my lips, and no sound came out.

"Don't. Please. Just—" He dropped his head between us with a sigh. When he looked at me again, I felt my walls crumble. "I can't lose you too."

Bast's skin, which usually resembled warm honey, now reminded me more of typing paper—pale and leeched of color. I gently brushed his hair away from the cut on his temple and he moaned, then went still once more. His eyes didn't open.

"Will he be okay?" I asked Auden, too afraid to look away.

What if he hit his head harder than I thought? I quickly checked his ears. No blood. He could be bleeding inside though, where I couldn't see.

"I was selfish," I whispered. "If I'd gone downstairs like we were told this never would've happened."

"The enchanted cells might have protected you from the Imps, but they were never made to hold a demon as powerful as a Shade." Auden moved closer and placed a couple fingers on Bast's neck. "This wasn't your fault, Kaya."

For once I didn't argue. It wasn't because I agreed with him, more that it hurt too much to voice the reasons of exactly why this was my fault. Gently, I lifted my hand to the bite on my neck. The demon seemed to be searching for something the second he stepped in the cabin. He'd sniffed us out and recognized me specifically. He paid Bast no mind until he attacked. Now that I thought about it, the demon hadn't blinked when Bast shifted into a massive wolf. No. He only had eyes for me. And when he bit me... *"What are you?"*

"Hey." Auden moved closer until he crouched beside me, concern making his eyes appear darker. "He's going to be okay. As soon as we hear the all clear, we'll get him to the infirmary."

I hoped Auden was right, because right now it looked like the demon was here for me and that meant I'd nearly gotten my new friend killed. Just like I'd gotten Asher killed. I focused on the steady rise and fall of Bast's chest and worked on blocking out the negative thoughts that tried to tear me down from the inside. The battered wood floor groaned, barely concealing the scuff of someone stepping closer and Auden spun, placing himself between me and the new threat. He was eye to eye with a cougar for barely a full second before she shifted.

"What happened?" Bast's mom grabbed a shirt out of the mess on the floor and pulled it over her head before kneeling beside her son.

Auden returned to his place beside me while the other adults fanned around the room in defensive positions. The male tiger approached the impaled Shade with a cautious sniff, and a low hiss escaped. What was left of the Shade's body slowly faded—melting into the sky like smoke over a bonfire.

"What the hell was a Shade doing here?" Captain Cesar questioned, toeing the demon's severed head with his boot. "And how did you manage to kill it?"

I'd let Auden answer that one. I was too tired to remember it all just now. My neck throbbed at the reminder of the demon's teeth and I pressed my lips together in pain. Bast's mother missed nothing. Her gaze landed on my bite wound, traveled to my bloodied clothes and hands, then to her unconscious son.

"There were no other demons on the island," she murmured, absentmindedly brushing a lock of hair from Bast's forehead.

"Ma'am—" I started, and she cut me off.

"Adira," she offered. "You may call me, Adira."

I swallowed and nodded. "Adira, the Imps—" She shook her head and I stopped again.

"Obviously a distraction for something bigger." She gestured at the Shade with her chin. "No other part of the island was attacked."

"That makes no sense," Auden frowned. "Why attack the outskirts of the community? And send a Shade, of all things, to do it?"

"Your guess is as good as mine, my prince." Captain Cesar abandoned his examination of the demon and knelt on the other side of Bast, opposite his mother. "But might I suggest we move the boy somewhere more secure in case more decide to appear?"

"Of course," Auden's cheeks burned. ". My apologies. Guards will be here soon. I'll have them assist us to the infirmary immediately."

Captain Cesar and Adira shared a brief look and the captain gave a subtle shake of his head.

"You have my gratitude," Adira smiled at Auden, but it was more of a grimace. "But we shall see to my boy. I'd much rather you tend to her wounds."

Her suggestion drew Auden's attention back to my neck and he cursed.

"It's still bleeding." He was close enough that I felt his breath on my skin as he got a better look at my wound. When his eyes finally met mine, my heart jumped. "Stay here," he ordered, and his firm tone told me not to bother fighting. "The captain and I will do a quick search of the perimeter and then I'll get you to the infirmary."

His gaze was searching, and when I said nothing against his plan, he responded with a soft smile and a gentle squeeze on my good shoulder. I watched them disappear through the hole in the wall and turned to see Adira assessing me.

"That's an interesting relationship you have with the prince. You two seem...close."

I couldn't stop my blush and shook my head. "He's the one who found me and brought me back. Now he watches me like a hawk."

She pursed her lips, thinking. "Perhaps."

I shrugged. What else did she want me to say?

"Be cautious, Kaya. Not all is as it seems on this island. A lot has changed."

I frowned at her warning, confused in more ways than one. "I thought you didn't like me."

She gave a light chuckle, but her expression was very serious. "My boy trusts you and you saved his life. That earns you a chance."

I glanced down at Bast, at the bruises and blood mottling his skin, and the guilt grew in me again.

"I didn't." My voice was almost a whisper the guilt was so heavy.

Adira snorted. "The demon's blood staining your hands and the front of your shirt say otherwise."

Again, I shrugged. What did it matter that I killed the Shade when I could've done it without allowing Bast to get hurt?

"If I shifted—"

Adira made a disapproving sound. "If you shifted, you'd probably be dead." I looked at her in shock. "If my boy's teeth couldn't do enough damage then there was nothing more yours could have done." I thought about Bast's long, canine teeth and knew she was right. "Thank you for standing by my son even after learning his truth. Not many would have done what you did."

"We're friends," I lifted my chin, daring her to challenge it.

She only smiled. The first real smile I'd ever seen from her. "So you are."

CHAPTER SEVENTEEN

It felt strange to walk in the sunshine after the shadows of the cabin. Between the Shade's bite stinging my shoulder and the images of Bast on the floor, it felt like even the warmth of the afternoon couldn't chase away all the darkness that lingered. Auden forged ahead; eyes peeled for any surprises hidden in the overgrown swamp. Even with his arms laden down with clothes—a gift to me from Adira— he cut a fierce picture to whoever dared approach. Not that anyone wandered this deep into the marsh. Adira hadn't exaggerated when she said the rest of the island was unscathed.

Birds chirped and went about their business while far off calls from the training yards mixed with the usual sounds of the community. I came to a sudden stop outside the boundaries of the girl's dorm. A quick look around revealed the small clearing where Auden trained me in potions. But it wasn't the memory of being bound with roots that shook me to my core. I almost died today. It wasn't the first time. Hell, it wasn't even the second or third time. But it was the closest I'd come to it and the reality of that was only now registering. When that Shade looked at me, I saw Asher. I saw his limp body and sightless eyes. I saw the untapped potential of his short life and hated that I'd run out of time to make up for it. I trembled where I stood, overwhelmed by my failures. A gentle hand on my cheek brought me out of my spiraling guilt.

"It's okay, Kaya." Auden's voice was soft as his arm slid gently around my shoulders. He drew me to his chest, and I didn't fight it. I couldn't stop myself from burrowing into his warmth, trying desperately to sink into his comforting scent. Tears stung the backs of my eyelids, but they didn't fall. I shook harder. "Let me run these clothes up to your room and we'll go to the infirmary." His hand ran soothing circles down my back. "The doctors will fix your shoulder."

"No." I pulled away and met with resistance. After another push, Auden let his arm fall from around me.

"No?" he asked, confusion mixing with growing disapproval. "Your shoulder is shredded. Who knows what poisons cling to you from that bite."

"If I was poisoned, we'd know it by now," I argued. "And my shoulder isn't *shredded*. The bite is more of a puncture wound if anything."

I started past him, toward the dorm. A few stragglers, either ditching classes or taking their sweet time to get there, loitered out front. A quick glance told me I looked worse than I felt, and I could only imagine the rumors that would circulate once I appeared before them looking like I'd just come out of a fight for my life. Which, I had. Auden stepped in front of me, holding the clothes once again, and I had to swing my good arm up between us to keep from crashing into him.

"I can't believe what I'm hearing." His eyes flashed. "Give me one good reason why I shouldn't throw you over my shoulder and tie you to one of the beds myself?" Panic stirred in my chest. He wouldn't. Not after last time. At the look on my face, he sighed, "You need to be looked at."

He was right. I knew he was. And the bite on my shoulder hurt like hell, but it wasn't as bad as he thought. Honestly, I was more messed up over how I got the bite, and what bit me, than the fact that I got bit in the first place.

"So, you look at it," I countered. His lips parted, a logical argument posed to strike, but I have him a beseeching look. "Please."

He swiped a hand through his tangled hair and spun away, almost dropping a shirt. Muffled curses reached me before he faced me once again, his brows knitted together over his clenched jaw.

"Fine," he barked, and a hint of a struggle crossed his face, softening it. "But if I think for one second you need more care than I can offer, we go straight to the infirmary. Deal?"

I nodded. "Deal."

Auden grumbled the whole way while I kept a couple paces behind him, worried that one more look at my shoulder would make him honor his previous threats. The loitering teens on the front steps fulfilled my every expectation of what played out in my mind. But Auden charged past them with a quick explanation of "training", like looking like death was an everyday occurrence when you worked with him. One of the guys winced when he met my gaze. By tonight no one would be jealous of me getting one-on-one time with the prince.

Minutes later, after a grueling climb up two flights of stairs, Auden dropped me at my dorm and left to gather the materials for my shoulder, even though he was still adamant that I be seen by a doctor instead. I thanked him again with a small smile and he turned away, grumbling about "stubborn shifters". I moved about my room until I reached the window. Students crowded the pathways and open spaces around the dorm, oblivious to the legit nightmare that went down on the other side of the island. Black ichor and tattered bits of Shade clung to my clothes and skin, mixing with the pink and red of my own blood and my stomach churned. Flashes of teeth sinking into my skin. Pain. Fire burning down my arm. I sank to the floor, my breaths coming in shallow, one right on top of the other, until my vision swam.

I had to get ahold of myself. This wasn't my first demon attack. This was my life now. What my future was always going to lead to. I was born to fight and kill demons, and I was pretty good at it. The abrupt change from the last four years was bound to have some consequences. At least, that's what I told myself. I went from being a normal teenager to four demon attacks in less than three weeks. I needed time to adjust. That was all. My little pep talk worked to calm me down and I was only mildly shaking when Auden came back through the door.

"I grabbed all I could from my room without having to raid the infirmary." He held a bag stuffed with the usual first aid supplies, although there were some extra-large bandages peeking out that I didn't have under my sink.

I moved to the desk chair and tried my hardest to keep blood off the wood. I decided to put a towel down instead and settled on that.

"How's the shoulder?" His voice was gruff. And right next to my ear, making me jump. Goosebumps danced down my arm and I rubbed them away.

"G-good," I replied, and he smirked.

"I'll be the judge of that."

He dug through the bag that he brought as I rubbed my sweaty palms on my thighs.

"What do you need to do?" I eyed the bottles and instruments he set on the bed. Was all that really necessary?

His smirk grew. "Change your mind?" At my glare his attention went back to the bag. "Relax," he chuckled. "Anything more than a bandage and you're going to the infirmary. Remember?"

His hands were gentle as they probed around the wound. I winced at a particularly sore spot, but Auden appeared calmer the more he examined the bite.

"It's deep, but it doesn't need stitches." He pressed some gauze against the little bit of blood that gathered. "You're lucky."

I grunted. Yeah. Getting bit by a fucking Shade made me real lucky.

"This might sting for a minute."

"Wait." I tried to pull away, but his hand clamped down. It felt like he doused my shoulder in alcohol and then set it aflame. "Why the hell did you do that?" I screeched, still trying to get away.

Auden pressed down harder on the gauze and the burning slowly faded. He wiped up the remnants of whatever he used to torture me and stuck on a clean bandage.

"If you wanted nice, you should've been looked at by someone with a good bedside manner." His hands were gentler than his words as he wrapped up. "The stitches on your other wound look ready to come out. You should have them looked at after the Choosing."

I didn't reply. With all that happened, I'd completely forgotten about tomorrow. The Choosing and dinner with my father all in one day. I groaned. There was so much unpacked baggage when it came to my father that I didn't even know where to start. Maybe I'd get lucky and all he'd want to talk about is what happened at the cabin. Reliving the Shade's attack would be less painful than anything else we could talk about.

"You should go clean yourself up," Auden gave a pointed look at my ruined clothes. "But try not to get the gauze wet if you can help it." He tugged on my torn shirt, and I gave a startled cry.

It felt like a sharp tear along my stomach, like ripping off a stubborn Band-Aid. It didn't hurt anymore, but Auden hands were already lifting the bottom of my shirt.

"Hey!" I jumped out of the chair and stumbled away, clutching at the ruined fabric like it would protect me from the heat in his eyes.

"You didn't tell me you had another injury," he accused and stalked closer. "Take off your shirt."

I couldn't move. Younger me would have absolutely melted at hearing those words, at seeing Auden glide closer with that look of determination on his face. But older me realized I was covered in blood and gore and that having someone as hot as Auden see your chest was way more nerve wracking than it was romantic.

"Excuse me?" I sputtered, and clutched the shirt closer, tacky blood and all.

"I'm not leaving until I'm satisfied you don't need more care than I can offer." He gently gripped my wrists and pulled them away. "Now, are you going to take off your shirt? Or do I need to do it for you?"

He smirked when my cheeks turned red.

"I-I..." I took a breath and shook my head. "I'm not hurting, I swear. It's just my shoulder."

He didn't let go and he didn't back away. He just kept staring. And staring. I was losing the ability to breathe the longer he watched me like that. If showing him I was truly okay would get him to stop, then...my hands twitched, and Auden released them. I gripped the bottom of my shirt and started lifting, but once the material reached my elbows, I realized I had a problem. I wasn't going to get it over my newly bandaged shoulder that way.

"Umm, is this enough?" I whispered, more nervous than I'd ever been.

Auden's soft laugh made me almost lose all the progress I'd made so far.

"Kaya, the shirt is barely above your belly button. And cute as it may be, that's not nearly enough." He placed his hands under my elbows and pushed up.

I winced as another sharp tear pulled at my skin, this time over my ribs. Auden cursed and dropped to his knees. His head was level with my still covered chest, leaving my arms crossed in front of me and bound in fabric.

"We need to get this off now." His face gave nothing away as he helped my arms back through the sleeves and eased the remains of the shirt over my bandage and then my head. "Now, let me loo—"

Auden cut off mid-sentence and I glanced down; afraid something was wrong. Was I injured after all? He was staring at my chest. I gasped, only making the problem worse by moving it closer to his face. He swallowed, trying to clear his throat, and when he opened his eyes again, they lifted from my chest, up my neck, and to my nervous stare in one long, slow scan. I bit the inside of my cheek and shifted from one foot to the other. His gaze felt like a brand, and I knew my skin grew flush the longer he watched.

From the corner of my eye, I saw him move. His hands slowly lifted and came to rest on my hips. The contact made me jump and he tightened his hold until I steadied. One of his thumbs made gentle brushes over my hipbone and my toes curled. My chest rose faster now but I couldn't help it. I was seconds away from hyperventilating. *Finally,* he broke eye contact, his eyes now ghosting over my chest, down my ribs, and back up again. He moved a finger over one of the spots that stung and glanced up at me when I flinched.

"Does it hurt?" His face was full of concern.

I shook my head. "Not anymore. That was one of the spots though."

He hummed his acknowledgement and continued his assessment. "I think it was the dried blood from your shirt peeling off your skin. I don't see any more open wounds, but I want to check your back just to be sure."

I spun around so quickly I almost fell. Only Auden's grip on my hips kept me upright. His laugh sent a warm breath across my spine, and I wiggled.

"Almost done."

"What am I supposed to tell them?" I blurted out, my nerves finding a way out in the form of rambling. But it was something else to focus on.

His fingers kept a gentle trail over the spots where blood dried. "Tell who?"

"Anyone; about the attack today. More specifically my father. We're supposed to have dinner tomorrow after the ceremony."

Auden let go of my hips and stood. I swung around, keeping my shirt spread across my front. He was across the room, grabbing his bag of supplies and frowned as he thought it over. I thought it strange that it took so long for him come up with an answer.

"I'm on my way from here to meet with my family and fill them in on all the details. As the head of the Council, your father will also be privy to that information, so speak with him about what you will." I nodded along, having figured that part out already. "But as for everyone else. I wouldn't bring it up."

"I'll admit, I don't have the best relationship with the rest of my classmates. But if someone asks me, are you telling me I should lie?" My breathing was back under control now. We were in safer waters, talking about anything but what just happened. "Why the secrecy?"

Auden knocked his head back against the door, exasperated, and rubbed at the spot between his eyes with every question I peppered at him. I could tell he was distracted. He kept staring at where my arms held my shirt in front of me and glancing away, the telltale tic in his jaw back with a vengeance.

"Shouldn't the rest of the community know about what happened today? I don't think it's right that we try and hide it. What's the point?" I pushed.

"Why do you always have so many questions?" He muttered. "Anyone else would take an order from their prince and move on." His eyes widened and he stepped away from the door. His hand hovered between us, as if he could take the words back. He couldn't. "Kaya, I didn't mean—"

"Was that an order then, *my prince*?" The shirt dropped as I stormed into his space, glaring up at him like his words didn't hurt. He may be taller than me, but I was sure my anger afforded me a few extra inches. "Should I bow now? Or will this work instead?" I showed him my favorite finger.

"I wasn't trying to say—I mean, I was frustrated— I—" He blew out a heavy breath. "Shit."

"Yeah." I agreed and walked around him to open the door. "Get out."

He didn't say another word, just stormed past me with his jaw clenched. In the hallway he half turned like he was going to really dig himself a hole and say something else, but he changed his mind and kept walking. I slammed the door and locked it. Next time I saw him, I was getting back that spare key.

CHAPTER EIGHTEEN

The dress fit me good. It was a little short, but not scandalous, and I liked the way it flowed and rippled around my thighs. I twirled once in front of the mirror, admiring how it moved and how the faint purple caught in the light. I wasn't usually one for wearing dresses and very rarely did I have an occasion to. But today I had no choice. The Choosing ceremony started at sunset and everyone was expected to dress their best. Part of me was dying to see what all the fuss was about, while the other half of me wanted to boycott on principle.

Unfortunately, attendance was mandatory, and I already walked a fine line as it was. I left my dorm before the crowds, preferring to take my time getting there. I hoped to snag a seat far in the back where no one would notice my less than supportive attitude. The pathways were more crowded than I was used to, but not overly so, and I moved around without garnering much attention. There were still stares. People still whispered, but it was easy to ignore them the further into the trees I traveled. Humidity made my hair frizz within minutes, but the cool breeze that moved through the shade more than made up for it.

"There you are!"

I spun on my heel, my dress floating around me a second later. Bast stood further down the path, looking absolutely stunning in a dress shirt and tie. The teal color played well with his caramel skin tone and his normally tousled curls were tamed. He looked great. Healthy. Like he hadn't been unconscious on the floor of his mother's cabin a mere twenty-four hours ago. Only a shallow cut and a small bruise on his forehead remained to prove that yesterday actually happened.

"I stopped by your room, but you'd already left," he panted. "You made me run all the way out here to catch you. And in my condition."

I launched myself at him, wrapping my arms around his neck and squeezing tight. He barely had time to catch me, but thankfully we didn't go down. Swamp muck didn't mix well with my dress.

"I'll give you a condition if you ever do that to me again," I threatened into his shoulder.

I leaned back and took a closer look. His face gave nothing away. No other marks or cuts to show of our life-threatening shopping excursion. Even the tiny bruise he had was partly covered by his hair.

"I don't believe it," I mumbled, more than a little jealous.

Bast's grin was slow, but cocky. "I know right? It's hard waking up this beautiful."

I rolled my eyes with a smile. His charm couldn't distract me for long. Eventually the corners of my mouth dipped, slowly taking that smile with every detail I remembered. Under my hair, the painstakingly concealed bandage felt heavy over the throbbing bite mark. If anyone saw it, they would assume it covered my stitches. That's how close the wounds were. I hated that I had to hide the bite, but Auden didn't think it was a good idea for the news of yesterday to spread further than those already aware. Which was bullshit. A little of my anger over his attitude still lingered. The stupid ceremony today was all about pairing the best of both our people to fight against the worst the demons could throw at us. Why wouldn't they want us to know what we're up against?

"Stop right there," Bast scolded, as the tip of his finger wiggled in front of my nose. "Whatever you're thinking, don't."

"I wasn't—"

"Ah ah!" He cut me off. "I can literally see you thinking about it. It's over. We survived. And today we're going to celebrate." He wrapped an arm around me and tried to steer me down the path. "All this emotion is frizzing your hair. If you don't stop now, you'll have your own radio frequency by the end of the day."

I ducked under his elbow with a frustrated growl. "Did yesterday not affect you at all?"

"Don't." He spun around; good humor gone. "We survived. We won. Don't linger on what didn't happen."

"How can you just let it go?" My rising voice brought more curious glances, but I wasn't concerned with what they thought of me. "I'm sorry that I can't be all smiles and rainbows after having been nommed on by a fucking Shade!"

Not many were around to hear my outburst, but Bast shushed me and pushed us deeper into the trees anyway. He strong armed me off the path and kept going until the thickness of the swamp closed in around us.

"Stop pushing me," I protested, stumbling over the tangled roots and vines. I caught my balance and spun to face him, prepared to either whack him over the head with one of the many sticks that tripped me or verbally fillet him with a few choice words.

His face stopped me. Guilt morphed his trademark, carefree smile into a pained grimace. The glow that surrounded him moments before actually dimmed as he shook his head.

"I didn't know," he whispered, brushing a light finger over the bruise on his head. "I'm assuming that's why your bandage is wider than usual? Is that where he bit you?"

I nodded and brushed more hair over my shoulder in an unconscious gesture. "Auden said I couldn't tell anyone about what happened, but I thought you already knew." I let out a frustrated scream, the stress and exhaustion of everything piling up.

Home no longer felt like home, and not just because Asher wasn't here. My people were different. Our traditions were different. The lies and secrets I was forced to keep grew with each passing day and all I wanted to do was scream them from the treetops.

"Why can't they know?" I shouted, feeling better already with just that small eruption, so I screamed it louder. "Why can't they know!"

Bast's hand covered my mouth and he stepped closer; even though the sun struggled to reach us here. Even though the broken twigs beneath my shoes were muffled against the wet leaves and decay that littered the ground, he too was worried that someone would overhear. His eyes glowed, and he cast them around as he tilted his head, listening. Only then did he speak.

"Things aren't as they seem here, Kaya." His whisper was scarcely louder than a breath and it trembled as he watched me, true fear in his stare. "You need to be more careful."

The hair on my arms rose to attention. "Your mom said the same thing."

"She wasn't wrong. She's—We—" he sighed, struggling over what to say. His troubles ran deeper than just the animal he shifted into and I found myself wondering how I'd missed this side of him. The side so good at keeping secrets. "You need to follow the rules. And even if you don't agree with them, pretend that you do."

"You can't tell me that you're honestly okay with what happened yesterday. We almost died!"

"Of course not," he replied, and I watched his eyes soften. "I never thanked you for saving my life."

I remembered him lying on the floor, so pale, and the fear grew inside me once more. The memory of Auden crouched next to us helped to calm me. We were safe with him. I was always safe with him.

"I didn't. Save you I mean." Bast scoffed. "Honest. I fought as hard as anyone to not be eaten by a demon. If Auden hadn't shown up..." I shrugged.

"What happened after I was knocked out?" he asked. "I remember being thrown, a flash of red, and then nothing."

In my mind, I saw Bast tossed through the air like a sack of flour. Gold and red sparks danced around him a second before he hit the ground. I didn't have much time to ponder it before the demon decided to snack on me, but now I wondered. What really happened?

"—that's what I'm more curious about."

"What was that?" Bast said, already moving on to his next topic.

"Auden. How did he know where to find you?"

Another good question.

I DID as I was told, shut my mouth, and silently followed Bast as he guided us out of the trees to mingle with the last of the lingering spectators. The atmosphere was thick with anticipation and excitement—an underlying current that spread from person to person. Grins were infectious and laughter even more so. Which made it all the more awkward to walk through it with the judgmental frown I couldn't scrub from my face. I tried focusing on something else.

The outdoor amphitheater was a far cry from the ornate palace where this usually *private* ceremony took place, but they tried, I guess. Thick, gauzy ribbons stretched across the half open roof, creating shade that danced and moved with the evening breeze. It didn't help with the humidity, though. With this many people squeezed into the crumbling stone walls, the moist air circled around and around like crumbs stuck in a blender.

As Bast led us to the lower rows, my gaze caught on the lighting. Small flames flickered in iron lanterns and bowls, adding contrast to the shadowed alcoves that housed the more esteemed guests: Council members, shop owners, and their families. I couldn't see their faces and the anonymity added to the mysterious feel of it all. The sun worked its way down, dragging us ever closer to the start of the ceremony. Its position, combined with the lanterns, created a warm ambiance that appeared more welcoming than the nature of the event would call for. But that was the plan, wasn't it?

Bring them in with warmth and laughter to hide the darker nature of the evening. I mean, people were going to be enlisted into breeding servitude tonight, essentially. Bast squeezed us in amongst the front two rows, the last of our class to arrive to our reserved section. We were given prime viewing to what would be our future next year. There went my plan of hiding in the back. My classmates vibrated with expectation, but I wanted to hurl. Those graduating this year stood on the ground floor, dressed in white to better stand out against the growing shadows and earth tones of the arena.

Two, uneven parallel rows of excited victims. There was no stage or platform to mark the Royal Family—one wasn't needed. They would've been recognizable even if I hadn't seen their faces almost every day of my life. Their matching dark hair and chiseled jaws were a dead giveaway. Auden's eyes glowed from within thanks to the nearby lanterns on either side of him. He and Asiel both flanked their father. Asher would've been up there too. The thought of him involved in this sham should twist me up inside, but at least it would mean he was alive and able to stand up to his father and older brother. Because make no mistake, Asher wouldn't have gone along with this crap. And as I watched Auden stand behind his father with pride, I fought to keep my eyes dry.

I fought the voice in the back of my mind that said he should recognize this as wrong. That he should be standing beside *me* in protest. Instead, he stood in front of my people, close enough to touch and yet so distant to the truth. I'm sure the lack of usual ceremony—crowns, pomp and fanfare, and the like—was again done intentionally to formulate a connection between the royals and the new graduates. A statement that said we were all the same and no matter the outcome of the Choosing, we were all doing our part to further the future of our community. It was well planned bullshit, and the crowd ate it up. The graduates stood tall and proud before their king and princes, preening under their attention. Couldn't they tell what was happening? Couldn't anyone? The division of our people was so obvious. The first row was all witches for crying out loud! With the familiars standing several steps behind, ready to be picked like ripe fruit.

This was nothing like what it used to be. As a child, Asher and I would hide in the palace and watch the ceremonies as new pairs were initiated. It was a private affair between the royals, Council, and the immediate families of the bonded pair. This was a joke in comparison.

"It's disgusting," I mumbled. Bast made a face but didn't respond. He glanced at someone behind me, but quickly looked away. The ceremony was about to start.

"My people!" The king's timbre easily carried across the natural acoustics of the amphitheater. "The time has come once again to celebrate the addition in our ranks. To welcome our brothers and sisters in arms as they vow to uphold our sacred duty of protection against the evil preying on our world." The candidates stood even taller if possible and beamed at the recognition. "Tonight, some of you will form a lifelong bond, one filled with honor, tradition, and great sacrifice. Others among you will fill a different role, but one no less honorable."

"Did he intentionally leave out the sacrifice part that time?" I whispered, not so quietly.

"Shh!" The reprimand came from somewhere to my right, but the offender didn't meet my eye. They all stared ahead, fixed on whatever came next.

At least three familiars wouldn't be paired tonight. That much was obvious by the uneven numbers of the class. Bast told me there was still a chance for the unchosen to be paired with someone older or out on assignment; someone not graduating this year. Familiars in repopulation had one year to find a suitable mate and settle in. Females could be chosen by a witch up until they conceived, then their time was truly up. While males could be chosen at any time until death or age made them unfit for duty. Regardless of whether or not they fathered any children. Only Asiel would have come up with something so sexist.

There were more female shifters in this class than males. One didn't have to be a genius to work out what those numbers meant. More than one female would be trapped tonight. I missed the last of the king's speech, but I wasn't upset about it. Whatever he said probably would have pissed me off even more. It blew my mind how blind my people were. Or maybe willful ignorance was easier than living with the knowledge that your worth was measured so low by your king and community. The growing division of our peoples sat like a heavy stone upon my chest.

The king waved a hand and the two rows faced one another. The class ranking—another ridiculous development— was announced this morning, so the graduates most likely knew their fates before the sun reached its afternoon peak. In the back row of familiars, toward the middle, stood a petite brunette. Her chin was tucked close to her chest and her shoulders trembled. As each witch stepped forward to claim their partner, her shoulders jerked. Like she was being stabbed in the gut each time a name was called that wasn't hers. There were three familiars left: that young girl and two others. The brunette openly cried while the others remained still, their eyes glistening in the torch light.

"How is anyone okay with this?" I growled, the girl's tears getting to me more with each passing moment.

"It's just the way it is now, Kaya," Bast whispered harshly, his eyes scanning around us.

I glanced to the side, and this time people met my eye. Hostility and disgust were clear on their faces.

"Oh, come on!" I flung a hand out at the three remaining shifters. "You can't tell me those girls are excited about their futures. I don't know why everyone's going along like this is the best night of the year."

More eyes landed on our row as my voice rose. Bast's hand was a painful vice around my arm, but I shook him off.

"Kaya—"

"No, this is unacceptable, Bast. How can we agree to being

treated like second class citizens? Like we're somehow worth less than our witch counterparts?"

"You better put a muzzle on your bitch, demon boy." Lincoln stood from his seat, easily towering over the rest of us as his lips curled into a snarl.

The murmurs of the audience faded as I turned to face the self-important shifter. "You know it shouldn't be like this, Lincoln. It was once an honor to be chosen by one of us, to create a bond stronger than any other in our world." I gestured at the poor brunette. The girl who was now looking right at me, along with a majority of the crowd on this side of the arena. I swallowed past a growing sense of unease and pushed on. "Tell me, does she look honored to you?"

Bast crowded my back and I couldn't shake his grip this time. He pulled, dragging me back through the rows as I kept my eyes locked with Lincoln's.

"I know you can kick my ass six ways from Sunday," Bast's voice was strong, but terrified as he barked in my ear. "So, I hope you recognize my bravery when I say; Shut. The. Fuck. Up."

My head whipped around in shock. I thought Bast supported my resentment of the Choosing.

"Run." With a final yank, he pulled us through the last rows and toward the exit. I tried to turn and see who watched us leave, but Bast gripped my shoulder with a firm claw. His nails made shallow marks against my skin and his lack of control told me all I needed to know about how much trouble I was in.

"Fuck," I cursed, increasing our pace.

"Yeah." He agreed, steering me further into the night. "Fuck."

The darkness of the night enveloped us as soon as we left the glow of the torch lights. Fireflies sparked here and there, lighting up in an unheard melody. It was cooler now, especially away from the masses. Goosebumps grew along my arms as an evening breeze wicked the sweat from the back of my neck. I wished I had a hair tie, but I'd only thought of covering my bandage this morning, not about how humid it would be or that I'd be running through the thick air like another horde of demons was on my ass. Bast didn't look down as he tugged me along the uneven path, expertly dodging rocks and tangled vines and weeds.

"You need to go straight to your dorm and stay in for the rest of the night," he ordered, not even out of breath despite the steady pace he kept. "Hopefully the heavy celebrations tonight will make their memories muddy by tomorrow morning and no one will say anything."

"I didn't do anything wrong," I argued, but even I could admit I sounded like a petulant child. "I only said what I was feeling. There's no crime against that."

We came to a stop at the fork in the path. Both dormitories were visible from here and Bast pointed at mine with a stern frown. "You're the one who said you were on probation. Asiel is looking for any reason to show you're not trying hard enough to fit in. Go. Before the crowds return."

We left the sounds of celebration behind us and bolted to the dorms.

CHAPTER NINETEEN

Most of the community partied it up at the amphitheater or at private residences deeper in the settlement. A few returned to the dorms, but I didn't think anyone saw me as I snuck out the side entrance. My beautiful purple dress was a ball under my bed and the oversized hoodie and leggings I now sported did a better job at protecting me from the mosquitos, even if it now felt hotter than the Devil's living room. The Ruling Island was surrounded by water and had a near constant breeze, so I wouldn't suffer for long. If I could get my feet to move, that is. I stood on one end of the bridge while the black water gently rolled on either side and tried to gather enough courage to cross. Dinner with my father couldn't be avoided, no matter how much Bast wanted me to stay inside tonight. I had a feeling I knew exactly how this dinner was going to go. Terribly. One hundred percent would bet my first-born child that tonight was going to be the rainbow sprinkles on top of an already shitty fucking night.

I ran across the old wooden planks without taking my eyes off the opposite bank. I didn't look at the beauty of the swamp or at the lit plantation homes that were my destination. I focused on ripping off the band aid and just getting my ass across to the other side. Panting, I gave myself a moment to gather my courage, and then started the small trek to my father's house. Easily the second largest home on the island, second only to—you guessed it—the palace, the old house was beautiful. There was no denying it. Painted a bright white and highlighted by the near full moon, the only color on the home was the red shutters and any vegetation that managed to take root along the walls and pillars. It was built in the Greek Revival style, all boxy shaped and symmetrical windows. The lights within glowed with warmth, offering a sense of safety and shelter against the wet and grimy world currently trying to swallow my Chucks. It was a good lie. But I knew the second I walked through those doors; I would feel nothing but cold. The last kernel of warmth left that house when my mother did.

I let myself in through the front door, not needing a key since my father never locked it. Who would he need to keep out? The entrance was just as grand and empty as I remembered. The tall ceilings and ornate chandelier might be impressive to some, but I'd grown up amongst the luxury and honestly didn't care for it. I preferred the small one-bedroom apartment Sensei maintained above the dojo. And the little shoebox of a room he made for me in one of the storage rooms downstairs. Those images felt like home. Not the plush, velvet carpet that led up the grand staircase. Not the textured wallpaper that ran from crown molding back to said plush carpet. The wooden accents from the furniture and railings would be more of a comfort, if they didn't shine so bright under the glaring light of yet another opulent chandelier.

There were five heavy, oak doors in this wing of the house and mine was directly at the end of the hall, sealed shut and probably unopened since I was last here. On the other side, was a time portal. A purple and black comforter sat neatly tucked around my childhood bed. Random posters littered the walls and clothes still spilled out of half-closed drawers. It was like walking back in time. A thick ball of emotions clogged my throat, making it hard to breathe without releasing a torrential rain of tears. My gaze ghosted over the back wall by the closet before I could stop it. Photos of all types—polaroid, candid, black and white— lined the wall in neat rows from floor to ceiling. Pictures of summers spent by the pool and afternoons hanging upside down from low tree limbs. Asher smiled so big in each one, safe with the false knowledge every kid carried with them; that nothing bad could happen to you. Invincible. That's what the pictures showed. A lie. I backed out of the room before I lost it completely and ran down the stairs to the dining room. This never-ending night had to have a stop button. But I couldn't hit it until after dinner.

My father already sat at the head of the table, picking at his food with immaculate manners. The gold in his hair shone like a crown from the candelabra in the center of the table and he looked far more at ease tonight than the last time I saw him. A place setting waited for me at the other end, six chairs on each side between him and me. I didn't think it was enough. I gingerly sat on the plump cushion and a servant moved forward to push in my chair. I hadn't noticed them standing along the back wall, but three others waited attentively, melting into the wallpaper like extra decoration. Who needed four servants to eat a basic dinner of...I glanced down; it looked like pot roast?

"I'm going to assume you've forgotten the dress code for dinner in your time away." My father's slender hands daintily cut the roast and his eyes didn't look up longer than the second it took to take in my appearance.

"I didn't forget," I said, scooting my chair in even further. The legs scraped against the hardwood, and I made a show of settling in. My father's pursed lips were the only outward sign that I'd annoyed him.

We ate in silence. Tension was an extra being at the dinner table, but not one that anyone acknowledged. The oppressive weight of my father's disappointment was enough to make me nauseous, but I continued eating and the clanking of our utensils against the fine china was our only conversation. The shriek of a knife cutting through roast to the bottom of the plate was my father's passive way of saying, *"you've aggravated me tonight, but I'm too superior to say it and let you know it bothers me."* The little scrapes of my fork as I tried to scoop the last of the potatoes was my response. *"I know. And I don't care."* Back and forth we went, until the servants cleared our plates, and one brought my father his nightly glass of brandy. I leaned against an armrest; my gaze locked on him as I waited for his hidden agenda. He didn't invite me here because his heart was overwhelmed with joy at the opportunity to connect with his missing daughter of four years. There weren't tears in his eyes because he missed me. There wasn't a smile on his face, his arms weren't wide open with love, and I knew nothing he said tonight would be what one would expect of a father in this situation—having a daughter returned home.

He didn't want to get to know me, to catch up on who I was now or what I'd been doing in my time away. He had *reasons* to call this dinner, and I bet my tight little ass it was about his image. It was one thing if his daughter died alongside the youngest prince in an unprecedented demon attack. But it was another thing entirely to know that she was alive, that she'd run away and was forced back like she didn't understand the utter privilege of being the offspring of the strongest familiar on the island. To top it off, she didn't quietly fade into the background and didn't try to ease the ripples her return might cause. No. She made a giant cannon ball when she demanded to be trained and to graduate with the rest of her class. Now she was a big ole' question mark. Would she embarrass him and be the lowest rank next year? Would she even rank? I saw the questions blistering behind his level observation, like magma simmering beneath the surface of a well composed volcano.

"You're to have a monthly allowance for personal necessities and are welcome to anything of want in your room upstairs for your dorm. Since you are so behind on your training, I think it best you stay on campus during breaks and weekends to better accommodate your extra classes. See to it you get what you need for the extended stay." He brought his arm down to rest along the table, the glass of brandy latent in his hand.

He awaited my response, poised like this was a casual conversation, but I recognized the first strike. I wasn't allowed in this house unless I was invited. This was no longer my home. What I took from that room upstairs was a gift he bestowed upon me out of kindness. And the allowance no more than what would be expected of him to provide for a daughter living on campus.

"That is, of course, unless you'd like to move back here. You could relinquish this useless aspiration of graduating next year and instead build a quiet life in society." My father swirled his brandy, the corner of his lip curling in what I'm sure he thought was a friendly smile. "You could continue your education of course, but there's no need to push for a pairing when we both know it isn't possible."

So that was his angle. He wanted me to quit. He wanted to stomp out the potential embarrassment before it got out of control, and he tried to sugar coat it in a way he thought would interest me.

I scoffed. Like he knew my interests.

At my obvious rejection, his smile dropped and was replaced with a concerned frown. "You don't have to put yourself through this, child. The objective set out before you isn't fair, or reasonably achievable. You could have a comfortable life here, with a mate and your own family."

I couldn't keep my face from scrunching at the suggestion and his fatherly frown turned into a full-on glare. He set the brandy down with a solid *clunk* and steepled his fingers beneath his chin, waiting. He'd made the first move, it was my turn to counterstrike. Only, I was in no mood to play games tonight.

"You're worried I'll embarrass you." I went straight to the point. "How will it look to the rest of the Council—to the king — if your daughter epically fails at being a familiar. They'll look at you and think you weak. That if your progeny is such a disappointment, it must be a reflection on your abilities to lead our people."

I smirked, enjoying how his hand tightened around his glass with every verbal knife I threw home. The grandfather clock chimed the eleventh hour and each peal echoed through the silence of the room. Neither one of us moved. We stared, searching for a weakness that wouldn't be revealed easily. And then my father smiled.

"You've embarrassed me enough for two lifetimes, so why would any of that bother me now?"

My brow creased in confusion. His image was everything to him but he acted like I already ruined it. He laughed the longer I tried to connect the incomplete scraps he threw at me, and I grew more apprehensive as his smile grew into a sneer.

"How did you think it made me look when my teenaged daughter ran away from the death of her would be future charge? She acted cowardly. And instead of coming back and facing what she'd done, she forced the prince to hunt her down and then offer to train her to save face."

Barbs. His word were hot barbs that hooked in my skin and

pulled with the weight of their truth. The pain was everywhere within me, and it took everything I had to keep it from showing on my face. But somehow, my father knew he'd struck true. My hands shook so I shoved them in my lap. My stomach rolled and I swallowed to keep my dinner down. Roaring overtook my senses, blinding me from his sneer and drowning out the sound of my racing heart. Every word. Every. word. How did he know how I felt about that night? He wasn't accusing me of being at fault for Asher's death, but he was right about everything else. I was a coward. I ran as my best friend hung by his neck from the pincers of a demon. He was tasted and nibbled on while I tucked tail and hid from my sins. My thoughts spiraled, I needed to say something. Anything before my father pounced again.

"That's not why Auden offered to train me." My words were quiet, but solid. I knew this to be true as well.

My father shook his head with another cruel laugh. "He spent all that time searching for you only to nearly die bringing you back. He *had* to say you were worth saving, if only so he didn't waste his time. If only so the king and his brother didn't resent him for ignoring his duties for so long."

"That's not true," I whispered, tears now clouding my sight. "He believes in me."

But a small voice in my spiraling mind whispered back little doubts. *He wasn't happy about bringing you back in the first place.* I remembered the glares and silent resentment as I made him travel across multiple states to catch me. *And then he had to feed you like a pet just to keep you from passing out. You're the reason they pulled over at the rest stop to begin with. He lost his team to a demon they could have avoided if you held your bladder. If you'd never ran away in the first place. If you'd died with Asher.*

"If you insist on this futile endeavor as some misguided attempt to spite me, do yourself a favor and at least keep your mouth shut." My father stood casually, tugging at the bottom of his dress shirt to straighten the wrinkles. "You lost the right to voice opinions when you abandoned your people. Tonight should have shown you where you stand with them."

Tears openly streamed down my face until the sleeves of my hoodie were soaked with them. My father left the room, content to let me wallow in my pain. The knowledge that I let him lure me into that verbal ambush—and worse, that he won— only made it hurt more. I ran from that house and didn't stop until the door to my dorm locked behind my back. I spent the rest of the night crying until my head swelled with the tears and my tortured thoughts pulled me under.

THE BELLS TOLD me I missed breakfast, but the endless chatter outside my door made me want to hide deeper in my blankets like the immature child my father claimed I was. At one point, Bast knocked on my door, but I didn't answer, and he eventually went away. Conversations up and down the hall, the slamming of doors, and the small sliver of sunlight moving across my floor told me the day was passing by like any other. Moving on just fine without me. Once more, there were footsteps outside my door, their shadow visible through the crack, but they too went away. I spent the day and most of last night replaying the brutal conversation with my father, so pissed that I let him get to me. I felt like a thirteen-year-old all over again, only this time I didn't have Asher to run to. I was alone.

I deserved to be, I knew, but that didn't make it hurt any less. Maybe what my father said was true. I was an inconvenience. I forced everyone to make room for me. Just like I always forced Asher to do what I wanted. Or when I forced Asher over the wall. I was selfish. My eyes stung with another round of tears when there was a knock at my door. I glanced at the bedside clock and the red numbers flashed past midnight.

"Go away," I called out, my voice muffled by my childhood comforter that now covered my bed.

To make matters worse, my father had my things delivered this morning, all of it still in boxes around my room. On the outside, it appeared a thoughtful gesture from a doting father. But I saw it for the calculated move it was. A sucker punch of sorts. A brash reminder that I'd run out of the house without the things I'd gone for. That was how my father knew he'd won that round. Not like my tears at the dinner table hadn't already told him. But he wouldn't be the man I knew if he didn't rub it in. The door to my room creaked open and the shadows from the hall lamps outlined a tall figure with broad shoulders.

"You missed dinner." Auden's voice pierced the room, and I stifled a groan. "Also, lunch and breakfast. But missing training, now that's personal."

He set a small plate on my nightstand with the vague shape of a sandwich on it. My stomach grumbled but I curled deeper into my blankets.

"Go away, Auden," I sniffed, and he crouched beside me.

"Hey," he whispered. "What's wrong? Are you not feeling well?"

No, I wasn't. My head pounded from a day and night's worth of tears. My stomach was going to claw its way out of my throat in rebellion, but more importantly, my heart hurt and having him here made it worse. My father's words echoed back to me. *He's only here because he has to be.*

"I said, go away, Your Highness." I managed to keep the emotion out of my voice, hardening it.

It didn't work. Auden tugged on my covers. Hard. Most of it slipped from my hands but I kept my head buried.

"Talk to me," he demanded.

One more tug and my shelter was gone. I sat up, fury rising, and I gripped it with all I had left.

"Another order, *my prince*?" My glare was directed at his neck. For all my bravado, I couldn't even look him in the eye. I wanted him out of my room before I lost it again. This simmering anger only did so much to hold the rest of the storm at bay. "Forgive me if I don't bow, but I wouldn't want to inflate an already massive royal ego."

Auden stood, towering over me once more. "Despite our previous spat, you know I'm nothing like that, Kaya, and this lashing out isn't going to make you feel better." He tilted his chin, trying to catch my gaze, but I refused to look at him. "I can't help you if you won't talk to me."

"Maybe I don't want your help!" I shouted, flinging my arms in the air. "I'm perfectly fine on my own without your egotistical, know-it-all, listen-to-me-I'm-a-prince, ass—"

A sharp tug on my chin stopped my rant. Auden was close, so close I couldn't avoid the concern etched in every feature of his frown. From the wrinkle in his brow, to the firm set of his lips, to the glow lighting his gaze. He held my chin gently between his thumb and forefinger, keeping me from looking anywhere else but right back at him. My face felt splotchy, my eyes puffy and red from crying, but he took it all in.

"Tell me the truth," his voice was a deep rumble. "And check the attitude."

Tears welled in my eyes again and I jerked my head to the side, but he didn't let me go. The silence in the room was deafening. My breath hitched and carried on in an uneven tempo as I tried to keep myself together. Auden's grip gentled until his hand cupped my cheek. He opened his mouth, but I beat him to the punch and uttered the first thing on my mind.

"Do you think I'm selfish?"

He drew back, visibly caught off guard by my question, but

shook his head. "You're the least selfish person I've ever met." He sounded confident, but I couldn't help but scoff. He swallowed and slowly settled on the bed beside me, our shoulders brushing. "You've thrown yourself in the direct path of danger twice now for the sake of someone else. Why in the world would you think you're selfish?"

Because I killed your brother and then ran away.

"My father..."

Auden jerked away with a curse. "Figures."

"What?"

"I'm guessing his demeanor hasn't changed since your return?" His jaw ticked as he waited for me to answer.

"You...you know about my father?" I'd never told him what my life was like at home, not even before. There was nothing he could have done, and I always tried to appear more grown up in front of him. Nothing screamed danger more to a boy than a girl with daddy issues.

"Asher mentioned a few things," he said, confirming my suspicions. No one else was privy to the truth. "I just never thought he'd still be like that. Especially after finally having you home."

My laugh was brittle, the laugh of a broken girl who knew better than to hope for what could never be. "If anything, I'm a bigger inconvenience than before."

"What did he tell you?" I felt Auden watching me again and my cheeks burned.

"That you only offered to train me because of all the time you spent looking for me. That I'd made you look bad, and it would be even worse if I failed." That I'm a coward who should've died the night Asher did.

"That's such bullshit," he sneered in disbelief. "I *saw* your face when my brother mentioned repopulation. And honestly, I knew how you would feel about it before it was even mentioned." His shoulder brushed mine again as he turned to face me fully. "You had such promise when we were younger and the grit you showed evading me only proved it was still there. You deserve to graduate, Kaya."

I didn't know how much I needed to hear his words until the heavy pressure on my chest eased. The worry didn't disappear, but a part of me recognized that while Auden's reasons were different from my father's, that didn't make my father completely wrong.

"So, why are we training in secret?" I asked before I lost my nerve. At his raised brow I added, "the attic?"

Auden threw his head back and laughed. A true one. Eyes closed, shoulders shaking, and infectious enough for a small smile to tug at my lips.

"It's not a secret," he admitted, still chuckling. "Your schedule will change too much to keep trying to use the gym between classes. The attic is private, consistent, and you can take your time without others staring."

I sat there, stunned. He really was looking out for me. And because he *wanted* to, not because he had to. But even with the truth staring me right in the face and coming from the source himself, it was hard to believe. My father's voice still rang in my head, mixing with my own self-doubts.

At my silence, Auden stood. "I can go tell everyone right now, if you want." He moved toward the door.

I smiled again, a small one. "Auden, its fine."

"No. No. I can see you don't believe me."

"Everyone's sleeping."

He shrugged. "If that's what it takes to earn your trust."

His hand was on the doorknob when I was moved. I launched myself at his back, clinging to him like a monkey to keep him in the room.

"I trust you," I panted, using all my weight to hold him back.

"Sorry, I couldn't hear you?"

I hit him on the shoulder. He heard me. "I said, I trust you."

He reached back and grabbed my thigh, his hand meeting bare skin. Before I could register the shock, he swung me around and threw me on the bed, his smile positively wicked.

"Asshole," I muttered, but I was only joking. My somber mood rapidly faded the longer Auden kept smiling at me like that.

I pushed up from the rumpled blankets and winced as my stitches dug deeper into my skin.

"What was that?" Auden asked, eyeing my shoulder like he could see beneath my sleep shirt.

"Nothing." Dammit. I winced, again.

"Kaya..." he growled in reprimand. "I told you to get those checked this weekend."

"Yeah, well it's been a busy past couple days, okay?" I batted his hands away, but he was quick at pulling down the collar of my shirt.

"They're scabbing over!" He scolded and I jerked away when he touched them. "I have half a mind to take you to get them out right now."

"I have an appointment tomorrow," I lied, pulling my shirt from his grasp.

He nodded. "Good. You need all the time you can get in your regular classes to get caught up."

"Yes, sir." I saluted and he flicked my nose.

He stood in the doorway, his indulgent smile making my heart skip.

"Get some sleep," he gestured at my rumpled blankets. "With those stitches out, we can really pick up training."

It took hours before I did what I was told; days spent

wallowing meant I wasn't as tired now. I had no plans to get my stitches out tomorrow and that posed a new obstacle. Without them, I'd be cleared to shift, and I couldn't begin to list the number of problems that would cause. I knew they couldn't stay in forever, but I needed a few more days to work out another plan. There had to be a way around this. What if I tried to figure it out on my own? If I could manage a full shift, it wouldn't be such a big deal to return to my regular classes. It's not like I expected to graduate without ever shifting again. But struggling in front of others while I figured out how to do it was out of the question. Who's to say that wouldn't be reason enough to pull me off of probation? All my father needed was one excuse and I'd be trapped here with a kid on the way as soon as I came of age. Not going to happen. My future was my own and I refused to allow it to be taken from me.

CHAPTER
TWENTY

The whole morning was a lesson in restraint. I woke up late and tripped getting out of bed. My stitches were itching like crazy and only added to my guilt about lying to Auden, and to top it off, there were hex bags on our table at breakfast. Small ones. But they pissed me off, nonetheless. I tossed them over my shoulder and couldn't stop grinning when they landed where I hoped they would. Snarls and chair scrapes drew the attention of those still lingering this close to the bell and anticipation built up inside me. My self-affirmations last night went a long way in giving me hope and I practically bounced with the energy coursing through me as I prepared to take my future by the horns and make it my bitch.

"Did you have to do that?" Bast ducked his head in a cower and I growled.

"You stood up to a Shade, but Lincoln still intimidates you?"

He didn't have a chance to respond. The douche canoe himself stood behind me, close enough that if I turned around, our chests would touch. Fuck that. I pushed my chair back, hard, until I heard a satisfying "oompf". There was plenty of space between us now and I stood to lean a hip against the table. A picture of unaffected. This new energy needed an outlet and a little scuffle sounded like the perfect opportunity.

"I'm surprised you showed your face today, little traitor." Lincoln rubbed the spot on his stomach where my chair hit him, and I smirked.

"Aw, did you miss me?"

His lip curled in a sneer, revealing a sharp canine. "I missed seeing you make a fool of yourself."

I scowled as his buddies laughed behind him. Why did bullies feel the need to travel in packs? It was like keeping your own audience on payroll. Pathetic.

"The way you carried on at the Choosing?" Another round of laughter. "Was seeing your future too much to handle?"

My brows knitted as I remembered that poor girl crying in the middle of the arena. It looked like Asiel and my father weren't the only ones who thought my future lie in repopulation. I looked forward to fucking up those odds. The bell rang and the cafeteria once more filled with the sound of chatter and clanking trays. But Lincoln didn't move and neither did I.

"Kaya..." Bast called.

Lincoln's glare shot past my shoulder. "Be gone, vermin. The little traitor and I have things to discuss."

I felt Bast behind me, softly shaking with nerves, but a subtle tang in the air told me his wolf was pissed. Finally. I knew he had a backbone. This wasn't his fight this time, though, and there was no reason for the both of us to be in trouble. I could handle Lincoln. Before Bast could go full wolf, I waved a hand.

"I'll be okay." I risked a glance and smiled. "I'll be right behind you."

After another tension fueled minute, I heard his footsteps recede at a steady trot. Lincoln wasted no time. His hips pinned mine against the table and I threw my hands up between us, pushing back. His chest was hard beneath my palms, muscles flexing in a way that sent off alarm bells in my head.

"What the hell, asshole." I stiffened and pushed harder, but it was like trying to move a boulder. Uphill. This wasn't a fight. As I struggled against him, his true intentions became more prominent. I gagged.

"We both know there isn't a witch on this campus that will choose you. But you won't be alone for long," he crooned, and pressed harder with his hips. The air left me between clenched teeth and my stomach turned. "With your bloodline and my scores, the Council will approve you as my mate in a heartbeat."

Now I was really going to throw up. "Both parties have to be interested, you sick bastard. And I find you sorely lacking."

He wrapped a meaty fist around my wrist and squeezed, crushing the delicate bones together. I held back my yelp but could do nothing as he forced our hands down his body.

"Maybe after a little taste, you'll see how far from *lacking* I truly am."

Vomit hit the back of my mouth as our hands kept moving. He had a solid grip on my sore arm and each struggle started and ended with sharp pains as my scabs pulled at the stitches.

"No." I ignored my throbbing shoulder and fought harder, our hands now at his belt.

He gave a quick jerk of his hips and I saw red. Claws punctured his shirt and skin and he released me with a curse. His throat was wide open. Exposed. I could almost taste the blood in my mouth as my inner cat curled to pounce. My swing stopped midair; claws pointed at the pulsing artery right below his jaw. Lincoln swallowed, too scared to move.

"I think a simple 'no' should have sufficed, don't you?" Auden stood at the cafeteria doors and casually strolled closer. Bast's head peeked around the corner behind him but darted away when the prince gave him a nod. I thanked every lucky star that Bast hadn't listened to me.

Auden was breathing hard, the rise and fall of his chest the only sign of his temper as he shoved Lincoln away from me. Auden whispered something in Lincoln's ear that made him blanche, all the color draining out of him before he took off without a look back. Auden turned to me next, taking in my claws still suspended in the air.

My face heated. "I know how it must look." My hand suddenly dropped, and I fell forward, catching myself on a chair.

"Like you were about to murder the boy molesting you and cheer in victory?" He snapped, temper still barely in check. Did he blame me?

"You forgot the part where I dance a jig on his cooling corpse," I snapped back.

Auden sighed, the anger leaving his features. "Are you okay?" I nodded, my cheeks still burning with humiliation. His fingers were gentle on my chin, but a muscle feathered in his jaw as he tilted his head. "None of that was your fault. You know that, right?"

I said nothing. It wasn't my fault Lincoln was a sick fuck, but it was my fault for poking at his anger and then failing to defend against it. I'd gotten cocky, thinking I could pick a fight and there wouldn't be consequences. Lincoln wasn't Braxton; human boys were nothing compared to the strength of a pissed off shifter. A lesson I wouldn't be forgetting any time soon.

"Kaya—" The pity in his voice was more than I could take and embarrassment made my blush linger a little longer.

"I have to get to class," I whispered, and Auden let me go.

"I'm here if you need to talk, Kaya. Always."

~

Lunch was hardly better than breakfast, and it too got off to a rocky start. Neither one of us wanted to go back to the cafeteria, so Bast skipped Fox's class and we went to a café on the edge of town. It was my first time being so close to the settlement in years. It was very different from the Ruling Island and that only made me like it more. Rather than landscaping and polished stone, the people of the community used the swamp around them to decide the shapes of their homes. Houses were built with water resistant wood, sealed tight against the constant moisture. No trees were knocked down to create yards, instead the homes were built into and around them until they became one cohesive unit. Sometimes you couldn't see the home until you were right on top of it. It was a different kind of beauty. One I preferred. But ugly could be found even in the midst of such artistry and this café owner was the blight on an otherwise picturesque part of town. I threw a fit, threatening the ornery shifter to within an inch of his life, but he refused to let Bast inside.

"Just let it go," Bast pleaded. "It's not a big deal."

I tore myself from his grip and took another threatening step toward the owner. "No. I want him to say it again. I want him to give me a reason to give my father why this restaurant insulted his daughter and her *friend*!"

The owner looked sick at the mention of my father, but Bast was too tender hearted to let me act on his fear. The owner offered our food to go and Bast accepted before I could spit more curses.

"Would your father actually do anything?" He asked after we left, making himself comfortable on the spongy ground where we decided to settle.

I snorted. "Hell no. But the owner didn't know that."

His deep laugh helped calm me more and the prejudiced shifter was soon forgotten. The sunny day was stifling, but peaceful under the canopy of mossy trees. Bast and I joked and teased, quickly healing the wounds left behind from the past few days and growing closer in our friendship. He told me about his father in whispers and halted sentences. About how his mom fell in love with a passing Creole shapeshifter, a *Rougarou*, that to this day he'd never met. He shared his dreams of meeting him and leaving this lonely island behind.

"When you go, take me with you." I was only partially teasing.

"As if your father would let you go again."

Silence overwhelmed us. I'd already filled Bast in on how that last encounter went and apologized for blowing him off when he came to my door. He was more than understanding, claiming his mother wasn't a big fan of my father either.

"She still resents him and the rest of the Council for not protecting us. He practically encouraged our ostracism."

"Trust me, I'm not surprised," I pushed my food around in its box. "I am sorry, though. Maybe you can petition the king?"

Bast choked on his drink. "The king?" He sputtered. "The royal family is worse."

I frowned. "Asiel is a dick, there's no denying that. And he has the king's ear. But Auden would help; I'm sure of it."

Auden was nothing like his older brother and the king listened to him when he was passionate about something. Just look at me and my situation. I'd be rotting in a prison cell or halfway through a mating arrangement right now if it weren't for him.

I shooed away Bast's objections. "Oh, come on! You have no problem calling him hot every other day."

Bast grinned, unapologetic. "I don't have to like him to appreciate how fine he is."

"It really is hard not to notice," I admitted.

We walked back to campus at a brisk pace. The hot prince in

question was waiting for me for our next training session. Butterflies danced in my stomach, and I couldn't stop them. Bast's talk of his hair, his chiseled jaw, the one time he saw him shirtless...how could I not be distracted?

"You probably wouldn't have to try too hard."

"What?" I'd zoned out, missing what Bast was trying to convince me of.

"To seduce him," he declared, growing smug at my blush. "You spend all that time alone together. Sweating. Grabbing. Twisting around each other's bod—"

My hands covered his mouth. "I get the picture."

Bast licked my palm and danced away from my answering swing. He wiggled his eyebrows and shimmied his hips, dancing in a circle around me while I tried not to laugh.

"I doubt it would work," I tried to trip him, but he hopped over my leg. "It's hard to seduce someone who's already seen you without your shirt on. If that didn't do it, I don't know what would."

"What?" Bast shouted and slammed into me. He gripped my shoulders and shook. "He saw your bubbies?"

"My *what*?" I detangled myself with a laugh.

"Your Bongos. Bumpers. Blorps." He frowned. "Your boobs, woman. When were you going to share with me that he saw you topless?"

My laughter dried up as Bast's glee grew. I reluctantly told him about what happened after the Shade attack, how Auden took care of my injuries to keep me out of the infirmary. The memory relaunched the heart-stopping nerves I'd buried, and I groaned, the residual embarrassment returning. How was I supposed to face him in training now?

"Did he kiss you?" Bast asked.

"No!" I rolled my eyes. "Don't you think I'd have said that first?"

“Do you want him to?”

I glared and he laughed. Cheeky bastard.

“I bet he’s better than any boy you’ve lip locked with when you were on the outside.”

My eyes widened at the dark gaze dancing over Bast’s shoulder. The corner of Auden’s mouth quirked up as he tried and failed not to grin. He held a finger to his lips and crossed his arms, settling in to hear Bast’s interrogation of my kissing history. My face was on fire, and I shook my head.

“Oh, well it’s okay if you haven’t,” he continued. “I’m a little shocked, but we all have to start somewhere.”

“That’s not what I...What I mean...I...” How did I explain to Bast that I’d never had the chance to kiss anyone yet? Braxton’s sloppy assault the night Auden found me didn’t count.

“Don’t be embarrassed,” Bast was still clueless to the presence behind him. And Auden’s shoulders shook with suppressed laughter. “Maybe your sexy prince can be your first.”

Fuck. Me.

“First what?” Auden stepped beside Bast who shot up with a squeak.

“Nothing,” he muttered, turning to me with wide eyes.

I glared at them both before turning around and running inside the girl’s dorm. Auden’s chuckles followed me all the way to the attic where we set up the training mats in silence, mostly because I ignored him. I felt him watching me as we moved around one another, like an awkward dance where I tried not to look at my partner.

“So, have you?” Auden broke the ice and walked closer to help as I struggled to roll the punching bag into place.

“Have I what?” I was out of breath, and not only from the strain of the bag.

“Have you been kissed before?”

I took a deep breath and stopped, facing him. "Yes."

His eyes narrowed and inside I smiled with glee. Wasn't expecting that, was he?

"Who?" He challenged, scanning my face for any hint that I was lying, but I wasn't.

"Asher," I smirked. "You should remember. You dared us to do it."

"That didn't count," he tsked, stepping closer, his confident smirk back in place. "It wasn't a real kiss."

I bumped into the bag behind me, not realizing the cat and mouse game Auden was leading. But now, with the bag at my shoulders and Auden only inches away in front of me, I was all too aware. I tried to pretend I was unruffled by our current position.

"Please. What constitutes a real kiss?"

Auden slowly, deliberately, closed the small distance between us, grinning playfully. He leaned down and I hardly dared to breathe.

"I can show you if you like."

I cleared my throat; eyes darting toward the door and warily took a step backward. My last one. There was no more room. Auden's grin turned lopsided as he moved in.

"Where are you going?"

I swallowed. "Nowhere."

"Hmm." His hand gripped my hip with slender fingers as he took that last step, his focus dropping down to my lips. A growl sounded deep in his throat as he tilted his head, and his nose skimmed my cheek. His other hand rested by my head, effectively caging me in. My body shook. Liquid heat pooled in my stomach. Lower. My inner cat purred, loving where this was going. But I...oh damn. Auden's breath was a warm caress on my ear.

"I'd love to be your first."

I ducked under his arm so fast he face-planted into the bag. I was away from him and on the other side of the room when his laughter reached me.

"I guess that's a no."

What was I thinking? I'd almost kissed Auden. *Auden*. My best friend's older brother. A prince. The guy responsible for bringing me back here. The only one standing between me and repopulation. The one who wouldn't hesitate to revoke his protection and throw me in prison if he learned the truth. I killed his baby brother.

"Hey, relax," He called from the other side of the mats. "I'm not mad."

I shook my head, not knowing where to go from here. He must have sensed my panic because he raised his hands and called me over with a challenging smirk.

"I'm sorry. I promise not to do it again," he swore, and my nerves eased. He then crooked his finger, the smug smile gone. "Come on, it's time to get serious."

CHAPTER
TWENTY-ONE

Raindrops made little ripples on the surface of the otherwise still water and tall grass rolled with each gust of wind that shook the treehouse. I scooched further from the window and the impending monsoon. It was that time of year; thunderstorms hit the bayou every afternoon, causing the water to swell and flood, then recede just as fast as it came. Sitting in a waterlogged, wooden box in the trees wasn't the smartest idea when there was lightning around, but I'd been hiding here since breakfast and still couldn't bring myself to leave. Asher was everywhere I looked.

Stacks of books lined all four walls of our childhood hideaway. The broken desk in the corner, the one that took us *ages* to get up here, was littered with Asher's methodical notes and my raunchy drawings. An old pair of shoes and his spare set of glasses. Cards frozen in an unfinished game, held captive under a layer of dust and mold. Our initials were carved into the massive tree trunk that pierced the center of the room and I ran my fingers over the grooves, remembering. It hurt to be here. Hurt so much I nearly had a panic attack when I first climbed inside. But now it was easier.

I thought I needed to avoid anything that reminded me of him. Out of sight out of mind. It served me well these past four years, but I realized now how wrong I was. Was it painful to remember his smile? To look upon his notes and bookmarked pages all waiting for the day he would never return to them? Hell yes. It felt like being gutted by a serrated knife. But Asher didn't deserve to be forgotten. He deserved every tear his memory caused, and every smile. I hadn't planned on coming out here. In fact, I swore to avoid our clubhouse even under the threat of death, but who was I kidding. I was always going to end up here eventually. I blamed a certain dark-haired witch for my impromptu trip today.

I hadn't seen Auden in two days. He was out on some scouting mission he didn't bother to tell me about. Not that I was missing him. And it didn't piss me off that he hadn't at least given me a heads up that he'd be gone for a while. Not at all. The last time I saw him, he was offering to give me my first kiss–which I said no to, but still, a girl could change her mind–

Wait. No.

I shook my head to try and keep that visual at bay. *Dammit.* Damn him and that devilish grin. And those warm eyes that seemed to look right through you. And his hands. Who knew that long fingers could be so attractive? Especially when they gripped your hips and–

Fuck!

I groaned and my head thunked on the wall behind me. Neither could be heard over the dying storm outside. Why couldn't I stop thinking about him? I got over my crush on Auden *years* ago. So then why did he affect me this way? It's not like there could ever be anything between us. Relationships between our peoples happened all the time, but a child between the two *always* resulted in another shifter. That meant a relationship between me and Auden was a no-no. I wasn't saying I wanted Auden's babies, but I also didn't go around making it a habit to dream about boys I couldn't have a future with. Not that I dreamed of Auden.

Shit.

A relationship with Auden was *not* happening. He needed to make little Wardwell babies to carry on his line and besides... there was the whole I killed his brother thing to get over.

"I'm questioning your intelligence if you think it's smart to be in a treehouse during a thunderstorm."

Speaking of Wardwell witches. The one insulting me from below was the only brother I actually wished a gruesome and painful ending for. Asiel. How did he find me?

"What do you want?" I called down, peering through the hole in the floor. The evil prince scowled and folded his arms, the unspoken threat zinging in the air between us. I slid down the rope and landed in front of him, choosing to confront him down here rather than risk tarnishing the memories held above. "What are you doing here, Asiel?" I tried to appear nonchalant, but it was hard to hide the nerves in my tone. He rose a delicate brow and my palms began to sweat, even as I glared. "What are you doing here, *Your Highness?"*

"Much better," he purred. "Can't a guy come check up on his little brother's plaything while he's away?"

I saw red. "*Plaything?*"

The rope I still held, flimsy as it was, I knew would be strong enough to wring Asiel's delicate neck.

He flicked a finger at me. "You do play together every day, do you not?"

My hand twisted around the rope until fibers dug into my skin. "We're training," I managed to get out through gritted teeth.

I released my weapon and turned away. I was dangerously close to treason. Again. But this time, there would be no second chances. If I attacked Asiel, I was done for. I needed to remove myself from the situation before I did something I would regret. See, I could be mature. My foot caught in a mud pocket and my arms flailed. The scabs around my stitches tore and my ankle twisted. I stepped with my other foot but it was stuck as well. Except...there was no mud around it. One tug. Two.

Asiel snickered and dread settled deep in my gut. One brief glance at his clenched fist told me all I needed.

"I didn't say you could leave." His laughter was gone by the time he circled in front of me. "I can't fathom why you'd want to avoid my company. I'm not really the bad guy you think I am."

Disbelief burst from me in a wheeze. "You can't be serious."

"A lot has changed since we were children, Kaya. I've had to grow up in ways you couldn't even begin to understand."

He wasn't the only one. Too bad I didn't believe a word out of his mouth. Asiel grown up? Was that a pig flying over the treehouse?

"It must be so hard to have all the power," I sneered. "And a daddy that lets you do whatever you want with it."

"You have no idea what you're talking about." His clenched fist began to shake, but there was no further pressure on my legs and I casually stood, brushing dirt from my knees.

"Oh really. The Choosing? Tell me that's not you playing God while daddy watches." I needed to shut my mouth. Every taunt was another excuse for him to throw me in repopulation, but I couldn't help it.

"You need to learn when to shut up," he snarled, getting in my face. "You ruined everything by coming back. I tried to protect you. To hide you in the community, safe, with a mate, but you just had to be difficult. Like always."

"What are you talking about?" I pulled away as far as I could without toppling over, but he was still so close.

His eyes were dark pools with small flecks of gold. Uneven scruff covered the lower half of his face, as if he couldn't be bothered and his upper lip curled as he looked me up and down.

"You're not worth it," he huffed, and stepped away. "Stay close to my brother, Kaya. And if he's not around, I suggest you make yourself scarce."

Asiel left without a backward glance, and I was left with so many questions. I spent the walk back to my dorm dodging the last of the raindrops and trying to shake off the eerie vibe I was left with. What did he mean he tried to keep me safe? From what? Himself? If that's why he sought me out today, he had a fucked-up way of showing it. I bypassed my room and snuck up the stairwell to the attic. Punching inanimate objects usually helped to put things into perspective, but it was doing little to help this time. The rain resumed pelting the window as I finished a warmup round. Each jab was punctured by a sting in my shoulder until eventually, a thin line of red dripped from beneath my sleeve. I followed it with my eyes to my elbow and watched it fall to the floor.

"Dammit." I whispered and pulled on my collar to see the damage.

My stitches were neat lines of black that burrowed into my skin. The scabs over them were cracked and blood leaked in each spot, streaking across my skin. I should've taken these out days ago. The thought of rejoining classes made me sick, but I couldn't go on with these things in my shoulder. Any further and they would actually disappear into my arm. Moving closer to the window, I grabbed a knife from the throwing set on the table and went to town. I quickly moved from standing to sitting when I began to sway too much, my equilibrium off while I stared at the tiny knots. A few minutes in and I was still beyond frustrated. The little threads sunk deeper in my skin when I pressed with the knife. It was a battle to not stab myself with my own weapon. More blood stained my shirt with no progress to show for it.

"Come the fuck on!" I threw the knife into the wall, where it stuck with a satisfying *twang*.

"I could've sworn I told you to get those taken out days ago." I jumped and spun, hand over my racing heart, to see Auden standing over me, arms crossed. When did he get back? "Why am I not surprised you didn't listen?" He finished softly.

"I forgot," I mumbled, as I now tried to pick at the scabs with my fingers.

Auden stepped beside me, his abs level with my shoulder. *And only a slight reach away*. I jerked at the stray thought and Auden's arm shot out.

"Be still," he ordered. "Let me look."

It was hard not to fidget when he looked at me like that. My toes curled and uncurled in my shoes as he took his time. Seeming satisfied with whatever decision he'd come to, he pulled a pocketknife from one of his pant pockets, pulled out the tweezers and then opened it to the little pair of scissors.

I snorted. "You're such a Boy Scout."

"Just hold still," he commanded. His hand gently moved up my arm, raising shivers in its wake. "If you'd gone to get them out like you were told to–"

"Ouch!" A stubborn scab clung to my skin like super glue, and I clenched my jaw as Auden worked to get it loose.

"Asher would've been better at this."

I winced again, for a different reason this time. "I don't want to talk about him." Asher's wound felt too fresh after the treehouse.

The snip of the scissors was the only sound until Auden took in a fortifying breath.

"Why not?" He asked. "We need to talk about it at some point. Now is as good a time as any."

There was no way I wanted to talk about Asher while his older brother had a sharp weapon this close to my jugular. I was guilty. Not suicidal.

"I just don't," I replied, and stood abruptly, catching him of guard.

His arm wrapped around the front of my waist, blocking me from taking another step. I avoided his gaze, choosing instead to stare at the wall of weapons.

"Sit down."

Those long fingers stayed firm on my hip until my ass met the chair once more. Then he got back to work on my stitches, working in a tense silence for a little longer before breaking it again.

"It's okay to talk about him." I felt his eyes on my face, judging my reaction, but his hands kept steady.

I shook my head. All the different variations of the truth built behind my teeth. Did I tell him I was sorry? Did I admit to everything? Pretend I didn't know where this conversation would eventually lead? I settled on the only safe version of the truth.

"I don't know what to say."

"That's a first," Auden choked on his laugh, and I glared when it caused him to pull on another sensitive scab. "Sorry."

His hands were as gentle as they could be as I watched his progress. A couple drops of blood began to bead where the scab was a little too attached, but he was doing a good job. Better than me with one hand, anyway.

"It's okay to miss him too, you know. I do. Every damn day."

My eyes stung at the emotion in his voice, and I nodded. "Me too."

His feeble smile matched my own and it was like catching a

glimpse of the old Auden, the one I knew before my life turned upside down. The kind boy who always listened to my problems and never made me feel smaller for voicing them.

"It's been so hard being here," I admitted. "Everything reminds me of him. The smells. The sounds. When something terrible happens, I find myself turning to tell him about it and then remember he's not there. How is that even possible? He's been gone for four years and all of a sudden I find myself forgetting that."

Auden let me speak, nodding as he continued to work. "It was like that for me the first couple years. Every day there was a new obstacle to overcome; something else that would remind me of him that I had to desensitize myself from."

I focused on our breathing. On matching my breaths to his until it no longer felt like my heart would break into tiny pieces and run away.

"You remind me of him sometimes," I whispered.

His smile was broad. "I'll take that as a compliment."

"It's your hair. You look kind of like how I imagined he would as he got older, only less..."

"Hot?" Auden smirked.

I wanted to smack him, but he still had the scissors against my skin. I settled for rolling my eyes. "I was going to say less muscle. He never liked training."

"It's fine if you think I'm the hotter brother," he teased. "You wouldn't be wrong."

"Shut up." I laughed. "You're so vain."

He shrugged but kept grinning. "You had no problem thinking it when we were younger. What was it you had written in that notebook?"

His face was composed in an innocent mask, while mine burned until I was sure I was a different color completely. He didn't mean...

“I have no idea what you’re talking about.” Inside I was freaking out. My diary! He read my diary!

“I’m sure it will come to you,” he continued. “It wasn’t something one forgets easily; you put a lot of work into that cover after all.”

Kill me now. I glanced at the throwing knife in the wall and wondered if I had enough time to grab it and stab myself before he got any further.

“Mrs. Kaya Auden Wardwell. I didn’t know there could be so many variations to one name. Or how many times it could fit on one page.”

I couldn’t hold it in anymore. “You went through my diary! That is just so...*wrong*.”

He wasn’t the least bit apologetic.

“We thought there might be some evidence to tell us where you ran to.”

“This is so embarrassing,” I whined, covering my face with my hands. “Just end me now.”

Through my fingers I saw him smirk and try not to laugh. His pocketknife sat on the floor by his knee, no longer needed, and I seriously thought about lunging for it.

“It’s alright. I thought it was cute. Everyone had a crush or two when they were younger.” He pulled out a jar of ointment I hadn’t noticed before, but I recognized the smell. This was going to sting.

He braced me with his other hand and rubbed the ointment over where the scabs had been. It didn’t hurt as bad as before, probably because the wounds were so tiny this time. He kept rubbing, causing warmth to spread and not just down my arm. He mistook my burning cheeks for latent embarrassment. “You were a kid. It was all in the past.”

“Right,” I swallowed. “The past.”

His eyes cut to me and a small wrinkle formed between

them as he stared. I bet he knew exactly what I was thinking. That the crush I'd tried so hard to fight wasn't in the past. It was very much real and still here. Shit. His eyes widened a small fraction and his fingers stopped moving. I couldn't look away, even though my rapid pants were so fast they resembled an asthma attack.

Auden inched closer, never taking his eyes off me. They danced around my face, checking to make sure I wasn't going to run this time. His hand was heavy on my shoulder. His breath warm on my cheek. Maybe I was going to get that lesson after all.

BOOM!

The thunder shook the window and we jumped apart. Auden still watched me, but the moment was broken, and I gathered what control I had left and stood.

"Thanks for the help," I gave a wobbly smile. "I'll see you for training tomorrow."

I hightailed it out of there before he could convince me to stay. I didn't think I had the strength to turn him down a third time.

CHAPTER
TWENTY-TWO

My heart raced so fast I thought it would give out on me right here in the middle of the trail. I swallowed and kept walking, anything to hold back the nausea that wanted me to blow chunks of my breakfast all over the soft bayou ground. I wasn't ready. In less than five minutes, my life would be over. Again. Instructor Lyra was going to make me shift, and just like last time, I would have to deny her. Free guesses on how that was going to go.

Four minutes.

The whole school would know how defective I was, and the news wouldn't take long to reach the Council. Asiel would be at my door before I even made it out of the gym. His sneer a haunting memory I couldn't shake.

Three minutes.

Auden would hate me. After everything he's done to keep me from repopulation...here I was, practically jumping to the front of the line.

Two minutes.

The algae-stained gym mocked me from the end of the

overgrown path. My classmates filed in. They were happy. Content. Safe in their falsified view of the world.

One minute.

A hand gripped my shirt and pulled me into the trees. Racing heart now in my throat, I swung blindly. My hand connected with a thin tree, and I yelped before another hand covered my mouth.

"Would you calm *down*?" The familiar voice was tinged with annoyance, and I swung again. "Ow!"

"For fucks sake, Bast!" I rubbed my hand and reminded myself not to wrap it around his throat. "You couldn't call out like a normal person?"

Bast's dark skin already showed signs of a bruise, right below the corner of his mouth. His tongue lightly inspected the welt, and I couldn't hide my sly smile.

"I didn't want to draw attention," he shrugged, like the consequence was worth it. "The others couldn't see you yet, so they won't expect you in class. No one knows you got your stitches out."

My frown was quick to form. "So, we're skipping then?"

"Yup," he popped the "p" and shot me a grin. "I've got something to show you."

I wasn't going to argue. He didn't know how close he came to witnessing a full-blown panic attack and anything that kept me away from that class a little longer was okay with me. We spun around and headed back toward my room, Bast leading the way. Surprisingly, he turned right at the fork, leaving the girl's building in the shadows and instead led us up the back stairs of the boy's dormitory. His room was identical to mine, as far as furniture and the layout. But that's where the similarities ended. This room was an explosion of creativity. The ceiling was decorated with glowing stars and planets, and I snickered when I saw neon lizards mixed in as well.

Dirty clothes were piled on the floor and hanging off the end of his bed. Drawers were left half open, his desk was a mess of papers, and his bathroom, thankfully, appeared clean. But it was the walls that really caught my attention. Floor to ceiling, door to window, sketches decorated every free space he had. Detailed portraits. Abstract scenes of animals and landscapes. No two papers were of the same subject.

"I didn't know you could draw." I couldn't hide my awe. My mouth hung open, taking it all in. "These are incredible."

Bast sat on his bed, booting up a laptop and blushing like he'd never received a compliment before. Which, he might not have.

"It's just a hobby," he ducked his head, hiding behind his curls. "What I wanted to show you is on here."

I skipped around his dirty laundry and settled beside him. "How come you get electronics in your room?" I pouted. "They confiscated the iPod I got from my father's house and that was way smaller than this."

"It helps to be invisible sometimes."

I bumped him with my shoulder but didn't comment. He knew I didn't approve of how he was treated. He moved the mouse to his email icon, clicked it open and entered a password.

"My mom sent this to me yesterday," he said, voice low. "It's security footage from the cabin. Of the Shade attack."

I sat on my hands to keep from reaching out and ripping the laptop from his gentle grip. Nightmares of the Shade still stalked me, and I wondered if seeing it again would send those dreams into overdrive, or irradicate them completely. The video took a few minutes to load and I glanced at the door, half expecting guards to break in and confiscate it.

"I thought the Council wanted that event silenced. I'm

surprised they didn't demand your mom hand over the footage."

"Oh, they did," Bast replied. "But she managed to conveniently misplace it."

"Good for her." I was impressed by his mom's disregard for the Council and their commands. My kind of woman.

The video was low quality but not grainy. The cabin's lowlights didn't provide much to see by, but when the section of the wall blew apart, the light from outside made everything clearer. We watched our digital selves crawl around the debris in our attempt to escape. I remembered that moment all too well, it was how my nightmares always started. The Shade was a swath of black in a humanoid shape that moved amongst the wreckage, only appearing in detail when he was corporeal. I watched us trip. The Shade smiled. Bast went full wolf and we attacked. Looking from the outside, I was surprised we survived. We were so small compared to the demon and weak in comparison. Then came the moment Bast went sailing across the cabin. I held my breath as digital me reached out. A red light flashed across the screen, diminished until it surrounded only Bast, then extinguished completely once he was on the floor. The video continued through to the end. I closed my eyes when the Shade bit me, but the rest was the same; Auden showed up, we killed the Shade, and the screen went black.

"What was that red light?"

"That's what my mom wanted to know too." Bast shook his head, at a loss as much as I was. "She was hoping you could tell us what you did."

"What *I* did?" He rewound the footage. Red stained the screen again. "That wasn't me," I swore, but it wasn't that convincing.

My mind ran wild. Unexplained moments from my childhood, some even more recent, came back in waves. The warmth in my hand when I reached for Bast in that cabin. The red glow that appeared the night the Amon demon tried to burn me to a crisp. The thousand and one times my antics with Asher should have killed us both.

"I—" I closed my eyes and took a breath. "How is this possible?"

The laptop was closed now. Bast set it on his desk and paced about the room, dodging piles of clothes as he thought.

"How am I a wolf?" He asked. "Genetics seems to be the most plausible answer."

"I've never heard of a single shifter with powers, B."

"There's a first for everything," he grinned, but I didn't return it.

Finding out I might have a hidden power didn't sit well with me. I was only marginally good at being a shifter, I didn't need this drama on top of everything else I had going on.

"Why don't you try it." He was still grinning.

My eyes bugged. "What, *now*?"

And that's how we spent the rest of the morning trying to recreate the mysterious red power caught on film. It was easier said than done. For one thing, I didn't know how it worked. If it was truly me, wouldn't I feel something? I looked inside myself but only found a bored cat, swatting at nothing and waiting for something exciting to happen. Her and me both.

"Maybe it's not an offensive power," Bast suggested, after another futile attempt of me flinging my hand out.

I was starting to sweat, my arms hurt, and I felt six different types of stupid.

"If you're suggesting you jump out the window and for me to try and save you, I won't object," I growled, beyond annoyed and done with trying.

He raised his hands in surrender. "Practicing in my room

isn't the best idea anyway. We should find a place more secluded next time."

"Next time!"

"You know, in case it works," he amended.

"We don't even know what it is!" I cried.

I felt another load of stress press down on my chest. It wanted to suffocate me, and I had half a mind to let it. Why couldn't I be a normal girl?

"I can't deal with this too," I moaned, and rubbed my temples. "My days are bad enough now that I have to rejoin Instructor Lyra's class."

The panic about that class was always in the back of my mind, never giving me more than a moment of peace. It took a lot of strength to not let it consume me. A strength that was weakening each hour I worried about it.

"Why do you fight her?" Bast asked. "It's easier to just do as she says."

"Easy for you maybe," I mumbled, then sighed. The weight of this one secret was too heavy to carry alone and I thought it would feel more like pulling teeth to get the words out, but they jumbled behind my teeth, fighting to be first after being held in for so long. "I... can't shift," I huffed in one breath.

The silence that followed would have been comical if I didn't feel so much like crying. Bast kicked a pile of clothes out of the way and sat on the floor in front of me, his face open and confused. No judgement. I immediately felt more relaxed.

"What do you mean? Have you never...?"

"Nope," I admitted, picking at my fingers.

"She might be able to help you," he suggested, meaning our Instructor. "That *is* what her class is for."

I shook my head and choked on the ball of dread in my throat. The thought of that vile woman finding out...I couldn't stomach it.

"No one can know, B. No One." My eyes pleaded for secrecy. "If the Council finds out...if my father...I won't graduate." We both knew what that meant.

Our shoes touched in a light game of footsies, and I smiled at Bast's attempt to comfort me.

"You know I won't tell," he promised. "And I'll help any way I can."

I nodded in thanks and wondered at what I'd need to do to make a shift happen. Why was it so hard for me? I heard others say that shifting into their animal form was freeing, but for me it was the exact opposite. It was painful and I came to dread it each time it felt like I was losing control. That's why I fought so hard to keep her in check. Repeatedly breaking multiple bones wasn't freeing, it was torture.

"I know I'm not supposed to hate it, but I do." Bast looked up in surprise at my confession and I frowned. I thought he of all people would understand seeing as he shifted into an animal that caused him such grief. It wasn't exactly the same, but it was close.

"You hate your animal?" He looked horrified at the very thought, and I realized I might have assumed wrong about him.

I shook my head, not sure how to explain it. "I don't hate *her*, just the actual shifting." My voice got smaller. "It hurts."

The corner of Bast's eyes turned down in pity. "Honey, it's not supposed to hurt."

"It's not?" I asked, hopeful.

"No," he scooched closer and leaned against one of my legs.

Our silence was both comfortable and contemplative. It was news to me that pain wasn't supposed to go along with this whole experience. I knew I shouldn't fear shifting, but that's just how it was for me. Maybe if I was guided by a mentor, like what was supposed to happen, my many attempts wouldn't have been so painful.

"We'll figure it out," Bast promised. "You're not in this alone anymore."

Some of my stress melted away. Friendship. I missed it. Someone who stood by your side no matter what and the confidence that came with that knowledge. The person who laughed with you over ridiculous things. Who you fought with but never truly stayed mad at. Someone who knew all your secrets and you knew theirs. Someone you could count on. My smile slipped when I thought of Asher, of the one secret that got harder and harder to keep, and hoped I never failed my new friend like I did my old one.

THE BOY'S dorm backed onto a thick part of the swamp, graciously providing enough cover for me to sneak out. The ground was spotted with sink holes and mud. Vines and overgrown vegetation reached out in a tangle of thorns and poison ivy; encouraged to grow to keep the two sexes apart. No set path cut through here, but students had worn down their own over the years. I silently thanked the brave few that came before to mark the easiest way and deftly avoided the swamp's attempt at breaking my neck. My stomach rumbled its displeasure at missing lunch; a common occurrence these past couple days, but I pushed through it. I had no time to eat before I needed to be in Fox's class. It was practical week, which meant we left the gym to engage in real-life situations. The goal was to get a feel for what awaited us on the outside. The probability of training drills being similar to a real demon attack were as likely as my father leaving the house in anything but a freshly pressed shirt, but it could be fun. I ducked under a fern, darted to the right and there...the garden. It was a quick jog to the amphitheater from here.

"Kaya!"

I stopped; shoulders hunched at the tone. Shit. What did I do now? Auden leaned against a trellis, arms and ankles crossed, and his face set. I could see the dent in his brow from here, and his jaw was clenched so hard he was in danger of chipping a tooth. If this were a cartoon, steam would be billowing out from his ears. I was used to seeing his anger, his glares, but it's been a while since one made an appearance and I found myself getting nervous. I thought we were in a better place. Auden separated from the shadows and strode toward me, his gate eating the space between us in seconds.

"I went to meet you after your class, hoping to walk you to lunch. Can you guess what happened next?"

"I—"

"Instructor Lyra said you never attended! And *then* I see you sneaking away from the male dormitories." He cursed under his breath and swiped a hand through his already tangled hair. He took a step forward, then stopped. "Whose room were you in all morning?"

I reared back. "Come again?"

I'd never seen Auden this worked up. And over nothing. His hands were fists at his sides. Slowly opening and closing like he couldn't control them. He looked down at me, nostrils flaring as a flush worked its way up his neck.

"Whose. Room."

"B-bast's," I stammered. "What's it matter to you?"

"Unsupervised visits are prohibited, Kaya. It's like you want to prove my brother right."

"I didn't do anything wrong!" I argued. "He's my friend."

Was he seriously about to lecture me right now? About hanging with Bast?

"Were you alone?" he countered, a disapproving arch to his brow.

"Yes," I snapped, officially annoyed. "Not that it's any of your business."

"That's where you're wrong," he hissed, his eyes frenzied.

I backed away and he paused, shaking his head. When he looked at me again, his gaze gentled.

"I don't know what you want me to say," I stated, calmly. Hands up like I was trying to ease an animal. "I'm sorry that I missed class, but nothing happened."

Auden blew out a breath, shoulders sinking. It was like a wave came over him and I watched as he deflated, the anger slowly leaving. Talk about whiplash. Pissed off one second and contrite the next. I'd seen enough horror movies to know that if he started laughing, I needed to get the salt.

"You know Bast doesn't see me like that, right?" Auden was already aware of Bast's preferences, but maybe reminding him would help calm him down.

A small voice whispered that Auden was jealous, and I lost the battle to keep a smile off my face. I twisted and stepped under the branch of a large cypress tree to casually lean against its trunk. When I turned again, Auden joined me in the shade.

"You were right the first time, Kaya," he sighed. "It's none of my business."

From a green-eyed beast to this moody shadow. I needed a manual on his mood swings.

"Then why were you so upset?" I asked, head tilted to the side.

Auden being jealous of Bast...it didn't make sense.

He gave a strained laugh and rubbed the back of his neck. "Because you ditched class to be alone with a guy in his room? Because just the thought made me want to turn into a caveman, throw you over my shoulder, and run in the opposite direction. Because of how you're looking at me right now." His voice deepened and his hand reached out, but he pulled it back just as quick with another curse. "I don't want to push you," he insisted. "You've told me more than enough times that you don't want to kiss me."

I think I was in shock. Auden *was* jealous. My heart skipped at the realization.

"I never said that." I slapped my hands over my mouth, panic blossoming. It was the truth, but should I really be encouraging this?

He scanned my face with an incredulous grin. "So, you do want to kiss me."

I dropped my hands. "I didn't say that either."

His chuckle was paired with a smirk and the combination did funny things to my insides. "You have to pick one."

Why did he suddenly seem closer? I didn't see him move but every time I took a breath, his scent overwhelmed me.

"I'm indifferently...undecided." I rasped, lifting my chin.

"Indifferent, huh?" He tutted. "Do I make you nervous, Kaya?"

I gulped. "No."

"You're a terrible liar."

My fingers dug into the bark at my back as I shook my head; maybe a little too zealously. He was so close now; one small move and I could touch him. Or he could touch me.

"I'm not lying."

"A pathetically ineffective liar," Auden repeated.

"Screw you." My face was heated as he both verbally and physically backed me into a corner.

Auden slowly scanned my body, and I swore he could see right through me. He took note of where my hands clutched at the tree, of how my chest rose and fell in rapid breaths. I watched him watch me, until finally, his eyes stared directly back into mine.

"Then tell me why you're so flushed." He took a step and

deliberately glanced at my chest then back at my face. "You're panting, squirming where you stand, and your pupils are dilated." He hit me with another grin, the corner of his mouth barely teasing up. "I don't need heightened senses to know you're attracted to me. I'm just reading the signs your body is offering and waiting for that pretty mouth to give me the okay."

I stopped breathing. I might have even died for a minute; either that or my heart exploded. I tried to choke down my nerves, but they grew with every second Auden stood there. Watching. Waiting. Fuck, how did he expect me to function after that? I opened my mouth. Closed it. My nails scraped more bark.

"I, uh—" I cleared my throat. "I'm going to be late for class."

If my hands weren't covered with tree, I would face palm myself. Why did I have to be so fucking awkward?

"Hmm." Auden gave me space, but still kept that smug, wide smile. "I think I see what's going on."

I scooted to the side, one hand on the tree. "Nothing is going on."

A few more steps and we were level with one another. He turned, his body tracking mine. "Agree to disagree."

One more knowing smile and he walked away. I was so fucked. This boy was going to be the end of me. I just knew it.

CHAPTER
TWENTY-THREE

Everyone was naked. I heard it's common to have nightmares of standing in front of your classmates with all your private bits on display...well, this was the opposite of that. I wrapped my arms around myself, subconsciously hugging my shirt closer, as the last of my classmates shifted.

"We're all waiting on you, Thornton," Instructor Lyra announced. "Now's not the time to be shy."

Little chuffs could be heard from the already shifted familiars. They mingled with the snickers from their awaiting partners. If ever in a situation that allowed, disrobing before shifting kept your clothes intact. Because, unfortunately, even though we lived in a world full of magic, no one had yet to invent a way for my clothes to travel with me when I changed into my animal form. It was either take them off first or shred them to pieces. The first and only time I fully shifted, I got stuck in my American Eagle sweater. It sucked more than you would think. And if it wasn't obvious, nudity wasn't a big deal to my people. It wasn't like you could carry around a bag of clothes when fighting a demon. Naked men and women were a common sight around here. But seeing and doing were two totally different experiences.

"I think I can serve my partner better in this form, thanks." I crossed my arms and settled in.

Instructor Lyra looked seconds away from strangling me and the other teachers present didn't appear inclined to stop her.

"That is not the assignment, Thornton. Stop being difficult and *shift*."

I refused. "Instructor Fox said you and the other teachers would play the role of demons for this practical and that our objective was to find our colored flag—I mean, target—and bring it to home base safely."

"That is correct," Fox confirmed with a definitive nod.

"Well, I know from personal experience that outside these walls, I can't just roam around in animal form whenever I want. And leaving my witch defenseless while I wait in the car or hide in some trees is not performing to the best of my abilities. I will shift when the moment calls for it and not a second sooner."

Instructor Lyra took a step toward me, but Fox put a hand out to stop her.

"This is a practical. She must perform as honestly as if she were on the outside." His gaze met mine. "I'll allow it."

Cace rolled his eyes beside me. It sucked that I was paired with this chauvinistic asshole again, but at least I'd dodged the larger bullet. Now I just had to find a way to complete this practical without having to shift. I glanced at Lincoln. Or get naked.

"Begin."

At Fox's command, all twenty pairs took off in random directions. We had no idea where our flag was hidden, but we were given a general direction and instructions to subdue any "demons" we came upon. The instructors would defend the flags, but Fox enlisted the help of off duty guards to provide more realistic practice.

"Your cat's sense of smell would be more beneficial to us," Cace spoke from beside me, his head on a swivel. "You'd smell the demons before we saw them."

"My senses are more heightened than yours, even in this form," I argued.

We stepped into the trees and my eyes automatically adjusted to the diminished lighting. Cace stopped as his human pupils took longer to acclimate, and I fought the urge to gloat. He really should worry more about himself.

He sighed, "Why do you have to be so difficult?"

A tree branch snapped to our right and I dodged before he had a chance to shout. A guard, dressed in all black and wearing a Halloween mask of—seriously? The devil? — lunged from the shadows of an overgrown fern. I caught his arm, ducked under it, and twisted until it was splayed out like a chicken wing. Cace hadn't even moved yet.

"Throw the damn potion!" I called out, breaking him from his stupor.

"Is that really necessary?" The guard whined. "You've already technically beaten me."

"Hush, demon," I growled, as Cace finally got his shit together and threw a bottle of fake potion.

The glass broke and a pungent, purple liquid stained the guard's chest. Now the instructors would know we'd taken one demon down so far. The fake demon sighed and ambled off into the trees to wait for his next victim.

"See," I grinned. "I told you we'd be fine."

Forty-five minutes later, I was at the top of a tall cypress, pulling moss from my hair and straining my vision. There. Our purple flag lay only a few more yards away, tied to the dock of our designated swimming hole. Nets and buoys cordoned off the area to keep out the gators, but when you could shift into a giant cat, who cared about an oversized lizard?

"I see it!" I called down to Cace, smugly.

I told him that if I'd been in animal form, I wouldn't be able to climb this high to find our target and he couldn't climb a tree to save his life. One branch up and he started to shake. He was slowly coming around to my way of thinking, but we hadn't come across an instructor yet, only guards. With the instructors playing Upper demons, I'd be expected to shift to team up with my partner. Luck was going to leave me sooner or later. My feet made contact with the earth and I brushed my hands together, ignoring the sticky sap now clinging to my fingers.

"Maybe we should circle around and approach from the water," I suggested. "Whoever's guarding our target wouldn't see us coming." Meaning *maybe* we wouldn't have to engage them at all, and I could keep my secret for another day.

"Yeah, okay." Cace agreed. "How about from behind the boat house?"

I stopped, eyes wide. "That's actually...not a bad idea."

Cace almost smiled but remembered who he was talking to and quickly switched it to a sneer.

"I wasn't looking for your approval." He stomped away, leaving me no choice but to follow or be left behind.

It really was a good idea. From the boat house, around the bend from the swimming hole, we could sneak into the water unseen. A small trip downstream, a quick snag of the flag, and we'd head back to base without being intercepted by an instructor. If only life were that easy. I knew better by now that nothing ever went according to plan. Not for me. The ground didn't shake this time, but there was still a demon inside the walls. A real one. Cace and I stood unmoving behind the boat house, neither one of us wanting to believe what we saw before us.

The king. Our king. Auden's *father* was standing in front of a demon. *Conversing* with it. I wasn't sure what type it was. An Upper level, if I had to guess based off its humanoid shape. Higher even than a Shade, possibly. It stood on two solid legs, encased in a rich black leather. A serpentine tail slithered behind it, the end flicking to and fro in an oddly hypnotic manner. I shook my head. The demon had no hair and no ears but tilted its head as the king spoke like it could understand him just fine. What was the king doing meeting with a demon? Why didn't he slay it?

For fuck's sake, I didn't even see a weapon on him.

"Shift, Kaya," Cace whispered, rising into a crouch. "If we can catch them off guard, we can—"

"What?" I whisper-shouted. "We can what? Die? Because that's what will happen if they see us." The stubborn witch pressed his lips in a firm line but didn't argue. "We need to get back to campus." I inched away from the boat house. "We're not equipped to handle this."

I'd learned my lesson with the Shade. Even with Auden's help, we almost died. The king was three times as powerful as Auden. And paired with an Upper demon? Fuck that. It was hard, so hard to silence the screaming thoughts in my head. The king was a traitor. How long had this been going on? Was Asiel a part of it? Did Auden know? I suppressed a hysterical laugh bubbling its way up my throat. We were so irrevocably screwed.

I clutched Cace's elbow and gently pulled him back with me, lest he got another idea about becoming a victim. My eyes didn't leave the king or his demon friend. Each breath I took was riddled with fear that they'd see us before we could escape. It would only take one small turn, there wasn't much for us to hide behind once we stepped far enough away from the boat house. Then it happened. Cace, or me—I wasn't sure which—got caught in a mud pocket and we both went down. It wasn't graceful and it wasn't quiet. I had a sickening sense of déjà vu as the demon's head slowly turned our way.

It had no eyes. A refined nose and large mouth were the only features it possessed. And when it smiled? My breakfast was in my throat. I had only enough time for one word when the ground shook.

"Run."

I was on my feet after the first tremor. Was the king calling more demons? My legs felt like Jell-O, like they weren't even attached to me as I stumbled and fought to remain upright. I clutched Cace's collar and pulled, but he moved like a newborn fawn; legs splayed in an awkward imitation of standing. The scent of rotting earth and dead fish smothered my senses and I gagged. A bony hand wrapped around Cace's ankle, and his eyes went wild, rolling with fear. He was yanked from my grip and landed on his stomach hard enough to knock the air from his lungs. A small head, bracketed by fins on either side of its beady eyes, floated at the shoreline. I followed its hungry gaze to where Cace clawed at the ground, the soft earth doing nothing to help him escape. I scrambled toward him, barely fast enough.

My nails dug into his wrists, leaving bloody half-moon shapes visible through the mud coating his arms. The ground was too soft. No matter how hard I pulled, there was nothing to anchor myself against. We slid with each tug, growing ever closer to the water and the hungry demon waiting inside it.

"Help me, Kaya!" Cace pleaded, his eyes round with terror.

I tightened my grip, feeling bone beneath my fingernails, but he slipped from my grasp as the Tennin demon pulled him to the water's edge like one reeled in a hooked fish.

"No! No!" Cace cried out, sinking all ten fingers into the mud.

I reached, stretched, moved faster than I thought possible in my human form, but it still wasn't enough. Cace disappeared beneath the water with a final scream and a flurry of bubbles. The water thrashed, turned a deep red, then stilled. The ground beneath me still shook, but the water was nothing more than ripples now. Until that bony hand returned to throw a steaming pile of skin and organs back onto the shore. What was left of Cace squelched with each new vibration and I finally lost the contents of my stomach. When there was nothing left, I wiped my mouth with the back of my hand then froze.

The Tennin was back, eyeing me as it tried to decide how to take the bones from my body next. My shoes slipped in mud and vomit as I clambered onto my hands and feet. I'd fucking bear-crawl out of here if I had to. Claws gripped the ground better than my fingertips and I was up and moving. The Tennin lunged, throwing its full body out of the water. It's slippery eel-like skin looked like rotting flesh and smelled like it too. The oversized appendages it used to tear Cace apart gave it enough reach to catch me in two strides. I dove to the side, barely missing its grip. One stride now. Mud was up to my wrists, the earthquakes doing nothing in my favor. Each movement suctioned me further and I knew I wouldn't be quick enough to dodge the demon a second time. Warmth built in my gut, fueled by fear and my absolute will to live. I refused to go out like this. My bones would not be stolen for whatever sick need this demon had for them.

The Tennin swayed on all fours, watching. Waiting. It was just enough time for whatever was in me to build, because when the demon charged, a bright red barrier sprung up between us. I heard the hiss of burnt flesh before I smelled it and the demon howled with rage. I focused. Again and again, I searched for the trigger to my power, but nothing moved inside me. *Please don't tell me I'm a one-hit-wonder.* The Tennin readied to pounce.

"Move!"

An iron net spread above me. I had seconds to roll out of the way before it landed over the Tennin, trapping it against the ground. The instructors and a few guards surrounded it, tossing potion after potion upon it. Words of power echoed over the receding tremors, and I lost control over my stomach again.

"Thornton!" Instructor Lyra shouted, keeping an eye on the witches at work. "Where is your partner?"

I glanced at the shoreline without really seeing. The memory of Cace's death would live on in my memory forever; there was no forgetting it. Their gazes followed mine to the messy pile of organs, skin, and torn clothes.

"Take her back to the others."

I heard the order but wasn't tuned in. I was aware of my surroundings just enough to notice that the king and his Upper demon were gone. Like they'd never been there at all.

From where I sat in the corner of the cafeteria, I could see everyone. Back in human form, and fully dressed once more, thank you. The usual jokes and endless chatter were gone, replaced with a weighted silence, fearful glances out the windows, and whispers from those spying on the guards near the doors. The ground stopped shaking before they brought me here, and I was pretty positive killing the Tennin is what made it stop. Honestly, I wasn't too sure how it all worked exactly. The king could let demons past the walls but couldn't disable the barrier spell? Or did he *want* it to go off as a warning? A head start? To keep up pretenses? I blew out a breath. Fuck. My head hurt. Another round of whispers escaped the guard's notice, but I heard them just fine. Cace. One of the tables behind me was talking about him. No one else knew what happened yet, only that he hadn't returned with me.

A gentle hand patted my arm. "Ignore them."

I hadn't had the chance to tell Bast either, but he could tell by my expression that it wasn't good. I slid my chair closer, not wanting to be overheard, but he shook his head. From his bag, he pulled out a pen and paper, then pushed them across the table.

You okay? Was scrawled at the top in his neat handwriting.

I shook my head and scribbled, *He's dead.* Bast paled and I added, *Tennin demon.*

"Oh shit," he breathed, and I glanced around to make sure no one paid attention.

"I saw something else."

Bast gestured back at the paper. I picked up the pen, but hesitated, not sure if it was safe to write it down. Then again, our king was working with the enemy, so safety was relative at this point.

We saw the king with a demon.

Bast's entire body stopped moving as he stared at the paper with an intensity I'd never seen from him.

"The Tennin?" He mouthed, deepening the lines around his lips as he scowled.

I shook my head again and wrote, *Upper.*

Bast stifled a curse with his fist. I eyed him carefully. He wasn't confused; he was furious, practically vibrating in his seat.

"What aren't you telling me?" I whispered, rather than take the time to write it down.

He looked over my shoulder, locking eyes with someone, and grabbed the pen.

My mother.

"Your mo—*pfhh.*" His warm hand covered my mouth, but I was too surprised to do more than glare.

Not here.

Bast removed his hand. The cafeteria doors squeaked open to reveal Instructor Lyra. Her eyes scanned the room, stopping on me for a breath, then ghosting past with a barely disguised sneer of disdain.

"The breach has been dealt with," she announced. "Please return to your dorms until the dinner bell."

She left without a backwards glance and my classmates swiftly followed. Bast crumpled our note and shoved it to the bottom of his bag. We kept to the back of the group as the guards escorted us to the dorms. Bast grabbed my arm and dove into the trees.

"Where are we going?" I gasped, keeping pace with his steady stride.

"You need to talk to my mother," he replied. "I can't tell you more than that."

"Can't, or won't?"

He pulled me down as another patrol wandered by.

"It's not my place, Kaya. She can explain it better." We stayed crouched as we crossed the path, only standing once we were far enough away to not be caught. "I bet you've figured out more than you think."

The problem was trying to think around the shock. I knew things were different now; the tone of the whole community was off. But I never would have assumed it was because our king was selling us out to the demons. Asiel I would believe—he was most likely in on it.

"I tried to protect you."

His words came back to me and they almost—not quite—clicked into place. I was missing a lot of pieces to this puzzle. Pieces I fully intended to get answers to. The outpost looked exactly the same, sans the Imps and with a new plywood décor over the windows and giant hole in the wall. We slid away a smaller piece and stepped inside to an empty room. The dust and damage were swept away and hidden, the clothes righted on what shelves remained. Soft voices came from below and we followed them through the back door and down the stairs. Magic made the holding cells impossible to escape and kept the water from flooding rooms *far* below the water table, but it couldn't keep out the mildew and dank air.

Past the cells was another small room, dominated by a large table. Five figures stooped around it, bent over papers they quickly tried to cover. I recognized all but one of the faces from the Shade attack. The other was a fair-haired man too lanky to be a familiar.

"What happened?" Adira asked, worry creasing her brow. "Students were sent to the dorms."

Bast looked to me for an answer, but I was too busy examining the room. The maps on the table and walls were of the community and surrounding swamp. Blueprints of the campus too. Weapons were stashed in the corners on top of large crates that I assumed held even more. All at once, the pieces finally clicked. Adira's hostility when Bast first brought me to the cabin, her worry over my father finding out, her telling me that things weren't what they seemed. The fact that this room looked like a war room...

"There was another demon attack," I said, finally finding my voice. "We were out on practicals and my partner was killed."

Adira's head tilted to the side as she looked me over. The room was silent, like someone hit pause and when she finally spoke, it was void of any feeling. "That's a tragedy, truly it is. But it doesn't explain why you're here."

"Because I saw the *king* working with a demon and I don't think that comes as a surprise to you."

The smaller witch—the one I hadn't recognized—cursed and moved toward me, but Adira stilled him with a hand.

"You would assume correct," she admitted.

"*Adira*!" The witch hissed. "Her father—"

"Is unaware that his partner converses with demons," she interrupted, voice hard. "That is not the issue I have with him, Nolen."

A small part of me swelled in relief that my father wasn't a part of whatever this was. He was a monster in his own right, but at least he was loyal to our people. It was clear to me now, we needed as many of those as we could get. Nolen shut his mouth, but his distrust of me couldn't be turned off. I felt it burning the side of my face as he held his glare.

"We've worked in secret to expose and overthrow the king." Adira's hand swept in a circle around the table. "For the past four years, those in this room have built and led a secret resistance, working tirelessly to gather enough evidence."

"Four years?" I whispered. Out of everything she just said, that's what my mind latched on to.

"Since the very night you disappeared."

CHAPTER
TWENTY-FOUR

We were alone. Adira took one look at my face and cleared the others out, much to my relief. I sank into an empty chair, still trying to wrap my head around today. Nolen spit curses the entire way out, and I was glad he wouldn't be present to hear what I had to say. Bast held my hand as the maelstrom of emotions overrode the working half of my brain and the door shut with a soft click as Adira pulled up a chair across from us.

"The room is soundproof," she offered. "No one can hear what is said."

I nodded but couldn't get my thoughts in order enough to do more. It was all connected. That's what I kept circling back to. The day Asher died, the king, the recent spree of demon attacks. The strange feeling that followed me since my arrival, how the community wasn't the same, *all of it.*

"I honestly thought you already knew," Adira admitted. "Why else would you have run?"

I blanched. She thought the king was why I ran? I swallowed over a dry throat and slowly shook my head. This went back to the first demon attack, to the night Asher died. How long before that was the king working with the demons? Would Asher be alive today even if we had stayed inside?

"W-we...Asher and I...snuck over the wall that day." I could still picture it clearly in my mind. The freedom. The relief at being away from my father. "There were demons. T-they got Asher before I even knew what was happening and I ran."

Guilty tears clouded my vision when I looked at Adira, then to my right at Bast.

"I didn't know they were there. I didn't know about the king. I swear!"

"Shh." Bast wrapped an arm around me. "Of course you didn't. No one knew what was coming. It's not like you climbing over the wall called them any sooner."

"But maybe it did," his mom murmured, finger to her chin.

"Mom!" Bast admonished, and I tried not to choke on my guilt.

"I only meant that some of the demons—whichever ones found them— were probably drawn to her," she amended. "Were you bleeding that day?"

I tried to think back, but nothing definitive jumped out at me.

"I always had scrapes and cuts back then, from training or running with Asher. It's possible."

But what did that have to do with anything? Why would the demons focus on me if they were after an entire island of people?

"So the demons were drawn to her, bust through the broken spell, thanks to the king, and continue to torment us for... amusement?" Bast asked, his arm still around me, and sounding just as confused as I was.

"None of this makes any sense," I moaned, dropping my head into my hands. There was so much more to this than I originally thought. Seeing the king betray us was one thing, but for four years, that he might have had something to do with killing his own son, it was inconceivable. If anything, he shared the blame for Asher. That didn't make me feel better.

"Buck up, kiddo. Things are going to get worse before they get better."

"Mom," Bast groaned.

"What?" Adira leaned back in the chair, arms crossed. "I've been saying it to you for years."

"Doesn't mean it helps," Bast mumbled, and I let out a soft laugh. It was good to see them act like a family, even now. I felt part of it and that was comforting in its own way.

"She's right," I sniffed and dipped my chin, ready to face what was next or fake it till I was. "What do you know?"

Adira watched me with a calculating eye and when I passed whatever inspection she had going, she nodded back.

"The question is, what do you?" she asked. "Bast showed you the video, yes?"

It would take more than one afternoon to get over what I saw on that security video but managing to replicate it was doing wonders at getting me to accept it.

"Yes," I admitted. "We tried yesterday to make it happen again, but it was useless."

Bast snorted. "It really was. We had no idea how to trigger it short of summoning another Shade."

His mother glared at him, like even suggesting it could bring down another storm of demons. Once today was plenty, thanks, and even though the Tennin brought the power out of me, I wasn't in a rush to try it again any time soon.

"I might have figured that out, actually." At their raised eyebrows, I added, "Sorta."

I told them in great detail—at Adira's insistence— what happened by the boathouse. I was pretty sure my fear was linked to activating the power. Either for myself or those I cared about, like what happened with Bast. The problem was, I couldn't control it. Even when I needed it. That Tennin demon would have turned me into a matching pile of goo if the instructors hadn't shown up. Even now, there was no power lying dormant inside of me that I could sense.

"Did the king see you use it?" There was a trace of worry in her tone, but you couldn't tell by her face. I bet she was great at poker.

I shrugged, now worried about the possibility. "I don't know how long he and that other demon stood around to watch." What if the king saw me? I pictured a manhunt like they sent after Bast and shuddered.

Adira nodded to herself before checking the time.

"It's of the utmost importance that you learn to harness this power," she told me. "Bast will help, and when your schedule allows, you will come here."

Bast shot me a grin and I rolled my eyes. I already knew what practicing with him meant; lots of throwing my arm at the wall and him trying his best to scare me.

"You children need to get back to the dorms before they notice you missing." Her strong hands pushed at our backs, practically shoving us out the door. I dug my heels in.

"You want me to go back?" My fingers caught on the door frame, but she pushed harder. "After what I just told you?"

"We can't exactly hide you here." Another shove and I was forced to climb the stairs.

"The demons are literally targeting me, and the king might have seen me use that power." The sparsely covered hole in the wall loomed closer and my words came out faster. She dragged me across the floor. "How can I go back to my dorm?"

Would putting my desk chair under the doorknob be enough to keep them out? What about my window? Maybe I could sleep in the bathroom for an extra layer of protection. Panic took over all future planning.

"The king won't make an outright move against you," Adira promised, and I let out a small sigh of relief. "He's playing the long game. But you need to be more cautious until we figure something out." She gave me a look. "Be careful who you choose as your friends."

The wooden board was moved back into place, and we were left outside to find our way back to campus. We stayed quiet as we snuck past more patrols and I thought over Adira's last warning. Bast was my only friend here and clearly, he was trustworthy. Who did she—I tripped and caught myself. Auden. She meant Auden. A sick feeling took root in my gut. Him being involved hadn't occurred to me. Was that trust? Or willful ignorance? The idea that he could be a part of this made me want to pull my hair out and my conscience played tug-of-war with itself. Auden wasn't like that. But he was the king's son. He was kind and goodhearted. But he hunted me down and forced me back against my will. He was my friend. But it might all be part of his plan. Back and forth I went, tallying a mental list of pros and cons. Nothing outright screamed his innocence or that he was guilty. Going right up and asking him was also out of the question. What was I supposed to do?

The door to my dorm shut behind me as I continued on the painful merry-go-round in my mind. I had no trouble sneaking back in and I didn't have the mental strength right now to analyze what that said about our current security or my overall safety. I pulled my desk across the room to block the door. At least I'd have a heads up if I needed to jump out the window.

Another summer storm battered the windows that night, washing away all evidence of the Tennin attack. By tomorrow, even the gouges Cace's fingers left in the mud would be gone, the earth wiped clean of yet another tragedy. The thunder played itself out hours ago, but the steady pitter-patter of the rain on the glass was soothing enough to lull me to sleep. At least, until the abrupt *thud* of someone trying to enter my room broke the bubble of peace. Muffled curses cut through the shadows after another attempt at the door. I rolled off the bed and landed in a crouch. The closest weapon I had was my knife under my pillow. It was clutched firmly in one hand as I backed away from my bed and toward the dresser. Open ground was safer to engage an attacker and I could always duck into the bathroom if I was overwhelmed.

The desk was roughly pushed away, allowing the tall figure to squeeze between it and the door. My palm grew damp with sweat, but there was no time to wipe it before the intruder crept closer. They aimed for my bed; hand outstretched toward my pillow. With a battle cry, I lunged, knife pointed down in a dangerous arc. The intruder spun, catching my wrist before the knife could make contact.

"I didn't think I pissed you off enough to warrant a knife in the back," Auden grimaced as he looked at the weapon inches from his chest. "I knew I was going to regret giving that back."

"What the hell!" I cried and pulled my wrist from his grip. "I could have killed you."

He had the audacity to smirk. "Nah. You've got to be quicker than that to get me."

Strangle him. I wanted to wrap my bare hands around his throat and strangle him.

"Do you mind telling me why you're sneaking into my room in the middle of the night?" I crossed my arms to keep my hands from doing what my brain demanded, pent up adrenaline forcing my fingers to tap.

"Care to tell me why there's a desk in front of your door?" He countered; one brow lifted in a challenge.

"To keep out the demons," I muttered, then rolled my eyes when he started to laugh. "After a day like mine, *anything* is better than nothing."

That sobered him and he plopped on the edge of my bed with a cringe.

"You're right," he apologized. "That's actually why I'm here. To talk about what happened."

"And you thought the middle of the night was the appropriate time?"

He gestured at the bed with a tilt of his head, his lips curled in a tease. "I won't bite."

My toes curled on the carpet. Something about that grin told me he would indeed bite...if I asked him to. I kept my arms crossed and sat on the floor instead, far from temptation. He blinked at my small act of defiance but didn't call me out on it.

"Are you okay?" He asked softly, after a moment or two of comfortable silence. My heart thawed a little more against him. That he would ask that before anything else...

"I convinced my father and the Council to let me speak to you because I had to be sure." He watched me with hooded eyes, his expression guarded. "I had to see for myself that you were alright."

Was it possible to swoon and be terrified at the same time? Because that's what it felt like. Auden was a classic knight in shining armor; protective, compassionate, and he made my heart flutter. It did something crazy to my insides when he allowed himself to be vulnerable with me. But at the mention of his father, a paralyzing chill settled over my limbs. Along with it came a horrible thought; what if Auden was checking on me *for* his father? It could all be a ploy to see what I knew or what I was willing to share.

"Kaya?" He moved from the bed to sit on the floor across from me, our knees almost touching.

He was close enough that I felt his warmth, but far enough that I didn't feel crowded. Only confused. He watched me with a concerned frown, and I could tell it was taking everything in him not to reach for me.

"I'm fine," I finally answered. "Really."

"You worried me for a second there."

The gentle rain cast a dark imitation on the carpet between us. I stared at the raindrops while mentally searching for a way to ask him about the king without blatantly accusing him.

"It's been a rough day," I admitted. "I never thought I'd see a Tennin demon. Let alone watch as it—"

I focused on the raindrops again, but now they reminded me too much of blood. So, I looked at Auden instead. He watched me in the silent way he always did; taking in every detail until all my secrets came clawing to the surface.

"How's your father?" I asked and held my breath.

I played a risky game, but I had to know. His brow wrinkled, making a deep V right in the middle.

"He's upset about the attack, of course, and what almost happened to you." I held back a snort but had trouble controlling the rest of my face. "Look, I know you have your feelings about how they ruled on your case, but—"

"I saw your father at the boathouse," I blurted, and his eyes widened.

I didn't mention the demon, or how they both looked at me like I was a prized catch on their line. I didn't shout or yell about how the king conversed with said demon like it was an everyday occurrence to meet up with your enemy and discuss a plan for destruction. How could I share how I felt if I couldn't tell him how seeing his father leer at me from beside an Upper Level demon nearly caused my heart to fail?

"Kaya, my father was in a budget meeting with Asiel when the attack happened. He confirmed it just today when I spoke with him." Auden marked every emotion that crossed my face, as if it would tell him why I acted so strange. I was too busy connecting the dots to do anything about it.

So Asiel *was* in on it. It really shouldn't have surprised me as much as it did. All his talk earlier of trying to protect me was messing with my head. Now Auden studied me like one did the crazies that wore tin foil hats and ran around downtown ranting about aliens.

"Are you sure you're okay?"

Maybe he didn't know. Please universe, say he didn't know.

I forced a sleepy smile. "Yeah, I promise. I must be confused with all that's going on."

Auden nodded. Whether because he believed me or because he wanted to, I wasn't sure. He slowly stood and waved a hand at my bed.

"I'll let you get your sleep then." We ended things on a more awkward note, but there was nothing to be done for it.

The cool sheets beckoned me like an old friend, and I crawled back into them, ready for all the crazy to stop for a moment. To think I ever thought this place was boring. Auden left the desk where it was, and I smiled into the pillow at his thoughtfulness. I still felt safer with it there. He'd almost shut the door when it creaked open again.

"Hey, Kaya?"

"Yeah?" I replied, already halfway to sleep.

"I really am glad you're safe."

Oh, my traitorous heart. How was a girl supposed to resist that?

CHAPTER TWENTY-FIVE

It was nightmare turned reality; but unlike in my dreams, I couldn't pinch myself awake. The gym was the same, rough wooden boards and dusty sun beams from the high windows; gouges made over time from the many claws that padded these floors over the generations. Someone should really fill those in.

"What are you going to tell her?" Bast asked, slowly shedding his clothes in preparation to shift.

I kept my eyes averted. "I still don't know."

"Maybe she will help."

I didn't respond. The chances of her helping me were just as high as Bast shifting into a cat. I sighed. At breakfast I'd resigned myself to two hours of taunts and maybe some resulting detention. But the truth was, I had no idea how she would react.

"Guess we're about to find out," I muttered to myself.

Instructor Lyra didn't walk, she prowled. She moved with a swagger that was part feline and part self-confidence. She knew she was a badass and had no problem flexing that self-knowledge all over her students. Someone like her shouldn't be threatened by the likes of me, and yet I got the sense that she was. Defying her didn't help my case, that was for sure. Too bad I was going to have to do it again. And again. And again.

"This appears all too familiar, Miss Thornton." Instructor Lyra's voice was nasally, and only made worse when she sneered like that and scrunched her nose. "The entire class is waiting on you. Or are you too pretentious to join us?"

My jaw dropped, taken aback by her accusation. She thought I refused to shift because I saw myself as above them? Where the hell did she get that idea? Lincoln chuffed where he sat against the back wall and my eyes narrowed. Never mind.

"It seems Miss Thornton thinks she doesn't need to practice like the rest of you." Instructor Lyra paced a circle around me. "She's special. Unique. Advanced beyond her years."

I'd had enough. "I never said any of that," I snapped, tracking her as she slowly slithered around me.

She arched a brow. "Then why not shift?"

This bitch...I bit my tongue. Nothing was going to get me out of this. I knew that coming in, but to see my classmates glare and hiss at me while she slandered my name was a tougher feat than I was prepared for.

"I'll tell you why," she continued. "You think your little time on the outside gave you experience. That your friendship with the princes and your father's seat on the Council make you above reproach. Well, it doesn't."

Chirps and growls of agreement echoed from my classmates and the skin on the back of my neck prickled with unease. They felt closer somehow, like a noose slowly tightening around my neck.

"You should be punished for your reckless behavior," she snarled. "And your father should have lost his seat for rearing such selfish offspring." I backed away from her, from the utter rage I saw in her eyes. How she kept her cat controlled was a mastery in self-restraint. Her fingertips remained blunt, even as she flexed them at her side. "We lost many good familiars in the original search for you." She let out a low hiss, her face briefly crumpling in despair before it returned to its usual mask of hatred.

She lost someone close to her in one of the earlier missions to find me. One probably sanctioned by my father before he realized I'd intentionally left. That's why her resentment was so strong. I never stood a chance with her.

"Now here you are, finally back, and what do you do? Spit on our traditions, refuse to shift, be so insubordinate and selfish that you cause the loss of yet another life!"

"What?" She couldn't know about Asher.

"Your partner, Cace. Tragically killed at the hands of a Tennin demon while you cowered on the ground!"

My relief at her not knowing about Asher was brief as her accusation set in. I turned red; my face overheated. Embarrassment. Fury. A small kernel of shame.

"That's not how it happened," I argued, but it fell on deaf ears. "You can't possibly be blaming me for his death." I had barely enough air to get the words out, but they heard.

The room went beyond silent. It was an unnatural stillness —one where I couldn't hear the rapid breaths of my classmates or my own racing heart. The thunderous roaring in my ears was the only sound.

"If you shifted, your partner would still be alive," her voice was made of steel.

That was bullshit and she knew it. One shifter and a young witch, armed only with jars of paint could not have taken down that demon. I backed further away from the intensity of her glare. A large head knocked into my lower back and sent me stumbling forward.

"Enough stalling," Instructor Lyra commanded. "Shift. Now."

My classmates closed in around me; all except Bast, who stood on the outside, eyes wide in horror.

Another headbutt. The swipe of a claw—enough to leave a sting but not break the skin. It was forbidden to harm another familiar while in their human form, they were waiting for me to shift. Again and again my classmates pushed me. All at the manipulative press of our instructor. It continued for an hour. I was knocked to the ground repeatedly only for the mob to back up, allow me to climb to my feet, and start again. My restraint held. I never sprouted a claw. Not one tuft of fur. And when the bell rang, I looked directly in the face of our instructor and smiled. Challenge accepted.

"There has to be a better way," I pleaded as Bast climbed up another branch. "It doesn't work if you kill yourself!"

The panic grew with each foot he ascended. I searched the area for something to break his fall, a pile of leaves, a tarp, a random mattress. *Anything*. There was nothing around but solid ground and rocks. Of course, that was Bast's entire plan. He wanted to climb as far up as he could and then jump off. The hope was that seeing him fall would activate my power. I thought it was too risky. Sure, it worked before when I needed it, but it also didn't work when I *most* needed it. For two days our lives were an endless routine of being harassed in class each morning and training out here until lunch. The harassment resumed in Fox's class and then we trained once more until dinner if I wasn't meeting with Auden. The grueling schedule wore on me. Practicals were cancelled in light of Cace's death but that made things no easier since the others blamed me for what happened. The school planned a memorial for Cace in the amphitheater tonight. One they made all too clear I wasn't welcome at.

"You've done it before," Bast called down. He was so high now that I couldn't see him. "Stop panicking and start focusing!"

Telling me not to panic only made it worse. I took in a deep breath and then let it out. Bast was right, I'd caught him already once before. I knew what triggered my power, but it was hard to find it inside myself. Our first day practicing, it took hours before I could call forth a red glow to my hands. By the fourth day, I could engulf any falling object Bast threw at me, including himself. But I couldn't hold the shield forever and timing was everything.

"Are you ready?"

"No!" I squeaked, still grabbing at my power.

It came willingly, warming my hands and throwing light into the shadows under the canopy.

"Here I come!" Bast announced, seconds before his high-pitched scream.

Branches cracked and leaves rained down. I focused more of my power into my hands and aimed it at the ground. Any second now. I pushed and a soft, red haze floated above the earth. It was see-through, but solid where it counted. Bast screamed until he hit it, bouncing once, twice, then landing on the ground with a soft *oomph* when my shield gave out.

He grinned at me while dusting off his pants. "Told you it would work."

My relief overshadowed the need to strangle him. He was right. As much as I hated to admit it.

"Hopefully your mom has safer ways to practice," I told

him, then smiled when he winced at the thought of his mom finding out how we trained.

Bast hooked an arm around my neck and steered me away from the tree-of-near-death. "We can worry about my mother later. Tonight, we party."

I sighed. "It's not a party, B. It's basically a funeral and I don't think we're wanted there."

The nighttime call of animals grew as the sun set. Fireflies burned along the path in no distinct pattern; here one minute and over there the next. The muggy heat of the day finally released its grip in favor of an evening breeze, and I wished we could just stay out here. The swamp meant no ill will against me and it didn't care that I couldn't shift. The murky waters didn't taunt and the Spanish moss threw nothing but a gentle caress when it touched my shoulders. Days of standing against my classmates had taken its toll, and I honestly didn't know how much more I could take.

"Look, curfew is an hour away, so the party will be winding down." Bast still tried to convince me. "We'll stop by, pay our respects, and then leave. Maybe grab a drink while we're there."

"This sounds like a horrible idea."

Bast stopped and twisted to face me. "You deserve to be there more than anyone. You nearly died too."

"But I didn't," I countered. "And they won't let me forget it."

The more we discussed it, the more I didn't want to go. But Bast was right on one count, I needed to pay my respects. In the end, we compromised. We snuck through the back tunnels of the amphitheater, avoiding every entrance that had voices emanating from it. The dark alcoves around the main arena made it easy to keep hidden and we sat in the dark, sipping our pilfered drinks as my classmates laughed and told stories about Cace.

"He sounded like an okay guy," I whispered. "Despite how he treated me in class."

I knew you couldn't judge a person based off one instance, I was proof enough of that, but it was hard to shake my original thoughts of him. His friends described a guy who was quick to laugh, a practical joker, and a fierce fighter. I knew the last part from experience. Cace was willing to take on the king and an unknown demon at the sight of their betrayal. So I knew I could add loyalty to the growing list of accolades. He didn't deserve to die how he did.

"Can we go?" I asked but already slipped into the tunnels.

The laughter from the arena cut deeper with each memory of Cace's screams. I vowed right then and there to get to the bottom of the king's deception and put a stop to it no matter what it took.

I walked into class the next morning still heavy with the scent of guilt. Nightmares plagued me until early morning and left me with brutal thoughts on how I could have been better—how I could have done better and tried harder to save Cace. Maybe it was that guilt that made me blind to the shift in dynamic today. Instructor Lyra wasn't here. I'd quickly learned to tune out her scathing remarks and harsh glares, so it took a minute to realize they weren't happening. At least, not from her. The rest of the class was all too happy to carry on in her absence. Lincoln first and foremost.

"Warm up laps!" He shouted. "I'm in charge today."

A shiver worked its way down my spine when he looked at me, and not in a good way. Instructor Lyra might be a bitch, but she was a teacher and beholden to the rules. She couldn't let things go too far even if she wanted them to. But with no adults in the room to keep him in check, Lincoln held no such reservations. We ran around the gym, everyone in their animal forms but me and Lincoln. I hardly kept up—two legs versus four—

and was repeatedly overlapped by all different breeds of feline. Bast tried to stay beside me but was chased away with claws and teeth.

"Had enough of being a traitor?" Lincoln came alongside me, shirtless and not at all out of breath.

I ignored him and pushed harder. His foot caught around my ankle and my knees met the hard gym floor. Pain ricocheted up my thighs and my claws dug into the hardwood before once again receding to blunt fingertips.

"Oops," Lincoln laughed, and offered a hand to help me up.

I smacked it away and resumed jogging, the pain in my knees already dulling to a subtle ache. After three more laps around the gym, he did it again. This time, I bit my lip on the way down. The scent of my blood worked the others into an excited frenzy and the speed of their laps kicked into overdrive. I crawled toward the middle of the room, but not fast enough. The first paw to the face took me by surprise. The blows left me dizzy and with a throbbing on my cheek that I knew would bruise. My body fell victim to a similar fate as I fell under the stampede. Curled into a ball, I could do nothing but protect my head and middle from the vicious onslaught. My inner cat hissed at each new bruise, then at me when I refused to let her out. I didn't know how long I stayed like that, squeezed into a painful ball on the floor, but when the hits finally stopped coming, my classmates took one final look before bounding out the door and into the daylight.

Lincoln crouched in front of me, and I couldn't stop the flinch when he reached out to move a strand of my hair.

"Traitors don't belong here, Kaya. Learn your place, or we'll show it to you. Every day."

He left and Bast appeared beside me, already dressed and glancing over his shoulder like they would come back any second.

"I'm so sorry," he apologized, over and over each step back to the dorms.

"Even your massive wolf can't go against a gym full of shifters, B."

"But I could've gone to get help," he grunted, helping me up the steps.

"Who would believe you?" I argued. "Honestly, it means more to me that you're here now."

Because the trip to my room would have been brutal without him. He left me in the middle of my bathroom, only after I promised to go to the infirmary if the pain got worse. Thankfully, a hot shower revealed nothing more than bruises and a small cut on my lip. My reflection in the mirror held my attention as I thought through my options. Was she the kind of girl to roll over and let others tell her who to be? Would she settle for the disrespect? The abuse? The answer wasn't hard to find. No. She wouldn't. If anyone laid a hand or paw on me again, I'd show them exactly what kind of monster lurked inside me.

I REFUSED TO HIDE. I knew there was nothing anyone could do about the bruises and I was no snitch, but I'd be damned if I was going to let Lincoln and the others shame me into hiding in my room. Bast and I sat through lunch with all the usual stares and then some. No one dared ask what happened, though I saw more than a few curious mouths agape. I smirked at Lincoln when I sat down with my full tray and casually ate like my head wasn't throbbing and my ribs didn't hurt with each breath. His eyes tightened, but there was nothing he could do to me in a room full of teachers and underclassmen. I wanted to be seen. I wanted my attackers to know that it wouldn't silence me. They hadn't won. What I didn't expect was how fast the rumor mill would spread, or how the tale of my bruises would spin so out of control. Not until Auden pounded on my door hard enough to make it shake.

"Let me in or I'll use my key," he threatened.

"How did you get another one?" I called back, exasperated.

Was there no end to his invasion of privacy? After the last time he broke into my room, *in the middle of the night,* I made him hand over his key. What was the point if he could just get another one?

"Kaya!"

With a very unlady-like huff, I unlocked the door and stepped back before it caught me in the face. It swung inward, revealing Auden in all his pissed off, royal glory. My hoodie hung on the back of the chair, so all my new bruises were on display. Auden sucked in a deep breath, his eyes dark and expressionless. Deadly. The fury was slow to show, but by the time he shut the door, it saturated the room. His hand was a fist around the doorknob. With his back still to me, I saw the tense muscles of his shoulders as he tried to get his anger under control.

"Who did this to you?" When I didn't answer, he spun on me and advanced until I saw the gold raging in his eyes. "Don't make me ask again," he commanded, voice gruff.

My hand unconsciously went to the bruise on my cheek, the skin already a light purple. There were matching marks along my arms, legs and torso.

"Lincoln tripped me," I finally said. The truth, but not all of it.

His long fingers encircled my wrist and held my arm away from my body. "You don't get bruises like these from tripping. Not unless there were stairs involved." His eyes flashed and his entire body went still. "Were there stairs involved?"

"No," I pulled, but he didn't release my wrist.

"Don't lie to me, Kaya. Not about this."

"I'm not!" When a last desperate yank did nothing, I glared at him.

He let me go and his fingers tangled in his hair instead. "I'm going to kill him," he swore, turning back for the door.

I lunged in front of him, my knees smarting at the sudden movement. Both my hands pushed on his chest, and it was enough to make him pause. He glanced down at me, his breath leaving his nose in hard bursts.

"Please let it go," I begged. "It will only get worse for me if you interfere."

Instructor Lyra already had everyone thinking I got special treatment. If Auden swooped in to save the day, it would only prove her right.

"You can't honestly expect me to see what he did to you and do nothing." Auden's brows rose, incredulous.

"I'm handling it," I promised. "I need you to trust me on this."

His mouth turned down, like what I requested was painful for him. But finally, his temper left him on an exhale, and he bent down to rest his forehead against mine.

"I don't like seeing you hurt."

A ball rose in my throat, and I had to swallow a few times to speak over it. "I don't like seeing you hurt either."

Slowly. So slowly, he brought both his hands to cup my face. He tilted my head, forcing my eyes to meet his. I watched, unblinking as his gaze shifted from my mouth to my eyes and back again. The tip of his tongue dipped out to lick his bottom lip and my heart jack-knifed against my ribcage. At the look in his eyes, the needy sound he made in the back of his throat, I wanted nothing more than to close the space between us. To press my lips against his. No matter how bad I wanted it, the small voice in my head screamed louder. This was stupid and reckless. Auden and I could never be. He was a prince, who might or might not know about his father's deal with the demons. Not to mention the baggage we knew I brought to the table. With a slight shake of my head, I ducked under his arm and fled for the safety of the other side of the room. Distance. We needed distance.

Auden groaned and slammed his hand against the door. "You're afraid."

I kept my gaze out the window and laughed, but it sounded disbelieving even to me. "Afraid of what?"

"Me. This." From the corner of my eye, I saw Auden step closer. "Us."

I kept my back to him and forced another laugh. "I'm not afraid of anything."

He scoffed at my obvious lie. "You can't even look at me."

I spun, ready to argue, but refused to move my eyes higher than his neck. I told myself it was because of his muscles and how his shirt clung to the shape of them. I knew from training where they flexed and hardened and how they felt when they lifted or pinned me. It had nothing to do with my avoiding the truth in his gaze. I kept the false mask on my face as Auden moved nearer, but inside I was a shaking mess. When he was no more than a foot away, I took a step back, unable to help myself. He raised a brow but kept coming. My lower back hit my desk and Auden closed the last bit of distance between us and a small sound escaped my parted lips. His eyes darkened and he groaned, his hands slipping past my waist. His grip tightened as he grabbed my ass, lifting me onto the desk and bringing us face to face. I automatically glanced down, but his fingers gently gripped my chin and forced me to look up into those golden eyes.

"Yeah, you're terrified," he whispered, his thumb brushing a ghostly path across my cheek.

And I was. I was scared of the way my heart raced so fast that I thought I'd pass out. I trembled at the strength of the feelings I kept boxed inside me. And yes, terrified. Terrified that I was falling for my dead best friend's older brother. Or worse, that he was falling for the person responsible for killing him. The way he looked at me made my breath catch, but it would strangle me whenever he inevitably came to the realization of what I'd done.

"Kaya," my name came out quiet and strained, our lips not even an inch apart. "Trust me, sweetheart," he whispered.

His large body crowded mine as our lips finally came together. Most first kisses were tender and gentle. This started that way, but maybe it was the tension leading up to this moment, the dancing around one another that turned the kiss heated and hungry. Auden opened his mouth to mine, gently guiding me. When our tongues touched, I started and tried to pull away, but his hand on the back of my head halted my retreat.

"Trust me," he whispered against my lips and kissed me again.

His hands were everywhere, tracing the dip of my spine, running his thumbs over my ribs, the swell of my breasts. He pressed his hand against the small of my back and pushed our lower halves together until I let out an involuntary whimper. My lashes fluttered open when he pulled away, the both of us breathing heavy. My entire body was awash in new sensations, most of them centering between my legs and Auden grinned as if he could read my mind. My lips tingled in a way I wasn't used to. Not even the small cut could take away from the feeling.

"Not bad for a first kiss," Auden smirked, his gaze catching on my lips again.

"It was...adequate," I panted, at a loss for words strong enough to describe what I felt.

"Now you've done it, sweetheart." Auden wrapped an arm around my waist and brought us back together. "Never give me a challenge I'm sure I'll win."

And he did. Again and again and again...

CHAPTER
TWENTY-SIX

My dreams were filled with hot kisses and golden eyes. I rolled over with a big smile, my fingers tracing my mouth like I could still feel Auden there. Yesterday was...unexpected. The afternoon's activities far outweighed my horrible morning, and I was absolutely giddy with anticipation of it happening again. It would be a lesson in restraint to not throw myself at him. With it being the weekend, however, my lips would get a well-deserved break while I instead spent the day practicing my new power. My grin faded as I thought about keeping it a secret from Auden. There was no denying how our relationship changed. We might not be together, or out in the open, but I was done fighting what I felt. I'd run out of excuses. I knew navigating these waters with my ever-growing secrets would only get trickier as time went on.

Despite the apprehension these secrets forced me to carry, I met Bast for breakfast with a genuine smile and optimistic outlook for the day. The cafeteria wasn't as full this late in the morning and it lacked the usual din from a million conversations. There were still plenty of stares, whispers, and overall feeling of unwelcome from a select few, but it didn't bother me today. I crossed the half-empty room with my tray, lost in my own thoughts and stumbled to a halt when I neared one of the corner tables. His black hair was tousled, like he hadn't bothered to fix it after I had my fingers in it yesterday. His mouth curled in an impish grin that only widened when he saw how it affected me.

I forced my feet to move and carry me to Bast, who was already scarfing down the last of his food. I felt the heat of Auden's stare as I sat, blushing despite how hard I tried to play it cool. My body had other ideas. How could he affect me like this from all the way over there? And without even touching me! My body knew the feel of his hands and like an addict, already craved more. I hardly tasted my food, so caught up in the reactions his gaze caused. Scrambled eggs, no matter how well seasoned, couldn't compare.

"Something's happened," Bast commented, his keen eye watching my every wiggle.

I shrugged and shoved more eggs in my mouth. It was hard to keep still.

"Spill." This boy was a bloodhound—no pun intended. I swear, he had a sixth sense for these kinds of things and wouldn't let it go until you divulged every minute detail.

"It's not a big deal," I started. Except it was. It really, really was. "But Auden came to my dorm after lunch yesterday."

"I was wondering how long it would take him to hear about the bruises," he said, and I nodded. Not long at all. "What did he have to say?"

I grimaced when I thought back to how ready he'd been to kill Lincoln. It wasn't an idle threat, either. Auden was fully capable of following through.

"That well, huh?" Bast snorted.

"I had to stop him from going after Lincoln," I admitted. "It would've only caused more problems for me if those two got into it."

Bast chewed on his lip and sat passively while he listened to the play by play of my detailed argument with Auden. It was the sudden shift in his expression that made me pause.

"What?"

"You didn't tell him the whole truth," he said, spreading the words like I didn't understand the significance of them.

"I didn't want him to interfere," I explained again.

Bast tilted his head. "Didn't want him to interfere or didn't trust him not to agree with them?"

Now he really lost me. There were no doubts in my mind that Auden would one hundred percent be on my side if I told him about Lyra's class.

"I trust Auden." At Bast's blank face, I glared. "I *do*. I wouldn't have kissed him yesterday if I didn't."

Orange juice sprayed across the table, narrowly missing my food. I watched with an amused frown as Bast hastily wiped it up.

"Please tell me, in exaggerated detail, what *that* was like."

Perfect. Hot. Worthy of a song, or at the very least a poem. Everything younger me dreamed of and then some. None of those words left my mouth. My red cheeks and inability to keep still under his scrutiny was enough for him to get the idea.

He let out a low whistle. "You've got it bad. Not that I blame you."

My embarrassment only worsened my blush, and I rolled my eyes. "It was just kissing, B. Nothing can come of it; you know that."

He nodded, face back to serious. "But do you?"

That got my hackles up. He knew I wasn't stupid. I wasn't going to pine for something that could never be.

"What's that supposed to mean?"

"You didn't tell him the truth about how you were hurt. You've yet to determine if he knows or even suspects his father's involvement with the demon attacks. And after talking with you about it, I know for a fact you haven't told him how you feel about what happened to his brother." With each finger he ticked down, my heart sank further into my stomach. "That sounds to me like you don't trust him. Yet, you're allowing yourself to be vulnerable."

I was going to be sick. My hands shoved my tray aside before the sight of the food made me throw up. I was torn, half of me in denial and still riding the high of that kiss, and the other half screaming Bast was right and to get out while I still could. I knew getting involved with Auden was a bad idea. There were too many secrets and too many unanswered questions on both sides. What would I do if I found out Auden knew about his father? Would that betrayal cancel out what I did to Asher? Auden might have no idea. Still, where did that leave us?

"Hey," Bast's hand was gentle as it covered my own. "I'm not trying to tell you what to do, or even discourage what you obviously feel for the prince. You just need to be smart about it. This is so much more than the two of you kissing."

I hated that he was right. Mostly because it killed the happy buzz I'd been floating on all morning. As far as our conversation about Asher, I knew I couldn't avoid it forever, but I hoped to have more time. The brisk walk to the outpost was grimmer than I'd imagined, what with the joyful conversation over breakfast. But the sunshine, singing birds, and lack of demons did a great job of lightening the mood and before long, we both wore smiles once more. Excitement simmered in my veins at the sight of the cabin. Learning about my power was swiftly becoming a highlight of my days. If I could get a handle on it, I'd never have to feel helpless again and my witch partner—

whoever that turned out to be—wouldn't suffer the fate of all the others I'd failed.

We squeezed through the hole in the wall and headed downstairs, this time fully prepared for the faces we would meet. What we weren't expecting was the tension and overall panic.

"We must disband! It's too risky." Nolen's squished face was overheated and ruddy. He wiped the sweat off his brow with a handkerchief as he stared down Captain Cesar.

"And I told you, that's not possible," the Captain barked. "We've come too far to stop now."

Adira's head tilted as she leaned on one fist, her eyes bouncing back and forth between the two witches like she was witness to a tennis match. The other two shifters in the room, the red headed tiger named Fin and his mate Larsen—who I later learned was a panther—sat playing cards in a back corner. Did the witches argue like this all the time? When Adira noticed us, she laid a hand on the table. That was enough to stop the bickering and now all eyes were on us.

Bast stepped forward, as attuned as I was to what we'd overheard. "What's going on?"

Adira waved that same hand at her son and beckoned him over for a hug. "Nothing for you to worry over."

"I beg to differ," Nolen snapped, pulling himself to his full, and still limited, height. "Do you truly plan to endanger your son just to further your own agenda?"

Her irises split; the cat-like glow reflective even in the dim light. "My son is at risk every day of his life thanks to his father and his chances only grow more dire after he graduates." She meant once the king put Bast on the front lines without a partner, since no one wanted him around. "Each of us in this room has nothing more to gain from this *agenda* than the knowledge that our people and those closest to us are safe."

Nolen flinched at the solid steel in her gaze and Captain Cesar gave a solemn nod, having argued this very point already. "There's nothing more to do, Nolen. We just have to be quick."

Bast and I wore matching expressions of confusion as Nolen stormed out of the room. Adira sighed, weary wrinkles creasing her face.

"Let him go," she called and the Captain returned to the table resigned.

"Anyone wish to fill us in?" I asked.

The shifters still played cards in the corner, content to stay out of the drama. Adira and the Captain exchanged a look before the latter let out a breath.

"The king reassigned the rotations at the other outposts. Longer hours, less breaks, and more missions outside the walls."

"We're losing numbers at an even faster rate than before," Adira added. "Almost as if the demons are waiting for our arrival."

It was highly probable that the king ordered our people right into an ambush. To what end, I couldn't figure out. There was a very real chance our drastic loss in numbers was directly due to the king's involvement with the demons and the very idea made me want to go on a rampage. So many innocent lives lost. And for what?

"Our spies closest to the king have warned many in time to save lives." By his grim and haggard appearance, I knew the Captain didn't think it was enough. "But now he's suspicious and when my men return—those still alive—to their posts, the buildings are left ransacked."

"He's searching for us," Adira's declaration echoed in the small room. "We need to be cautious and do nothing that will draw any ill-timed attention to the cause."

That last bit was directed at me. I had no plans to attract the king; last time was enough.

"Training," she ordered, and I shuffled from the room while their plotting continued.

THE ROCK HIT the cabin wall right next to my head. Large enough to take two hands to lift, it broke apart into sharp pieces that rained down at my feet with jagged edges. Bast and his mom stood across from me with a pile of similar rocks ready to go.

"Catching something is different than blocking it," she shouted to me. "Think about what you do with your hands when blocking a strike, then do that."

My power engulfed my hands as I waited for the next volley. We'd been at this for hours and I had nothing to show for it but a headache. When I caught objects with my power, I aimed at the ground and pictured it like a big catcher's mitt. But that wasn't working. Maybe if I pictured it in front of me...More shards exploded as I barely dodged Bast's well aimed throw.

"Dammit!" I growled, when a particularly large piece grazed my arm.

Why was this so hard? Blocking versus catching wasn't *that* different.

"Move," Adira pushed Bast aside and drew a small knife from the sheath on her calf.

I wasn't one to question the woman who single handedly led the charge against the king, but holy shit she had to be nuts if she planned on throwing that at me. Sunlight caught on the thin edge as the knife flew end over end toward my face. There was no time to think. No time to plan how to make my power obey. I crossed my arms in front of me, hands still aglow, and prayed. Seconds went by and when I realized I wasn't screaming in agony, or dead, I opened my eyes. The knife lay useless on the ground, stopped by a shinning red shield arcing over me.

"Cool! You have your own force field," Bast hooted, and threw another knife at it.

The shield held for longer than the one with the Tennin demon. I attributed that to all the practice I'd been doing since then. Adira made me take the shield up and down a hundred times until I could call it at will and hold it. When it faded no matter how hard I tried, she called an end to the day. Sweat dripped down my temples and gathered at my lower back. The muscles in my limbs shook like I'd actually done something with them. Using my power was a full-bodied workout.

"Get some rest," Adira told me, one of her rare smiles on display. "There's no sense in being so tired you get stabbed."

I helped them pick up the fallen knives and daydreamed about the day I wouldn't have to hide my power. No other familiar in known history had one as well as the ability to shift. Even those with mixed heritage. It was why some witches didn't like to mix; their child wouldn't be able to throw a potion and activate it with a word of power. And a witch of the royal line...forget it. The telekinetic ability was left in only three; our people couldn't afford for such a strong gift to be lost.

"Do you know where my power comes from?" I asked, when all evidence of our training was cleared.

I'd thought about it a lot lately, where these powers came from. Both my parents were familiars and neither had an extra gift as far as I knew. It definitely wasn't something my father would keep quiet about if he had.

"I'm not sure, child." Adira patted my arm. "But I'm looking into it. I have some leads."

"Really?" I asked, excited. "What leads?"

She shook her head. "When I know for sure, I'll tell you."

I knew better than to argue. So, with a sigh I squashed my curiosity and headed to the dorms. At the start of my hall, I changed directions. All that dodging and straining for my power tore at my muscles. A little light stretching in the attic before a hot shower I knew would do wonders. The room was empty, and the mats cleaned from their last use. This time of day, the sun wasn't shinning directly through the window but there was still plenty of light to see by. I went through an old cool down routine Sensei taught me, feeling both sad and nostalgic at the memory. I'd yet to get word out to him that I was okay and knowing he was worried about me didn't sit well on my heart. I reminded myself to write him an email the next time I was on a common room computer. I still had no idea what I would say, but something was better than nothing. It was strange to think that my definition of family changed as I went through different stages of my life. As a child, if one were to ask, I'd tell them my family was my parents. Pretty straight forward answer. But after the death of my mother, my father became a stranger and Asher became my family. After Asher, Sensei. Now, I'd come to see Bast and his mom as my new family and they gladly welcomed me even though I wasn't convinced I deserved it. I swore to work every day to fix that.

CHAPTER
TWENTY-SEVEN

A thunderstorm greeted us Sunday morning, so Bast and I took our training to the attic. Now that it was easier to call forth my power, we had a little fun with it. Bast threw different items across the room, ranging in weight from a small knife to a sandbag. I'd catch them or block them depending on the item. I'd gotten quite good at both. What I needed the most practice on was maintaining the connection to my power for an extended period of time. I worked on that each night in bed, calling that red glow to my hands and holding it until I couldn't. There wasn't much more we could do without time and experience.

"Can we try something a little different today?" I asked, deflecting another knife with a wave of my hand.

"Sure. Do you want to try using your shield to block the door again?"

I smiled as I thought back to that ingenious idea. We figured if my power could catch someone falling or stop a speeding projectile, why couldn't it keep someone out? It took way more energy and concentration than anything else we tried, but it worked.

"Actually, I was thinking about working on my shifting."

Bast hadn't pressured me for answers since the last time we talked about it and by the look on his face, I knew I caught him by surprise.

"What brought this on?" He asked. "I thought you were going the rebel route, you know, stick it to the man and all that."

He wasn't wrong. Even if I could shift, I probably still wouldn't on principle, not after what that class put me through. It was no secret how I felt about this toxic environment, but I knew I was going to have to do it eventually and I wanted it to be on my own terms.

"You know I've struggled with it," I admitted. "I would just rather it be my choice when the time comes."

We worked together to clean the room while Bast suggested ideas on how to help. The main problem with practicing was we couldn't do it if I couldn't *actually* shift. That put a bump in any plans we came up with and we ended up sitting across from one another in the center of the mats.

"What does the doorway look like for you?" I finally asked, and then winced at the personal question. "Sorry if that's too invasive."

Bast gave me an easy grin, "It's fine. I don't mind."

The doorway appeared different for each familiar. Located somewhere in the back of our minds, it wasn't accessible until our sixteenth year. I'd heard some describe it as a pool they jumped into, or a light switch they flicked on and off. It was how each person mentally visualized the conscious decision to give in to our animal half.

"Mine appeared as this bright light in the middle of the forest." There was a genuine look of happiness on his face and a small kernel of jealousy took root in my chest. "I told my mom as soon as I saw it and she coached me through what to do next.

Of course, you know what happened after when I came out a wolf on the other side." My growing jealousy snuffed out. Bast hasn't had an easy journey either and somehow, I kept forgetting that. His cheery attitude and open heart did a lot to hide his rough life. "What about you?" He asked, bringing me back to my own problems.

"It wasn't as smooth for me," I told him. "One night, this doorway just showed up and I knew what it meant. I was excited. It was so perfect."

I was smiling now as I remembered it. The doorway looked just like the entry to the treehouse— my safe place. And after years of missing Asher and being away from home, it was like being given a gift. Up until I realized I couldn't open it because I was surrounded my humans. Then, I started to see it for what it really was, more punishment.

"And now?" Bast gently encouraged.

I suppressed a snort. "Now it's weathered, cracked, and tangled in vines."

Worse yet, I could feel the door fading, but I didn't tell him that.

"Hmm," Bast chewed on his lip as he thought. "Could your attitude toward shifting be affecting your connection?"

"My attitude?" My brows rose, but not in anger. It's not like I could deny it.

He gave me a playful shove. "Yes. Your attitude."

"Possibly."

I hadn't thought of it like that before. Granted, it didn't take long for my doorway to start looking a little janky. Maybe my power had something to do with it. As I said before, no other familiar in known history had a power *and* the ability to shift. Maybe one cancelled out the other eventually? Would I have to choose?

"We're not going to figure this out on empty stomachs," Bast declared, moving to his feet. "Lunch?"

At that moment, the creak of the attic door made us both turn to see who found their way up here. It wasn't a known spot. Auden's head poked through, and his eyes lit upon finding me.

"There you are," he said, making his way over.

My heart kicked into overdrive with each step he took. Butterflies took flight in my stomach and all serious thoughts Bast and I had moments before left me in a wave of heat. One minute in my presence, and all my hard work was trashed. Bast's nostrils flared, as he noticed my change in scent. I refused to be embarrassed.

"So, lunch?" he asked again, then gave Auden a strange look.

Auden returned it and I watched their silent communication grow into full blown awkward before having enough.

"I'm not very hungry," I replied, and both their attention switched back to me. "I'll grab something later."

The cafeteria kept supplies available for sandwiches if anyone missed a meal. But I honestly wasn't hungry at the moment. Bast left after another stare down with Auden and I thought back to our conversation yesterday about trust and whether or not I should be placing it with the son of a traitorous king. Why did things have to be so complicated?

"You guys have hung out a lot, lately," Auden commented, his head still turned toward the door where Bast disappeared.

"Yeah, because we're friends." Why did he act like he didn't already know that?

"What do you really know about him?"

My eyes narrowed. We'd already had this conversation. Auden knew there was no reason to be jealous where Bast was concerned and if kissing him brought it back out, then I was going to have to second guess doing that again. He didn't look angry though, more...suspicious. Maybe it wasn't jealousy. Could Auden be uncomfortable with the fact that Bast was a wolf shifter?

"Are you referring to his animal?" I asked, defensive on Bast's behalf. "Because I don't care about that, and I didn't think you were one to care about it either."

"What?" Auden replied, shocked. "I *don't* care about that."

I crossed my arms. *Something* was bothering him.

Auden raised his palms. "Really. I wouldn't care if he shifted into a flamingo."

Wrinkles creased on his forehead and for the first time, I noticed the dark circles under his eyes. Auden looked haggard. His messy hair was more unruly than usual and even his clothes seemed a little rushed. Was it a bad night's sleep or secret keeping for his father?

Ugh. All this doubt gave me a headache. I wasn't usually this skeptic and for it to be over someone I cared about...

"There's been some rumblings about your friend and his mom," he voiced, obviously uncomfortable with the conversation. "People are complaining that they're not supporters of my father and other traitorous whispers. I just don't want you to get mixed up in whatever it is."

I switched between outraged and suspicious, never landing long on either. The question wasn't who was saying these things about Bast and Adira, because everyone was against them. No. The real truth was whether or not Auden was trying to use me to gather information for his father. I truly believed he cared for me. But I wasn't sure yet about everything else.

"Who's saying these things?" I demanded. "People in the community? The Council?"

"I don't know exactly—"

"Don't know or refuse to say that it's coming from your father?"

The words sat between us, angry and loud. Thunder rolled outside but it sounded amplified in the large room and the growing storm mirrored the expressions slipping across Auden's face as I waited for an answer. He settled on shock with a bit of irritation.

"Come again?"

"You heard me." I wasn't in the mood to repeat myself, and I didn't have the courage to ask twice.

"No. The news wasn't from my father but I'm sure he's been made aware of the rumors."

"By you?" I held my breath. This was it. If Auden worked for his father, even unknowingly, I didn't know what I'd do. Cry first. But not sure about after.

His gaze softened. "No."

My relief was instantaneous. Auden wasn't working with his father. He was being played like the rest of us. His honesty was more than skin deep; it was who he was. So, if he said the rumors weren't from the king and that he wasn't the one who reported them, I believed him. That didn't make the news any less dangerous. Adira would need to be cautious for a while. And it didn't mean I could suddenly divulge all my secrets like Auden wasn't loyal to his family. It was a big weight off my chest, though.

"Why do you have so much animosity toward my father?" Auden's voice hadn't lost its rough edge, he was still upset.

"Because he made Bast's life the way it is." The truth was out of my mouth before I could take it back. Auden frowned with such confusion I had no choice but to share the heartbreaking story of Bast's childhood.

How the king did nothing to protect him when he shifted the first time. How he allowed the community to run his mother to the edge of the island like a pack of wild animals and how he continued to allow their mistreatment. Bast wasn't even allowed in most businesses in the community all because of something he couldn't control and didn't ask for. The hex bags, the abuse; it wasn't right.

"My father is powerful," he whispered. "But he can't control his subjects on matters where there is no law." I opened my mouth to argue, but he covered it with his hand. "That doesn't mean it's right or that something shouldn't be done about it."

There he was, that honorable gentleman that he couldn't hide. I pulled his hand down but didn't let it go. Turning it over, I grazed his palm with my finger, thinking.

"Okay, but this thing between us isn't going to work if you can't get along with Bast."

Auden's hand closed around mine and I looked up at his smirk. "What thing between us?"

Talk about self-conscious. I tried to pull my hand back, but he held it in a firm grip.

"Well, aren't we friends?" I asked, my mouth going dry.

"Sure we are," he confirmed, and I felt a little less like dying. "But I was kind of hoping to be more."

I took that back. I was definitely dying. Auden's eyes danced with mirth as he held my gaze. There was no stopping my blush and we were too close to back away now. He'd seen it. When my tongue finally came unglued, I'd gotten over the shock. Somewhat.

"We can't be more, Auden. You know that." It physically hurt to say the words, but one of us had to be realistic.

"I'm not next in line for the throne, so I have no immediate duties to fulfill."

"That doesn't actually solve anything," I sighed.

"How about this," Auden pulled on my hand, hard enough that I bumped into his chest. His arm snaked around my waist and pulled me even closer. "We play it by ear and see where this goes. Because I really like you." He drew back just enough to look in my eyes. "I like spending time with you." His other hand drifted up my side, over my shoulder, and along my neck until it cupped my cheek. "But I especially like doing this."

This kiss was filled with the same urgency and the same longing as the first. My eyes fluttered shut and my fingers wasted no time reaching up and burying themselves in his hair. His lips moved over mine, encouraging, and when I flicked my tongue against his lip, he growled. Lifting me against him, he pushed me into the wall. My legs rose of their own accord, wrapping around his waist with the support of his hand on my thigh. His mouth found the sensitive spot where my neck met my shoulder and he grazed it with his teeth and my next breath came out a moan as warmth coiled low in my belly. My muscles tensed, fueled by a liquid heat coursing through them with each swipe of his tongue. He pushed against me harder, his breathing just as frenzied as mine. I bucked against him with a whimper. Something was growing, a pooling of sensations between my legs that ignited with each roll of his hips.

"Auden," it was supposed to be a protest, a warning to slow down, but it came out more like a moan.

"I've got you sweetheart," his voice thickened as he rolled his hips harder. Faster.

He scooped both his hands under me, palming my ass and adjusting me in such a way that...*holy fuck.* He lined us up perfectly, my thin leggings not even an obstacle against the hard press of him, and I sank my teeth into my lower lip to silence my scream.

"That's it, Kaya," he whispered against my neck. "Let it go."

As if I could stop it. I erupted. Starting from my toes and branching into every part of my body, my nerves tingled as millions of pinpricks of pleasure speared through me in wave after glorious wave. Auden's hips gently rocked against mine as I came down and I kept my face buried in his neck as feeling slowly returned to my limbs. He peppered small kisses along my neck, the side of my face, and my hair until I unwrapped my legs from around him and he let me go. I thought I'd be more embarrassed to lose control like that, but Auden had such a satisfied grin on his face that it was hard to do anything but match it.

"You're beautiful," he spoke against my lips in one more kiss.

The storm had settled outside the window, but the one in my chest was just getting started.

CHAPTER
TWENTY-EIGHT

I rode the rest of my weekend on a high, satisfied for the first time in almost every aspect of my life. The parts I still worked on couldn't dull the shine of the rest. That was until Monday reared its ugly head. I was prepared for Instructor Lyra. Neither she nor Lincoln would break me. I didn't care if the whole class ganged up on me again. My good mood couldn't be shattered. But it wasn't Lincoln standing in the middle of the room today. The newcomer had dark, rich hair somewhere between black and brown, cut close to her head and slicked down. She wore the usual attire of a witch on duty, black cargo pants, matching shirt, and combat boots. The class tentatively gathered around, cowed by her less than friendly disposition. Instructor Lyra was a hard ass, but this woman was something else. Unease took root at the base of my spine, burrowing deep until I shook with it.

"I see you're all aware of our visitor today." Instructor Lyra's voice rang out, a heartbeat before she appeared. "I've asked her here today to help those of you struggling to conform to what's expected of you."

My palms grew damp with sweat when her eyes landed on

me. The corner of her mouth twitched in a barely concealed smirk, and I knew I was fucked. Beside me, Bast stepped closer as a sign of solidarity, but I didn't want him dragged into whatever shitshow was about to go down.

"You all may call me, Nakela," the newcomer announced, hands laced behind her back as she surveyed the class. "I've been active in the field for the past fifteen years and faced the worst demonkind could throw at me. There is no job I can't handle."

Her gaze slid to me and I visibly gulped. Her eyes were like spears, metallic and cold. They pierced through the uninterested façade I hastily donned like scissors through paper.

"Miss Thornton." My name rang like a bell and my classmates fell away.

Bast was the only one to remain by my side. I gently pushed him, lest he capture Nakela's attention next.

"I've heard you've been having trouble shifting." I cut a glare at Instructor Lyra, but Nakela moved into my line of sight. "Don't worry about her, she only wants what's best for you."

I laughed. "Did she tell you that?"

Her skin tightened around her eyes, but she plastered on a fake smile. "She brought me here to help you. She knows I can get results."

I didn't want to think about how she planned to get those results. My heart was in enough of a panic without my imagination getting involved. Something told me her plans weren't sanctioned by the Council.

"You're not a familiar," I said, moving to the side, only to be blocked by a ring of students. "I fail to see how your 'expertise' will help."

"Humor me," she dared, and it wasn't like I had a choice.

Silence fell and the sunshine with it, like the world held its breath for what would come next. There were still streams of dust particles hanging stagnant in the air, but they did little to distract me from the situation.

"Close your eyes," Nakela began. "Visualize your door."

It seemed simple enough, so I shrugged and did as she asked. Her footsteps made soft scoffs on the hardwood that I heard even without tapping into my extra senses. She circled again. I tensed, not trusting her behind me, but kept my eyes squeezed shut. The door in my mind was exactly as I described it to Bast, weathered and damaged, looking much older than my seventeen years of life. Cobwebs littered the upper corners while brittle vines creeped across the threshold in silent wait for a victim. This was no longer the peaceful gift I thought it once was. Time and resentment warped it into something else entirely. Even so, I sensed my inner cat pacing on the other side.

"Once you've located the doorway, step through." Nakela instructed, like it was as simple as that.

If that were the case, I wouldn't be here right now. I heard the soft breaths of everyone in the room as mentally, I stepped closer to the door. The hinges were rusted and tarnished, but I wrapped my hand around the doorknob and gave a half-hearted push.

Nothing. It wouldn't budge.

A soft hiss filtered in from the other side when I tried again with the same results. My eyes opened to a watching gym and the instructors patiently waiting. I hadn't even sprouted a claw.

"Again," Nakela commanded.

I rolled my eyes and searched for the door. This was going to be a long, boring class if all she did was repeatedly tell me to open the door and—

"Ouch!" My eyes sprang open at the sharp pinch on my arm.

The bitch pinched me! I stared at her, incredulous. Were we in the fifth grade?

"Close your eyes and try again." There wasn't a smirk this

time. Her face was set like marble, leaving no room for argument.

I'd barely approached the door when another pinch to my side forced me away with a curse. "I fail to see how this is helping," I growled, my pupils flickering in anger.

The slight reaction pleased Nakela and she shared a look with Instructor Lyra. "Fear and intimidation did nothing to spur your animal half into action," she explained, her voice sickly sweet, as if she spoke to a child. "I've found pain to be a great motivator in times of need."

She was certifiably insane. I glanced around the room to catch the reactions of my classmates. Some of them looked properly disgusted, but they kept their mouths shut. Others, like Lincoln, smiled in an almost gleeful way as they waited to see how this lesson would unfold. Nakela no longer waited for me to close my eyes, and she was past telling me to open the door. She moved right into trying to force the change out of me. Her hands whipped out with lightning speed, landing in soft spots all along my body. The pain was sharp and immediate but faded quickly. Frustration welled inside me as I failed to dodge her attacks.

"Enough," my voice was rough, my inner cat right below the surface.

The pressure of my claws against my fingertips, the prick of my canines along my lower lip, the feel of my skin stretching as fur broke through in spots. My body was on sensory overload. After days of bullying and harassment, this was the final straw. I promised myself I wouldn't roll over and allow the mistreatment any longer. And that included assault from an uppity witch that didn't know how to take no for an answer. The next time her hand came at me, I blocked it, twisting my wrist until I gripped hers. Her eyes briefly widened at the challenge...and then she struck. Her foot swung low at my ankle, intent on knocking me down. I jumped over it with ease and used my momentum on the way down to pull her forward, directly into my knee. The feel of air leaving her lungs was more than satisfying and there was no stopping the grin that split my face.

"You bitch," she wheezed, dropping all pretense with a glare. Instructor Lyra made to intervene, but Nakela held out a hand, the other still cradled across her stomach. "She's mine."

I didn't expect her to move as quick as she did and that was my fault. When she lunged, I tripped over my own feet trying to dodge. Her fist grazed my jaw. The pain was fleeting, but I was still pissed she made contact at all. My animal grew more agitated as we fought. Bits of her attributes escaped in the form of strength and speed, but not enough to completely immobilize Nakela. Her experience was obvious in how swiftly she moved and in knowing exactly where and when to strike. I held my own though, landing just as many blows as she did.

"You will shift before the day is through," she promised, switching up her attack to grab the front of my shirt in an unbreakable grip.

I slammed my forearm down against hers, trying to free myself. She held strong with a sinister smile and twisted. I flipped over her hip. My back met the hard floor and all the air left me. As I tried to recover, she straddled my waist.

"Your resistance is admirable, if not a bit stupid." Nakela clutched my wrist and brought it up in front of her.

I was too busy trying to breathe to put up much of a fight as her stubby hand wrapped around my middle finger. My first breath barely filled my lungs when it left again on a scream as Nakela yanked, breaking the bone with a sure *snap!* My inner cat went nuts, tackling the door from the other side. But she failed to break it down. Instead, claws sprang free and sliced Nakela's skin to ribbons. She hardly blinked. Her fist wrapped around my index finger.

"That was close," she goaded. "But I know you can do better than that."

The next break hurt worse than the first. I bit my lip until I tasted blood, refusing to scream a second time. The doorway in my mind trembled and cracked. Not enough. My hips bucked and caught Nakela off guard enough to throw her forward. She still had a hold on my broken hand, but my other was now free, and I scooped it around her elbow. My leg moved outward and in a flash we flipped. I scrambled away, keeping my broken fingers close to my chest. My eyes were wild—the pupils split as I scanned the crowd for an exit. This had gone too far. Teachers weren't allowed to fucking break bones and while Nakela was the one who technically did the crime, Instructor Lyra stood by and watched. Faces swam around me in a blur of shocked masks, terrified frowns, and leers. They stood shoulder to shoulder, surrounding me and Nakela with no room to escape. Both of us were breathing heavy. My fingers were bent at odd angles and her arm was shredded. Neither of us were willing to back down. Nakela held her hand out to the side where a fully charged cattle prod magically appeared.

Oh, fuck.

I frantically battered the doorway in my mind, my animal fighting just as hard from the other side.

"Your petulant tantrum is over." The end of the cattle prod sparked as she pointed it at me. "It's time to shift."

Her grin revealed bloody teeth from one of my earlier blows and it enhanced the crazed look in her eye as she stalked me. I kept as much distance as the crowd would allow. It was only a matter of time before that thing made contact if I didn't think of something quick. She stabbed. I dodged. We circled a few times and she tried again. This nerve-wracking dance drew us closer together with each turn, our room to maneuver growing smaller as the others crept closer. Fur broke out on my back, hidden under my shirt. Another crack in the doorway that came too late. The cattle prod grazed my arm, and the shock was agonizing enough to blur my vision. My heart beat like a drum inside my chest, threatening to give out as the electric current tapered off somewhere in my elbow. My animal and I worked in tandem to break the door down. Nothing else would save me. No one was coming to stop this, and I didn't know how far Nakela would take it. Already she sprinted around like a mentally altered ringleader, high on trying to tame the large cat in her cage. With some kind of sick battle cry, she leaped, arm outstretched, and prod thrust forward. I tried to twist, to turn, to get away, but there was no room. The barbs struck in my lower ribs and dug deep.

Currents of fiery agony coursed through me, down to the ends of my hair. It felt like peeling skin from my muscles. She twisted the prod, digging it deeper, adding more pain. That was it. The doorway disintegrated and my animal flew to me. The scream that ripped from my throat morphed into a roar as claws replaced fingers, teeth elongated, my bones broke and reformed until a near-rabid snow leopard stood over Nakela. My coat was thick and decorated with dark spots, the camouflage doing nothing for me in the openness of the gym. But it didn't really matter, because my prey was right where I wanted her. Her weapon lay a few feet away, blue streaks of electricity still sparking on the end. She moved her hand as if to reach for it, but a low rumble from my chest stopped that. My large paws curled above her shoulders, close enough for me to see her chest rising and falling in rapid succession. To scent the sweat leaking from her pores and saturated with fear. I gave her a feline smile, all teeth, and that scent increased until it bathed the room.

"See," Nakela called. "I knew you could do it."

She smiled. She actually fucking smiled like she'd accomplished something and that it was over now. And if *I* was in charge, maybe it would be. But I wasn't. The snow leopard attacked, clamping her teeth around the witch's neck. She stopped just short of crushing her trachea, choosing to enjoy the taste of blood oozing from where her massive canines punctured skin. The room gasped and the leopard enjoyed that too. The power she now held in her jaws. Nakela wasn't above pleading for her life, especially when she realized no one was going to interfere. Stupid witch, that wasn't the shifter way. We didn't interrupt the hunt of another.

"P-please," she whimpered, and the snow leopard bit down a little harder just to make her squirm.

The scent of urine added to the others. The prey wet herself. Playing with food was an old past time of cats, and one my leopard was completely engrossed in. So much so, that she didn't hear the opening of a door or the new footfalls moving ever closer. She was too busy growing excited for the feel of life's blood pumping into her mouth and down her throat. Only a little more pressure...

"Kaya, don't!"

I growled, fully in sync with my animal half when it came to someone ruining my fun. Auden and Bast stood across from me, one with eyes wide and a mouth parted in shock, the other meeting my gaze with an unblinking determination. I growled again. A challenge. Daring either of them to come closer.

"You don't want to do this," Auden swore, his eyes darting between my mouth and the pulse jumping in the witch's throat. It was just one little nick away... "You're not a murderer," his voice was soft, and somehow closer.

He knelt on the ground now, within arm's reach. His scent saturated the air around me and the familiar rush of comfort I associated with it did more than anything else to calm the need to maim the woman beneath my teeth.

"You're not a murderer," he repeated. "This isn't who you are."

My eyes softened as they stared back into his and I whined. I *was* a murderer, but I didn't want to be. Gently, I commanded my leopard to open her mouth and we stepped back. Instructor Lyra rushed to Nakela's side, pointing at students and assigning them roles to help her. They left in a flurry of shouts, in a beeline for the infirmary. With my killer instinct off, I sat back on my haunches and waited as Auden tried to calm the room. I realized now was the time to explain myself. To tell what happened before the truth could get jumbled and confused. I couldn't be punished for this, right? I was only defending myself. And I didn't actually kill her, I just came really really close. My mind was in turmoil as I desperately searched for the doorway back. Where were the hinges, the vines? Nothing was where it was supposed to be! It spun in a kaleidoscope of colors, all bleeding into one thought. Another whine stuck in the back of my throat and Auden was in front of me. His hands grasped either side of my head, his long fingers sinking into my fur. Our gazes locked and he cursed under his breath.

"Everybody out!" he ordered, then glanced around the room to make sure they obeyed.

Once we were alone, he returned his full attention. I panted, my sides heaving with my panic. Auden's hand sank into the fur behind my ears. His warmth spread as he ran that touch down my neck, lifted, set it on my head and started again.

"You can do it, Kaya," he promised, never stopping his touch. "Take a breath. I'm here now."

I calmed as his words soothed both the pain and terror. A soft glow caught my attention and there, in the back of my mind, was the doorway. It was still rough, but the vines and cobwebs were nowhere to be seen. The snow leopard walked back through and after a new wave of pain as my bones rearranged, I fell into Auden's arms, naked as the day I was born. There was no strength left in my limbs. The forced shifting, the bruises, the cattle prod, it all took a toll and the tears rolling down my cheeks couldn't be stopped. I hated crying. My eyes swelled, my nose ran, and I looked like an over ripe tomato. I curled tighter around myself, burying my head into Auden's chest to muffle my sobs. His arms tightened around me, both comforting and excruciating where they touched charred skin, and he rocked me. I'd never been held like this before. Like I mattered.

Auden's hand gently slid from my shoulder to just above my elbow.

"I need to see what hurts," he spoke softly. "Can you show me?"

I shook my head and curled tighter. "Everything."

The air left his nose in a loud burst. I could picture the frown on his face; the lowered brows and his lips pulled into a tight line. Auden wasn't used to being denied and after all this time, it still frustrated him when I did it. I felt his eyes roam over the parts of my body he could see. My pale skin the perfect canvas when it came to displaying injuries. Each bruise stood out in stark contrast, cuts gleamed a deep red like marker on paper, and without my clothes, there was nothing to hide it all.

"Let's start with this arm," he crooned, gently gripping the one I held closest to my chest.

Despite my protest, there was little resistance when he pulled it away from my body. It hurt too much. My hand looked tiny compared to his. Tiny and mangled. Two of my fingers bent awkwardly at the second knuckle and the throbbing told me they were beyond swollen as well. Auden's next exhale was shaky.

"Why?" That one word carried so much. Fury for the act, disbelief at the damage, and sorrow for the suffering endured.

I shook my head.

"Kaya," Auden warned. "I'm trying very hard to stay in control right now, but not knowing what happened to you is *killing* me, sweetheart."

"They thought pain would make me shift," I mumbled into his chest and another wave of tears followed, soaking his shirt.

Auden's teeth ground together he clenched his jaw so hard. His touch on me remained gentle even though I could feel the absolute tension shaking the rest of his body. His muscles were wired, ready to snap on those that caused this, but he held it together because he knew he was needed here instead.

"And that's why you had your teeth at the witch's throat," he assumed, without the slightest bit of condemnation.

I shifted in his lap, uncomfortable with reliving my recent torture and he adjusted his hold. The movement knocked his arm into my side, and I yelped. My vision turned white, then fuzzy around the edges as new waves of agony shot down the left side of my body. Auden didn't bother asking this time. He moved away and turned me just enough to get a look at the blackened chaos that was my lower ribs. Charred skin and jagged welts took center stage as Auden released a string of curses so loud the guards on the wall probably heard him.

"What the hell did this?" He snarled and released me; fearful he would accidentally hurt me in his rage.

I brought my knees to my chest and wrapped my arms around them. His eyes fixated on my side, still visible even as I tried to disappear into myself. I was shaking now. Adrenaline wore off and there was only so much I could do to hold myself together when it faded. Auden quickly shrugged off his shirt and pulled it over my head. It took the both of us, and a lot of patience on his part, to get my arms through their proper holes. When we were done, the black fabric bunched just under my ass and Auden's bare chest rose and fell with shuddering breaths. I didn't even make a comment about his chiseled abs or how the sight would normally make me grow wet in unmentionable places. That alone told me something was very wrong. But it was the two Auden's swaying in front of me that finalized the knowledge that I was going to pass out. Before I could, strong arms swept under my legs and around my back, careful to avoid any tender spots. I felt weightless in his arms. My head lolled onto his shoulder, and I fought to get the last words out before the darkness came for me.

"It was a cattle prod," I mumbled.

The words came out slurred, but the hitch in his stride told me he heard. His lips pressed a gentle kiss to my temple, warm and safe.

"I'm going to fucking kill them."

CHAPTER TWENTY-NINE

Nobody died. Not that afternoon and not the next morning when I woke up sore in my own bed. Auden had no time to kill anyone as glued to my side as he was. He remained as the doctor poked and prodded, popped my bones back into place and splinted my fingers, all while asking an endless number of questions. An unnamed emotion took root in my chest. It swelled each time I looked to my right and saw him listening raptly to the doctor's instructions, when his arm remained a firm support around my waist as we walked back to my dorm, and every time the proof that he cared was waved in front of me. Even now, the evidence lay scattered around my room like clues to a puzzle I'd long ago solved but didn't quite believe. It was in the pain medicine, carefully separated into proper doses next to the water bottle on my dresser. It was in the fog still lingering on the corner of the bathroom mirror, leftover from the hot water in the tub Auden insisted I climb into, even with his shirt still on. He cleaned and inspected each bruise and scrape, despite a trained physician having already done so, then stood outside the door while I removed the shirt and soaked away the rest of the pain.

There was no permanent damage from the assault, despite feeling like there was. Physically, my fingers bent and wiggled once more, the bruises were only skin deep, and my heart took no lasting damage from the cattle prod. *Physically* I would be okay in a matter of days thanks to a familiar's quick healing abilities. But mentally, that was a whole other story. The memories weren't something I could scrub clean in the bath. I couldn't shove them into a dusty box in the back of my mind and forget about them. What happened in that gym that day changed everything.

"Fuck," I sighed, pulling the comforter over my head. Hiding didn't work either, but it was nice to pretend.

The shaking started again down at my feet. It traveled through my legs, tapping each individual muscle on its way north until I felt like a live action Operation game—the one where I could never *not* cause the little red nose to light up with a harsh *bzzz!* Different parts of my body took turns rebelling. My claws tore at my clean shirt when they suddenly burst through my skin. The fur on my right arm was still there, challenging me as I tried and failed to get my animal half under control. She was forced back behind that door after finally being let out and it pissed her off. The heavy comforter over my face muffled Bast's soft knock, but I still heard his feet scuff across the floor.

"Maybe a little food will help," he suggested, offering me a classic PB&J on a paper plate. "It will only be a temporary fix though."

I sighed again and scooched higher in bed until my back rested against the wall. "I know, but now is not the time for her to have a temper tantrum." I bit into the sandwich and half the triangle disappeared. The glass of water vanished next to clear the peanut butter. "I'm expected in front of the king and Council in an hour."

Auden sent the warning not too long ago. He tried, but he

couldn't keep me away from the meeting this time. His word and detailed retelling of yesterday's events only covered the end part and even though I told him everything that happened, the Council still wanted to hear my side of things before judgement and punishment would be passed on Instructor Lyra and Nakela. Auden said if it were up to him, they'd be dead already. I'd be lying if I said that didn't make me smile, to know he was just as bloodthirsty for justice as I was.

"Maybe you should shift a little first, before you go," Bast tried again, for the fiftieth time and I rolled my eyes rather than shout.

"The doctor—"

"Said no shifting for a few days. I know I know," he sighed.

I nodded and went back to the sandwich. Let him think the doctor's orders were what held me back. The truth was more complicated to explain. How did you tell another shifter, one who loved their animal half despite the grief it caused, that you feared yours? That the thought of shifting wasn't the cure all he claimed it was.

"I'm not sure the doctor is right in this case, though." Bast kept pressing, like he might know I fibbed a bit on the orders to keep my animal half contained. "A shifter that stays apart from their animal as long as you have risks losing the ability to shift altogether. Or insanity. Slower healing..."

"I get it!" I snapped, then felt immediately guilty for yelling.

He took it in stride, and I finished the sandwich. Hopefully, feeding the beast would keep her calm long enough for me to make it through this interrogation disguised as a hearing. The fear over the next hour far surpassed the very real consequences Bast warned me about. I'd known my whole life that a shifter and her animal needed to have a cohesive relationship; one could not exist without the other. Survival seemed more important at the time as I learned to lock her away and survival was what I worried about now. I was going before the king for the first time since I saw him at the boathouse. There was no telling how this would go.

"He's going to kill me," I whispered, sinking back down into the safety of the blankets.

Bast took the paper plate before crumbs could be spilt on the sheets and set it in the small trashcan. "Not if you stick to the plan," he countered. "Do we need to go over it again?"

We really did because I couldn't see how this wasn't the perfect opportunity for the king to get rid of me. I attacked a witch, a prominent one high in the guard with years of experience and connections, *and* I was still on probation.

"Mom said that you need to remain calm and act normal," Bast knelt at the side of the bed so he could look me in the eye. "Give no indication that you saw the king with the demon."

"But he saw *me!*" That was the problem with this whole 'plan'. I could ignore the big demonic elephant in the room all I wanted, but the king knew that I knew. I was as good as dead the second I walked into that room.

"And he would rather keep his secret than oust you, or you wouldn't be alive right now. Just keep playing his game and it will be okay."

I took a deep breath. We'd been over this a thousand times. The king would have killed me already if he wanted to. Adira was unsure of his overall master plan; they couldn't figure out why he was working with the demons, but they knew one thing: whatever the plan was, it was crucial his involvement not be revealed yet. We had to hope that was a strong enough deterrent to keep me alive a while longer.

"Are you sure about Auden?" Bast asked. "He doesn't know about his father?"

There wasn't a doubt in my mind. It was one weight out of a

million off my chest. I expressed my utter faith in him once again and Bast held up his hands for me to stop.

"If you're sure, then you'll be safe. Auden won't let anything happen to you and the king isn't about to reveal himself in front of his son and Council just to kill you when he's had ample opportunity elsewhere." His new point did more to calm me than any of the previous strategic talk from his mom. Auden would be there, and with him at my side I could face anything. "Be on your guard," Bast warned.

It stuck with me as Auden and I crossed the wooden bridge to the Ruling Island. A breeze rolled across the black water, peaking in small waves that vanished under the wooden slats beneath my feet. Trees bent with the small gust as we passed until it looked like they bowed. The magic of the island was in full effect, almost like it put on a show for my final walk across the green lawns, between the grand houses, and up to the thick doors that barred the entrance to the Council chambers. Did the island know something I didn't? I took a quick glance at Auden. He was the picture of calm and composed; arms relaxed at his side so his fingers could graze mine as we walked. The corner of his mouth twitched each time we touched so I swung my arms wider, ensuring it happened with every other step. Long fingers wrapped around mine, bringing our game to a close just as we turned the hall. A few feet away, on the other side of the imposing doors, was the large room where my fate was already determined once this year.

"Are you ready?" Auden queried, watching my face closely for any signs I was going to bolt.

I schooled my features, pulled back my shoulders and nodded. A small thought side railed my bravado and I stepped back. "Will they be in there?"

He didn't need to ask who I was talking about.

"No," he shook his head, a gentle smile curling his lips. "But you'd be okay even if they were."

The doors opened from the inside before I could respond. Show time. The room hadn't changed since my last visit; high windows allowed in bright light behind the raised bench that separated us from the king, Asiel, and the Council. The various members eyed me as I walked closer, their scrutiny not as painful as I thought it would be— definitely not as bad as last time when they took stock of my breeding attributes. I shuddered at the memory and moved further into the room, avoiding looking at the center for as long as I could. I knew each gaze personally that awaited there. On the left would be Asiel, his near black pupils fixed on my every move. My father would be to the right; the coldness of his gaze a complete opposite to the warm color they once shined with. Right in the center sat the king with his perfectly styled hair and warm Wardwell gold. I bowed to give myself more time before I had to look at him. It was confusing to look at the man I'd grown up revering and see all the little faults somehow invisible to everyone else. The gold in his eyes was several shades lighter, making the black more dominant and the skin around his face and neck drooped with wrinkles I hadn't noticed before.

"Welcome, Kaya!" The king's voice boomed across the room, and I startled. Auden stepped up beside me, his fingers once again grazing mine in a brief touch. "I'm sorry to see you return to these rooms under such circumstances."

I gave another slight bow to hide how much I was shaking, "As am I, Your Majesty."

When I straightened, my father leaned forward ready to begin. The king held the final decision, but it was my father and the Council who would run the trial. I was thankful the accused weren't here to stare daggers into my back while I revealed all the details of their act of betrayal. It was hard enough to speak them to the three men I was pretty sure weren't on Team Kaya anyway. Spilling my trauma to a roomful of old witches and shifters intent on judging me was as hard as I thought it would be. My mouth felt dry after only a few sentences and the tentative hold I had on my inner cat was tested the second Asiel started speaking.

"I'm sure you're aware that we've already gotten statements from the accused before you arrived today, yes?" Asiel's superior attitude wasn't easy to swallow even when you were prepared for it. I nodded rather than risk opening my mouth to answer, who knew what would come out. "Then I must mention that we've been informed about the multiple instances where you chose to be difficult in class. Refusing to shift being first and foremost, but also disrupting class and overall complaining about how things are done."

As Asiel ticked down my faults on each finger, I risked a glance at my father. His diplomatic mask held firmly in place to hide his true thoughts, but I was used to reading it like he read Council reports each night with a glass of his favorite alcohol. Disappointment—that one wasn't new. Irritation, that one was also a treasured favorite. But there was one emotion I couldn't make out. It caused a new crease in his chin that wasn't there before and a small kindling of hope sparked that it might be a sign he was on my side after all.

"Are you suggesting she *deserved* to be attacked by a seasoned guard and then struck with a cattle prod, brother?" Auden left the silent role behind to argue with Asiel and I was glad for it, but a showdown between the princes would do me no good.

"There was a lot for me to adjust to upon my return," I admitted, recapturing the attention of those behind the bench. "I've learned better since then." Asiel leaned forward to spear me with another one of my faults, but I kept going. "I *was* having difficulty shifting. I spent so long holding my animal back while living with humans that when put under pressure by Instructor Lyra, I fell back onto old habits of keeping my cat at bay."

The key to a good lie was to have just the right amount of truth mixed in. I did have trouble shifting and a lot of it had to do with spending my formative years among humans. Instructor Lyra's pressure to shift certainly hadn't helped, but I would've come to her for assistance if she hadn't greeted me with animosity from day one. Auden watched me along with everyone else as I spun my tale with emphasis on how I was treated.

"While your control is admirable," the king finally commented. "I worry that if you can't shift, it will be a handicap to you and whoever you eventually partner with."

Well, shit. I didn't have an argument for that.

Before I could give in to panic, Auden stepped up yet again. "Her level of control over her animal was ideal in this situation or Nakela would be dead right now."

Universe, please don't let Auden tell the entire room how he had to coax me away from killing the witch. I know he's only trying to help, but that would be very, very bad.

"I'll also add that what happened yesterday was not approved training protocol." The support came from the last person in the room I'd expect... my father. "Weapons are not to be used against students in a shifting class and no permission was requested or given for a guest instructor to be teaching, let alone *torturing* my daughter."

Asiel sat back in his seat, properly subdued as the rest of the Council nodded along with my father's points. No one wanted to argue with a man about whether the torture of his daughter could be overlooked. Not even the king. My throat swelled with tears as they dismissed me to determine the rest in private.

Auden escorted me out, but only as far as the bridge since he would be a part of the final decision once deliberations were over.

"You can breathe now, Kaya," he chuckled when I fell against the railing, his arm rushing out to make sure I didn't fall in.

"I just didn't expect that," I whispered, still in shock. "My father never once....he..."

Auden rubbed soothing circles on my back. "Maybe hearing details about his daughter's attack has changed his view on some things," he suggested.

I doubted it. It was more likely that he played the role of outraged father since it was expected of him, or he refused to let the slight against our family name go without punishment. Both served his own image. I hated to be so cynical, especially after seeing him today, but that was the man he'd proven to be time and time again. The pity in Auden's gaze was more than I could take; paired with his touch it was a little overwhelming.

"I'll come see you tonight when the verdict's been reached," he promised, dropping a light kiss to my forehead. "Go get some rest."

For once I had no desire to misbehave after being given a direct order. There was no fight left in me today; my body used it all to heal and keep that damn snow leopard behind that door. I fought off another round of shivers, surprised the sandwich suppressed them for so long. I rushed across the bridge and down the nearest path to the dorms. Spending the rest of the afternoon in bed became my new goal. Right behind getting my inner cat to calm the fuck down.

CHAPTER THIRTY

The night was cool as it ghosted through the open crack in my window, bringing with it the scents of summer and a piece of calm. I felt better after a full afternoon of rest. My side still hurt when I moved, but the lingering nausea finally faded, and I found myself growing bored as the evening dragged on. It was ironic that the one time my world was peaceful, I craved excitement. Not that I was in any condition for it. Besides having enough bruises to resemble a dalmatian, my damned inner cat had no chill. There was a driving need inside me that demanded I shift and run through the swamp until my paws were caked with mud, as some unlucky prey filled my jaws with their blood. One quick glance out the window showed the moon was full: a perfect night for hunting.

My skin itched just thinking about it and fur broke free along my arm before I could stop it. Triple checking the door in my mind did no good when my animal half was sneaky and talented at hiding. I couldn't keep this up forever. The sound of metal springs and a soft click was easy to pick up with my cat this close to the surface. My doorknob turned in one smooth motion and the heavy wood swung inward, allowing the moonlight to illuminate Auden kneeling on the ground with a pair of lockpicks in his hand, his grin as wide as a Cheshire cat's as he took in my raised brow and crossed arms.

"I took your key so you would knock first, not so you could turn to a life of crime."

He tucked the picks into his pocket and sauntered in, relocking the door behind him. "Please. B and E isn't new to my resume."

The audacity.

"Oh really? Break into a lot of girl's rooms do you?"

The bed creaked as he flopped down beside me. His head rested on his hand like he wasn't the least bit guilty, and the room grew warm. He was so close I felt his body heat even through my thick comforter. My hands twitched with the desire to cross those last couple inches separating us and feel along the dark skin of his forearm—over the thick veins that flexed when he moved.

I swallowed. "Did something else happen after the hearing?"

They reached the verdict within an hour of my leaving. Auden already came by once today to tell me. Both females were reassigned outside the walls to permanently remain on duty for the foreseeable future. They could only occupy the outposts outside the community, but it was better than being subjected to a set time in a prison cell. The Council was desperate for warriors due to our falling numbers, so every able-bodied fighter was badly needed. The same technicality that saved me, saved them, but I didn't care how they were punished, as long as they could no longer hurt me.

"No," Auden replied. "No changes since this afternoon, that I know of."

"Then why are you here?" It sounded harsh, but it didn't knock the smile from his face. Actually, it deepened.

"I swung by to make sure you were settled in your room for the night," he sat up, the sudden height difference forcing me to lean back. "The full moon is when they reset the wards and some small voice in my head told me I'd better make sure you stayed put."

I rolled my eyes. I had no plans to go anywhere; sleep was all that was on the agenda for tonight. The shrill song of a winged predator snatching its quarry squeezed in through the open window and another thought came to mind.

"Are you worried the demons will attack tonight?"

The wards were at their weakest when the casts were being laid. With all the recent attacks, I wouldn't put it past the demons to try again.

Auden rubbed his jaw as he stared out the window. "They haven't done that in a while, but I'm a little on edge with the bad omen tonight, if I'm being honest." He gestured at the moon and the hazy orange glow surrounding it. "When there's a circle around the moon, it means trouble isn't far behind."

A heavy cloud took that moment to drift across the room and bathe us in darkness. I held back a hiss at the eerie harbinger and dug my fingernails into my palms until it passed. New racing heartrate aside, I didn't want Auden to think I was incapable of riding out the night by myself.

"You don't have to stay," I told him, as I fought the urge to get up and close the window.

His head tilted to the side. "No wild urge to shift and run through the trees?"

He meant it as a jest, but he was so close to the truth I couldn't laugh. How did he...? His knowing smile made me want to slap him.

"I've got her under control," I lied through clenched teeth. "I'm not stupid enough to go out on an unsanctioned shift across campus after you warned me of a bad omen."

Honestly, how stupid did he think I was?

"Forgive me if I don't trust that," he replied with a laugh, obviously not reading the attitude of the room. Mainly mine.

"What are you going to do, stay here and watch me?"

He made a show of sliding off his shoes, first the right, then the left, before wiggling until his back rested against the wall. "That's exactly what I'm going to do."

"All night?" I squeaked, my annoyance gone at the possibility of me and Auden alone that long.

His lips tightened as he suppressed another smile. He enjoyed making me uncomfortable. "At least until I know you won't go sneaking out to howl at the moon or something."

"That's Bast," I deadpanned, and then had a brief wandering thought about whether that was true.

He never told me if Rougarou suffered the same curse as a werewolf when it came to the full moon. I would assume not if he was allowed to stay on campus. I had to ask next time I saw him if the moon made him all itchy. It definitely had an effect on me tonight. Keeping my animal locked up for so long, only to let her out and steal her prey, didn't make us the best of friends right now. She wanted freedom and I was terrified of it happening again.

"Hey, you okay?" Auden's teasing grin was replaced with concern, his thick lashes fanning his cheeks as he looked down at me.

"Yeah," I nodded as another wave of anxiety rolled over me. "Just anxious about the wards now I guess."

Lies. I was worried I'd turn into a big furry cat with a penchant for chewing on witches.

Sheets rustled as he moved closer. "You know I'd never let anything happen to you."

And just like that, my heart skipped for an entirely different reason. Gone was the doubt and uncertainty of keeping the leopard in check. Right now, she was just as interested as I was about the change in Auden's scent. Her ears perked, tail flicking back and forth as she and I both waited to see what he would do. I couldn't help but take it all in, even as I tried to focus on how the gleam in his gaze made my stomach clench in anticipation. Instead, I was all too aware of what I wore—Auden's borrowed shirt—and how it rested high on my thighs. His warm fingers grazed the sensitive skin as they took the weight of his body, allowing him to plant his hand on the bed right next to my hip. He leaned in, his hooded lids lowered, until his breath tickled the shell of my ear.

"Are you still nervous?" The warm air caused goosebumps to breakout all over my body.

I shook my head. I was full of lies tonight. My breaths were uneven and just shy of panting. He hadn't even touched me, and I was ready to melt into a puddle. I knew what he tasted like, knew how it felt to have him between my thighs and I wanted more.

He hummed, using his other hand to skim the tender skin at my neck where my pulse fluttered like crazy. "Are you sure?" he purred. "You're trembling." A small kiss to my throat followed by a gentle suck had me gasping. A new wave of shivers made me wiggle and he pulled away. "I guess I have to try harder to distract you."

He pressed against the center of my chest until I lay back and his body followed mine until he completely covered me. His weight stayed on his elbows, but after a little nudge with his knee, my legs opened enough to cradle his hips and take some of that burden. One arm was still by my head, while his other hand slipped into my shirt. My hips bucked. Already I was needy. Heat pooled where our bodies met, and I chased that feeling with another roll of my hips.

Auden pulled back with a smirk. "Shh," his voice was a low rumble that had my legs tightening around him. "So greedy."

I was seconds away from whining. Need rippled through my body like a firestorm demanding to be both stoked and put out. His lips were firmer as they grazed the column of my throat. I tilted my head to give him better access and was rewarded with a slow lick followed by a deep grind of his hips.

"Oh," the air left me on a moan, and I fought in vain to get it back while Auden continued his strategic onslaught.

I quivered and shook with each pass of his lips, each rock against that sensitive spot at the apex of my thighs. His free hand now traveled sensually up my ribcage, tracing a path of scorching heat to my breasts. He lingered there, pulling and teasing my nipples into hard pebbles he could roll between his fingertips. My eyes squeezed shut as I got lost in the volley of sensations; hyper aware of every place he touched and all the places he still could. As if he read my mind, Auden's hand left my shirt to drift down my body. When I felt him push my knee out, everything below my waist clenched. My hands were busy themselves, running over his sculpted abdomen, scraping my nails along the light dusting of hair above his belt, and the sound of his halted breathing was enough to set me on fire.

The look he sent me was so hot it burned as he rubbed his hand down my inner thigh, pushing my legs wide. His touch started light as his fingertips made little circles, but when he felt how ready I was for him he growled against the side of my neck and pressed harder. I gasped as my hands squeezed his sides, as my mind blanked at the sheer pleasure he was causing. His movements stopped and I opened my eyes to find him staring at me. After a moment, I realized he was waiting for permission. Holding my breath, I dipped my chin. He slipped a finger beneath my underwear and gently thrust it inside. My muscles clamped around the digit, greedy to keep it inside when he pulled back. Whimpers escaped as Auden played my body like a well-tuned instrument, wringing more sounds out of me I didn't even know I could make. Pressure pushed at my entrance and my hips moved away on reflex.

"You can handle another finger," Auden's voice held a dark promise as he licked the shell of my ear.

My mouth opened in a silent shout as a second finger slid inside, joining the first and pumping carefully. I tensed at the stretch, but Auden kept his strokes gentle.

"Relax," he rasped in my ear, working me slowly. My body gradually eased until I met each of his thrusts with a roll of my hips. "Good girl, let me in."

He twisted his fingers and I gasped, burying my face in his shoulder to hold back the scream I felt building in the back of my throat. I strained against the rising wave inside me, against the burning, suffocating pressure of my lungs as I tried my best not to alert my entire floor about the dirty things Auden's hand was doing to me, and how much I liked it. He slowed and alternated between scraping his teeth across my nipple and sliding a finger inside me. Another nip with his teeth, then he'd slide out. My hips moved on their own accord as I unconsciously chased that relentless storm of pleasure spinning just out of reach.

"Not yet, sweetheart," he murmured. "Not yet."

My fingers thread through his hair, pulling as he continued his torturous touch. It was all too much, the growing peak that once looked so far away was now right here and far too big.

"Please," I whimpered, not sure if I was asking him to stop or keep going. I was painfully aware of his every movement, his fingers twisting inside me against that one spot, his mouth against my throat, and his hard arousal rubbing against my leg.

"Open your eyes, Kaya," he commanded, his voice pitched lower. "I want to see what I do to you."

My lashes fluttered open as his thumb joined the rest of his fingers that were driving me out of my mind. It rubbed above the other two; around and around, up one side and down the other. My climax started in my toes as a numbness, a tingling that grew stronger the higher it traveled until it reached my thighs. Higher. Auden moved faster when I began to mumble incoherently, and I ignited. Everything building within me took off, sending me so high I felt weightless. Our breathing was the first thing I noticed when I came back down, and it was the only sound in the room that could be heard over the blood roaring in my ears. Auden was still hard against my leg, but his hands weren't rushing me as they fixed my underwear and pulled my shirt back over my stomach. He obviously hadn't finished, and I grew excited at the thought of bringing him the same pleasure... but it also made me pause.

Was I ready to go that far with him? And was it right for me to let it continue when he still didn't know the truth about me? I wasn't thinking before, too caught up in the moment, but now —my guilt grew as we kissed and touched our way closer, as *something* sparked between us that threatened to burn me from the inside. Auden felt it too, I could tell, and when he touched me like he just did, I knew I couldn't do this to him. He deserved to know who he was getting into bed with, even if it ruined everything. My hands on his shoulders gently pushed him away until there was enough space for me to see the evidence of my effect on him.

"What's wrong?" he panted; brow creased with worry. "Did I hurt you?"

I couldn't help but laugh at how absurd it sounded. That was the farthest thing from pain I'd ever felt.

"No," I snickered, also out of breath. "But we need to talk before we go any further."

The more I thought over what I was about to do, the quicker all those good feelings fled. Auden's cheeks burned as he cleared his throat. He awkwardly climbed off me and sat back on his heels, his hand rubbing at the back of his neck. I focused on his face and the secondhand embarrassment I saw there rather than the intimidating tent at the front of his pants.

"I, uh," he coughed. "Since I was your first kiss, I already assumed you'd never done this before." His eyes widened when the words left his mouth, like he didn't mean for them to come out. "I didn't come here tonight with plans to steal your virtue, I mean."

My nerves left me on a giant wave of confusion. What in the hell was he going on about?

"My *virtue*?" My eyes felt wider than my face. "What is this, a medieval romance?" He opened his mouth to ramble some more, but I cut him off. "Just, shut up. That's not what we need to talk about." I took a deep breath; better to get it over with. "I need to tell you the truth about Asher."

The mention of his dead brother put a hard stop to the touching. He sat further on the bed, back against the wall as I tried to gather what was left of my courage. I'd opened the door, there was no choice now but to step through it; that didn't make it any easier. Auden's infinite patience was not a boon in this situation. His eyes followed me as I got up and paced the room, not with malice, but...soon. I expected nothing less from him when he learned of what I'd done. Shit. I really didn't want to do this. The door in my mind squeaked on its hinges and I slammed it shut at the last second. Stopped in the middle of the room, hands clenched by my side, and eyes squeezed shut—yeah, I'm sure this was helping the situation.

Auden's hand worked to open my fingers. "Is it that hard to say?"

My laugh was short and mocking. Hard? This went beyond hard. It was unfathomable. Eyes still closed, I decided to start at the beginning. My hand tightened around his, as if I had the right to steal comfort from him while simultaneously smashing his heart with a hammer.

"That day, my father was being worse than usual, shouting and cursing at me until I wanted nothing more than to escape from that stupid island and his expectations I never could seem to fulfill."

As the words spilled out, the memories came with them. The unforgiving heat of that day and how it stuck to me like the threats and insults my father casually threw, the rough stone of the wall and the dried-up, broken bits of ivy that clung to it.

"Asher didn't want to go," I blew the breath I'd been holding in a harsh laugh. "You know how he was, always the rule follower. But he'd go anywhere for me, do anything, because I was good at manipulating our friendship." I always knew how to get Asher to do what I wanted. He got in trouble only because I dragged him along to whatever my stupid scheme was for the day. "I *forced* Asher to climb that wall even though he didn't want to. He was scared of heights, but I didn't care. I told myself I was helping him overcome his fear."

I remembered that first taste of freedom as I looked out over the unprotected bayou, at all the free space without a single guard around to report to my father. The trees were perfect for climbing, the ground strong enough to run on, but still mushy, and all that Spanish moss dripping from their limbs made the grove look like a secret hideaway all our own. Here came the hard part. I tried to let go of Auden's hand, I didn't deserve the comfort, but he held on tighter than I did. I was too much of a coward to open my eyes and see the hatred I knew was forming.

"I was so foolish, so *selfish*, that I didn't think there would be any demons outside the protection of the wards. We hadn't heard of any nearby in years so what could it hurt to be a little daring?" We hadn't had any reports, but our whole existence was centered around protecting humanity, who was I to think I knew more than the entire history of our people? "I didn't know, Auden. I swear I didn't know the demons had him until it was too late. Asher was grumpy with me, and yelled, but I didn't know...I—"

I stopped, too choked up to say anything else. Visions of Asher's limp body hanging from the demon's pinchers made me sob. He was never coming back, never going to smile again or pick a new book from the library, never be here to tell me it was going to be okay. Because it wasn't.

"Look at me," Auden demanded, the sharpness of his request hit me right in the heart. "Kaya, look at me, dammit."

I opened my eyes on another sob, not ready but knowing it was time to face my fate. Auden's hate was just the tip of the iceberg. Once the rest of the Council knew, they'd make what happened to Instructor Lyra and Nakela look like a birthday party. Asiel would delight in any chance to punish me, and I wasn't sure what happened to the king, but keeping his secret would never be easier. Auden stood in front of me, holding my hand as I met his dark gaze. He forced my chin up with a finger when I tried to look away. He was so still.

"You've blamed yourself for my brother's death this entire time?" His voice was soft, but deep and with no hint of the rage I thought there'd be.

"*I* made him climb the wall. *I* forced him past the wards," I replied, coldly. Did he not get it? I killed his little brother. How many times was he going to make me say it?

"Is this what you've been carrying around with you? Why you didn't come home?" He asked in complete disbelief. "You were just a kid!"

I shook my head; this couldn't be happening. Auden was supposed to hate me when he found out. He needed to hate me as much as *I* hated me.

"I was old enough to know better and you can't tell me

some part of you didn't blame me. I saw how pissed you were when you found me in Miami." I would never forget that first meeting. Auden looked ready to strangle me and I hadn't even said a word to him yet.

"Because when I found out you were still alive, that you'd ran away, I realized I'd spent the last four years alone when I didn't have to be! I lost both of you!" He shouted, the emotion I saw in his eyes finally making its way out. "I needed you here after I lost the only person in my family that understood me. But I never, *ever* blamed you for Asher's death, and I still don't. What happened was an accident, Kaya. A tragic, horrible, accident."

"No," I couldn't stop shaking my head, couldn't get his voice out of it either.

"Yes," he insisted, bringing both his hands up to cup my face. "What will it take to make you believe me?" He wiped the tears from my cheeks with his thumbs and I saw a glimmer of gold spark to life deep in his eyes. We shared the same breath and somehow it was more intimate than any kiss. "I think I'm falling in love with you," he admitted, and my heart came to a full stop. "I always have, you know, when we were growing up, but now it's different. I want more with you. More moments annoying you, more truths, more battles to fight by your side even when you don't need me to. I want all your kisses and all your other firsts. I want to help you see yourself as I see you, as I know Asher saw you; this strong, loving, *least selfish* person I've ever met."

The crying didn't stop for hours after that, but Auden held me through it all. I fell asleep with my head tucked into his shoulder and his arm curled around my waist. I never told him I loved him back, but we had time. My future rolled out before me in a thousand nights just like this one and for once, I couldn't wait to wake up the next morning.

CHAPTER
THIRTY-ONE

I dreamed of death. Screams echoed like a high-pitched ringing, coming at me from every direction no matter how I tossed and turned. I pulled the pillow over my head, but it couldn't keep out the shrill shouts or the squelching sounds of weapons sinking into flesh. Tearing. Clawing. Visions of demons wrenched me from my restless sleep and I sat up, pushing my tangled hair from my face with a large breath. Auden was already awake and peering out the window, his body angled behind the curtains to keep him hidden from anyone who may be lurking below. It wasn't a dream; the screams were very real and coming from inside the dorm.

"What's happening?" I already reached for the first pair of pants I could find, not caring if they were dirty. A sports bra was thrown on next.

Auden cursed and ducked away from the window just as a dark, leathery wing struck the glass. A spiderweb of cracks spread from one corner to the other as the Revenant backed up to try again.

"Go!" Auden ordered, opening the door and pushing me

into the hall just as the glass gave way and the demon broke in with a screech.

The hallway was chaos as students and guards ran around with no sense of direction. Our rooms weren't safe, as we'd just seen, but where else were the students supposed to go? Outside sounded like a battlefield and if more Revenants were out there, we risked being plucked from the ground like appetizers with a toothpick. I pressed against the wall as panicked classmates ran by, some armed with weapons and others already shifted. My leopard behaved for once but I felt her just below the surface, ready to break free if I needed her. At the look of things, I just might. Auden grabbed my hand and dragged me along behind him, against the current of fleeing students and toward the back hallway that hid the stairs to the attic. Tucked inside, our rapid breathing was the only sound besides the now muffled screams.

"We're hiding?" I asked, not liking the idea. "There are Revenants out there, they need our help!"

"You're going to go up to that attic and barricade the door with whatever you can find," Auden ordered, the look on his face made it clear arguing wasn't an option. "The room is stocked with weapons, but if you do what I say, you shouldn't have to use them." His grip moved to my arm, and he held on tight as we moved up the stairs. "Cover the window with whatever you can find and then stay away from it. Do you hear me? Do *not* let the demons see you."

"Auden, what's going on? Why are you hiding me instead of letting me fight?" We'd stopped at the top of the stairs, but he still hadn't let go of my arm. "If this is about last night—"

He opened the door and pushed us inside. Neither one of us risked turning on the light as the sounds from outside resounded off the high ceiling and cavernous room. Auden was already on the other side, pushing unused furniture and other stored, forgotten items across the window. It wasn't completely covered, but if I stayed away from it no one would know I was in here. Fear rose within me as I watched him stalk around, checking the weapons and pocketing a few he might need. He wasn't planning on staying in here with me. Outrage fogged my vision at the thought of being pushed aside and hidden like a child. I didn't train my whole life just to cower when the fight decided to come find me.

"This looks oddly familiar," I said, coldly. "Remember what happened last time you told me to stay put and then left to go fight by yourself?"

Auden calmly tucked a knife in his boot then spun to face me, his arms crossed and feet spread as he braced for battle. "I remember exactly what happened. You tore your stitches and I had to drag you back to the infirmary to get fixed up. Again."

"I was referring to that little part of how I saved your ass," I pulled my shoulders back and met his defiant stare, unblinking. "You have me to thank for all your organs still being inside your body. You're welcome."

He shook his head and stalked past me, heading for the stairwell. I followed, close on his heels, with no intention of being left alone to twiddle my thumbs. Auden hated help and claimed that he worked better alone, but he needed me. We made a pretty great team when he trusted me.

"This time will be different," he vowed, spinning to keep the open door at his back. "Because you will be safe in here until I come back to get you."

"Un-fucking-likely," I growled.

"You will," he threatened. "Or I will tie you up and tuck you in the corner like the naughty schoolgirl you pretend to be."

I jabbed my finger into his chest and bared my teeth. "You don't get to tell me what to do just because I let you in my pants."

The battle raged outside, but in here we were locked in our own stalemate. I was tired of being left on the sidelines when it came to him trusting me. I was either competent or I wasn't. He either trusted me, or he didn't. He may not after last night—especially after last night—and that knowledge twisted my heart until it nearly cracked, but I refused to back down.

"This has nothing to do with that," he insisted, stepping closer until I had to tilt my head back to look in his eyes. "The demons are drawn to you. I'm just trying to keep you safe."

"What?"

His thumb brushed across my cheek as a muscle ticked in his jaw. "You've been the target of a demon attack five times since I found you. Five. Three of those times resulted in an infirmary visit and here we are again."

"That doesn't mean—"

"A damn Revenant broke through your window! What more do you need?"

Knowing what I did about the king, I realized he might be on to something. Fuck. The Amon demon in Miami, the Buer demon at the rest stop, the shade, the Tennin, and now a Revenant through my own window—the demons really were after me. But why? Was it to keep me silenced? Because of my power? I wrung my hands in front of me as the implications of being a target sunk in. Everyone around me was in danger. Auden was— my head swung up, eyes wide. Auden needed to get out of here. If they were truly after me, he was safer as far from this attic as he could get, winged demons outside or not.

"I'll stay away from the window," I promised, and he released a sigh of relief.

"Barricade this behind me." He left a final kiss on my forehead before shutting the door, his footsteps fading down the stairs.

I did as I was told, finding whatever I could to push in front of the not-so-sturdy door. The shrieks of hunting Revenants didn't fade as time moved on. Shadows swooped across the walls each time one flew past, their size easily taking up half the wall. Through all the shouts and sounds of battle, I kept my ear tuned for one voice in particular. Fear of death wouldn't keep me away if Auden needed me. I just hoped it was all over soon so I could yell at him for risking his life, then kiss him until my heart stopped trying to claw out of my chest.

IN THE SHORT time we had to act, the attic seemed like the best place to go; it was secure with only one exit, plenty of space to maneuver, stocked with weapons, and easy to defend. But as the Revenant rammed into the window a third time, I realized even the best plans weren't foolproof. All my textbook reading on Revenants blurred behind adrenaline and shattered furniture. The window long ago surrendered to the bulky weight of the demon's body, the small shards of glass still attached to the frame failed to even leave a scratch. Smaller than the one that broke into my bedroom, this demon was more of a teenager in size.

"Goody, we're the same age," I muttered, backing away from the still impressive wingspan.

Talons tipped each wing and its fangs dripped with saliva as it scented the air with a forked tongue. The floorboard beneath my shoe creaked. Yellow eyes snapped to me, narrowing when they saw me lunge for the door. Furniture still blocked my route, and I had no time to try and move it. The Revenant roared its delight at seeing its prey trapped and my cat hissed a warning from the other side of our mental door. I stopped fighting her. A brief burst of pain, popping joints, and stretched skin, and my snow leopard was there, prowling the west wall with a feline grin. At the sight of my claws, the demon bared its teeth. Now we were evenly matched. The ancient floor groaned beneath our combined weight and any moment I feared it would give out and we'd go tumbling to the level below. We circled one another, the mats and punching bags becoming obstacles in our game of patience; seeing who would strike first. Either demons didn't have much or this one was as impulsive as any other teenager. It swiped for my head, the reach impressive and a little scary as it almost hit me from across the room. I ducked and flexed my paws before moving in and scratching at the fibrous underside of the wing. My hooked nails sliced through the membranes like butter, resulting in a cry so shrill my ears flattened to my head in pain. There was an answering call from downstairs, and suddenly, the door to my only exit shook under the force of another intruder.

Two places at once. It was impossible to fight the Revenant *and* defend the door at the same time. That old dresser wouldn't hold for long and even though there was one less demon appendage to worry about, the pissed off teenager wasn't done with me yet. The injured wing dragged on the floor as it moved, more cautious than before, but no less malicious. Wood curled away in deep gouges where its claws sank into weakening boards and the door shuddered in warning behind me. I was running out of time. My sensitive hearing isolated the heart chamber on the right side of its chest, a little toward the center and wide open for a desperate attack. I knew from Mr. Laveau's lessons in demon anatomy that the heart would be protected from a frontal attack by bony plates attached to the ribs, but there was a small weak spot on the side where I should aim. One claw was all it took.

Splintered timber zinged over my head as the dresser made its final stand and failed. The weak door and even weaker lock would be next, and I'd face an enemy on both fronts. I had to move *now.* Crouched low, I weaved around the Revenants attempts to slice me, creeping ever closer to its tender center. My first swipe was blocked, forcing me to duck under the broken wing to keep from being skewered. The demon's enraged roar invigorated its partner on the other side of the door. I heard nothing but the steady beat of my heart and the ringing in my ears. There were no more shouts of pain or threatening demon snarls; nothing penetrated the bubble of piece that settled over me once I had my target in my sights.

My second swipe was right on the money. My foreclaw sank into the demon's chest, through thick tissues and past the bony plates surrounding every spot but this one. With a single hook, I punctured the heart and the Revenant froze, releasing a final death cry so loud it shook the walls. I dodged its falling body and shoved my leopard through the door faster than I ever had, shifting just in time to throw my hand out and seal the broken doorframe in a shield of red. It took a moment to adjust to my human senses, to block out the buzzing in the back of my head. A deep voice breached the confusion, coming from the other side of my shield.

"Kaya!" Auden's bellow was full of fear. I barely made out his black hair through the cracks in the wood.

I dropped my shield. The door ruptured inward and there he was, sliding across the floor to scoop my naked body up into his arms. His hands and shirt were covered in gore, but I didn't care. My nose flooded with the scent of summer rain, and I almost cried in relief. He was alive. He was safe. Our hands were grasping and clingy, moving over one another to check for injuries.

Auden's gaze caught over my shoulder at the dead Revenant and my lips curled in a half-smile. "Guess the plan didn't work after all."

His deep chuckle resonated through his chest as me

pulled me close. His lips laid kisses along the crown of my head, the side of my face. We lay there, wrapped around each other as our hearts slowed and eventually beat in sync. The calls for help trickled away to nothing and I knew today's battle was over. For now. I wanted to ask how bad it was and what damage we took to our numbers this time; I knew it wasn't good. But I needed a few more minutes to revel in the feel of Auden's arms around me and the knowledge that we made it. The calm couldn't last forever, and there was work to be done.

I tried to pull away first, but Auden was reluctant to let go. "I was terrified," he whispered into my hair before leaning back to look me in the eye. "I heard the Revenant on the other side of the door. The thought of you trapped in here, alone..." His throat bobbed. "I've never been so afraid in my life."

"You came back for me, that's what matters," I told him, knowing there was no real way to keep me safe when the building was bombarded by demons.

"I tried to get to you, but the door wouldn't open," he shook his head. "It was like something held it closed. There was a flash of red and then suddenly it was gone, and I broke it down."

Now would have been the time to tell him about my power. It was the perfect segue. His fear and worry should theoretically override any suspicion or potential mistrust he might have for me not telling him sooner. The words wouldn't leave my mouth. How did you explain something you knew nothing about? Sure, I could do a few party tricks—tricks that saved my life— but I couldn't begin to explain where the power came from or why I was training with Bast and Adira instead of informing the king and Council. Once again, life threw a complicated wrench at my face, and I was forced to duck instead of catching it.

"How bad is it out there?" I asked, gently steering him away from the topic of the door. I immediately wished I hadn't.

Auden's shoulders slumped, "Bad. The Revenants attacked the dorms and community simultaneously." The grief in his eyes shined. "There was significant loss of life."

A sick part of me wondered how the king would cover it up this time. The other demon assaults were brushed under the rug, even when the leftover blood proved we took substantial damage. Classes resumed as usual the next day, sometimes even within the hour, and no one ever said anything about it. I knew they were all thinking it, though. Adira said there was unrest lurking in the underbelly of the community. Too many unresolved concerns and not enough action from the king and Council made people ask questions. Our little community was about to turn on its head, I only hoped we all made it out the other side when it finally happened.

CHAPTER THIRTY-TWO

Half the girl's dorms took damage, including the now unusable attic. The boy's building didn't fare much better, and all homeless students were now being reassigned to cots in the cafeteria until further notice. Some chose to stay back with their families in the residential part of the community but having to share a sticky floor with bitching teens wouldn't be enough to make me go back to my father's house. Unfortunately, a summons from him wasn't something I could ignore. The cardstock arrived by personal messenger, engraved in gold like the other and too pristine looking against the backdrop of all this destruction. A small part of me wondered if this was his way of checking on me after the attack, but experience squashed that hope with a sledgehammer. He read the reports already and knew I was okay, if at least alive and not bleeding out somewhere at the top of a tree after being dropped by a Revenant.

The Ruling Island took no damage, not a shingle out of place on the meticulously maintained homes. Which made sense. If the king wanted to launch an attack on his own territory, he wouldn't want his house to take damage in the process.

It only made me hate this place more. Back on campus the stairs were stained with blood and broken glass littered the pathways. Trees were destroyed and torn to bits after bearing the weight of the massive monsters that barreled through them. You couldn't turn a corner without seeing the destruction and loss, but here...life went on like nothing happened. The elite were untouched, and the inequality didn't sit well with me.

My father sat at the head of the dining room table, just as he had the last time we spoke. He wore a crisp white shirt, sleeves rolled to the elbows and starched until wrinkles ran at the sight of it. Not a hair out of place, he would be considered handsome sitting there in the late afternoon light. He had that rugged, older gentleman thing going for him if you could look past the elitist attitude and scathing remarks. The hair on the back of my neck stood on end when I stepped fully into the room and saw the king seated at the other end of the table. Servants lined the wall between the two most powerful men on the island, waiting to spring forward before either one could lift a finger. They quietly ate their meal, only stopping when my father noticed me lingering in the doorway.

"Kaya, you may enter," my father gestured me forward, then wiped his mouth on the handkerchief in his lap. "Tobias and I were just having a late lunch."

I kept the sneer off my face as I stepped closer. They were enjoying a lush meal while their people lay screaming in the infirmary over the bodies of loved ones and their own tragic injuries. Bile rose in the back of my throat at their callousness; they really were made for each other. My father appeared no different to me than he had my entire life. There were no signs or symptoms that he wasn't the same lion shifter that led the king's forces when they were younger, who could lop off a demon's head faster than a witch could throw their potion. For a while I wondered how he could let the king, his own partner, continue a relationship with the enemy. Adira claimed he didn't know, that he's in the dark like the rest of us. Or maybe, my father was just a cold-hearted asshole who wouldn't care even if he knew the truth.

I dipped a quick bow when the king looked at me, his keen gaze raking over my still visible bruises and new scrapes.

"I'm so glad to hear you're okay, dear girl," the king's tenor echoed across the room. "My son said you tangled with a Revenant all on your own!"

"It was but a fledgling," my father casually waved his hand, like defeating a demon of that size was an everyday occurrence.

They bantered back and forth over the fighting quality of Revenants as they aged and squeezed in jokes about the ones they fought in their youth. Neither one took note of the blood stains my shoes tracked on the carpet. They didn't comment on the hollow look in my eye or the disgust now blatant as I watched them. I thought my father called me here to demand I stay at the house now that my dorm was unlivable. But when I saw the king, that changed. I no longer feared either of them; I feared what would happen to our people the longer they continued to be in charge.

I cleared my throat. "Was there something you wanted, father?"

Both men stopped and turned to look at me. The intensity of their gaze, as well as the look they shared, sent my instincts back on high alert. The servants along the wall maintained neutral faces, as if they were part of the décor and weren't witnesses to whatever was about to happen. I readied myself for the worst.

"I have questions about your friendship with the Creole boy," my father finally said. "I've heard rumors about him and his ilk, and it concerns me that my only daughter is spending so much time with them."

My shoulders remained tense. "Bast and his mom have been nothing but kind to me."

They shared another indecipherable look. Auden's mention of rumors came back to me, and I worried that's what this meeting was about. Did the king know about Adira and the group's plans? If my father had any inkling about what they were up to, they were in extreme danger.

"That may be so, my dear," the king pushed his plate away and wriggled his finger at the door behind my father. "But we have an inside source that claims they may be using you to get close to the powerful people that surround you. And ultimately, to get to me."

I frowned, playing ignorant even as my breaths went shallow. They knew. All I could picture was running back out the door and warning the others before the king had a chance to kill them. There would be no trial, that I was sure of. With the community in turmoil, it would be all too easy to take out a few extra people and blame it on the demons. I was willing to bet that's what the king's been doing all along. The corner door that led to the kitchen squeaked on its hinges, revealing a small, lanky man with mouse-brown hair and a large nose.

I stepped back, caught off guard at the sight of Nolen nonchalantly strolling from my father's kitchen. That lying, two-faced, asshole. My father's eyes scanned my face for even the smallest kernel of recognition and when he leaned back in his chair, I knew he saw it.

"Please escort my daughter to her room and guard the door," two shifters in black flanked me at his command. "These are dangerous times, and I wouldn't want her to get caught up in saving the wrong people."

The grand staircase was even more imposing when one was ushered up the carpeted steps like a prisoner delivered to death row. My childhood room stared back at me with all the comforts of a less complicated life, but it couldn't help me now. I wouldn't bury my head in the sand while innocent people—people trying to change our community for the good—were murdered. There was no point going out the way I came in; fighting with the guards would only cause a commotion large enough to draw the exact attention I wanted to avoid. My window opened onto a small balcony that to anyone else might appear too high to jump from. But for a snow leopard, it was a piece of cake.

Dusk fell over the bayou as I snuck my way around, no longer sure who was working with the king and who wasn't. The cabin was alight with activity, more people coming to and fro than I'd ever seen here. Boxes were packed and taped shut and filled with everything from clothes and food to weapons. Idling trucks stood to the side ready to carry the supplies away to their new destination. I shifted and pushed my way through the boarded entrance to grab the first set of clothes I could find. Once I was no longer naked, I ran down the stairs where I knew I'd find the others. Adira directed what felt like a hundred people, but was probably less than thirty, as they moved around the basement headquarters like ants swarming a dead roach.

"Adira!" I shouted over the din and her eyes lighted on me immediately. If my mismatched and oversized clothes didn't tell her something was wrong, the dread on my face did. "Nolen betrayed us. He's at my father's house right now with the king and they plan to march on this place tonight!"

It all came out in a rush. My heart pounded so hard I thought I would pass out and Adira rested a hand on my shoulder to stop me from swaying.

"Alright everybody, listen up!" The room came to a standstill, each set of eyes trained on us and ready to listen. "Our plans have been leaked. Take whatever is in your hands and load up the trucks; everything else stays behind. Move!"

They scattered, clamoring up the steps and into the trucks like the hounds of hell were on their heels. The engines roared to life and puttered into the distance until I heard nothing but the rapid whispers of those left in the room. Captain Cesar helped Bast carry a large box of ammo while the mated shifters, Fin and Larsen, ran to start the jeeps hiding out back.

"I'll see you up there, yeah?" Bast hugged me tight. There was so much left unsaid between us; so much happened in the last twenty-four hours that we hadn't had a chance to talk about. I worried that we wouldn't get that chance. He disappeared with the captain before I could do more than nod.

Adira remained at my side, watching them go. "The plans are in motion far sooner than intended, but there's nothing that can be done to stop them now." I nodded, only half understanding what she said. "The attack on the dorms was the final straw for many people. At the very least, more are seeing the king as an incompetent leader who's no longer capable of protecting their children. Things will happen very fast from here; you need to be prepared to make a choice and soon."

"What kind of choice?" I asked, but I think I already knew.

"You will need to decide with who you stand. It's already too hot for you to remain, but I won't force you to come with us if you choose not to." Her hands squeezed my shoulders and something like pity flashed in her eye.

I wasn't sure what to do. I'd come here with the intent to warn them about my father and the king, but foolishly thought my involvement ended there. What would my father say when they found me missing from my room? Or if they caught me trying to sneak back in? There was no safety for me here if I'm deemed a traitor; not even Auden could save me from such a fate. And Auden...I wasn't ready to let him go yet. He wouldn't believe me without proof, and I had none to offer him. A conspiracy of demons and murders and secret partnerships but no concrete evidence to show for it. Shouts came from outside the cabin. I'd run out of time to decide.

Adira split us up, ushering me toward the back exit while she took the front and distracted anyone waiting for us there. Bast and the others were already in the jeeps further in the swamp where they wouldn't be found. It was full dark now and I was glad the hoodie I'd grabbed was black, making the shadows gather around me and claim me as one of their own. The soft mud felt cool against my bare knees as I knelt and peered around the corner of the cabin. It was hard to make out their numbers when they blended in with the night as well as I did but tapping into my extra senses revealed them and the things they couldn't camouflage—heartbeats, soft steps, the scratch on an arm. There were too many to take on by myself and so closely packed together, even my leopard wouldn't be able to sneak around them. Maybe if I—

Pain and then darkness. The yowl of a pissed off cat followed me into unconsciousness.

I CAME to with a pounding head and the taste of copper in the back of my mouth. Male shouts hurt my tender senses and I flinched as they argued, it felt like a drill in my brain. The back of my head throbbed, and my hair was plastered to it, leaving a small part of my neck free to feel even the slightest movement of air. My fingers reached to touch it, but they were wedged between my back and the wall and locked in metal. Handcuffs. Mere slits were all I could see out of; my eyes refusing to cooperate. I made out three figures, blurred and out-of-focus.

"Admitted from her own mouth, was it not?" That voice haunted my nightmares lately, the ones where Asher's ghost came back to tell on me, and his father strung me up on the outer walls for revenge. Was this a new one?

"She was led astray by her best friend," the next voice argued. I knew that one. Auden was always on my side, and it made sense that he would be even in my nightmares.

"She was cautioned away from that *thing* multiple times and has chosen to ignore all the warnings." The king's voice sounded further away now, and I noticed one of the shadow figures walked in the opposite direction.

The one shaped like Auden made to step forward, but the third figure stopped him with a hand on his arm.

"Stand down, brother."

My eyes were too heavy to keep open, even that little bit, so I gave in to the nightmares and let them take me where they willed.

When my eyes opened again, it was still dark out and I knew I wasn't dreaming. I was locked in a cell. Slimy and dank, I shivered at the touch of the slick stone against my legs and tucked them inside my hoodie. It barely helped. The air held the permanent scent of mold, rich and earthy, but sour like milk gone bad. Hardly wider than my spread arms and less deep than my height, I could only lay down at a diagonal angle and it would have to be on the floor, because there was no furniture. A deep pot in the corner looked suspiciously like what they used before the invention of outhouses, and I scooched as far away from it as I could.

It finally happened. I knew all those years ago that I'd one day end up here. The other cells beneath the king's mansion held no prisoners, only rats to keep me company. I feared ending up here for so long that the reality failed in comparison to what my imagination came up with. There were no torture racks or old bones; I even had a small window at the top of the bars. It was as tiny as a brick, but beggars can't be choosers. I wondered how the others fared. Did Adira get away? She wasn't down here with me, but I hardly saw her as one willing to be taken alive. Bast was long gone before the king's men showed up, so there was still hope that he remained out of reach.

"Kaya," my whispered name pulled me from my contemplations.

Auden stood on the other side of the bars; his face paler than I'd ever seen it. I staggered to my feet, ignoring how my head swam, and tripped my way over to him. I wrapped my fingers around the bars, scared to touch him. Was he real? Did he still love me? His arm reached through to gently cup my cheek and I leaned into the warmth. Tears built behind my eyes, and I let them fall.

"It's okay. I'm going to get you out of here," he promised, wiping the tears as fast as they fell. "We'll convince him you weren't apart of this. I know you were just in the wrong place at the wrong time."

I stopped nuzzling his hand and moved back until he couldn't reach. Angst creased the corners of his eyes and drew his mouth into a tight line. His bottom lip trembled before his tongue gave it a firm swipe as he watched me distance myself. I couldn't escape the earnest plea in his gaze, it called to me and ripped my heart out. I thought we had more time. The plan was always to tell him eventually, once I had proof. I was going to ease him into the idea and be there for him when the truth tore him apart. Instead, I was the one being shredded to pieces as I looked at him from behind rusted bars.

"I wasn't there by accident," my voice sounded hollow, even as it finally rang with the truth. "I've been working with Bast and Adira to elect another head of government until a suitable replacement can be found for your father." There it was, out in the open.

Auden's mouth dropped and then closed. Over and over like a gaping fish out of water. "No," he tilted his head, refusing to believe what was right in front of him. "That kid was a bad influence on you. It's his words you're speaking, not your own."

I waited in silence for his brain to catch up. For his intelligence to mark all the strange moments and conversations we never finished or I avoided. All the times he watched me disappear into the dorms, only to meet with him later coming from a different direction. My heart broke as he connected the dots. I thought it would be a gradual thing, but the dying organ felt more like a sharp blade of glass so cold it burned as it went in. It took root in my chest as his disbelief turned to despair, and his despair into rage. The gold in his eyes cooled, like chips of ice. That hatred I was so afraid of seeing slowly grew, erasing all the features of the boy I used to know. In front of me now stood a stranger, lacking the warmth and kindness he was known for.

"Who are you?" The simple question was delivered with such revulsion; it was like a punch to the gut.

"Think about it for a minute, Auden," I rushed to speak before his anger got the best of him, but I could see him slipping away. I didn't know how to stop what I started. It was a runaway train falling off the tracks, over the hill, and away forever. "I wouldn't do this without a good reason. If you would just let me explain—" He leapt away when I reached for his hand and that hurt more than anything that came before.

I eyed the stone floor to hide the fresh wave of tears. My betrayal gave him every right to hate me, I reminded myself. I knew this was coming, remember? It's just that, it didn't seem to hurt so bad when I was prepared for it. This was like losing my mother and failing Asher all rolled into one.

"You know me," I pleaded, but he was unmoved.

"I thought I did." Each word exchanged created more distance between us until his face was enveloped by shadows.

"You do," I insisted, and his mouth turned down slightly, the only movement I could still see.

"I'm not so sure anymore." Even his voice was unrecognizable. Flat and lacking emotion, he sounded like an empty shell of himself. I ached to reach out and hold him, to take it all back and pretend this was a bad dream. My heart couldn't take him scorning my touch again and he refused to come close enough for me to try. His light steps were the only clue that he left. There was no goodbye or chance to come to terms with his rejection. Nothing but the echo of falling water as my tears ran dry.

I sat against the mildewy wall with my head slumped between my knees. I stared for hours at the spot Auden left, wishing he'd come back once he worked through his anger, but the squeaking of rats fighting over their own shit turds was the only sound in this dank dungeon. I never knew emptiness could feel so excruciating. Wasn't it supposed to be a lack of feeling? My limbs were numb if that counted, but everything in my chest was on self-destruct. Hot and cold. Dead and alive. Is this what my life had come to? I had nothing to live for but the rise and fall of the sun through my sad excuse for a window and the hope that the king would offer me a quick death. I didn't waste breath on prayers for my father to save me. He probably wiped his hands of me the second the king told him I was locked in this cell and not safe in my room. Auden was gone, lost to me forever. That's what I kept circling back to, like a clogged drain filled with glass shards. When he left it took some time to come to terms with it. He wasn't who I thought he was; my other half, the one who loved me and swore to see the better parts of me. But to be fair, I wasn't the girl he promised that to. That girl was a misguided runaway who thought the worst of herself but was trying to be better. The real me, the one sitting in this tiny cell was the girl I always knew would catch up eventually. She was cunning and cruel, manipulative until she convinced even herself of her own innocence.

The screech of metal hinges warned me someone was coming down the steps before the scuff of their shoes. A pair of long legs came into view, covered in a pair of green tailored pants, then a pressed shirt. Asiel stopped at the bottom of the stairs, facing me through the bars with his signature smirk.

"Well, I can't say I didn't see this coming."

Even his smug arrogance couldn't get a rise out of me, not this time. There was no point. He seemed almost concerned over my lack of response and stepped closer to the bars to get a better look at me.

"I *told* you to lay low and make yourself scarce, did I not?" His tone was no less accusatory than usual, but something in it was different. There was a new cord— honesty. For once he wasn't wearing the façade of a spoiled prince high on his own power. "I've spent months trying to draw attention away from you and it's all gone to hell now. So, thanks for that."

My eyes narrowed, taking in his calm stance that screamed indifference. His hands were tucked neatly in his pockets, his head tilted at just the right angle to claim bored innocence, but it was there in his eyes. More gold than I'd ever seen swirled around his pupils, drowning out the black and making his gaze almost...kind. Lost pieces of that damned puzzle started coming together like icebergs drifting toward a waterfall. Asiel insisting he be the one to find his brother after the Raka attack, him demanding to be at every meeting his father ran, his warning to me at the treehouse, shit, even his plans for repopulation.

"You know about the king." He said nothing, but the slight tilt of his chin confirmed everything, and I choked on my own breath. "Why haven't you done anything?"

"Because I wasn't sure," he shrugged, hands still in his pockets like he was on an afternoon stroll. "There were a bunch of little things since the first night it all went to hell; my brother died, you disappeared, and the demons broke in for the first time."

"I remember," I grumbled, still licking the old wounds.

"Well, my father was never quite right after that and at first, I began to question his sanity." Asiel paced back and forth in front of the bars as he told his tale of how the king slowly transformed. Unnoticed by all but a devoted son, he changed habits and beliefs over the course of four years until our laws and community resembled what it did today. "I started following him," he said. "And when I saw him meeting with a demon for the first time, I knew. *That man isn't my father.*"

He stared at me, waiting for my gasp of surprise or maybe a swoon, but all I did was raise my brow.

"Come on!" He shouted. "You can't tell me you already guessed that."

I shook my head. "No, we just thought he was working with the demons. Why do you think he is one?"

"Because he doesn't use his powers anymore. Not once in four years."

"That's it?"

Asiel threw his hands in the air and stalked away; whispered curses and grumbles about not knowing a good plot twist filtered through the bars. When he came back, all the mischievous smirks were gone, leaving behind a solemn man who looked like he carried the weight of the world on his shoulders.

"Regardless of what I think," he whispered. "When the king took an interest in you, I knew I had to hide you. I tried to conceal you in the population, out of sight out of mind, but you refused to go quietly. *Then* you continued to stir up trouble like it was your single goal in life."

"I'm sorry?" I wasn't sure what he wanted me to say. How was I supposed to know Asiel hid an actual conscience behind his asshole persona? "I thought you were out to ruin my life."

"Say what you want about me, but I care about my people," he growled. "We are *dying*."

I nodded. This part I knew. There were hardly enough of us left to defend ourselves, let alone the humans we were charged with protecting. If the king really was a demon in disguise, it picked the perfect role. How better to take out your enemies than from within? If we imploded on ourselves, we were doing all the work for them. I think I understood Asiel a little better now. He was dealt a pretty good hand growing up, but the responsibility he wasn't prepared for hit him over the head and he'd risen to the challenge to the best of his ability. I didn't agree with most of his decisions he claimed were to protect our people, but I had no room to speak. My decisions haven't been the best lately either.

"I need to get you far away from here." Asiel crouched now, close enough that his voice wouldn't carry. "Your friend and his mother escaped and have successfully evaded any attempts to retrieve them. You and their group are our last chance at saving our people."

I looked around the room, noting the heavy chains around the door as well as the rusted lock that I already tried and failed to pick. Asiel wasn't whipping out a key, so I assumed he wasn't going to spring me himself.

"I have a plan to get you out of here. What do you say? Want to run away again for old time's sake?"

I thought I was past running. For so long it was all I knew and once you do it long enough it's a pretty tough thing to stop. I ran so hard I almost lost out on new friends and a chance to feel loved by the boy I'd give anything to wrap my arms around one more time. I should have told him how I felt. Stupid. I thought I had more time and that his acceptance of my greatest secret meant nothing would keep us apart. I saw a future. I saw happiness. Now, all I saw was another endless road and forever spent looking over my shoulder. But I'd already come to terms with who I was and what my actions justified. My people...they didn't deserve this and if I had a chance to save them, then I would take it and fuck the consequences.

"Auden is our head of defense right under my father," Asiel warned me. "He's been in back-to-back meetings, and I haven't been able to get to him. If we do this, if you run, my brother won't forgive you."

"I know," my voice was dull, lifeless.

"He will come after you."

"*I know.*"

Asiel smiled, the first real one he ever directed at me. "Then let's make a deal."

THE END